D0276863

EX LIBRIS

By the same author

Stillriver
Keeping Secrets
Without Prejudice
Fear Itself

The Informant

Andrew Rosenheim

HUTCHINSON
LONDON

Published by Hutchinson 2013

1 3 5 7 9 10 8 6 4 2

Copyright © Andrew Rosenheim 2013

Andrew Rosenheim has asserted his right under the Copyright, Designs
and Patents Act, 1988, to be identified as the author of this work

This book is a work of fiction. Any resemblance between these fictional
characters and actual persons, living or dead, is purely coincidental

This book is sold subject to the condition that it shall not, by way of trade
or otherwise, be lent, resold, hired out, or otherwise circulated without the
publisher's prior consent in any form of binding or cover other than that in
which it is published and without a similar condition, including this condition,
being imposed on the subsequent purchaser

First published in Great Britain in 2013 by
Hutchinson
Random House, 20 Vauxhall Bridge Road,
London SW1V 2SA

www.randomhouse.co.uk

Addresses for companies within The Random House Group Limited can be found at:
www.randomhouse.co.uk/offices.htm

The Random House Group Limited Reg. No. 954009

A CIP catalogue record for this book
is available from the British Library

ISBN 9780091937263

The Random House Group Limited supports the Forest Stewardship
Council® (FSC®), the leading international forest-certification organisation.
Our books carrying the FSC label are printed on FSC®-certified paper. FSC
is the only forest-certification scheme supported by the leading environmental
organisations, including Greenpeace. Our paper procurement policy can be found at
www.randomhouse.co.uk/environment

Typeset in Sabon LT Std by Palimpsest Book Production Limited,
Falkirk, Stirlingshire

Printed and bound by CPI Group (UK) Ltd, Croydon CR0 4YY

For Laura and Sabrina

Part One

Los Angeles
Late September 1941

1

BILLY OSAKA WAS missing.

He hadn't punched in at Northrop near Hawthorne Airport where he worked the occasional night shift for extra dough – the airplane production lines had ramped up threefold in the last year. He hadn't gone by the offices of *Rafu Shimpo*, the Japanese-American news-paper, not even to say he wasn't filing that week. He hadn't answered Nessheim's knock on the flimsy door of his three-room railway apartment in Boyle Heights, and he hadn't been seen by his neighbours – or those who spoke English at any rate. There'd been no sight-ings of him locally: at the drugstore on the corner or Curley's bar, where Billy drank a beer now and then and sometimes cashed a cheque, or at the grocery store, where even Billy had been known to buy a quart of milk.

Normally Nessheim would not have been surprised. Billy was easygoing but also impetuous, like a classy thoroughbred who sometimes didn't want to race. Once he'd disappeared for two weeks without letting Nessheim know where he was going; when he finally appeared he said he'd been up in Portland, helping out his cousin with the salmon catch. When Nessheim had looked sceptical, Billy had shrugged and admitted that he'd been touring the Sierra with a girl.

But this time was different. Three nights before, when Nessheim had gone home after a long day at the studio lot, he'd found an envelope slid under the front door of his rented ranch house above North Hollywood. Inside there was a note, written in thick pencil: *Urgent. Meet me at the Blue Fedora at 5.30 tomorrow.*

It's important. Billy O.

But Billy Osaka hadn't shown.

In the bleached morning sunlight of Los Angeles, Nessheim turned off Hollywood Boulevard and moved south on Argyle Avenue, wondering why Billy had wanted to see him so badly. He was only an occasional help to the Bureau, usually when a Japanese translator was required, and though he seemed to know everybody, the information Billy provided was never worth a lot. Raw ore rather than gold.

Nessheim slowed down and pulled into the lot of American Motion Pictures, driving through the flimsy gates, feeble imitations of the grander ones at MGM. He stopped at the barrier and Ernie the guard came out of his sentry box, gimpy on his pins. He had thinning hair and sloping shoulders and a handshake soft as pie. A retired cop from the Pasadena force who had come to California from Minnesota thirty years before, he got a kick out of talking to a fellow Midwesterner who still carried a gun.

'You packing today?' he asked with a smile.

'Sure thing,' said Nessheim.

'I do miss my sidearm,' Ernie said wistfully.

'And it misses you,' said Nessheim in what was an established routine. Ernie chuckled as if he'd never heard it before.

There was a sudden revving of an engine. Through the windscreen Nessheim saw a convertible speeding towards them down the lot. Nearing the barrier, it braked sharply and came to a halt on the other side of the sentry box. The car, a deluxe Packard coupé, was a vivid green chartreuse with whitewall tyres and too much chrome.

Nessheim figured it belonged to one of the new actors. They would arrive like a rocket in a burst of vainglory; a month on the AMP studio's factory-like production line usually brought them back down to earth.

From the car a male voice shouted: 'Hurry up, Pops, and open the gate!'

'Hold your horses, I'll be there in a minute,' Ernie said amiably.

'I'll push your horses right up your ass if you don't get a move on!'

Ernie was old and slow and utterly harmless, and Nessheim leaned over to get a look at the speaker. He could make out the profile of a young man's square-chinned face, a blue short-sleeved shirt and two hands drumming impatiently on the steering wheel.

'Take it easy,' Nessheim called out through the passenger side window.

'Says who?'

'Says me,' said Nessheim.

'Does Me want to have horses shoved up *his* ass too?'

Nessheim was usually slow to anger, but this guy had jump-started the process. He opened his door and got out to confront him, but just as he stood upright again the other driver accelerated. His car was so close to the wooden barrier that at first it bent slowly back like a hunting bow, then suddenly snapped like a toothpick. The car surged through. As it sped out the gates, the driver extended his middle finger in farewell.

Nessheim looked at Ernie. 'Who the hell was that?'

Ernie shrugged. 'Some smart-ass kid. He parked in Mr Pearl's place, but when I asked Rose said it was okay.' Rose was Pearl's secretary.

'Well, Pearl's the boss.' Nessheim pointed to the ragged wooden stub, all that was left of the exit barrier. 'Though I don't think he's going to be happy about that.'

He waited while Ernie lifted the entry bar, then drove into the studio grounds. He went past the long window-less wall of Studio One, then by the executive offices. They were housed in a three-storied stucco building with wide gables and two decorative but entirely redundant chimneys. In front there was a short strip of carefully tended lawn and a row of small palm trees, planted the spring before. In the distance, at the back of the lot, sat Studio Two, recently built to help the fledgling studio's push into A-movies. It was immense, the size of an airplane hangar: sixty feet high and a football field long, with vast doors that slid open on tracks.

Its sheer size made it easy to overlook the low-slung building that ran between it and the executives offices, and was more like a Nissen hut than a proper building: single-storey, it had a foundation of concrete blocks supporting painted walls of metal sheets and a slanted tin roof. Here worked the studio's roster of writers, as well as Nessheim. If you could call it work.

Parking in front, he paused at the entrance to let a workman come out first. He was carrying a stuffed armchair and Nessheim watched as he dumped it unceremoniously on the pavement outside, where it would sit until the owner, some writer whose contract hadn't been renewed, came to collect it. Nessheim had seen it happen often enough: there was a high turnover among the scriptwriting ranks. As Teitz, a long-term survivor, had remarked, the bad ones got canned and the good ones left for better places to work.

Nessheim walked down the thin central corridor which a resident wit had nicknamed the Ink Well. It split the offices, from which he heard the sporadic clack of typewriters and the more consistent noise of people talking. He stopped halfway down at an open door. Looking in, he saw that Lolly Baker, the single secretary for the entire roster, wasn't there – otherwise half the writers would have been there too, gathered around the coffee urn, flirting with her. Less than fifty yards away in either of the two studio sound buildings, there were women galore – chorines and showgirls, child star wannabes and romantic heroines, secretaries and make-up artists and assistants – but since the writers were banned from going on set, these women might as well have been a mile away.

The writers occupied tiny cubicle-sized offices and were made to double up, working in conditions so cramped that one of them had once complained he had to go outside just to change his mind. By contrast, Nessheim's room at end of the corridor was embarrassingly spacious. Entering it, he closed the door behind him. He took off his suit jacket and hung it and his gun and holster from the hook on the back of the door. He didn't like taking his gun with him to work, but when he'd asked if he could go without it, the answer had been a flat no. R.B. Hood, the Special Agent in Charge of the LA Field Office, was a stickler for Bureau regulations, and he liked making Nessheim toe the line.

Nessheim sat down and looked out the window, where he saw a man in a clown suit trying to pull a donkey with a rope through the open doors of Studio Two. Mornings inside Two were currently occupied by the filming of a family farm picture, set in the Civil War, intended to replicate the success of *Gone with the Wind*. There were only two problems with this plan: every other studio was doing the same thing, and every other studio was doing it in colour – which AMP's budget didn't run to. In the afternoon the main sound stage was used for *The Red Herring*. Nessheim would be there in his role as adviser, ostensibly to ensure the accuracy of its depiction of FBI men at work. The truth was, though, that accuracy was not his real priority. *You're just there to make sure the movie makes the Bureau look good.* Tolson himself had said this when he'd agreed to move to LA.

There was a tap on the door. He sat up straight as it swung open.

'Gee, did I startle you?' It was Lolly. 'You looked a million miles away. What's her name?'

He laughed. 'Billy Osaka – sound like a girl to you?'

'Sounds like a Jap.'

'He is, sort of.' Billy's dad had been Japanese all right and Billy had inherited his Oriental colouring, and spiky dark hair. But he was tall, over six feet, as tall as Nessheim, with high cheekbones and a jaw and dark-blue eyes he himself attributed to his dead Irish mother.

'I don't like Japs,' Lolly said without malice.

'Yeah, but I bet you'd like Billy.' He knew that women admired the kid's striking looks and liked his easy, cheerful manner. 'Say, do you know who owns a new green convertible?'

'No, but I'd like to.'

Lolly stood there smiling in her gawky but attractive way. She wore a cotton dress, eggshell blue with white polka dots that didn't line up where the side hems met. Nessheim figured Lolly must have made it herself. She was tallish, maybe five foot seven, with a pretty face framed with blonde ringlets the size of silver dollars. Together with pale blue eyes and a good figure, the effect was striking – if Lolly's looks might go in ten years' time, their allure was immediate enough to make anyone forget about the passage of time.

Like any girl who'd moved to LA, Lolly wanted to be in the pictures, though she didn't talk about it much, since when she opened her mouth her Hollywood prospects receded. The sight wasn't appalling, but it wasn't that good either: her two front teeth overlapped like the X of a railroad crossing sign.

Finally she recalled the purpose of her visit. 'Mr Pearl's office called.'

'What about?' Nessheim asked mildly.

'You're invited to lunch at his house on Sunday.'

Nessheim stifled a groan. In nine months at the studio he hadn't broken bread with the owner, and he saw no reason to spoil an unblemished record.

'Here's the address,' said Lolly, putting a slip on his desk. 'Rose says don't dress up, and bring your trunks if the weather's nice. She says he's got a humdinger of a pool. Even Johnny Weissmuller's swum there.'

'I bet,' he said, wondering if there was any way to get out of it.

He noticed that despite having delivered her message, Lolly wasn't going anywhere. She stood in front of him, nervous as a filly. 'You've got another invite,' she said, pointing to his desk.

On one corner he noticed something new – a card the size of a jumbo postcard. He held it up and read:

Help Your Comrades in Arms

**You are invited to an evening of entertainment
and education to help support our Soviet brothers
in their struggle against the Nazi enemy.**

Monday October 13 at 8 p.m.

**The Arabia Ballroom Cash Bar
All proceeds to *Help the Soviets Fund*
Organized by *Writers for a Free World***

'This is for me?' he asked. Lolly nodded and he looked at the invitation again. 'Who are the Writers for a Free World?' He wondered if there were writers *against* a free world. Presumably Goebbels had some on his staff.

Lolly shrugged. 'I think they're Guild guys, but they'd get in trouble if they used the Guild name for this.'

'You bet they would. Who sent it?'

'Waverley.'

'He did?'

Lolly said, 'Teitz told me Waverley used to make fifteen hundred a week when he was at MGM. Could that be true?'

'Probably.' John Waverley had an ear for dialogue and a sense of pace that had once put him in the top drawer of screenwriters. A tall, good-looking man with a wave of hair he swept back as if it were an inheritance, he came from a high-toned family out East. He had a natural grace (just bordering on hauteur) that had once inspired awe in studio owners, immigrants virtually to a man. But politics had proved his Achilles heel. He had joined the Party early and had worked hard to radicalise his fellow writers; when, briefly, the Guild had been broken, Waverley had been a prominent casualty of the victors' hit list. Thereafter he had found work only on the most humiliating terms – and finally ended up at AMP, content to work on the company's second-rate productions for second-rate pay as long as he was left alone to continue the struggle for a better world. Which for Waverley meant a Communist world.

Nessheim pointed to the invitation. 'Are you going to this thing?'

Lolly flushed. 'I don't know.' Flustered, she pointed wildly at the Ink Well corridor. 'Half those guys have asked me.'

'I bet they have, Lolly. You're a good-looking girl, despite your age . . .'

'I'm twenty next May,' she protested.

'That's what I mean,' teased Nessheim. 'You're getting a bit long in the tooth. You ought to take one of these guys' offers before it's too late.'

Her face swung from outrage to hurt; for a terrible moment Nessheim thought she was going to cry. So much for banter, he thought.

'I better get going,' Lolly said. 'Don't forget about Mr Pearl's invitation.'

When she'd gone he looked out the window again. The donkey was still there, but now two grips had come out from Studio Two to help pull the recalcitrant animal inside. The donkey had its feet braced in the dust and would not budge. There seemed something admirable about its refusal.

He knew he should go to the benefit, yet Nessheim could think of nothing more dire than an evening of Communist propaganda disguised as entertainment, even if Lolly seemed to want him to take her there. He thought about how good she looked in her thinning cotton dress – and how young, for all her nineteen years. If he took her out, and maybe took her in, he'd feel like a creep. Thank God he was spoken for.

There was a knock on the door, but this time it didn't open.

'Come in!' he called impatiently, wondering who was being so polite. The door finally opened and a woman peered in. She wore a forget-me-not-blue linen jacket and skirt and looked out of place in the studio – more like a businessman's wife than an actress.

'Are you John Waverley?' She had an accent Nessheim couldn't place.

'You've come too far. He's two doors down – on the left of course.'

'Naturally,' she said with an amused smile. 'Many

11

thanks – I am sorry to disturb you.' She stared at him with deep-set eyes the colour of chocolate.

'No big deal. I wasn't up to much.'

She continued to look at him, long enough for it to start to seem peculiar. Then her face suddenly creased into a transforming smile and she laughed. 'That's honest of you,' she said.

It was his turn to laugh. 'Honesty in Hollywood. Remember this moment.'

'I will,' she said, still smiling, and closed the door.

Back to work. He took a form from the drawer and started to fill out his expenses, which putatively went through the LA office, where Hood had spotted them – and been flabbergasted. 'Fifteen years in the Bureau,' the SAC had complained, 'and I've never had to complain that an agent's expenses were too *small*.' What Hood didn't know was that any expense of consequence went through the Bureau's office in Mexico City, then got rerouted for approval by Assistant Director Guttman back in D.C. It was just one more strange aspect of this odd posting.

He pushed his expenses away, deciding he'd do them later, and wondered where next to look for Billy Osaka, and why Billy needed to see him.

When Nessheim had arrived here eight months before, he'd been given a list of four paid contacts from the Japanese-American community, used mainly for translation. One had died, one had returned to Japan, and one had told Nessheim that he wasn't interested in working for the FBI any more. This left Osaka, though Hood had not been encouraging: 'He's not even a real Jap,' the SAC had complained. And now Billy had gone missing, even though with his mishmashed blood lines he stood out in LA like a split nail in a manicure bar.

Nessheim thought he had better tell Guttman that he

had a missing informant. He considered calling him; he'd had a phone installed, which collected dust on the window sill, since he rarely used it and it never rang. But calls through it went out through a switchboard, where it had been known for some nail-buffing bored operator to listen in.

Nessheim got up and took his jacket and gun, then left the building. In Lolly's office a crowd of writers had gathered round her desk, and she was laughing.

He walked out past Eddie in his booth, who seemed surprised to find anyone leaving the lot on foot. Western Union was only half a mile away, an easy walk, despite the heat that had hung over from summer. But then it was always summer here, he thought irritably, his mood darkening as he started to sweat.

He didn't like LA.

He didn't like the fact that its most famous product, the movies, was a mirage, put together in a soulless town that pretended it was glamorous as well – like a snake-oil salesman claiming the magic of his elixir made him magic too. He didn't like the low-lying smell of gasoline and hamburger grease the minute you took a drive downtown. Which was every minute if you wanted to get anywhere.

He didn't like the way that some mornings' daylight was the colour of bone, some the colour of late corn, or that the city had hills in some parts and was as flat as a map in others. It was a jellyfish of a city, translucent in the middle because there wasn't one. He didn't like the trapped heat, held in by the minor mountains to the north and east, unrelieved by the ocean south and west of town, or how the clouds could hang low like a dropped ceiling. He felt hemmed in.

He didn't like the fact that the place had been settled by conmen and illusionists, and that its

13

population was so heterogeneous and yet so unequal
– he had a natural curiosity about the Mexicans and
Orientals, but the bigotry of everybody else made his
interest seem subversive. He didn't like the place's
disconnect with the country he had grown up in; LA
never felt to him like it belonged to the rest of the
nation, and made him yearn for his native Midwest.
He missed seasons, fresh water and trees that were
made for snow – maples, birches, beech and oaks,
the trees of Wisconsin. Here the trees seemed alien
– juniper, pepper trees and eucalyptus, even the palms
he'd always thought were confined to the South Sea
Islands.

And no one here seemed to know where Europe was,
or what was going on there. No one seemed to understand or even sense the menace of Nazism, though as
for Japan, California seemed to think the Pacific Ocean
was an Oriental carpet the sons of Nippon were about
to walk across.

Finally, he didn't like LA because he didn't choose
to be there – unlike other recent arrivals, who came
West to leave a wounding world behind. Hopes had
been crushed everywhere else for a decade, but here
optimism spread like mint, a phoney optimism since
people were merely buying time before being let down
again. Unlike everyone else, Nessheim wasn't fleeing
anything or looking for something. He'd come here
because he'd been pushed, but at some point he would
push back.

He'd do that after Annie Ryerson came – she was
due out at Christmas with her son Jeff. He hadn't seen
her since January, after he had gone to Washington and
accepted Guttman's offer of this cockamamie job. He
had spent time then with Annie – good calm time. She
wouldn't sleep with him, which took some getting used

to, yet it was kind of nice to wait; or so he told himself, wondering if he should put saltpetre in his cereal. He felt confident he was going to be with her, and confident that would get him out of LA.

Western Union was in a squat, light-grey granite building with four tellers, older men wearing eyeshade caps like bookies, with pencil stubs by their side. He filled out a form at the counter, and paid his forty cents. His message was simple:

OSAKA GONE AWOL. N

He looked at his watch. It was 12.30. He retraced his steps, but at Vine he turned right and walked away from the studio for a block, until he came to Elsie's Diner on the corner of Hollywood Boulevard. The studio didn't run to a canteen; if you didn't bring a packed lunch Elsie's was the closest bet, if not a good one. It was already crowded and he headed for the one free stool at the counter, until a shout came from a corner booth.

'G-Man!'

It was Teitz, motioning him to join his party, even though from their empty plates it looked like they had finished lunch. Waverley was there, and Nessheim hesitated, but Teitz kept beckoning him. He went over and saw that Stuckey, a rewrite man, and Debts Grenebaum, who was fresh from another Broadway failure, were also sitting on the dark-brown leather banquettes.

'Have a seat,' Teitz said, moving over to make room. An ex-reporter, perky and full of the gossip he called news, he was a self-confessedly mediocre writer who had carved out a collaborative career – functioning as a junior partner with anyone he could hook up with; when he couldn't find a partner he transferred to shorts, the little documentaries the theatres ran as trailers for their shorter pictures.

'We were talking about the war,' said Grenebaum. Like Teitz he was a studio veteran, though he returned to New York whenever he could get a play produced. His work was 'progressive' and often compared, usually unfavourably, with that of Clifford Odets. 'Just drop the O from Odets and you've got our boy,' Waverley had once declared, and after that Grenebaum was known as Debts.

Waverley himself was sitting at the end of the table, against the window, dressed in a coal-coloured turtleneck and a fawn blazer. Teitz was wearing a madras jacket and his standard jaunty bow tie (this one was green) but none of the other writers ever dressed up – they either wore ties pulled down an inch or two or didn't wear a tie at all. They liked to tease Nessheim for his G-Man uniform – the Bureau's dress code set a high bar and, like the gun, the banker's suit came with the job.

'You got to hand it to the Brits,' Stuckey was saying, as Nessheim sat down and picked up a menu. The special, chalked up on a board above the counter, was corned-beef hash, poached egg on top a nickel extra. 'Everybody thought they'd cave in by now. But I don't see how the Germans are going to invade. They've lost the air war, so if they try to cross the Channel the Royal Navy will make mincemeat of them.'

Waverley dismissed this with a wave of his hand. 'Frankly, if one fading colonial power is taken over by its fascist progeny, it doesn't matter very much – except to the capitalists. But if the Soviets lose, that will be a disaster for everyone.'

Nessheim looked up from the menu. 'I'd have thought you'd be happy to have anyone fight the Nazis. Even the fading colonial Brits.'

Waverley looked at him as if he were a flea who had jumped the wrong way. 'You think my enemy's enemy is my friend? That's absurd. Where were the British when the Republicans needed help in Spain? Where were they back in July when Nazi Germany invaded the Ukraine?'

'Hang on a minute. Three months ago the Soviets were *allies* of the Nazis.'

'What else could they do? The West wouldn't lift a finger to help our comrades. The Russians had to protect themselves.'

'Fat lot of good it did them,' said Stuckey. He was tall and heavy set, but his black-rimmed glasses made him look more contemplative than tough. He had none of Teitz's bounciness, but he carried himself with a calm modesty which Nessheim admired.

Waverley shook his head impatiently. 'Stalin knew who the enemy was. But with the rest of the world undermining him, he needed to buy time.'

'By sleeping with the enemy, I suppose,' said Stuckey. He took a toothpick and began working it between his two front teeth. Somehow he managed to do this gracefully.

The waitress came with a pitcher of ice tea. As she refilled glasses, Nessheim ordered the corned-beef hash without the egg and Teitz used the interruption to change the subject – he was keener on people than politics. 'So tell us, G-Man, what's new in the world of interstate crime? Have you found another Lindbergh baby?'

Nessheim said, 'Taste, Teitz, taste.'

Grenebaum, normally silent, spoke up. 'Too late,' he said glumly. 'Taste is a Teitz-free zone.'

Even Waverley laughed at this. Nessheim said, 'I'll leave Lindbergh to Hoover. I'm looking for somebody else.'

'Who's that, some Red?' asked Teitz, and Waverley gave a derisory snort.

Nessheim said, 'A kid named Osaka.'

'Billy Osaka,' said Teitz, his face lighting up. 'Everybody knows Billy.'

'Sounds like a Jap to me,' said Waverley sourly.

'Can't a Jap be a comrade too? I thought you were a democrat at heart,' said Nessheim.

'I am. Unlike the Japs.'

When Nessheim's food came the others paid and left for the studio. Except for Stuckey, who stayed behind and ordered a cup of coffee. When it came he lit a Camel and looked at Nessheim.

'So what are you working on now?'

'*The Red Herring*,' he said.

Stuckey gave a small smile. 'It's art of course, not "proper-gander". With the added bonus of letting the public know all that you FBI guys are doing on its behalf.'

'Yeah,' Nessheim said without enthusiasm.

'Don't let the Count fool you. He's a peasant from Puglia, even if he quotes Vorkapich and Eisenstein.'

'But I thought he was an Italian nobleman.'

'I think you'd find on close inspection that the title was acquired the day he got off the *Super Chief* and arrived in Hollywood.' He took a final drag on his cigarette and stubbed it out in the table's ashtray. 'But what else are you up to, Nessheim?'

'Oh, you know, helping out with this and that. Mainly that.'

'Do you see much of Buddy Pearl?'

'Very little,' said Nessheim.

'He's a Jew of course.'

'Of course,' Nessheim said, though he had never given it much thought. He hadn't mistaken Pearl for a

Mayflower descendant, but for Nessheim, growing up in rural Wisconsin, the only important distinction had been between Lutherans and Catholics.

'A Jew, but of the tough rather than sweet rabbinical kind. Don't get me wrong, I haven't anything against them – those guys are my pals.' Stuckey gestured at the seats Teitz and Grenebaum had just vacated, then took another toothpick from the little cup that held them and twirled it lightly between his fingers. 'In my experience, the Jews are good to work with – all bluster at first, then perfectly reasonable when you stand your ground. But I imagine Pearl is different: it can't be easy to do business with him.'

'I'm not doing business with Pearl,' Nessheim said firmly.

Stuckey nodded. 'I know – the Bureau's your boss. But I still don't envy you.'

'He's invited me to lunch.'

'That means he wants something. I'd watch your back. What Buddy wants he usually gets, though I think he's finding the movie business a little tough to crack. I mean, who starts a studio in the middle of the Depression?'

The Count was on loan from Warners, which was thought to be a coup by AMP executives, since he shot fast and didn't use a lot of film. His Italian accent grew stronger when he was stressed, but today he was not only perfectly intelligible, he was actually friendly to Nessheim. Normally he ignored him. 'Art,' he had declared when Nessheim had first appeared, 'I make Art, not proper-gander.'

Nessheim had repeated this to the residents of the Ink Well, who'd all laughed. Teitz had said they should call the Count 'Goose'. Grenebaum had broken his standard silence and been more scornful. 'This guy doesn't make art *or* propaganda. He's no Leni Riefenstahl, that's for sure. This guy makes *junk*.'

They were in the final three days of the eighteen-day shoot of *The Red Herring*, the fourth in a series of Bureau-endorsed movies featuring Special Agent Edward Parker – played by a tall, lantern-jawed actor named Harry Dedway, who had begun his acting career as a horse-riding extra in cowboy movies. There had been bigger FBI-loving pictures made by bigger studios, but these were some years back. Hoover, who had not been pleased by James Cagney's playful portrayal of a Special Agent in *G-Men*, was now on a mission. He was determined to show the FBI as a team of crime-busters, a force of integrity, relying on the clinical science of forensics, which was why, in the interests of 'accuracy', Nessheim was here. AMP's FBI pictures were all B-movies, using two cameras at most, but they had made good if not spectacular money so far, largely because they were cheap to make – the budget for this one was sixty grand, Nessheim had overheard one of the Count's assistants say, and they were bang on target and a day ahead of time.

There hadn't been much for Nessheim to do during filming – they'd shot on location in the Valley the week before, where he had driven out just in time to point out that no one could fire a tommy-gun with one hand. Now they were filming the movie's climax – the arrest by Special Agent Parker of a young woman who had murdered her fiancé, embezzled $20,000 from a bank and done her unsuccessful best to seduce the FBI man. Presumably her crimes involved crossing state lines, as otherwise young Parker would not have been called in to solve the case. But this was the kind of nit-picking (*neet-pecking* as the Count called it) which Nessheim had learned – if only for the sake of an easy life – to forgo.

The Count sat throughout the afternoon on a dolly, right behind the cameraman, who drove it up and down for trucking shots, while a second but static camera focused on the femme fatale and Agent Parker as they had their final showdown. Periodically, the Count would call Nessheim over and ask if the scene was realistic, especially when Parker disarmed the suspect. Nessheim, wanting to justify his presence, demonstrated how this would be done and the Count filmed the scene three times.

At last Nessheim managed to escape back to his office, where he finished his expenses while the writers wound down for the day – the sound of popping corks and loud laughter replacing the erratic clack-clack of type-writer keys. He waited around until six o'clock in case Guttman replied to his telegram, but nothing arrived. It didn't seem to matter very much; he was used to waiting around these days.

Part Two

Part Two

Washington, D.C.
Late September 1941

2

IT WAS ONLY a matter of time, Harry Guttman told himself as he turned onto the slip road into Rock Creek Park. The Nazis were halfway across Russia, the Japanese were bullying most of Asia. At some point, America would enter the war, and as far as Guttman was concerned the sooner the better. And this sense of imminent conflict – worldwide for a country that never liked to look beyond its borders – made the evening's rendezvous seem a waste of time.

What did Thornton Palmer want?

Guttman parked his car with a sigh, then wiped his sweaty forehead with the back of one hand. He realised that, despite ten years working there, he would never get used to the Washington heat. Even in September, as dusk neared he felt he was sitting in a breezeless bath of hot air. Under his shirt he felt a tiny rivulet of sweat trailing down across his gut. It tickled.

The only other car in the rough gravel lot was a maroon Chevrolet, parked underneath two beech trees on the far side of the log boundary. Enough daylight remained to see the couple necking on its front seat. This remote corner of Rock Creek Park was a natural Lovers' Lane, so it seemed normal enough to Guttman. But the car had New York plates, which didn't. Guttman fumbled for a pencil in his jacket, then wrote down the numbers on a scrap of paper just in case.

I should have been a cop, he thought – an ordinary cop, that is. Kevin Reilly in the D.C. force had said so often enough. Years before Guttman had tried to join the NYPD, halfway through his education at CCNY.

He withdrew his application when the woman clerk downtown had told him, not unkindly, that they weren't taking any more Chosen People that year. Funny, then, that he should end up with the Bureau, since everybody knew that Hoover didn't like the Jews.

Guttman got out and locked the door of his ageing Buick – he would be going home next, so he hadn't brought a Bureau car. Glancing at his watch, he hoped this wouldn't take long. It had been difficult enough to get the helper to stay and look after his wife Isabel. If he were very late, the woman might say no next time.

He walked across the lot onto a timbarked trail that ran through the woods. Trees towered above him. He wished he knew more of their names. That's an oak, he thought, passing an angled trunk with bark ridged like a grill-steak pan, though maybe it was a willow, sitting as it did by a runaway split of the park's eponymous creek. He wasn't sure, he realised, and felt irritation at his ignorance. He was a city boy by origin, who'd made it out of town, but never seemed to have time to get to know his new surroundings. Two springs before he'd planted a maple in the backyard of his Virginia house, but the maple had died by August. He told himself it would all be different when he retired. Less than twenty years to go.

When the path split he took the thinner branch to the right – Thornton Palmer's instructions had been very clear. Though why they had to meet way out here was a mystery to Guttman. *You'll understand when we talk*, Palmer had said.

They had met once before, for a background talk about Argentina, now part of Guttman's new South American empire. At the time, Palmer had been Deputy Consul in Buenos Aires, but was back in D.C. for his annual leave. As Guttman remembered, he hadn't known much about Nazis or German sympathisers – said to be plentiful in Buenos Aires. In fact, Palmer hadn't seemed very interested in Argentina at all.

There was no one else in sight – in half an hour it would be dark. Thornton Palmer – what kind of name was that? The WASP ascendancy's habit of giving themselves two surnames reminded Guttman of a Masonic handshake, exchanged to tip the wink to fellow members of the clan, those upper reaches of American society filled with ancestral names clinging like burrs. Doubtless Palmer belonged there. He'd gone to Yale, hadn't he?

On the phone Palmer had said it was urgent, but Guttman had learned long before that one man's drama could be another man's yawn. He would have sent somebody else, but there wasn't anybody he could trust to handle this unorthodox approach. The Bureau was full of bushy-tailed new recruits: the Director had been quick to leverage the possibility of war to persuade Congress to bolster his ranks, and 2,000 agents had become more than 6,000 in less than two years. But they were too green to decide whether Thornton Palmer's urgency was justified or, as Guttman suspected, so much hogwash.

The path turned left, making a sharp bend around an unkempt clump of rhododendrons. Ahead, set back on a semicircle patch of grass, a man sat on a bench smoking a cigarette. Guttman recognised him from their previous meeting.

Palmer must have seen him, but he didn't move until Guttman left the path and approached the bench. Then he stood up. He was a big man, well over six feet, a good five inches taller than Guttman and equally broad in the shoulder. Well dressed, in a beige suit that looked J. Press, a broad, striped tie and smart English brogues.

'Mr Guttman?'

'Call me Harry, Thornton.'

Palmer shook hands firmly, like an ex-jock. He had such conventional facial features – straight nose, good cheekbones and a strong jaw – that women would have described him as good looking, though few would have said it with any excitement.

'Thanks for coming,' Palmer said.

'Sure. It's a bit of a hike from Foggy Bottom, isn't it?'

Palmer nodded. 'That's why I picked it. You might see somebody you know, but I'm not going to.' He gave a quick, confident laugh and Guttman thought either he was a good actor or he wasn't nervous at all. Palmer couldn't have been much more than thirty, but there was an air of self-assurance to him – and a receding hairline – which made him seem older.

Guttman gestured at the bench and they both sat down. From there they could see the path, twenty yards away, though Guttman didn't expect anyone to come along this close to dark. He just hoped he'd be able to find his way back to his car. Palmer had thrown away his cigarette, but now he reached in his jacket's side pocket and brought out a pack of Pall Malls. 'Smoke?'

'No thanks,' said Guttman and watched as Palmer lit his own with a shiny silver Zippo lighter. His hand looked steady enough and he blew the smoke out with obvious pleasure. On the path's far side the creek hiccuped and gurgled over its gravel bed, invisible from the bench.

'So what's this about?'

Palmer hunched forward, elbows on his knees, putting his hands together. He had clean-looking hands, which seemed to glow like Ivory soap in the disappearing light. Guttman reflexively clenched his wrists to hide his fingernails, chewed down to the quick, flecked with traces of ink.

28

Palmer said, 'I've been told you're in charge of catching spies working in America.'

'I used to run the Intelligence division, if that's what you mean.'

'Yeah. There've been a lot of articles about the Nazi agents you guys have rounded up.'

Guttman shrugged. It was true that the papers had enjoyed a field day earlier that month, when thirty-three members of the Nazi Duquesne spy ring had been brought to trial, hailed by Hoover as the greatest round-up of spies in American history. Hoover insisted the publicity helped keep American citizens vigilant, although there had been other incidents where the Bureau hadn't performed so well that never saw the light of day.

'Is this about Nazis?' Guttman asked.

'Wrong side,' said Palmer airily. He could have been describing a football game.

Guttman suppressed a sigh. So this is why he was here – Palmer wanted to blow the cover off some Red. Doubtless someone from his Boola Boola days at Yale who'd subscribed to the *Daily Worker*. 'So,' he said, not trying to disguise his disappointment, 'which Commies do you want to tell me about?'

Palmer looked taken aback. He said, 'Actually, I'm here to talk about myself.'

Nothing in Palmer's file had suggested anything unusual about him. Guttman said warily, 'Are you a member of the Party?'

'No. And I never have been.'

'I don't think you've got much of a problem, Thornton. Lots of people were pretty pink for a while, what with the war in Spain and the Depression here. Even Mr Hoover can forgive a youthful indiscretion, especially if you weren't a Party member.'

'That's not what concerns me,' said Palmer curtly, shaking his head.

Guttman bristled slightly. 'So what does concern you?'

'Six months after I started at State I was approached. By the Russians. They wanted me to spy for them.'

Guttman was nonplussed; he hadn't expected anything like this. Nazi infiltrators he was all too familiar with, but Soviet agents? It seemed ridiculous. The Russians didn't even have an ambassador after the signing of the Berlin-Moscow pact two years ago, and before that the embassy had been sparsely staffed. Throughout the Thirties they had been too busy failing to feed themselves (and putting 'counter-revolutionaries' on trial) to worry about spying on anybody else, much less a country as remote as America. And the Nazis were flooding through the Ukraine and heading east at a hell of a lick. Even by blitzkrieg standards, the German onslaught had been extraordinary. It was hard to see how Stalin would hold on.

Sceptical, he asked, 'Why did they come to you?'

'I think they thought I'd say yes.'

'Because you were sympathetic?' When Palmer shrugged, Guttman asked bluntly, 'Were they right?'

Palmer looked at Guttman. 'I'm not a spy, if that's what you're asking.'

'So what made them think you were ready and waiting to work for a commissar?'

Palmer looked defensive. 'Having a conscience isn't about which class you've been born into,' he said.

To Guttman, Communism meant complaint – what did the likes of Thornton Palmer have to complain about? He said, 'Maybe you'd better explain. Let's start at the beginning.'

Palmer's face flushed slightly; it seemed the conversation wasn't going according to plan. He seemed less confident now and when he spoke it was with the hesitancy of a reluctant storyteller. 'It began the summer of '33 when I went to Europe with the Whiffenpoofs.'

'Whiffen-what?' asked Guttman.

Palmer gave him a patronising smile. 'It's a singing group at Yale. Very famous – well not that famous, I guess. Every summer it tours Europe. My year we started in France, then crossed into Germany. I saw Nazism up close. Not a pretty sight. Then we went to Vienna.' He smiled at the memory. 'We gave a concert in the concert hall – the Musikverein. Afterwards there was a reception in the Imperial Hotel, hosted by the Mayor.'

Guttman wondered what this travel history had to do with espionage. Palmer said, 'I met a young woman there, an architect. She was beautiful – tall, blonde – and spoke very good English. We were staying in Vienna another two days and she offered to give me a tour.'

'A tour, huh?'

'Yeah,' said Palmer in a half-mumble. 'You see, I hadn't known a lot of girls. She was pretty remarkable,' he added, then looked embarrassed.

The guy had probably been a virgin, thought Guttman.

'What was her name?'

'Kristin.'

'Kristin what?'

'Does it matter?'

'Could do,' Guttman said. When Palmer didn't say anything, he decided not to press. 'Was Kristin political?'

'It wasn't called Red Vienna for nothing. This was in its dying days. Kristin was a believer: she worked for Karl Ehn, the architect of the Karl Marx-Hof housing project, and her own apartment was in the complex. It was huge, you know; it stretched for nearly half a mile.

Everyone there was working together to create a new kind of community.' There was a hint of passion in Palmer's voice for the first time. 'It was probably the purest experiment in socialism ever seen, and it scared the hell out of the rest of the world.

'Then the tour moved on. I wrote. She wrote. I missed her like hell. When we got to Rotterdam there was a telegram from Kristin, begging me to come back to Vienna. So I did – and when I got there I stayed two months. I'd graduated that spring and was supposed to start work at Brown Brothers right after Labor Day. Instead I showed up just before Halloween. The bank – and my folks – were none too pleased.'

'What did you do in Vienna?'

'I met people. Kristin had lots of friends. Most were Austrians, of course.'

'Communists.'

'Socialists, Communists, progressives – nobody wore a tag, everybody was of the Left. Considering what happened later, they were right.'

'Go on.'

'One of her friends was Russian and he was tremendously worried about the rise of fascism in Europe.' He looked at Guttman almost reprovingly. 'As he had reason to be.'

'His name was . . . ?'

'Milnikov. Or that's what he said it was. I have no idea if he was telling the truth. He'd been chased out of Germany, that I do know, and he was always on the alert, even in Vienna.'

'And he tried to recruit you?'

'In a manner of speaking. He worked on me, that's fair to say; his big bugbear was what he called Western Liberals. He thought they were too naive to understand the struggle that was going to take place in Europe between right and left. He said a person had to choose, had to take a stand, had to act – and not just theorise.'

'Is that how you were feeling anyway?' said Guttman, trying to sound sympathetic.

'Yes, I suppose so. You see, the summer before I drove with a friend out to the West Coast. We went the southern way, through Oklahoma, and I saw suffering there first-hand. *The Grapes of Wrath* has nothing over the reality – all those people who went to California didn't find things much better there. So Milnikov must have decided I was making all the right noises. I probably was – you have to understand, I never thought I'd see him again. Especially once I got the boat at Rotterdam and sailed home.'

'Why didn't you stay with Kristin?'

'Kristin was going to come to the States the following spring. Then we'd get married. That was the plan.'

And go farm apples in Vermont, thought Guttman cynically, but he said nothing. He sensed this story wouldn't have a happy ending.

'I wrote her every day and she wrote back, but halfway through January her letters stopped. At first I thought it was because she was so busy – the reports made it sound like a civil war was breaking out in Austria. Whole parts of Vienna were under siege. When I hadn't heard anything for three weeks I started to get worried. I didn't know what to do. I tried calling – it was quite complicated; the overseas switchboard is routed through London or Paris. The operator couldn't get through. Then I tried to reach some of her friends but I couldn't locate anybody. I was getting desperate when suddenly Milnikov showed up in New York.'

'What a coincidence.'

Palmer shrugged. 'It didn't seem that odd at the time;

he was visiting with a Soviet Trade Delegation. When we met he told me he had terrible news. Kristin was dead – she'd been killed in the street-fighting after the Government reclaimed the Karl Marx-Hof buildings. Over two hundred people had been killed. Kristin was one of them.'

Considering his first love had been murdered, Palmer's voice sounded curiously unemotional. 'For a while I was really shook up. I didn't know what to do – though I knew I couldn't stay at the bank when the world seemed to be falling apart. Fascism was on the rise all over Europe and I wanted to help fight it. But there wasn't any place to fight – you have to remember, the war in Spain was almost two years off. Still, I knew Europe would be the battleground and I thought I should go there.'

'What changed your mind?'

'Milnikov. After the Trade Delegation left he stayed in New York – I didn't realise why until much later. He said if I really wanted to defeat the fascists then I shouldn't go to Europe – I'd just end up getting killed when the fighting started. I needed to play a part that was more important, where I could influence events and make sure America didn't go the way of Germany or Italy. Father Coughlin was reaching his peak and the Silver Shirts had formed and Gerald L. K. Smith was talking about running for President – there were more fascist groups starting up than you could shake a stick at.'

'Did this Milnikov say how you should fight the good fight?'

Palmer looked annoyed. 'Not then –' he started to say, then stopped. After a pause, he resumed. 'I took the Foreign Service exams six weeks later. I passed them easily enough and I had some good contacts – half my mother's family were diplomats. Joining wasn't a problem.'

I bet, thought Guttman. People weren't stupid at State – not stupid at all. But they tended to be well-born and well-connected.

'I worked in Washington for the first six months. I didn't hear from Milnikov during that time; I assumed he'd gone back to Moscow. But then one day he called out of the blue and said he was in Washington, working on trade relations – we'd just signed the first agreement ever with the Soviets. We had dinner and we talked about Europe. By then the war in Spain had started and Hitler had moved into the Rhineland. Milnikov must have sensed my frustration – I was in the Western European Division, but felt I was just spinning my wheels, watching from the safety of a desk while the fascists made their move. After dinner we went to a bar and it was then he made his proposal.'

'What did he want?'

'He wanted me to feed him information.'

'What kind of stuff?'

Palmer looked impatient. 'They didn't want the base-ball scores, Mr Guttman. They wanted cables, reports, assessments, all kinds of things.'

Guttman raised his eyebrows.

'It could have been done easily enough. Take them home, photograph everything, transfer them onto micro-film and let them off at safe drops round the city. Security is so lax that it wouldn't be noticed if they were gone overnight, not if the next day I put them back. No one would ever be the wiser.'

'Golly,' said Guttman, mentally noting that something had to be done to tighten things up at the Department of State. He could envisage how delighted Hoover would be to tell Cordell Hull what a loose ship he was running.

There was no point beating about the bush. Guttman said, 'So did you?'

'Absolutely not.' The young man looked sternly at Guttman. 'I told you that. I'm not a traitor.'

'But you were sympathetic – you felt you weren't doing enough to fight the fascists.'

'I wasn't, and we weren't. But that didn't mean I would work for the Russians. Look, I'd heard enough things about people being recalled to the Soviet Union, then disappearing forever. In Spain, once the civil war started, some comrades were keener to shoot Trotskyites than kill Franco's soldiers. And of course there was Kirov and all the show trials.'

'So what happened when you said no?'

'Nothing. Milnikov was obviously disappointed and said if I changed my mind I should get back to him. Then I got posted to Argentina.'

Guttman sat back, trying to take it all in. He said, 'Why didn't you report any of this?'

'Hard to say. I suppose I still believed in the cause of anti-fascism – but not in the creed of the Communist Party.' He paused. 'And I was scared about what might happen.'

'To you?'

'No, to my Aunt Matilda,' he said dryly.

'So why are you talking about this now?'

'Events.'

'The Nazi invasion?'

Palmer laughed. 'Hardly. That's been positively heartening.' He threw his cigarette down, but didn't stamp it out and it glowed like a ruby lozenge in the dark. 'Look, the pact with Berlin killed any sympathy I'd ever had for the Russians. I know all the Party arguments justifying it, but it's all baloney. At the very heart of things Russia has no moral core. Not under Stalin. I'd

36

have been helping a regime that is in every substantial way as bad as the Nazis.' He looked defiantly at Guttman. 'I mean that.'

Lighting another cigarette, Palmer took a big drag and sat back on the bench. Guttman said, 'Tell me, did Milnikov try to recruit other people at State?'

'I don't know. If he did then he also did a good job of keeping us apart. That way if you guys found one spy, you wouldn't find the others.'

Guttman's disappointment must have shown, for Palmer added, 'I do know one man he approached. He's one of the reasons I'm here.'

'Yeah?' said Guttman encouragingly. 'Who was that?'

'Another Yalie, but a little after my time there.'

'Small world.'

'It gets better. He was also a Whiffenpoof and, yes, he went on the European tour the summer before I did. When they got to Vienna, he met a girl . . .'

'Don't tell me. Kristin?'

'Yes, and tragically she was killed by the Nazis, though the version he was told had it happening in Linz.' He shook his head and chuckled. 'At some point they're going to run out of ways to kill her off.'

'How did you find this out?'

'There was a Whiffenpoof reunion at the Yale Club in New York. The present group sang, then we all gathered in the bar. I got to talking to this guy, and he mentioned Vienna. Then he told me about this girl he'd met and she sounded kind of familiar – unsurprising, since she had the same name. Kristin Pichel.' Palmer didn't seem to realise he had supplied the surname. 'I didn't know whether to sock the guy or laugh; I think he felt the same way. Fortunately, we both had a sense of humour and we got to be friends. It took a while before the other stuff came out.'

'So they approached him too?'

'Yes.'

He hesitated, as if uncertain whether to cross a line. Guttman guessed what it was. 'But unlike you he said yes, right?'

'Right,' said Palmer through tight lips.

'Does he know you're talking to me?'

'No, and I don't feel so good about it. He's got more to lose than I do. He works for a bank in New York and he's married and has a family to feed; I'm not and I don't. Plus, he has one credential I never had. He joined the Party after he came back from Vienna. If that came out he'd lose his job lickety-split, whatever FDR likes to say about democratic bygones. The Russians have that over him. He wasn't happy helping them, but he had no choice.'

'What did he do for them?' What could a banker have done for the Russians?

'He told me he was asked recently to send a money order to the Coast.'

'That's all?' Guttman said. Even the Russians had the right to move money around.

'It went to a Jap bank in LA. A big sum too.'

'Who was getting the money?'

'Some Russian, I assume.'

'Then why a Jap bank?'

'That's the funny thing,' said Palmer. 'The Russians have put some people on the Coast. The banker knows that much – he just doesn't know why.'

They all say that, thought Guttman; not even the most voluble informant ever spilt all the beans at once. 'He's the only other recruit you know?'

'Yeah, though he knew of another one. A scientist at Princeton – a real whizz-kid.'

'Albert Einstein,' said Guttman facetiously. He must be tired.

'No, though the guy did work with Einstein once.'

'I could use these names.'

Palmer thought about this for a moment. 'I don't know the scientist's,' he said at last.

'The banker then?'

'I wouldn't feel comfortable giving it to you just yet.'

Comfortable? Jesus Christ. Guttman wondered momentarily if this was all horseshit. He said gruffly, 'You said this Yalie is one of the reasons you're here. What's the other?'

Palmer exhaled noisily and when he spoke he sounded depressed. 'They've approached me again.'

'Recently?'

Palmer nodded. 'When I was in Argentina, there wasn't much I could do for them there – so they left me alone. That was for almost five years, but then the wizards of Foggy Bottom decided they required my talents back here; I was recalled two months ago. I didn't tell anyone I was back, except my parents. But the Russians knew. Oh yes, they knew all right. Three days ago I found a note from someone who said he was a friend of Milnikov. It had been pushed under the door of my apartment, even though I never told them where I lived.'

'What's this new guy's name?'

'Kozlov. He wants to meet me next week.'

'Okay,' said Guttman neutrally.

'I'm not going to show. They'll name another time, and I won't show then either. Then they'll turn on me. That's why I wanted to see you.'

'What will they do? They can't say you spied for them, for one thing, and for another you didn't, and for another it's not as if they could reveal to the US government that they have a spy network anyway.'

'They're cleverer than that – they'll claim I *offered* to spy for them. Naturally, they'll say they turned the offer down, and as a gesture of good faith they want to let my superiors know about it. It will be something like that. So I figured I'd better act first; I want it on the record that I reported their approach right away.' He looked up and added suddenly, 'I'm going to have to go soon.'

'Right,' said Guttman. If they could set it up properly they could catch the Russian in the act – not at this next meeting, but in future when Palmer had something to give him. 'I think you should meet Kozlov,' he said.

'Why?' Palmer asked. For the first time he sounded genuinely worried. He wasn't acting any more.

'Play him along, see what he wants. You said yourself, if you don't show, he's going to try and do you in, one way or another.'

'But he's going to want me to have something.'

'We'll cross that bridge when we come to it. You don't have to promise him the moon – you can say security's tighter than before you went to Argentina. Say whatever you want – just don't turn him down flat.'

'I don't know . . .'

'Listen. If you want the Bureau to help you, then you have to play it our way. Don't think you're off the hook because you've spilt your guts now. We should have been having this conversation five or six years ago.'

He watched Palmer until at last the man nodded his assent. Guttman said, 'Now, when are you supposed to be meeting him?'

'Next week – we haven't set a day yet. He's going to call me.'

'Do you know where you'll meet?'

'I suggested here,' said Palmer. He gestured behind him. 'About a quarter of a mile in.'

40

'*What*? You're meeting this guy here, in the park?'

'Sure,' said Palmer stiffly, as if his judgement had been impugned. 'I told you, nobody I know is going to see me here. What's the matter?'

Jesus Christ, thought Guttman, where do I begin? 'I want you to call me after you've seen him.' He reached into the side pocket of his jacket and took out a card, which he handed to Palmer. 'Then I'll want to know the arrangements for your next meeting.' He was thinking that's when the Bureau could pounce.

'I better get going,' said Palmer.

You and me both, thought Guttman. They rose simultaneously and Palmer extended his hand. Guttman shook it, trying to hide his unease.

'There's one thing I don't understand.'

'What's that?' asked Palmer, anxious to go.

'How did the Austrian woman know to single you out? I mean, why you?'

Palmer looked startled. 'I don't know for sure. It might have been someone at Yale who tipped them the wink. Or somebody out West – you know, that summer I told you about.'

'You can give me names, can't you? Who it might have been.'

'Not yet. I have to know you'll keep me in the clear. I better go now.'

And without even saying goodbye, Palmer walked away. Guttman stared as the big figure moved slowly into the dark of the woods.

Guttman himself turned and went back to the path, peering ahead of him as he picked his way carefully towards his car. His hesitant progress matched the uncertainty he felt. What Palmer had told him was on the face of it downright crazy. The Russians were a ragtag outfit, one step out of the peasantry, none more so than

Stalin himself. It's true they were relentlessly paranoid – look at Trotsky, hounded by assassins until one had succeeded last year. But the Russians were barely familiar with America; they had only established diplomatic relations after Roosevelt became President.

He stopped short as he neared the car park, not knowing exactly why, until he realised he had heard something. *Someone*, he decided – it had been the sound of a footstep off to one side of the path he was on. He peered into the darkness and there was a sudden movement, of a dark shadow – no, it was two shadows. Then the two shadows merged into one. Were they embracing? Another couple like the two he'd seen in the car. Time to get out of here, he thought, as the shadowy figures stayed in a clinch. Then they unattached themselves, the shadow split in two, and Guttman saw they were walking into the park – away from the car park, he thought dumbly.

He heard a voice, low and quiet, yet it came over crystal clear. What had it said?

He moved on to the car park and was unlocking the Buick, ready to start up the car and race for home before Isabel's helper blew her stack, when suddenly he thought about what he'd heard. A monosyllabic word like *Duh*. Or was it *Da*? *Yes* in Russian. Was he imagining things?

He didn't wait to think it through. He ran back along the path, inexplicably panicked, scared he was too late. There was no sign of the couple. He called out, 'Palmer? Are you there?' He heard nothing. This time he shouted as loud as he could. 'Palmer? Thornton Palmer! Where are you?'

He stood hearing only the little bubbling current of the stream that ran along the side of the path. Even the birds had gone down for the night – nothing rustled in the undergrowth. He pulled his weapon, wondering why he was so nervous, holding it out in front of him, ready to shoot – shoot what? He'd end up shooting Palmer by mistake. 'This is the FBI!' he shouted out in frustration. It sounded ridiculous. What the hell was he doing?

'Palmer!' he shouted for the last time. He listened as the sound of his own voice receded into the darkness. Still, the only reply was the sound of water moving through the gravel bed. Guttman felt powerless, which he didn't like, and afraid, which he liked even less. Especially since he didn't know what he was scared of.

Part Three

Los Angeles
End of September 1941

3

NESSHEIM LIVED ALONE in a dead-end street on the edge of Laurel Canyon; a winding road that climbed up to the ridge of the Santa Monica Mountains, then toppled into the San Fernando Valley. His place was a ranch house of stone and wood built into the side of a hill, which slanted down steeply from back to front.

He rented it furnished from a widow lady, who, after her husband died, moved to Glendale to live with her daughter. The place had three bedrooms, which seemed luxurious to Nessheim; he slept in one, used the second as a study and never set foot in the third. He liked having a house to himself and spending his time there alone. He was too old to have a roommate and tired of boarding-house life. A Mexican woman came in once a week to do his laundry, iron his shirts and clean the place; otherwise he could count on the fingers of one hand the times anyone else had been in the house.

He parked in the open garage, then came out again to climb the stone flight of steps to his front door. He had just put the key in the lock when a woman's voice said, 'Did your friend find you, Mr Nessheim?'

He turned to find Mrs Delaware, his nosy neighbour, standing at the bottom of the steps. She was wearing her customary apron – Nessheim sometimes wondered if she wore it to bed. There was never any sign of a Mr Delaware; Nessheim didn't know if he had died or just grown tired of the apron. 'What friend was that, Mrs D?'

'I thought you'd know; he certainly seemed to know you. At first I thought he was a realtor – he was in the backyard.'

'Was he Japanese?' he asked.

'Oh no,' she said and Nessheim remembered there were covenants here that kept the Japanese from buying a house. 'More European-like. I think maybe he was German.'

'Why? Did he sound it? *Vere is young Jimmy Nessheim?*' he said, mimicking the accent of his aunt's late husband – Eric had come over from Germany in the Twenties and never lost his thick Bavarian overlay.

Mrs Delaware laughed. 'Gee, you sound like a Kraut yourself.'

'He didn't leave his name?'

She shook her head. 'He acted like you were expecting him.'

'You sure it wasn't just some guy from the utility company?'

'I've never seen one in a three-piece suit before. Besides he was out back and your electric meter's in front like mine.'

'Well, thanks for letting me know,' he said and turned back to his front door.

Inside he checked his mail – a letter from his mother (he got one every week) and the other in the familiar handwriting that set his heart beating hard. He made himself open his mother's first. It was her weekly missive, full of small-town news and small-town dramas. He'd worried about her when his father had died very suddenly the year before. She'd sold what was left of the farm and moved to town, where she worked part-time in a store and, it some-times seemed, full-time seeing her friends. He was starting to realise how lonely life must have been for her out at the farmhouse, especially when her husband had been forced to work in another man's dry goods store. Now Nessheim's mother seemed to be thriving, and though she thanked him as always for the money he sent her every month, it didn't sound as if she really needed it. He realised that part of him wished she weren't adapting so well to life without his father; the part of him that wasn't adapting so well himself.

He went out to the kitchen where he'd had his one luxury installed – a Frigidaire. He liked his drinks cold, and in a place where you could go swimming on Christmas Day this was the only way to guarantee it. He took out a red-and-white can of Acme beer. It tasted thinner than the Wisconsin brews he was used to, but was ice cold. He drank half of it quickly and sat down to read Annie's letter.

Annie was too Vermont to indulge in many frills, but she did like proper stationery, heavy, cream-coloured, like that of her great-aunt, Sally Cummings, but without the embossed sender's address on the back of the envelope. He tried not to tear it too badly as he opened it; he kept her correspondence in a drawer, neatly stacked in their envelopes.

Dear Jimmy,

I am sorry not to have written for so long – and do understand how pleased I am to get your letters. Your life seems so interesting these days – and I laughed out loud at your description of the 'Count'. I am so glad you've kept your sense of humour, even if not everything about the job is to your taste.

We are doing pretty well here. Jeff likes school, though he still prefers football to anything he learns in class. He has grown about a foot in the last six months and eats half a horse a day.

Otherwise, life is much the same. Justice Frankfurter continues to put up with my non-existent shorthand and has settled in at the Court. Harry pokes his head in on occasion, and I have helped out a few times when his wife's sitter has let them down. I don't mind at all, but I have to say that Mrs G does seem to be failing.

I know I said we hoped to visit for Christmas this year, and I hope you will not feel too disappointed that I've had to change our plans. For the first time since – well, since Great-Aunt Sally invited me to live with her – my parents have asked Jeff and me for Christmas. It's not a reconciliation I have sought, or really even care about, but I think it's important for Jeff to know his grandparents and where his mother came from. It's not as if he's ever going to know his father's family. So, much as I'd prefer to be catching a train, crossing the country knowing you were at the other end, I think it's important that we go to Woodstock for the Christmas holidays. I do hope you will understand.

And I hope you'll understand when I say that I am worried about you. I sometimes feel you are letting yourself be tied to the past, when you should be making a future for yourself. After all, that's what California's for. And I could not forgive myself if I thought I was in any way responsible for keeping you from living life to the fullest.

Be in touch when you can, and believe me that I am sorry about Christmas.

Love from Jeff and me,
Annie

He put down the letter and took a long pull from his beer. At least she had used his name, since she could just as easily have started the letter 'Dear John'. He could read between the lines of that and then some. Annie was not freeing him so much as pushing him away, done in the nicest possible way – 'I could not forgive myself if I thought I was in any way responsible for keeping you from living life to the fullest.' Which meant, *Find another girl, pal.*

Any woman who changed her mind and went to see her parents for Christmas wasn't in love with the man she'd been planning to visit. Not that Nessheim believed she'd be welcomed with open arms by that grim old couple in Woodstock, Vermont – she'd described them well enough: the penny-pinching storekeeper father who didn't like to laugh; his haggard wife, who on his account was scared to. Nessheim knew that Annie hadn't until now seen or heard a word from them for over five years – when she'd taken her illegitimate little boy south to D.C. and joined the household of her powerful socialite great-aunt.

She didn't love Nessheim – that was clear as a trout stream. Sure, she was fond of him, but he had an older sister who was fond of him as well. How could he have misread the situation so badly? Had Annie fallen for someone else? He doubted it – a single mother with a bastard child was not a hot ticket in a woman-filled town like Washington, D.C. She'd had a fiancé once before, but he'd had hidden motives to say the least. So there she was, after the bust-up with her great-aunt, living with Jeff as lodgers with some old lady in Arlington, trekking in on the bus to work for the Justice, trekking back, watching every penny, making the light bulbs last. And it didn't have to be like that at all, thought Nessheim bitterly.

He stood up and went through to the kitchen, then out down the back steps into the yard, where the scarlet-tinged leaves of the persimmon tree were preparing their autumn finale. He could see that there was going to be an abundance of fruit this year and he made a note to water it. Think of something else, he told himself; think about work. But his was not a job fit for a man in peacetime; it would be even worse when America entered the war, which Nessheim thought inevitable. But even war wasn't going to change things for him, or get him out of this place.

He'd made it as far as the medical in the recruitment office in Fond du Lac, fifty miles from his Wisconsin hometown. He hadn't told a soul he was trying to enlist other than Annie, for he'd learned by then just how far tentacles – Hoover's, Tolson's, even Guttman's – could extend. There had been twenty minutes when he thought he'd made a successful swap from civvies to uniform. But then a recruiting sergeant had come in and pulled him out of the line; Nessheim remembered the odd looks of the other enlistees as he left the room. He'd been taken to an office where he found the same doctor who had cleared him thirty minutes before sitting with a full colonel. Fingering a folder on the desk in front of him, the doctor had said, 'It seems you haven't declared all your medical history.'

Someone must have tipped off this doctor about the Chicago consultant who'd ended his football career; or about Nessheim's stay in a New York hospital after he'd almost drowned in Long Island Sound.

'Who's been telling tales?' he had asked mildly.

'None of your business,' the Colonel had snapped. Then, more softly, 'Nice try, fella. But it's no go. And the Bureau needs you anyway.'

The Bureau, the goddamned Bureau. It wouldn't be so bad if he were working in the field again, but his recurring dizzy spells – sole relic of that football injury – had put paid to that. He was a desk man now, confined to holding the hands of the phoney Count, doing the odd errand for Guttman, and pacifying the local SAC by keeping an eye on the pinkos who Hood thought were rife in the Hollywood ranks.

He was thirty years old and what did he have to show for it? Momentary glory as an all-American football player, cut short by an injury that had lost him his scholarship. Pure chance had landed him a post under Melvin J. Purvis, the Chicago SAC, legendary pursuer of Dillinger. Purvis had encouraged him and helped him move from being a clerk to becoming an agent, against most odds and many regulations.

But Purvis had made the mistake of becoming famous – which meant goodbye Melvin, once Hoover decided to move against the upstart. Along with all the other Purvis loyalists, Nessheim had been about to be bounced to the Butte office or its obscure equivalent when Harry Guttman had stepped in and turned him into an undercover agent – furtively, since it was against Hoover's own proscriptions.

He put a hand now against his side and felt the scarred ridge of skin that a bullet wound had left him as a souvenir. Twice he'd almost been killed working for Guttman, and he wondered if there was going to be a third time. Who was this stranger Mrs Delaware had reported seeing?

He went inside, intending to take a shower. The doorbell rang as he was starting to undress. Mrs Delaware again? It didn't seem likely. When he answered the door he found an old man standing at the top of the stairs wearing the blue uniform of Western Union. His eyes bulged when he saw Nessheim's holstered Smith and Wesson.

'Maybe I got the wrong place,' the old man said.

'Who are you looking for?'

'James Nessheim,' he said, looking down at the name on the envelope he held. His other hand was crippled, the fingers curled like a hook, hanging lifeless by his side.

'That's me.' Nessheim took the envelope and signed for it. The old man said delivery was pre-paid, but seemed happy with the quarter Nessheim gave him on top. When he'd gone Nessheim went back inside and opened the envelope. Even by Guttman's laconic standards the reply was short:

FIND HIM.

4

IT WAS SATURDAY morning and Nessheim rose and showered, then put on a pale linen suit and the silk tie that a rich girlfriend had bought him in Chicago almost a decade before. He left the house and started his car, then went down the hill to Hollywood Boulevard. There was very little traffic at the weekend, though a small black Austin followed him down the hill and along the Boulevard. When he parked his car at the corner of Vine the Austin went right on by. He didn't get a good look at the driver, though he was pretty sure it was a man. No hat, short hair.

He crossed the Boulevard and went into Albert's Barber Shop. It had a spinning candy cane barber's pole in front, and elaborate lettering traced on its wide front window: *Men's Hair Dressing, Toiletries and Shaves.* He'd first gone there for a haircut soon after arriving the January before, and now made a habit of coming every Saturday morning for a shave. There were four barber chairs with mirrors on the wall facing them, which made the room seem larger than it was, an effect enhanced by a floor laid out in a chequerboard pattern of large black-and-white tiles. Against the other wall customers could sit and smoke cigars and read the papers in one of a line of comfortable red leather chairs, which had tin ashtrays sunk into their chrome arms. At the back of the shop were two coat-racks and a shoe-shine stand with two chairs – Arthur, the 'shine boy' (who looked about a hundred years old), sat on a low stool when he wasn't making a show of slapping polish on or snapping his chamois rag. Today he was fiddling with the radio for the broadcast of the ball games starting three time zones later back East.

It was less than a mile from the studio, but Nessheim had never seen anyone from the AMP in the barber shop. He liked the place: it seemed an oasis of calm after the hectic craziness of the Ink Well. You'd sit down and Albert would pump the chair up, then tilt it back until you were almost looking at the ceiling. He swathed your face with hot damp towels to soften your beard, lathered the cup of shaving cream, then applied the foaming soap with a soft badger brush that he'd dipped in hot water. You lay back with your eyes closed, sleepy and content to let the man take a lethal straight razor and shave you so close and so effortlessly (never even a nick) that when you stood up five minutes later your face was pink and smooth as a baby's bottom. You handed over two bits and left the shop a new man, ready for the week ahead.

It was quiet this morning and as Albert stroked the sudsy lather from his throat Nessheim listened to the Braves game, crackling through its various relays.

'You think that Ted Williams will hit .400?' Albert asked as he wiped away the remaining bits of soap with a towel.

'Could do it,' said Nessheim. 'I'm a DiMaggio fan myself.' Jolting Joe had hit in fifty-six straight games earlier that season; if Williams did hit .400 they were two records that looked likely to last a long time.

'What a year,' said Albert, wiping his razor between swipes.

'Enjoy it while you can.'

'What do you mean?'

'Next year those guys may be wearing a different uniform.'

'Nah, the Sox would never trade –'Albert stopped as

he suddenly understood. 'Don't remind me. I got a boy who's coming up to draft age.'

Shaved and trimmed, Nessheim drove south, then east on Wilshire towards downtown, where even two miles away he could see City Hall, looming high above its neighbours, the sole building exempt from a city-wide height limit of 150 feet. He turned down Spring Street, and its heavy-set financial office buildings, plonked right in the flat bottom of the bowl which made up most of the city.

He managed to park right outside the Federal Building, since only a few employees worked at the weekend in the Mussolini-style edifice. Inside only one elevator was working – a new automatic one. He took it to the eighth floor, where the guard at reception looked half-asleep as he pushed the sign-in book towards him. He walked down the corridor to the open space where most of the agents had their desks. Looking down he spied the Los Angeles River, swaddled in its new channel of cement, recently poured to control its tendency to flood – it had broken both banks earlier in the year.

His office was a sawed-off desk tucked in one corner, and most of the time he arrived to find that someone had taken his chair. He averaged one visit every other week, so he couldn't really complain. Now the room was almost empty. In a corner two agents were poring over a map they'd spread out on a desk; another agent, by the window, was on the phone, looking bored. He glanced up and Nessheim gave a casual wave and kept going towards the filing cabinets on the room's north wall. The long-term files were kept in a locked room down the hall, but more transient stuff, including recent reports from informants, were kept in the bank of three-drawer filing cabinets, next to the SAC's office. Hood had given him a key only reluctantly, after

Nessheim had pointed out that he couldn't very well keep his files at home – nor at the studio, which, as Hood knew, was full of snooping pinkos.

The SAC's office door was open and he peered in; there was no sign of Hood. Not unusual for a weekend, since he was a big family man, his desk studded with framed photos of his wife and kids. He advised bachelor agents that they should get married if they wanted to advance at the Bureau.

Nessheim went back to the filing cabinets and unlocked the middle filing cabinet. *M, N, O* – he pulled back the heavy letter tab and scrutinised the files behind it. *Ockermann, Olley, Ormand,* then the one he was looking for. He pulled out *Osaka* and walked back to his corner desk, grabbing a chair on the way. He wanted a coffee, but decided it could wait. Opening the file he took out its pages and read them very carefully.

Billy Osaka had been born in Honolulu, Hawaii, on March 19, 1916, son of Taro Osaka and Mary Osaka (née Mitchie). He had moved to the mainland in 1935 aged nineteen, where he attended UCLA for two years but left without a degree. His two references were teachers there – an English composition lecturer and an Associate Professor of Political Science – though neither had been consulted since Osaka's work for the Bureau was occasional and hardly top secret.

Billy had begun work as a stringer for the Japanese-American newspaper *Rafu Shimpo* in 1938, and was first approached by Special Agent Danforth in spring 1939 when fears of a Japanese invasion led the Bureau to start identifying fifth columnists within the Japanese-American community. Osaka had been asked to help identify subversives who might be working for Japanese intelligence, and to serve as a translator. He was put on a retainer of $10 a month, which suggested scepticism about his value; unsurprisingly many of Agent Danforth's notes of their meetings recorded Osaka's complaints that he wasn't paid more.

Not that his intelligence seemed to justify a pay rise: as Danforth noted, most of it was available from public sources. When the Japanese Ambassador Kichisaburō Nomura had visited Southern California earlier in the year, he had been feted at a lunch by Japanese-Americans. Osaka had filed a confidential report saying the Ambassador had held meetings with two local Japanese-American dignitaries. Since both had been openly described in *Rafu Shimpo* as the organisers of a lunch in Nomura's honour, Osaka's disclosures were of limited value to say the least. Particularly since Osaka had written the *Rafu Shimpo* article.

Nessheim checked that the address Osaka had most recently supplied was the same one in Boyle Heights which he had already visited. He was about to close the file when someone said, 'Well, if it isn't Clark Gable himself.'

Nessheim looked up, to find Cohan standing across the desk, his pinched face looking like it had been caught in a trap. 'Morning,' he replied, hoping to limit their exchange. Cohan was the SAC's deputy and Nessheim thought him the worst kind of gung-ho agent, happy to climb the career ladder by kissing the ass on the rung above him, while stepping on all the hands on the rung below. Cohan had got married in spring and spent his honeymoon in Washington; rumour had it that he had taken his new bride to visit the Bureau training facilities in Quantico. Rumour also had it that his wife was rich, which explained why Cohan lived on the edge of Beverly Hills.

'What gives us the pleasure of your company at the weekend? I'm impressed.'

Nessheim said, 'I could ask the same of you. Why aren't you home with your new bride? Something up?'

Cohan said, 'Nothing you need to worry your sweet buns about.' But he couldn't help boasting: 'We got a spic drug ring in our sights. There's a raid set for tonight and R.B.'s coming in to check we're all prepared.'

Nessheim wondered if R.B. Hood was going to lead the raid himself. He was a cautious man, but no coward – and traditionally SACs were first through the door. This added another subtler danger to the obvious one of getting plugged, since a successful raid always made the papers, and the publicity rarely sat well with the Director in D.C. Look at Purvis, after Dillinger's death: his endorsement had been stencilled on half a million boxes of Wheaties. Within two years Hoover had driven him out of the Bureau.

'When's SAC due in?' he started to ask, but then the man himself appeared. The agents called Hood 'Dick Tracy' behind his back, with respect if not affection. He was tall and ramrod straight and as prudish as a small-town minister, which made sense given that his father had been one in Kansas. Hood Junior didn't smoke, drink or swear. His one concession to human weakness was a vanity about his appearance. Today he wore a khaki suit and a panama hat with a band the colour of smoke. He saw Nessheim and stopped. 'Where's your report?'

'Sorry, boss,' said Nessheim. He was damned if he'd call Hood 'sir', and Hood was never going to invite Nessheim to call him 'R.B.'. 'Something's come up – one of my sources has blown. I can't find him anywhere.'

'Who is it?'

'Billy Osaka.'

R.B. frowned. 'I told you he was no good. It's a waste of time worrying about him. You can't trust the Japs.

Their loyalty is to a different country, whatever they tell you.' He paused. 'By the way, there's some Red shindig I want to know about. It's raising funds for the Communist brethren in Moscow. You'd think it was a little late for that – *too* late if you read the papers. Still, it's worth finding out who's behind it. You have good sources – use them.'

'Okay,' said Nessheim, whose 'sources' amounted to gossip overheard in the Ink Well and Elsie's Diner. It looked like he would have to go to the Writers for a Free World benefit after all. But there was a silver lining, he realised – he'd ask Lolly to go with him. Why not? he asked himself, since he was no longer spoken for.

Hood went into his office and Nessheim put the Osaka file back, then walked to the other end of the floor, where the typists sat in an open bullpen. There was a small working library by the window and the view here was a spectacular one of the Santa Monica Mountains to the west and north. He could just make out the dip of Laurel Canyon.

He found a Bureau Directory, wondering if there would be a field office in Hawaii – it was just a territory after all, not even a state. But it was listed, along with the SAC's name: Robert Shivers. He found a piece of typing paper in the bullpen and wrote out his message in block capitals: INFORMATION REQUIRED ON LA INFORMANT BORN IN HAWAII NAME OF WILLIAM OSAKA. He gave Billy's date of birth, his parents' names, then asked for details of Osaka's upbringing and education in Hawaii, any known addresses where he resided, any living relatives, and any criminal record. It was standard stuff, a Scoop search as it was called in the Bureau. He signed the sheet and stuck it in the Work Waiting basket.

He left the building and got into the Dodge. Driving east, he crossed over the Los Angeles River on Olympic Boulevard and went past the Sears Roebuck Building, an immense concrete tower, one of nine depositories across the country. He'd grown up with the company's catalogue, remembered how his mother would read through it in the evenings, carefully choosing those items she couldn't find in the general store in Bremen.

Boyle Heights was north according to the map so he swung left, entering a neighbourhood of small streets with shabby old houses and little bungalows, just east of the river. Boyle Avenue, the main street, was bustling with people. There were fruit and vegetable stalls, fresh produce piled high, and the array of small shops were almost all Mexican or Jewish. He crossed Fourth Street, then drove into the quiet residential neighbourhood on First Street, with its pale stucco houses and brick apartment buildings, a school and a Catholic church.

He parked, took off his tie and left it on the passenger seat. He didn't want to be taken for a bill collector, or a detective. As he approached the tall wood-frame house, a young woman came out and stood on the porch. She wore baggy shorts, a pink shirt and bobby socks, the dress of a classic American girl, except that she was clearly Japanese. She looked upset, like she had been crying; seeing Nessheim she wiped her eyes, then quickly came down off the porch and cut across the front lawn, heading away from him. He watched her, but she didn't turn around.

He went upstairs to Billy's apartment and knocked, but no one answered and he couldn't hear any sound from inside. He tried the other upstairs apartment, but the couple he'd seen on his previous visit weren't in, so he went downstairs and knocked at a door on the ground floor. An old Japanese lady answered the door, wearing a housecoat and oversized slippers that had fluffy balls on their toes.

'Sorry to bother you,' Nessheim began, then realised from her uncomprehending expression that she didn't know English. He was about to make his excuses and go when a man's voice called from inside the apartment.

The old lady said something and seconds later a man appeared. He was Japanese, in thick, blue work pants and a T-shirt, and looked about ten years older than Nessheim. He was stockily built, with powerful arms. His hunched stance suggested he was a stoop labourer, days spent in back-breaking labour picking strawberries, melons, asparagus and squash, crouched down with a stem knife. 'What do you want?' the man demanded. A grain of rice hung off his upper lip and he wiped it off impatiently. His lack of any accent suggested that he was American-born.

'I'm looking for Billy Osaka.'

'You come round before?'

Nessheim nodded. 'I was looking for him then too.'

'What kind of trouble is he in?'

'He isn't. I'm a friend of his. We were supposed to meet up, but Billy didn't show. I haven't been able to get hold of him since.'

The man looked dubious. 'You want me to tell him you came by?' he asked.

'Please,' said Nessheim and the man looked surprised.

'Who do I say it was?'

'Tell him Nessheim.'

The man nodded. 'I'll tell him.'

'Sorry to trouble you.'

He was halfway through the front door when the man called out. 'You tried his grandmother's?'

What grandmother? According to the file, Osaka's family was in Hawaii. 'I don't know where she lives.'

'In Little Tokyo. Above a restaurant; a fish place. That's why he moved out here – he couldn't stand the smells. He said his grandmother didn't mind it. She used to ask for the fish guts and use them as fertiliser for her window boxes.' He gave half a smile.

Nessheim nodded. 'Thanks,' he said, thinking that there were quite a lot of restaurants in Little Tokyo.

'I hope you speak Japanese.'

'Like a native.'

The man laughed. As Nessheim started to leave he added, 'Or you could try Ferraro's.'

'The restaurant?' A fancy place on Wilshire Boulevard, with a menu so expensive it didn't have prices. It didn't sound like Billy's kind of place.

'Yeah, but he doesn't go there for the food.' He looked at Nessheim meaningfully. 'The game's in the back.'

Nessheim drove home and spent the afternoon in the relative coolness of his study reading *What Makes Sammy Run*, which had done the rounds of the Ink Well in spring. At 7.30 he ate a liverwurst sandwich and drank a bottle of beer. Then he changed into his best lightweight suit – a grey, double-breasted number he had bought after he'd been promoted to agent. Six years before, yet it seemed an age. He put on a white shirt with a semi-stiff collar and carefully tied his tie – a striped one, maroon and white. From the inner pocket of a jacket in his closet he unearthed a roll of fifty-dollar bills and peeled off six of them, which he folded in half and put in his trouser pocket. Then he went through his wallet, taking out his badge, Bureau identity card and driving licence, substituting a different licence with a Chicago address. He left his gun behind.

Ferraro's was not an average spaghetti-and-meatballs Italian joint. Its entrance was on Vine and had a wide yellow stucco front with smoked glass that allowed customers to look out, but did not extend the privilege in reverse to the hoi polloi on the sidewalk. There was a doorman and valet parking, but Nessheim put his car a block away. He didn't expect to have to make a quick getaway but he wasn't taking any chances.

The doorman stood in front under an awning, wearing a full-length coat, which had gold-braided epaulettes on each shoulder, and a commander's white cockaded hat. Nessheim walked past him, nodding politely. A neatly trimmed privet hedge ran parallel to the sidewalk, and when he came to a gap in it he went through the opening. Ahead of him stretched a colonnaded walkway, running along the side of the restaurant and ending at a squat single-storey annexe in the back, behind the restaurant kitchens.

'Can I help you?' It was the doorman. He was quick to have caught up to Nessheim so fast.

Nessheim turned round and let the doorman scrutinise him.

'I was told there was a game tonight.'

'Are you expected, sir?'

Nessheim forced a wry smile. 'I wouldn't have thought so.'

The doorman was shaking his head, so Nessheim reached into his jacket side pocket and brought out a fin. Folding it with his fingers he tucked it into the breast pocket of the doorman's coat. 'Jackson told me about the game.'

'Jackson?'

'Yeah. Tell them Jackson from the studio.' He figured there had to be a Jackson at a studio somewhere.

'Wait here a minute,' said the doorman. He looked back at his post and swore. 'Where's that crazy carhop?'

'Don't worry. You go find him,' said Nessheim.

The doorman shook his head. 'No can do. You better come with me.'

They walked back to the entrance of the restaurant, where under the awning a lectern stood in a corner with a house phone and a drawer for the customers' car keys.

The doorman picked up the phone. 'Susie,' he said, 'put me through to Ike.' He waited a moment. 'Hi, it's Dave in front. I got a guy who wants to join the game. Says Jackson sent him.' He paused. 'That's right – Jackson. From "the studio".' He paused again and eyed Nessheim's suit. 'Yes, he is.' Then he hung up the phone. 'You're in,' he announced.

Nessheim went through the opening in the hedge for a second time and down the colonnaded walk, which had a line of stout agave in large pots on either side. He came to a large metal door; it looked heavy as a vault. Next to it he pushed the buzzer and after a moment the door swung open.

'Come on in,' a balding man in a tuxedo said. He looked like a maître d'.

Nessheim stepped through the doorway into a large room that was bathed in golden light coming from two oversized chandeliers dropped from a high ceiling. There were perhaps two dozen people in the room. Closest to Nessheim, two men with blonde wives in tow were playing blackjack under the disinterested eyes of a pudgy-faced dealer, who slid the cards out of the shoe with stubby fingers. Nearby a small group was watching a big man with an open-necked shirt throw craps down the wooden alley, and around the roulette table half a dozen people squealed when the wheel stopped on zero. Everyone was well dressed; even the waitresses were classy-looking, with black skirts and crisp white blouses.

'Are you here for the poker?' the maître d' man asked.

'That's right.'

'Both tables are full right now. Why don't you sit and have a drink at the bar? There'll be a space free soon.'

He went and sat on a wooden-backed stool. The bartender wore a white shirt and black bow tie, but no jacket. He was Nessheim's height, but squarer in the shoulder – he wouldn't need a bouncer if there was trouble.

'What'll it be?' asked the bartender.

'Bourbon and branch.'

'Branch?' He looked amused. 'Where you from, buddy?'

'Chicago.'

'What brings you west?'

Nessheim said, 'Poker.'

'First time here?' Nessheim nodded and the bartender chuckled. 'You'll find a good game in the back room.'

A few minutes later a man walked out through a curtain at the back of the room and the maître d' came over. 'You're on,' he said and Nessheim followed him through the curtained doorway.

Here in a much smaller room five men sat around a round table with cards and chips on its baize. Nessheim took the one empty chair and watched in silence as the hand was played. The tubby man on his left won a small pot with King high.

'Chips?' asked the dealer with a smoker's rasp. He wore a tuxedo too.

Nessheim pushed all three hundred dollars across the table and got stacks of five-dollar chips pushed back. There were fifty-seven of them, so the club was taking 5 per cent off the top. It didn't seem unreasonable.

'Ante up,' said the dealer. Everyone threw in a chip while he shuffled the cards.

'So what are we playing?' asked Nessheim, his voice all innocence.

The dealer looked surprised and momentarily stopped shuffling. 'Five-card stud.'

'You got any better ideas?' asked the tubby guy next to him.

'No, I'm happy,' said Nessheim.

'Oh good,' said Tubby. 'He's happy, Fred, so you can deal now.'

Fred dealt and the cards came shooting out, sliding eel-like across the felt until they halted just short of the waiting hands. One down, then one face up.

Nessheim showed a deuce and held a four in the hole. He folded at the first bet and did the same for the next three deals. He was trying to feel his way in. The college poker he'd played had been social rather than serious: five-card draw, which made it less a matter of calculation than of blind hope – almost any hand, however poor, could be redeemed at the last minute by a drawn card. Stud was different – immoveable odds and everything down to betting and bluffing.

He watched in bewilderment as a forty-dollar pot went to a pair of threes, and then as an Ace high, bet aggressively by Tubby, got a showing pair at the end of the table to fold. Two hands later Nessheim lost sixty dollars when he tried to bluff Tubby, and lost with King-eight against the other player's King-Queen. Despite this, Nessheim felt more confident now, and was doing his best to show it, talking a little too much, ordering another bourbon and water when the waitress came round.

Then he got some cards. He won a hand with a pair of tens, though all but one player folded and he only won twelve bucks. On the next hand he held an Ace in the hole. Tubby had King showing, and further up the table a man with brillantined hair also showed a King. He bet twenty dollars and Tubby and Nessheim seed him. Through the next two rounds no one showed a pair, but Tubby bet so aggressively that Brillantine man folded, King notwithstanding.

With the final card to play there were almost three hundred dollars on the table. With that kind of money at stake, Nessheim figured Tubby didn't bluff, so he was ready to fold after the last card came out. Instead he found his heart beating like a drum when he was dealt another Ace.

Tubby pushed two neat stacks of chips into the middle of the table and grinned at Nessheim. 'Raise you another two hundred.'

'I haven't got enough cash left to call,' Nessheim protested.

Tubby gestured at the dealer. 'He'll take your note. But I feel bad taking your money.' Not that Tubby looked very upset. 'You can raise me to the moon and I ain't gonna fold. Fish don't fly over rainbows in this part of the world.'

Nessheim nodded at the dealer who counted out two hundred dollars in stacked chips and pushed them over to him. Nessheim thought fleetingly of Guttman – and tried not to imagine the expression on his face when he saw Nessheim's next expenses.

'I'll call you,' said Nessheim suddenly. 'With the two hundred in lieu.'

Tubby slowly turned over his hole card. Sure enough, he had another King. He looked momentarily jubilant – until Nessheim turned over his second Ace.

There was a little gasp of admiration at the far end of the table. As Nessheim raked in the chips, he glanced at Tubby, who was staring at him angrily. Tubby said in a mimicking voice, '*So what are we playing?*' He shook his head in disgust. 'You been around a bit, buddy. Where you from?'

'Here and there.'

'How did there get you here?'

Nessheim finished stacking his winning chips. 'A guy I met told me about the game. He said he played here a lot. Funny-looking fellow – kind of Japanese. Billy something.'

No one said anything. Noise from next door suddenly seemed louder. Tubby put his hands on the table, nodding thoughtfully. Nessheim saw he had a scar the size of a stick of gum running along one side of his neck. When Tubby spoke he almost spat out the words. 'You're telling me you heard about this game from *Billy*?'

'Something wrong with that?'

Tubby shook his head at Fred the dealer. 'Count me out. I need a drink.'

Without Tubby the game seemed to lose its intensity and the betting was more restrained. When he turned to summon the waitress, Nessheim saw Tubby standing by the door, talking with the maître d'. After another round, in which Nessheim folded early, the maître d' appeared at Nessheim's side. 'Could I have a word in private please?'

'What about?'

'I'll explain in a minute.'

The other players weren't looking at him any more. When he stood up, Fred pointed to his chips. 'They'll be safe there,' he said.

The maître d' led the way towards the back of the room and into a small corridor where they found a closed door. When the maître d' knocked a voice called out 'Come in.'

They entered a small dark office that was lit only by

a table lamp on a desk. A man sat behind the desk, dressed in a grey banker's suit with thick pinstripes and a scarlet silk tie. He looked about fifty years old and had a handsome face, though a birthmark sat in a small red patch under one eye. His hair was slowly going a distinguished grey.

'Have a seat,' he said, pointing to the empty chair on the other side of his desk.

Nessheim sat down and the maître d' left the room. 'Is there a problem?' he asked. 'I was doing okay out there.'

'Don't worry – you got plenty of time to lose it.' The man leant back in his chair until only the very front of his face was in the lamp's light. 'George tells me you were asking about somebody.'

'I was?'

'Evidently. Guy called Billy Osaka.'

Nessheim was thinking how to answer when there was a knock on the door and George the maître d' reappeared. 'We got company,' he said.

'Oh yeah?'

'It's Foyle again. And some of his men.'

'Christ. Better send him in.'

As George went to get the visitor, the man behind the desk looked at Nessheim. 'Sit tight. This won't take a minute.'

A few seconds later the door swung open and a cop came in, wearing a peaked cap and a double-breasted uniform coat lined with brass buttons. His face was big-boned and Irish and – when he looked at Nessheim – very unhappy. The last thing Nessheim needed was to be busted in a raid by the local cops, carrying a phoney identity card.

The man behind the desk said, 'This is an old associate, Commander.'

'I don't care who he is. You're late, Ike.'

Ike shrugged, and the cop looked at him angrily. 'I've told you, and told you to tell your boss: this isn't Cleveland. So don't fuck around. When I name a date, you keep to it, got it?'

'Okay. But I've got this for you,' said Ike. He reached in his top drawer and brought out an envelope. 'Or do you want to turn it down and stay pissed off?'

The cop called Foyle hesitated, then reached out for the envelope and grabbed it like a candy bar. Nessheim looked down at the floor as the cop shoved it into his inside jacket pocket. 'It better all be there,' he said.

'Of course it is. With a double sawbuck thrown in for late delivery.'

'Next time . . . on time. Got it?'

'You bet,' said Ike cheerfully, and the cop went out the door, banging it shut behind him.

Ike looked at Nessheim and shrugged. He didn't seem fazed. 'I've creased palms in a lot of towns, but the LAPD take the biscuit. Anyway, where was I? Oh yeah, you were asking after Billy Osaka.'

'That's right.'

'Is he a friend of yours?'

'I wouldn't say that. I'm looking for him, though.'

Ike stared at Nessheim and pursed his lips. Then he said, 'You mind my asking why?'

'Maybe.' Ike continued to stare at him and Nessheim relented, since otherwise he wasn't going to get anywhere. 'I've got business with him.'

'Join the crowd. Don't tell me: he owes you some money.'

'Something along those lines.'

Ike nodded and his mouth hinted at a smile. 'He could be hard to find. Some people think Japs all look alike.'

'Not Billy. Maybe because he's only half-Jap.'

'That's true,' said Ike, and Nessheim realised he had been checking that he really did know the guy. 'But it would still be pretty easy for him to disappear in Little Tokyo. There must be twenty thousand people living there.'

Nessheim didn't react, and Ike said, 'You know the neighbourhood?'

'A bit,' he allowed.

'Well, that's more than I can say.' He sat up a little in his chair and put his hands on its arms. 'So here's the thing: I got my own wish to see Osaka, and I want to piggyback on your search for the guy. I'm offering you a thousand dollars to let me know where he is. It's got to be reliable – don't just give me rumours. But if it's real, you get a grand.'

'I want to see him first.'

'Okay, but I don't want damaged goods when it's my turn. Understood?'

'Sure – I want the money he owes me, not his hide.'

Ike nodded. 'And another thing: I don't want any trouble with the Tokyo Club. They've got their turf and we've got ours, and that suits me just fine; I've got no bone to pick. But I can't have Osaka coming here to play, then not clear his debts. Make sure they understand that's what it's about – nothing more, nothing less.'

'Got it,' he said, though he hadn't.

'So we have an understanding?'

'It sounds that way to me.'

Ike extended his hand across the desk and as Nessheim shook it, asked, 'You got a name, pal?'

'Rossbach.'

'A Kraut, huh?'

'One hundred per cent.'

'Okay Mister Rossbach, is there a way I can reach you?'

'I'll give you a phone number.'

There was a pad on the desk and he reached for it and wrote down his home number, then slid it over to Ike, who looked at it and said, 'You got an address maybe?'

Nessheim shook his head. 'It's Osaka you're looking for. Not me.'

5

SUNDAY WAS MISTY and overcast when Nessheim drove to Pearl's house in the foothills of Bel Air. He drove through gates a lot fancier than those at the studio, then the drive curved sharply and swung round a line of eucalyptus; behind it he saw a mocha-coloured clay tennis court, sitting in the middle of half an acre of lawn that was tightly mown in stripes of dark green. Another curve and he glimpsed the roof of the house before it disappeared, blocked by a pair of native oaks. At last the drive straightened out and he pulled up in a circle of packed gravel that had a little statue of Mercury in the middle, standing on top of a bubbling bird bath. But by then his eyes were on the house – an immense villa, three storeys high with a flat roof. Its stucco walls were painted pink, its window frames glossy white. The place looked like it was built of candy cane.

His was the only car in the turnaround, and he wondered if he had come in the wrong entrance or, worse still, was the only guest. He didn't really know Pearl, and wanted to keep it that way. They'd spent twenty minutes together when Nessheim had first arrived; it had been an amiable conversation in which Pearl himself had been the chief topic of conversation. 'Doing a Goldwyn,' Teitz had described it, after that mogul's habit of conducting a non-stop monologue about himself, pausing only to take breath and say, *Enough of me about me. What do you think about me?*

Nessheim had turned down the offer of an office near Pearl's in the executive quarters, preferring to keep his distance among the studio's proletariat of writers. Since then Nessheim's relations with the studio owner had been confined to the occasional phone call. He thought of them as the Happy calls. 'Is Mr Hoover happy?' Pearl would ask, and Nessheim would say, 'The Director is happy.' And that was it. He couldn't think of anything he'd done to merit this invitation, especially if it meant lunchtime alone with Pearl.

Now a teenager in white trousers and a white polo shirt came around the corner of the house and waved to him. The kid ran up to the car and Nessheim said, 'No rush.'

The kid caught his breath. 'Mr Pearl doesn't like to be kept waiting. I figure his guests might feel the same way.'

Nessheim let the kid drive off with the Dodge, then walked up to the front door, which was half-open. He knocked once and walked into an empty entrance hall dominated by a majestic staircase, which rose in a vertiginous sweep of white struts topped by a black banister. It looked like a grand piano had been tipped over on its side.

A young Hispanic maid appeared and asked for his coat; she smiled when he pointed out he wasn't wearing one and he noticed how pretty she was. A door to one side opened and Mrs Pearl came out. It had to be, Nessheim figured, since Hollywood Wife was written all over her: she was tall and tanned, with shoulder-length, wavy blonde hair that looked fresh from the beauty parlour. She wore a silk dress, patterned with blue-and-red peacocks and a string of impressive pearls. Two rings, one a big diamond, sat like capital investments on her wedding finger.

'I'm Faye Pearl,' she said in a voice that was all cigarettes and smoke. 'And you are?'

'Nessheim. I'm with the FBI.'

She looked momentarily startled, then gave a hostess

smile. 'Of course. Buddy mentioned you'd be here. Do come in: it's a buffet, nothing formal – just a lot of friends of ours. Which means movie people, since Buddy doesn't have any other kind of friends any more.' She turned to the maid who was now standing by the door. 'Anita, don't just stand there. *Comprende*? Work – go to work.'

He followed Mrs Pearl through into a vast living room, which had large windows that looked out over a square of formal lawn, framed, in Italian style, by tall cypresses. There were perhaps thirty people in the room, almost all standing up, though there were several clusters of chairs and sofas, covered in fruit-coloured fabric – orange and lemon and plum. At the far end an oil portrait hung above the fireplace of a woman who looked familiar, and Nessheim realised it was a younger Faye Pearl.

The guests were mainly men, dressed in smart weekend suits, holding drinks and talking in small groups. At the near end of the room French doors opened on to a long sun porch with a glass roof. There silver chafing dishes lined the serving tables, which were covered with starched linen tablecloths.

Faye crooked a finger and a black waiter came up. 'What would you like to drink?' she asked Nessheim.

'A beer, please,' he said and the waiter went over to a bar in the corner.

Faye said, 'I don't know how many people you'll know here, Mr Nessheim.' He looked around, but didn't see a single familiar face except for Buddy Pearl. Nessheim noticed Faye catch her husband's eye. As the waiter came with his glass of beer, Buddy gestured at Nessheim to join his group, so he excused himself to Mrs Pearl and made his way over.

'Ah, Agent Nessheim,' said Pearl expansively. He wore

a blue blazer with shiny brass buttons, his white shirt open at the neck. 'Come meet some people.'

There were half a dozen men standing in a semicircle and Nessheim tried to take in their names as he shook hands with each in turn. One little guy was named Mayer, another Loew, another Warner. Suddenly it clicked: these were Pearl's fellow moguls. He wondered again what he was doing there.

One whose name he didn't catch asked him, 'How is Edgar these days?'

'I haven't seen him for over a year,' said Nessheim, which was technically the truth since he hadn't *ever* seen Hoover.

'Is he coming out to the Coast any time soon?' the man named Warner asked. He was dressed sharply in a grey suit with small black checks.

'I haven't heard,' said Nessheim.

'I have,' said Pearl. 'I had a call from him about two weeks back. He was checking on the progress of our latest Bureau picture. It's looking good, isn't it Agent Nessheim?'

Nessheim nodded. 'They'll be wrapping up tomorrow or Tuesday.'

Pearl said, 'Mr Hoover told me he's thinking of coming out later this Fall.'

'Before the Santa Anita season ends,' Warner said. He added with a smirk, 'His friend Clyde likes a flutter.' Someone gave a knowing smile.

A much younger man came across the room. He was a little short of six feet but square-jawed and muscular. Pearl beamed at him. 'TD, you made it.'

'Have you got the keys to the pool house? I left some stuff out there.'

'Sure thing. Say hi to these gentlemen. This is my boy,' he said proudly.

TD nodded curtly at the group and made no attempt to shake hands. Pearl said, 'TD's got one more year at USC. Then I'm hoping he'll join me at the studio.' When TD frowned, Pearl protested, 'Well you can't play pro football. That's a mug's game.' He looked around for support and his eyes fastened on Nessheim. 'You played some ball, didn't you, Nessheim?'

'A bit.'

'In high school?' asked TD, sounding unimpressed. He didn't seem to recognise Nessheim from their encounter at the studio gates.

'Yeah, and college too.'

'Really?' TD seemed surprised. 'All four years?'

'Nah,' said Nessheim, who didn't want to play it up. If Pearl thought the sun shone out of his kid's backside, Nessheim wasn't going to put a cloud in the way.

Pearl said, 'TD here was varsity all three years. They'd have made the Rose Bowl if they'd started you,' he said to his son.

TD nodded. There was no aw shucks modesty about Pearl's kid, thought Nessheim. One of the moguls asked TD, 'What position do you play?'

'Quarterback,' he said. He was looking hard at Nessheim. Maybe he did recognise him after all.

The mogul turned to Nessheim and politely asked, 'What about you?'

'I went both ways. Safety and end.'

He sensed the moguls were getting bored of the football talk. Pearl took a bunch of keys out of his pocket and handed them to his son. As TD walked off, Warner announced, 'On the way here, the radio said Kiev's fallen.'

A man with receding hair laughed. 'Kiev? I left there when I was five years old after they murdered my uncle in a pogrom. My mother carried me, and my father carried a sack of gewgaws to get us started in the New World. So I'm not shedding any tears for Kiev.'

A quiet-spoken man said, 'If Kiev's fallen, the Nazis will be heading for Moscow next.'

'Good for them.' This was Mayer and everybody looked a little surprised. 'Listen, I'd rather do business with Hitler than the Commies any day. That's what I want Joe to understand. He's got to realise we're Americans first and Jews second.'

The receding-hair fellow said knowingly, 'The Russians will fight like rats. If Moscow goes they've had it. That's why I can't see it falling myself.'

'Maybe,' said the quiet-spoken man, 'but they better watch their backside. They've got divisions on the Manchurian border. If they pull them back to fight the Germans, the Japs will be in like a shot.'

Warner piped up, 'Not if the Japs invade us first. Then the Reds won't have to worry about their eastern flank.'

'Let the Japs try,' said Mayer. He looked at his watch. 'Is the Ambassador due any time soon?' There was a slight impatience to his voice.

'Don't worry, he'll be here,' Pearl said. 'You know Joe – if he can keep Gloria Swanson waiting, why worry about a bunch of *haimishe* Hebes.' He laughed but seemed a little antsy. He glanced at Nessheim, 'You should get some lunch, Agent Nessheim. You must be starving.'

Nessheim knew when he was being dismissed. He nodded at the semicircle of potentates and made his way to the sun porch. Two black men in white shirts served him from the hot dishes. It was nothing fancy, but still quite a spread – creamed beef, hot tongue, barbecued drumsticks, breast meat served cold in slices, potato salad, coleslaw with carrot bits, beets in vinegar, tomato vinaigrette and lettuce mixed with avocado. There were three kinds of rolls.

He took his plate and looked around; people were eating in little groups he didn't feel comfortable joining. Spying some empty wicker chairs by one of the windows, he went and sat down. It had started to rain and the windows were streaked with long runs of water. He was gnawing on a drumstick when a man joined him, stylishly dressed, in a double-breasted suit with a white dress shirt and a rich blue tie with a Windsor knot.

'Mo Dubin,' the man said, leaning over to shake, with a soft enormous hand that felt boneless. He was rumple-nosed, with a face that looked older than the rest of him.

'Tell me,' said Mo, leaning forward close enough that Nessheim smelt the earthy stink of Pall Malls, 'have you ever seen a bigger bunch of jerks?'

Nessheim sat back and tried not to laugh. 'You tell me.'

He said, 'You work for Buddy?'

'Sort of.'

'Say your name again, pal.'

Nessheim told him and Mo looked at him carefully. 'A *landsmann?*' When Nessheim looked baffled Mo laughed. 'I didn't think so. Though all those guys are Hebes like me. Yet they're standing there like the six apostles, waiting for the Ambassador.'

'Who?'

'Joe Kennedy. Having been bounced out of his post in England, he had the nerve to tell them they should hold back on criticising Hitler or it could go badly for the Jews over here. I used to know Joe – what a schmuck.'

'So why's he coming here?'

'It's more why are *they* here waiting for him?' Mo gestured disdainfully to the group around Pearl. 'It's because they're scared. Not Buddy – he's known Joe even longer than I have. But the others –' he shook his head in disgust. 'They'd cut a deal with Hitler himself if they had to. They're having some hearings in Washington – the isolationists and anti-Semites are having a field day. Hollywood's run by the Jews, they say; Communism is being insinuated into the nation's motion pictures. Honest to Christ, three minutes with Louis over there and you'd know he's terrified of Commies.'

'It's true that Mr Mayer didn't seem very hot on war with Germany.'

'Who is? But sometimes you do what you gotta do.' Nessheim nodded and Dubin went on, 'Mayer's a buffoon. Oh, I know he makes a great picture, but what's that got to do with anything?'

Nessheim didn't have an answer; it summed up his own view of Hollywood. 'Are you from LA?'

'Is anybody? I'm just visiting for a while. Though not many of these schmoes seem to have been out here much longer.' He gestured with a bent thumb towards the living room. 'Listening to them, you'd think they all lived in New York. You hear more talk about Second Avenue than about Hollywood Boulevard.'

'Are you from New York?'

'Nah,' said Mo. 'I'm just a rube from Shaker Heights.'

A connection clicked for Nessheim, but only vaguely. 'What brought you out here?'

'The weather,' he said cheerfully, pointing outside, where the rain was now steady. 'And I do some jobs for Buddy. We used to be partners.'

'In the movies?' Nessheim asked.

Mo gave a curt laugh. 'Would you see a movie made

in Cleveland?' He added casually, 'It was the liquor business.'

'How long were you in that for?'

'Long enough,' said Mo and he and Nessheim looked at each other. Prohibition had been over for eight years, but it was clear that Mo's and Pearl's venture had pre-dated its expiration.

Mo said, 'So if you don't work for Buddy, which studio are you with?'

'I'm at AMP all right. I advise on the crime pictures. I'm with the FBI.'

Mo made a great show of patting his jacket pockets, then guffawed. 'Nothing to declare,' he said.

Nessheim shrugged amiably. He'd had worse reactions to working for the Bureau. 'I'd cuff you if there were.'

'I bet you would,' Mo said jovially, but he looked less comfortable now. He took his empty plate and put it on the side table next to him, ruffling its fabric cover. 'Excuse me a minute; I got to make a call. Nice speaking to you.'

Nessheim nodded. 'See you later.' He sensed Mo was unlikely to return.

Dessert was being served at the buffet tables by two Hispanic women, though not the pretty one who'd greeted him at the door. He saw Louis Mayer with a plate of strawberry shortcake, edging his spoon into his plate while a fat man in an off-white suit whispered in his ear.

He got up, suddenly desperate for air. It was now raining hard outside, but he didn't want to move back to the living room and the moguls. There was a glass door to the garden at his end of the sun porch and he went towards it. No one paid any attention as he quietly slid open the door and stepped out onto the veranda.

It was paved with small ceramic tiles that were slick

from the rain. Nessheim moved gingerly along them until he came to steps leading down to a small section of mown lawn, which was bounded by a high evergreen hedge. He descended and crossed the lawn, then went through a low archway cut into the hedge and looked down at a big rectangular swimming pool, long enough for laps, wide enough for water polo. Behind it sat a long low cabana of pale pine. As he came down to the level of the pool, the rain was starting to soak into his suit's shoulders. On the surface of the pool the rain dropped *plink plink plink*, and steam rose as it hit the heated water.

He decided to take shelter under the timbered portico of the pool house and wait until the rain tapered off. There were two doors in the cabana and he hoped one would lead to a bathroom. Then he heard a noise that sounded like moaning. The wind?

He picked the second door and pushed it open slowly. Inch by inch the changing room came into view. The room was unlit and it took a moment for his eyes to adjust. But gradually he could make out the wooden floor, the benches that ran against two walls, their green cushions . . . and then in the far corner a pair of legs. Brown legs, their knees bent, with another pair of legs wrapped around them.

It was two people, one lying on top of the other. He saw uppermost the muscled figure of a naked young man – tanned except for his ass, which stood out in the dark room like a pale moon. A woman was underneath him, making the moaning noises Nessheim had heard outside – it was hard to tell whether from pleasure or pain. Her skirt was hitched up high, almost to the waist. It was a white cotton skirt, though darkened in places by water stains – she must have been caught by the rain.

84

The woman turned her head and suddenly a pair of dark eyes was staring straight at him. It was the maid he had met in the entrance hall. The man, he realised, was TD. The look on her face was not embarrassed or surprised, but simply resigned, as if his presence was just one more humiliation.

He turned and moved back through the open door, closing it quietly behind him. He took a deep breath. What a risk the pair were taking – but then, who would be stupid enough to come out in this rain? *Bring your trunks*, Pearl's secretary Rose had said, but there would be no swimming party today. Not that it seemed TD would care what anybody thought.

Nessheim walked past the pool as the rain belted down. When he came to the opening in the hedge, he hesitated – he didn't want to face Mo Dubin again or answer the inevitable question about why he had got so wet. He went left instead, walking on a neat gravel path that went around the house, functioning as a walkway and a French drain to keep water away from the house's foundations. Even in this torrent the gravel was absorbent and dry, crunching with every step he took.

He had turned the corner when he realised he was about to pass a large window. He moved out into the garden instead, sheltering briefly under a jacaranda tree, orange and green-leaved at this time of year. He peered at a ground-floor room of the house and realised he was looking into a study. A man sat behind a desk. Expecting it to be Buddy Pearl, he was surprised to see Mo Dubin sitting there instead. Someone else was in the room, standing in front of the desk. Nessheim took a small step forwards to get a better view.

Any thoughts of returning to the party vanished. It didn't matter to Nessheim what they were talking about;

it was enough that the other man was there. Time to go. He retreated further into the garden, moving behind clumps of white oleander. He'd fetch his car himself and make his excuses. Right now it was crucial that he wasn't seen. Not by Mo Dubin while he was talking to the other man, and especially not by the other guy – Ike, the manager from Ferraro's.

It took him several minutes to find his car, but at last he located it behind the stables. Its keys were in the starter. He was drenched by now and drove out quickly, waving with phoney cheer to the parking kid as he went through the turnaround in front. Back on Bentley Avenue he headed towards Santa Monica Boulevard. A hundred yards down he saw a woman walking along the winding road. It was the maid again.

She was walking quickly through the downpour on short powerful legs, her calves packed with a walker's muscle. She was carrying an umbrella, but the wind had picked up and she had to stop every few steps to keep its spokes from bending inside out. Nessheim drew alongside her and stopped; reaching over, he pushed down the window and said, 'You want a lift?'

She turned, ready to say no to a stranger. He said, 'I saw you at the party. You know, in the Pearls' house.'

She hesitated and he could see that she was tempted. Even with her umbrella the girl's white skirt was wet with rain. He reached over and pulled the handle, then pushed with his fingertips until the door opened. 'Come on, you're getting soaked.'

She took down the umbrella and hopped in, then closed the door.

'There, that's better, isn't it?' he asked. She was even prettier up close, with unblemished skin the colour of light caramel, and those dark, wide-set eyes.

She was silent as he put the car in gear and pulled

away from the kerb. 'Do you speak English?' he asked after a moment. She nodded, but didn't say anything.

They drove for a minute in awkward silence, Nessheim beginning to regret his chivalrous gesture. 'Are you from across the border?' he finally asked.

'I'm not from Iceland, if that's what you're wanting to know,' she said in entirely unaccented English.

Nessheim laughed and she gave a reluctant smile, adding, 'But don't tell Mrs Pearl that, please. She's happier with help when *ellas no comprenden Inglés.*'

'I won't tell any of the Pearls,' he said pointedly.

The girl sighed. 'That was you, wasn't it?'

'What was me?'

'You know. In the pool house.'

'None of my business,' he said, keeping his eyes on the road.

She said quietly, 'Just drop me at the bus stop if you don't mind. It's about a mile down the hill.'

He nodded. 'What's your name, by the way?'

'Anita. Why?'

'No reason. But listen, I hope you're not doing things you don't want to do.'

Her mouth puffed derisorily. 'Doesn't everybody? That's what jobs are for.'

He glanced over and saw that her uniform skirt was drying out – except for an oyster-coloured streak halfway down. He had seen for himself how that had got there. He said, 'You could talk to Mr Pearl. You know, ask him to get the kid to lay off.'

She turned and he could sense her eyes on his. 'What are you, mister, my knight in shining armour?'

Galahad, he wanted to say, but kept his mouth shut. She went on, 'First of all, Mr Pearl thinks Junior's so wonderful his poop don't smell. Second of all, do you know the expression "like father like son"?'

He looked at her in surprise. 'You mean . . . ?'

'Pull over. There's my stop.'

He slowed down and stopped. She opened the door right away and got out quickly. 'Thanks,' she said, with the door half-open.

'You got enough for the bus?' he said feebly. He didn't want her to leave angry.

'Why?' she demanded. 'You want to pay for that so you can fuck me too?'

He drove home feeling faintly sick. He lay down in his bedroom, trying to lose the image of TD pumping away in the pool house, then of the disdain in Anita's eyes when he'd offered her money for the bus fare.

He thought about Annie's letter, but tried to lose that thought and pictured his mother's Sunday back in Bremen, Wisconsin: church, then maybe lunch with his Aunt Greta, then a quiet afternoon of the radio and her knitting. He wished he were there – no, that wasn't true.

He got up and went and sat in the backyard now that the rain had stopped, replaced by the mid-afternoon sun. The news was disheartening: Leningrad was still under siege and in a separate development German troops were moving towards Moscow. Hitler had declared that Russia was broken and would never rise again. Nessheim wasn't so sure. He wished there were some way that both the Nazis and the Soviets could lose their war. He turned to the sports pages, but didn't find his usual satisfaction there. Northwestern had lost again, but for once it seemed utterly unimportant.

His surprise at what he'd seen in the cabana had been trumped by learning that Buddy Pearl was just as bad as his son. But what did he expect? Mo Dubin had been refreshing in his candour about their shared Cleveland past, and Ike's presence suggested that it was something Pearl had not shaken off.

If these guys were looking for Billy Osaka, Nessheim needed to find him before they did. He didn't know why it mattered, but he was glad something did.

6

HE STARTED OUT at six and made it to Little Tokyo half an hour later, slowed down by the traffic on Santa Monica Boulevard, full of trippers back from Sunday jaunts to the ocean. For an hour he cruised the streets, ignoring the irritated honks from cars forced to a snail's pace as he checked out the storefronts for restaurants. Eventually he parked on Third Street and walked the main body of Little Tokyo methodically, like a man searching a large patch of grass where he'd dropped his keys.

It was a different world, as if a construction crane had swung its boom across the Pacific, lifted part of Japan and plonked it down a few streets over from LA's City Hall. For blocks at a time his was the only white face – Sunday evening seemed no time for outsiders. The old, the young (separately and as families) seemed to be out for a stroll. They were neatly dressed: the older men wore ties, the women skirts and dresses, with sweaters against the growing chill of the evening. The stores were all closed, but the residents seemed to have gone out in order to see each other, not to window shop. He was noticed but not stared at, although on one corner a bunch of small boys giggled as one of them pointed a finger at Nessheim and said *Bang*. Nessheim laughed, then realised he must look like a plain-clothes cop, since why else would a well-dressed white man in a sharp-brimmed hat be walking the streets of Little Tokyo so industriously?

He felt out of place, but not disliked or feared. Yet the Japanese provoked those feelings in everyone else.

90

Were they feared because they were hated or hated because they were feared? The Chinese weren't much liked either, but they were usually merely mocked by white Americans; the Japanese possessed a pride that made them impossible to deride. No one could doubt their accomplishments – which may have been part of the problem. It was said they controlled the agricultural production of Southern California and most of its markets, as if the two were a tandem tap that they could turn off at will – despite the fact they weren't allowed to own the land they worked. It was taken for granted they had no loyalty to their new country and would rise up if war broke out, helping the invading warriors of Japan to create a new Nippon of the Pacific states, from Tijuana to Tacoma.

By eight o'clock it was dark and he had covered every street of the square mile. There had been plenty of restaurants and once he'd spied a window box, but when he went inside to ask, a waitress in the restaurant told him a young couple lived upstairs.

He returned at last to his car, ready to head home. Maybe the farm worker at Billy's house had got it wrong; or maybe he'd decided to send Nessheim on a wild goose chase. Either way it had proved a waste of time. The failure nagged at him and he pulled over, this time on San Pedro Street, under the yellow light of a street lamp. He reached for the glove compartment and took out a road map for the city, almost his first acquisition when he'd arrived in LA. He got outside and spread the map on the hood. He checked that he had covered all the streets of the neighbourhood, then looked for alleyways he might have missed. Nothing.

Starting up again, he noticed that the needle on his gas gauge was close to empty, then remembered he'd passed a gas station further east on Fourth. When he drove there an old Japanese man in overalls came out. Nessheim held up one finger. 'Give me a dollar's worth.'

The old man slowly put gas in the car, then walked up to the driver's side. 'Check oil,' he said brightly. 'Waw-tuh?'

Nessheim shook his head and handed over a dollar bill. A sudden impulse made him ask, 'Is there a restaurant near here?'

The man looked at him uncomprehendingly. Nessheim mimed someone eating and repeated his question.

The man nodded this time and pointed down Hewitt Street. Nessheim drove slowly along the street, but it didn't look promising: an empty lot, a row of houses with badly kept front porches; in the distance a warehouse with security lamps lighting up its forecourt.

And then he saw it. To his left as he drove past the warehouse towards some factory buildings that stretched south to Palmetto. It was a small restaurant, little bigger than a coffee shop, with lettering in Japanese above its one big window. It sat in the middle of half a dozen storefronts, housed in three-storey brick buildings that must have been built at the turn of the century. Above the restaurant's sign, on the second floor, two sash windows fronted on to the street; light came through one of them. Each window ledge held a wooden box full of waxy red flowers. Begonias, Nessheim thought, as he pulled over to the curb and turned off the engine.

As he got out a Japanese couple emerged from the restaurant. The man gave an appreciative belch and his wife tittered. He waited for the couple to turn the corner, then peered through the restaurant's window. It was empty now, except for a solitary waiter brushing off a tablecloth. Next door there was a hardware store and between the two shop fronts there was a single doorway with a buzzer.

He went to it and looked at two handwritten labels taped to the side of the doorframe. They were in Japanese and English, and the two words he could make out were *Kikuchi* and *Oka*. He stood for a moment, wondering which could be Billy's grandmother, then tried the door. It wasn't locked and he opened it wide, revealing a thin dimly lit hallway with a narrow staircase of steep steps. He entered the hall, closed the door quietly behind him, then stood and listened. All he heard was the thump of a carpet cleaner next door, banging against table legs in the restaurant.

Nessheim went up the stairs slowly, one step at a time. At the second floor a gallery doubled back, leading to the next flight; halfway along there was a door. He stopped outside it and looked at his watch. It was 8.30. An odd time for a stranger to be visiting an old lady, especially on a Sunday night.

He tapped on the door and waited. There was no sound from inside the apartment. He knocked again, louder – *rat-tat-tat*, like a quick triple smack on a drum. No response.

He tried the door knob and the old brass handle, darkened by years of use, turned easily. Little Tokyo was famously safe – full of one tribe looking after its own – but he was still surprised that the old lady didn't lock her door at night.

He went in cautiously and found himself in a small hallway. Light came from the front of the apartment – the same light he had seen from the sidewalk. Straight ahead he saw the kitchen, lit by an overhead light with no shade, and he stepped onto its scuffed linoleum floor. Now he heard music from a gramophone or radio upstairs. 'Hello,' he said softly, not wanting to scare the old woman. No one replied.

He went back to the hall and into the sitting room.

An oiled paper blind, yellowed with age and half pulled down, shed just enough light for Nessheim to make out the room's spare furnishings: a tatami mat on the wood floor, a small teakwood table against the wall and a snub-armed easy chair, covered in scarlet velvet darkened by wear. In a corner sat a miniature carved altar with a tiny statue of Buddha. Next to it there was a half-closed door. He walked across and stopped just short of it.

'Hello,' he said again and realised his hand was moving towards the holstered gun inside his jacket. He gave a solid knock to the door, then pushed it open. Looking through the doorway he saw a bed which had been stripped down to its mattress and a chest of drawers. This must have been Billy's room. No wonder he had moved out – Nessheim could smell the evening's cooking from the restaurant below.

Hearing the faint thud of a step upstairs he walked back quietly through the living room and into the kitchen again. He noticed another door in the corner, which must lead to the old woman's bedroom.

It did. He slowly turned the door knob and looked in, but the room was pitch black. Suddenly he was assailed by a terrible smell and he gagged. Holding his breath, he reached for the light switch just inside the door and flicked it on.

The old woman lay in the middle of the bed, covered by a single sheet, her nightgown visible only at her shoulders. She was lying on her back, her head slightly raised on a white pillow, dark thinning hair flowing on each side of her face. Her lips were pursed and tight, and her expression strained. The tendons of her neck looked as taut as the strings of a violin.

He moved closer to the bed, trying to ignore the powerful stench. The old woman seemed to be wearing a single-strand necklace the colour of tarnished silver, but he saw that the filament strand wasn't jewellery at all but a piece of wire, tied taut around her neck. It encircled her throat and ran back in a single silver thread to the headboard, where it had been looped around an upright post and tied in a slip knot.

Any movement would have tightened the encircling 'necklace'; if the woman had tried to lift her head even slightly she would have succeeded only in reducing her air supply. And if she had panicked and thrashed around, she would have strangled herself quite quickly.

Nessheim slowly pulled back the covering sheet, revealing a white cotton nightgown that extended almost to the woman's brown and wrinkled feet – the toenails were long and yellowing. Her arms extended down her sides, but her hands were tucked under her bottom. Nessheim put his hand around one of her forearms, no thicker than his wrist, and tried to move it out from under her. He couldn't and he realised her hands had been bound together behind her back, so she couldn't untie the bracelet of wire around her neck.

He moved back from the bed and this time he did pull his Smith & Wesson from its holster. He would phone the police, though he hadn't seen a phone in the apartment. He would ask in the restaurant down-stairs, but first looked around for anything he wanted to find by himself. In the corner of the room there was a heavy pine dresser with a half-mirror on top that had an envelope tucked under one corner. He picked it up and saw that someone had written on the front in Japanese:

転婆

The envelope was unsealed and held a small wad of bills, which Nessheim took out and counted. There were ten fifty-dollar bills. He rolled them up and put them in his trouser pocket, then separately stuffed the envelope into his jacket's side pocket.

Downstairs the waiter didn't want to open up, shaking his head when Nessheim stood at the glass-fronted door. He changed his mind when Nessheim held up his badge, and he called over his shoulder. The owner came out from the kitchen and unlocked the door. He was stocky, with fat cheeks and a mastodon jaw. 'What you want?' he demanded when Nessheim showed him his badge.

'I need to use your phone. The old lady upstairs is dead.' Not sure if he'd been understood, he pointed to the ceiling. 'The old lady,' and he drew a finger across his throat in a universal language.

The owner's eyes widened in surprise and he led Nessheim back to the kitchen and an old-fashioned two-piece phone on the wall. 'Thanks,' said Nessheim. He was about to dial, then remembered the envelope in his pocket. 'Hey, look at something for me, will you?'

He handed the envelope to the owner and pointed to the ideogram on its front. 'What does that mean?'

The owner looked at it for a moment. 'It's in Kanji,' he said.

'Great, but what does it say?'

'Grandmother.'

The patrol car was there in five minutes; the homicide detective took half an hour. His name was Dickerson and if his suit was his Sunday best then he didn't go to church, though it suggested he was honest – a cop on the take would dress better than that. Nessheim waited in the hallway while the cops took Dickerson through the apartment. When Dickerson came out, he told one of the patrolmen to call the coroner. 'I don't want the old lady moved until he's seen her. Got it?'

He turned to Nessheim. 'The beat cop said you're with the FBI. Mind explaining what you were doing here?'

'I'm looking for the grandson. He used to live here, then he moved to Boyle Heights. I came round to see if he'd come back to the bosom of his family.'

Dickerson gave a tight smile. 'I thought R.B. didn't like jokes.'

'Yeah, that's why he's the boss and I'm in a stiff's apartment on Sunday night.'

'Tell me about this grandson. What's his name?'

'Osaka.'

The beat cop interrupted. 'Billy?'

'Yeah. You know him?' Nessheim asked.

'Everybody knows Billy in Little Tokyo.'

Nessheim said, 'The old lady was called Oka – don't ask me why it was different.'

Dickerson said, 'Maybe she was his maternal grand-mother, huh?'

'His mother was Irish, so I don't think so.'

'That's right,' said the beat cop. 'He's only half-Jap.'

'Why are you looking for him anyway?' asked Dickerson.

'I was supposed to meet up with him last week – at his request. He said he had something important to tell me, then he didn't show. No one else has seen him either.'

'Did he have any money troubles?'

'You know anyone who doesn't?'

Dickerson fingered his tie, which had a large grease spot near the bottom. 'So where do you think this kid is? It looks to me like we want to find him, don't you think?'

'I don't make him for this one, detective. She was his grandmother.'

'Sure. But who knows why people do what they do? This ain't a burglary gone wrong – not the way that old woman died.' He shook his head. 'The killer knew her, well enough to get in without any fuss.'

'I found this.' Nessheim handed Dickerson the wad of bills. 'It's five hundred dollars.'

'Why did you touch anything?' asked Dickerson, sounding peeved.

Nessheim stared at him. 'No point tempting anybody was there?'

Dickerson looked furious at the implication. 'I want to talk to Osaka,' he barked.

Nessheim didn't say anything Dickerson didn't need to know about the envelope in his pocket. If Nessheim couldn't find the kid, maybe the LAPD could – before Mo's mob got there first.

Part Four

Washington, D.C. and New York
Early October 1941

/

7

THE MEETING WITH Hoover and Tolson this week was scheduled for noon, which was cutting it fine in Harry Guttman's view. Nothing got in the way of Hoover's lunch, and this Friday Hoover and Tolson would not dally long over their midday meal in the Mayflower Hotel, since they had a train to catch for New York. Increasingly Hoover liked to spend his weekends there, enjoying a nightlife at '21' and the Stork Club that had no counterpart in D.C. He and Tolson usually caught the Embassy at three o'clock at Union Station, and they weren't going to risk missing it (or lunch) because of their weekly meeting with Harry Guttman.

Marie, his secretary, came through the doorway. She was trustworthy yet completely undeferential; Guttman sometimes wished it was the other way round. A redhead and a big-boned gal with wide high shoulders, she was always nicely turned out, which was all the more impressive, Guttman thought, since he happened to know she made most of her own clothes. Her face was distinctive rather than pretty, with elongated lips and a flattened nose, but she carried herself well and the visiting field agents always seemed to find reason to hang around her desk, to Guttman's annoyance.

'You want to speak with Kevin Reilly?' she asked.

He had thought of Reilly only the week before. 'Sure. Put him through.'

He waited for the buzzer, then picked up his phone. 'Hi there.'

'Harry, you're like a bad penny. You only turn up when I'm having nightmares at work.'

'What is it this time, Kevin?'

'You better come see for yourself. I'm in Rock Creek Park; we could have a picnic. Though when you've had a look, you might lose your appetite.'

Reilly met him at the parking lot and they walked in together, past the bench where he and Palmer had sat the week before, and another 200 yards into the park. From there Guttman could see the creek – and a pair of uniformed cops smoking and talking quietly. When he and Reilly came into view, they stubbed out their smokes and pulled back their shoulders.

The grass around them had been trampled by many pairs of feet, and a man's body lay in the middle of the exposed area. It had been hauled out of the water; the clothes were still wet. The corpse lay face up on his back on the bank. Guttman took a quick look and wished they would turn him over.

'I did warn you, Harry,' Reilly said.

Guttman forced himself to look again. The dead man had been shot in the face – at very close range since he no longer had a nose, just a blood-soaked hole which resembled a second mouth. The force of the bullet had pushed one eye socket upwards, into a grotesque show-man's wink. On one cheek a piece of bone balanced pristinely – unless it was a splintered tooth, since the upper lip of the man's mouth was caved in. Blood had run down the man's neck, soaking the lapel of his khaki-coloured jacket. It had also reached his silk tie, where it added a rough smear to the stripes, and had dried to the colour of prunes.

'Poor bastard,' said Guttman.

'You know who it is?'

'Don't you?'

Reilly shook his head. It had rained that morning and

he wore a light raincoat over his cheap suit. 'If he had a wallet on him, it got taken. Though I can't believe this was your average stick-up.'

'It seems a little excessive for that.' Guttman remembered his futile bellowing into the dark. 'I don't suppose there were any witnesses.'

Reilly laughed derisively. 'What do you think?'

'How'd he get found?'

'Pure chance. He could have been there a long time,' he said, pointing to the bushy undergrowth around the creek. 'Some lady walks her dog here early in the morning. She came off the path to let the bow-wow take his crap and spotted a shoe heel sticking out of the water. She took a closer gander and started screaming; one of the park rangers heard her. When we got here she was still shaking – I thought any minute we might have another stiff on our hands.'

'Why'd you call me?'

'We found this in the grass over there.' Reilly reached in his coat pocket and handed a small card to Guttman, who didn't bother to look at it.

Reilly said, 'Maybe it's a coincidence – your calling card found thirty feet from a dead man who's had his face blown to smithereens. But I thought I should let you know.'

Reilly and Guttman had worked together before, but there was nothing pally in his voice now – he was a homicide dick who liked everything in its rightful place. Guttman said, 'His name's Thornton Palmer and he worked at the State Department. I saw him last week – about halfway between here and the car park.'

Reilly scratched his head. 'Are you in the habit of meeting diplomats in Rock Creek Park?'

'His choice of venue.' He stopped suddenly, realising

he had moved a foot closer to Palmer's body. He didn't want to look at it again. 'We through here?'

'Sure. I'll walk back with you.'

They rejoined the path and trudged along in silence for a moment. Then Reilly said, 'What did he want to see you about?'

Guttman sighed. 'I can't say just yet.'

'Can't say or won't say?'

'Take your pick,' said Guttman. He looked at Reilly. Once his Irish features – green eyes, a residue of freckles and the tangerine-coloured hair now starting to fade – had made him seem younger than his years, but now he looked as tired as Guttman felt.

Reilly said, 'Why can't you talk to me, Harry?'

'I'm sorry, Kevin, I just can't.'

'For Christ's sakes, Harry,' Reilly said impatiently as Guttman turned his eyes back to the path, 'I'm not going to ask the Chief to call Hoover, and you know it. But see it my way: I got a dead man with no face left and nothing to go on except that he met with an FBI assistant director only a long piss from where he got slammed. Do you blame me for wanting an explanation?'

'I have a new job at the Bureau, keeping the Nazis from setting up shop in Latin America. Palmer worked at the embassy in Argentina, so we had business to discuss.' He looked at Reilly with as much sincerity as the lie let him muster. 'That's as far as I can go.'

Reilly dropped his head and scratched his hair. 'Okay, but why did he want to meet you here? What's wrong with a coffee shop?'

'State and the Bureau have been having a bit of a ding dong lately. You know how these things go. Palmer didn't want to be seen with an FBI man.'

Reilly waved a hand dismissively. 'All right, all right. Beats me how you guys manage.'

'I don't know that we do,' said Guttman. He was thinking of what Hoover was going to say, and not looking forward to it. He looked at his watch – if he took his time getting back to Connecticut Avenue, the Director would be on the train for New York.

8

On Monday, three days later, Guttman was waiting for his postponed meeting with Hoover when Clyde Tolson appeared in the doorway of his office. Tolson wore a soft grey suit with a white handkerchief deftly folded in the breast pocket. He had been to the barber's: his hair was close cropped above his ears and the faint aroma of talcum powder drifted into Guttman's little room.

'I was just coming, Clyde,' said Guttman, starting to stand up. He'd been due on the fourth floor in five minutes.

'Relax,' said Tolson. 'The Director's had to go to the White House. It's just you and us chickens today.'

Tolson's presence always made Guttman feel uneasy; Hoover's Number Two had a disconcerting curiosity that could be unpredictable – he would lean over and pick up a confidential file, then ask why it had been pulled and when, or suddenly ask what a Field Agent from Topeka he'd seen on the floor was doing visiting the Washington HQ. Usually he contented himself with an acerbic remark about the state of Guttman's desk; fortunately Marie had come in twenty minutes before and done her daily sort out.

Today Tolson was in a rare playful mood, tossing a scrunched-up ball of paper from hand to hand as he ambled in and plopped himself down in the chair across Guttman's desk. He kept tossing the wad of paper, like an ex-ballplayer, which he often said he was – he'd boasted to Marie that he'd been all-Conference halfback. In a rare moment of disloyalty, Louis B. Nichols, Head of Records and Press Relations, had confided to Guttman that there was no record of Tolson playing any football after high school.

'What's going on at 1600?' Guttman asked lightly. He noticed that one of Tolson's sideburns had been trimmed higher than the other. 'War been declared?'

'Well, the boss is certainly waging one of his own. It's Donovan again.'

Guttman nodded. Hedley Donovan was Hoover's latest bête noire – ever since the President had appointed him Coordinator of Information during the summer. Hoover had a monopoly on the domestic side of intelligence – FDR had announced that two years before – but he didn't want anyone peeking over his shoulder. So far Roosevelt wouldn't budge, and Donovan remained firmly in place.

'Anyhow,' said Tolson, 'tell me what's new in Rio de Janeiro.' He said this without urgency.

'Not a lot. But there is something else I wanted to raise.'

'Go ahead. I'll be seeing the Director at lunch.'

Guttman took a breath. 'Ten days ago I met with an official from the State Department,' he began. 'His name was Thornton Palmer.'

'You mean the guy in the papers?' Tolson asked, sitting up in his chair. Palmer's death had been splashed all over the pages of the morning's *Washington Star*, though Kevin Reilly had taken his time letting the news out, since Palmer had been found on Friday.

'That's the guy.'

'Holy smokes. What did he want?'

'I assumed it would be about Argentina. I first met him when I was touring State to learn about South America. He was back on leave from Argentina, so I picked his brain about BA. But that wasn't what he wanted to talk about.' Guttman paused. 'He told me he'd been approached by the Russians.'

'What for?' asked Tolson without much apparent interest.

'They wanted him to spy for them.'

Tolson stared at Guttman, then laughed out loud. 'I've heard some good ones in my time, but that takes the prize. Look, right now I wouldn't think espionage is much of a priority for Comrade Stalin. He's not even sending money to the CP here any more.'

'I was sceptical myself. I asked him what the Russians wanted him to do. He said they wanted information from the State Department. Classified stuff.'

Tolson laughed again and Guttman was tempted to join him. Then suddenly Tolson said, 'You say this was ten days ago. Why didn't you report it right away?'

That was the thing about Tolson: you were starting to think you were talking to the equivalent of an affable insurance salesman, when suddenly he caught you out.

Fortunately Guttman was used to this. He said calmly, 'I did do a note for the file.' It had been written after Palmer had been found dead, but he wasn't going to tell Tolson that. 'Palmer wasn't very credible – to me at least. When I pressed him for specifics, he was evasive.'

'Did you tell Tamm?' asked Tolson. Tamm had replaced Guttman as the man in charge of Domestic Intelligence.

'No, I was going to tell you and the Director first. As I say, Palmer didn't seem credible and he didn't give me any proof.'

Tolson snorted. 'When did he say they approached him?'

'1935.'

Tolson was shaking his head. 'You know, for all the problems we've had with the Nazis, the Russians have never tried to penetrate us. We'd know if they had.'

Guttman wasn't about to argue. Hoover – and so by

default Tolson – was convinced he had a complete overview of espionage activity in the United States. Until he'd met Thornton Palmer, Guttman would have agreed. 'I told him I'd need evidence if I was going to help him.'

'Help him? How?'

'He said the Russians left him alone after he first said no, and then he went to Argentina for a few years. But once he was back he said they approached him again. I guess he wanted protection – it wasn't clear.'

Tolson said, 'The papers suggest Palmer killed himself.'

'They didn't find a gun.'

Tolson shook his head. 'He was in the water. The gun would have been washed away.'

It seemed an odd way to kill yourself, standing in the middle of a creek, but Guttman let this pass. 'Maybe. But then again, maybe there was something in what he told me. I mean, why make up a story like that?'

'Who knows?' Tolson shrugged indifferently. 'He sounds unstable – a fantasist.'

Guttman said, 'Don't you think we should follow this up?'

'What's there to follow up? He didn't give you anything specific. You said so yourself.

'He claimed he wasn't the only one the Russians approached.'

'Did he give you names?'

'No. He said one of them also went to Yale – but after Palmer.'

'That's a big help,' Tolson said sarcastically. Guttman sensed he was ready for his lunch. Tolson went on, 'You have to admit, Guttman, they don't sound like your average Reds. It's not as if Palmer was a . . .' He hesitated.

'A what?' asked Guttman.

'Come on, you know as well as I do that most of these Communists are foreigners or Jews.'

'I'm a Jew and I'm not a Communist,' Guttman said, his voice rising a notch.

'I'm not saying all Jews are Commies.'

Guttman wasn't going to argue – it was undeniable that so many members of the Party were Jews. What was the distinction he'd been taught at CCNY – between necessary and sufficient conditions? Which one was being a Jew? It never seemed sufficient to him; he was American first, he liked to think. But certainly it seemed necessary when he was talking to the likes of Tolson, if only because it wasn't something Guttman could get out of. It was too late to change his name, even if he'd wanted to – and besides, with his schnozz and dark eyes, plus a bulky build that seemed to be made out of corned beef and pickles and chopped liver, he could have been a poster-boy Yid for Goebbels.

He said, 'Palmer claimed the Russians had sent money to the West Coast recently – he heard about it from his Yalie friend. It went to a Japanese bank.'

Tolson waved a dismissive hand. 'Hitler will give money to synagogues before the Russians help the Japs. They hate each other.' He sighed and looked at his watch. 'This gets more and more far-fetched. Just turn it over to Tamm.' Guttman's face must have shown his dismay, for Tolson said sharply, 'What's the matter Guttman? Don't you like your new responsibilities? The spics getting you down?'

'I didn't say that.'

'You're not in charge of this stuff any more. That was the deal, remember?'

'I remember,' he said coldly.

'It's Tamm's business now. Though I can't believe he'll waste his time on this.'

That was true. Edward Tamm was constitutionally incapable of following a hunch (and probably incapable of having one). Intelligent, thorough, efficient, he followed orders like nobody's business and was terrier-like pursuing a lead, especially one coming from a superior. But he was totally unimaginative – yes, he had proposed naming the Bureau the Federal Bureau of Investigation back in 1935, but that didn't exactly require the soul of a poet.

Guttman hesitated. 'The thing is . . .'

'What?' Tolson asked bluntly.

The thing is I believed the guy, thought Guttman. Maybe not at the time, but afterwards, when I went through our conversation in my head. Palmer had been scared, but he hadn't acted crazy. Not in the slightest.

He couldn't say this to Tolson, because he had no proof – in that sense, Tolson was as rigid as Tamm. Guttman tried one more time nonetheless: 'I've got Nessheim out on the Coast. I thought maybe he could have a sniff around – about this money transfer, I mean. Just in case Palmer was telling the truth.'

Tolson was already shaking his head. 'Absolutely not. Nessheim's not there to play hero any more. He's doing just what the Director wants at that studio and he's going to be plenty busy in the months ahead. We're going out there in a little over a month and after that he'll have his hands full.'

'With what?' asked Guttman. Nessheim might be an anomaly, since Guttman was supposed to operate only south of the Rio Grande now, but he was still his agent.

'With the movies, of course. The Director has plans. So drop this business: that's an order I know the Director will confirm. I gotta go now. Next time we meet, let's stick to Rio de Janeiro.'

9

IT HAD BEEN an early start for Guttman, after a restless night for Isabel, which meant a restless night for him as well. He had risen in the dark and driven over the bridge and across most of Washington to catch the 5.15 Crescent for Philadelphia. There, at 30th Street Station, he'd grabbed a roll and a paper cup of coffee before boarding the Pilgrim, heading north for its terminus at Boston.

He was allowed to travel first class on business, but this trip wasn't going to appear anywhere on the monthly expenses sheet he submitted to the Director, so he had bought a seat in the ordinary day coach. He would have liked the comfort of one of the Parlor cars they'd added to the sleepers in Washington; you could recline like a potentate in the soft swivel chairs that sat on either side of the aisle. He had tried not to think of the hot breakfast he was missing – bacon and eggs and toast, steaming hot coffee – as he chomped on the dry roll.

Only Isabel knew where he was going. Even the trusted Marie was in the dark; when he had told her he was taking a day off, she had raised an eyebrow, since Guttman never did that. Sure, he took his vacation – all two weeks of it – but otherwise attended to his job on a clockwork routine. He had ignored the eyebrow.

New Haven looked grim on first view: an industrial shoreline of rusting tankers, oil depots and dilapidated factories. As the train pulled into the station Guttman got up, suppressing a yawn. He disembarked and walked through the citadel-like grandeur of the station. Funny how America had made such monuments of train depots – massive waiting rooms with high painted ceilings and marble floors. Did it cheer people up, he wondered? If you were starving would you rather go hungry in grand surroundings or drab ones?

Out front there was a line at the cab stand and he doubled up with two students who were also heading for campus. They were in high spirits after a jaunt to New York, which they were discussing as the taxi set off. The cab drove them away from the harbour, through a neighbourhood of old brick tenements and dingy stores, then down a wider street with banks and an insurance building. The students were talking about their fancy dinner in a French restaurant, a play they'd seen which sounded like *Lady in the Dark*, and jazz they'd listened to at a club downtown in Greenwich Village.

Two rich kids, then, in expensive blazers and striped shirts, having a heck of a time. Guttman didn't resent them – they'd been polite enough to ask if he wanted to share the cab – but he did hope they knew how lucky they were. What a contrast with his own college days: he'd lived at home and attended CCNY, then shared rooms with two friends in Hell's Kitchen, while he worked in a Midtown jewellery store and took law classes at night.

By then he'd met Isabel. Although their meetings were furtively arranged (his parents would not have approved of their inter-faith romance), they had conducted their courting in public. They'd share a sandwich on a park bench by the New York Public Library or if they were feeling flush go to an automat – which seemed fitting, since they'd first met at the one on 42nd Street, where he'd bought a piece of cherry pie by mistake and Isabel had offered to swap her own slice of apple pie for his.

Later she had liked to joke, *We took a short-crust to matrimony*. Her parents wouldn't have been wild about these meetings either, but they'd been dead almost twenty years – leaving Isabel to be raised by nuns in a Polish Catholic orphanage on Long Island.

Isabel had been such a live wire when they'd met. An only son, Guttman had been forced to shoulder adult responsibilities prematurely, but Isabel's sheer enthusiasm for life had made him feel his own youth – he'd been like a reluctant bather at the beach, who shivers at the first tentative steps into the water, only to be collected by a sudden embracing wave. She knew how to tango, drove a car faster than he did and was the only girl he'd met who could ride a horse.

He hadn't hesitated two seconds about marrying outside the faith, not when it was his beloved Isabel he'd be marrying. If he and Isabel had had children, technically they wouldn't have been Jews either – sometimes Guttman could picture the son he'd never had. Slender as Isabel, with skin the colour of milk and fair hair that hinted at his Polish antecedents. But still named Guttman and doubtless made to pay accordingly.

He thought of Isabel again, now lying half-immobilised at home with creeping paralysis. He had known for ten years she was going to predecease him, but he remained terrified of her dying. He knew some people thought he would be unfettered then, even free. Sure, he thought grimly, free as a bird without a mate. There was something to be said about the certainty of a wife, especially when you loved her.

The taxi went round the New Haven Green, a large common shaded by lines of tall elms and bisected by neat paths. Along the north side the driver pulled over at an entrance with high iron gates. 'Old Campus,' he announced and the two boys hopped out. One of them handed a dollar bill to Guttman. 'That should cover us,' he said, and Guttman thanked him.

The driver went on down College Street, passing a Gothic building of grey stone with gargoyles and intricate scroll work around its thin mullioned windows. It looked like the refectory of a medieval monastery and Guttman thought wryly that it was almost as nice as the City College of New York.

'What's that?' Guttman asked.

'Calhoun.' He saw Guttman's puzzlement in his rear mirror. 'One of the colleges.'

'It looks older than the *Mayflower*.'

The driver laughed. 'There're ten colleges and believe it or not, every one was built in the last ten years. They had stonemasons come in from all over the world,' he said proudly.

They turned down another side street, signed Wall Street, and halfway along the block pulled over by a plaza, ringed on two sides by buildings. 'That's the university offices,' the cabbie said, pointing to a colonial-style mansion. It could have been lifted straight out of Fifth Avenue, the house of a Morgan or Carnegie.

Guttman paid the driver and entered the building, where a secretary directed him upstairs. It seemed eerily quiet, like a men's club. As he climbed the stairs he looked at the portraits of past Yale presidents lining the wall and realised he *was* in a kind of men's club. He found another woman sitting in an outer office and explained who he had come to see. She had him sit down while she went through a door into another room.

'Mr Goodman?' The man who came out through the same door was younger than Guttman had expected – mid-thirties, possibly forty.

'It's Guttman,' he said, rising from his chair. Isabel had made him wear his best suit – from Hecht's in D.C.

– but looking at the spruce figure this man cut, Guttman wondered why he'd bothered. The man was about six feet, lean and loose-limbed with straight brown hair he had tried to comb back, but which fell in a soft comma across his forehead. He was dressed in a dark blue serge suit and a tie with an insignia on it – a Yale tie, Guttman figured.

'Sorry, Mr Guttman. I'm Franklin Vail. How can I help you?'

He handed his card to Vail. On the phone, the woman Guttman had spoken to had been less than helpful, even snooty once she'd heard the New York intonations of his voice – a drawbridge had gone up. He had felt like Popeye: *Iyam what Iyam.*

He said now, 'I was hoping you could give me some information.'

Vail paused as he looked again at Guttman's card. 'My assistant told me you'd called the other day. Have you come all the way from Washington?'

'That's right.'

'I hate to think you've made your trip for nothing, but I'm not sure I can be of any more help than my assistant.' He said this politely but perfunctorily. Guttman sighed inwardly. It had been a gamble coming all this way. He felt cross, and was tempted to show it. But it wasn't as if Guttman could call on Hoover to twist an arm or two. Not when he wasn't even meant to be there.

He sighed again, this time openly, while Vail waited impatiently. Guttman said, 'I don't need much of your time, Mr Vail.'

'I've got to meet someone for lunch,' Vail said, looking at his watch, an elegant number with a caramel leather band. But he seemed to understand that Guttman wasn't trying to throw his weight around. 'I've got a minute,

I guess,' he said reluctantly, and ushered Guttman into his office.

It was a large high-ceilinged room with a view of the plaza. The walls were lined with prints of Yale from the last century and the shelves on the bookcase held bound volumes of the *Yale Daily News*. Out the window Guttman could see dozens of students walking towards a massive neo-classical building that ran along one end of the plaza.

'Where are they all going?' Guttman asked, pointing towards the students.

'Lunch,' Vail said pointedly.

'I'll get to the point. I'm here because I'm trying to identify someone and I haven't the faintest idea how to go about it. I need your help.' He put out both palms to show he came as supplicant not cop.

Vail regarded him with a first flicker of interest. 'Who are you looking for?'

'A Yale graduate.'

'What class?'

'Upper,' said Guttman and Vail smiled for the first time. 'Actually, I don't know for sure. Nineteen thirty-five or thirty-six or thirty-seven. I don't think it could be beyond that range. Certainly not any earlier.'

Vail made a note on a lined yellow pad on his desk. 'What's his name?'

'Ah, there's the rub,' said Guttman and Vail gave a token smile. 'I don't know.'

Vail leant back in his chair. 'A Yale graduating class has almost five hundred students, Mr Guttman. Do you have any more information than that?'

'A bit. He was friends later on with someone from the class of 1934.'

'You don't know his name either, I take it?'

'Oh, I know his name all right.'

Vail gave him a look of patronising compassion. 'Then I suggest, Mr Guttman, you ask him to tell you the name of the man you're looking for.'

'I would if I could. *His* name was Thornton Palmer and he was found shot dead in Rock Creek Park five days ago.'

'I read about that!' Vail exclaimed. 'An alumnus.'

'That's right,' Guttman said.

'*The Times* made it sound like suicide. Yet you say "shot dead".'

'Officially, the cause of death is still unknown. I should have chosen my words more carefully.'

He looked at Vail, who seemed to get the message, for the Yale man then said, 'What's this got to do with the man you're looking for?'

'He may be able to explain what happened to Thornton Palmer.'

'I see. Do you know anything else about him?'

'Yes. He was a Whiffenpoof.'

Vail's eyes widened and Guttman added, 'I know that's a singing group, but that's about it.'

Vail said, 'There are about a dozen Whiffenpoofs every year. They're all seniors – they start singing in other groups as freshmen and then, if they're lucky, they get picked to be Whiffenpoofs in the spring of their junior year. It's quite an honour.'

'I'm sure.'

'You don't sound convinced.' Vail laughed. His tone had changed. He was cordial now. 'Listen, I tell you what – I'm having lunch with a Professor at Mory's.' Guttman must have looked blank. Vail suddenly burst into song:

To the tables down at Mory's
To the place where Louis dwells.

118

Breaking off, Vail explained, 'It's a club, a kind of restaurant really, where the Whiffenpoofs sing every Monday night. On the walls they have photographs of the baseball and football teams, and if memory serves me right, of each year's Whiffenpoofs. Let me have a look and if I find them I'll write down the names. Would that help?'

'It would,' said Guttman, thinking he was going to see a little more of Yale than he'd planned.

Guttman killed an hour, stopping on Chapel Street at a small restaurant where he had a pizza pie for the first time, served by the Italian owner. Its melted cheese was piping hot and the crust crispy and slightly burnt. He wolfed it down with a soda. He was worried about Isabel, but resisted the temptation to call home. Mrs Davis, Isabel's helper, grew impatient with his concern, and lately she had seemed impatient about everything. He wondered how nice she was to his wife. Isabel said she was 'fine', but then Isabel knew how much he worried about her; she would have been loath to add to his list of anxieties.

He strolled back to Vail's office and this time he was ushered in right away. Vail was waiting for him with a list. A long list. 'I took down the names for five years,' he explained. 'I think my lunch partner must have thought I was nuts.'

'Or starting the Whiffenpoofs fan club,' Guttman said. He looked at the names unhopefully. Now all he had to do was locate seventy addresses of Yale men and find all those who lived in New York.

'Is that any use?' asked Vail anxiously.

'Thank you, it is. I'm just trying to figure out how I'm going to track these people down.'

'I can help with that,' Vail declared and Guttman

119

could see his interest had been well and truly piqued. There was a little private eye in everybody, Guttman thought. Vail said, 'The alumni association will have all their addresses – everybody gets a magazine sent to them once they've graduated. But it might help if we could narrow things down a bit. Do you know anything else about our mystery man?'

'Yes I do. He lives in New York – or at least he works in the city. And he's a banker. He must be an officer of the bank,' he added, thinking of Palmer's description of the transferred money. 'I mean, he's not a teller.'

Vail snorted at the very idea. 'Leave it to me,' he said. Guttman could see that he now considered himself part of the investigation. 'I'll have names for you tomorrow.'

'That would be great. You've been a big help, so I'm reluctant to ask for any more assistance. But I was wondering . . .' he paused, like a fly fisherman mending his line.

'Go on,' said Vail cheerfully. This guy was well and truly hooked.

'I wanted to know a bit more about Thornton Palmer, the dead man. A sense of who his college friends were and what his interests had been. Especially anything political.'

'Oh,' said Vail, obviously surprised. He must have thought Palmer and the mystery man had been involved in something else. What, wondered Guttman? Narcotics? Bank robberies? The white slave trade?

'Yes, I'd be interested in knowing if he'd joined any organisations or agitated about political stuff. That sort of thing.'

'Well, the biggest organisation on campus nowadays is the America First Committee. But Palmer was here well before any of that started. I'll see what I can find out.'

'Great,' said Guttman. It seemed the likes of Franklin Vail couldn't conceive that a Yale man might have had progressive sentiments.

10

THIS TIME GUTTMAN used his mother as an excuse. He told Marie she was failing badly and that he would be gone for at least a day on compassionate leave. It wasn't that he didn't trust Marie, he just didn't want her to get caught up in his subterfuge. If he ran afoul of the Director, Hoover would take no prisoners and Marie would lose her job as well. With a child to raise and no husband any longer, she needed the job.

Vail had called him the day before, excited as a kid. He had come up with the names of five Whiffenpoofs living in or around New York. The first on the list had a home address in Queens, which ruled him out – Guttman was confident a Yale-educated banker wouldn't be living off Astoria Boulevard. The second had graduated from Columbia's medical school and was an intern at Mount Sinai; a third had been drafted the year before and was currently stationed at Fort Sheridan in Illinois. That left two names and both had connections with the banking business, though the one named Oliver Mason at J. P. Morgan had gone on sick leave four months before and had yet to come back. Given Palmer's time frame for the money transfer that seemed to rule him out as well, and left only Roger Sedgwick, class of '35, who worked in midtown at the Manhattan Savings Association. He lived in Westchester County in a town called Brewster, but Guttman wanted to confront him in his work environment. He had found that people felt more vulnerable there.

About Thornton Palmer, Vail had less useful news. He had spoken with the Dean of Palmer's old residential college, Jonathan Edwards, and learned that Palmer had been a solid but unremarkable presence. He'd played intramural football, sung for a year in the Glee Club, dated a girl from Smith College and achieved an academic record notable only for the strict uniformity of his grades – straight Bs. Vail's questions about any political activity had been greeted with disbelieving laughter by the Dean, followed by an emphatic no.

So much for the upper-class radical. It would certainly make Guttman's life simpler if all of this led nowhere, he thought, remembering the memorandum he had found on his desk when he'd returned from New Haven:

```
To: Assistant Director Guttman (SIS)
From: The Director
I wanted to speak with you in person but
learned you were taking the day off.
  Mr Tolson has spoken to me about your
recent meeting. I have since talked with
Secretary of State Hull who informs me
that Thornton Palmer had a history of
medical problems and difficulties with
alcohol. The Secretary also reports that
Palmer's superior considered him unreli-
able and prone to self-aggrandisement.
  Given this information, I have
instructed Special Agent Tamm to refile
your note and to consider the matter
closed, barring any further disclosures.
As Mr Tolson instructed, you should
transfer any information you have forth-
with to Mr Tamm.
  I hope you had an enjoyable vacation.
  JEH
```

Guttman got into Penn Station before noon and took

the 7th Avenue line one stop to Times Square. He was in a hurry, determined to see Sedgwick, then scoot back to Penn Station and head for home. Mrs Davis had complained. 'That's twice in one week, Mr Guttman. It's a lot to ask.' He had given her an extra ten dollars.

He took the shuttle over to Grand Central and ascended into the grand concourse of the station – another railway monument with a high vaulted ceiling. Through the cathedral-like windows light streamed in attenuated trails, illuminating motes of dust like snowflakes.

Outside on 42nd Street it was cooler than in Washington, and when passing cloud obscured the sun he was glad he'd brought his raincoat. The sidewalks were crowded: women in neat two-piece suits, hats tilted at an angle, men in grey fedoras, hurrying along. He had forgotten the sheer bustle of his native city, where no one ever seemed to stand still. Even the architecture here seemed to be in transit, the equivalent of a hundred Washington Memorials soaring skyward, their thrust modulated by the mount backs that seemed the builders' new rage. By contrast Washington was a city of neo-classical buildings, immobile as statues, a place so intent on *dignitas* that it seemed to slow your breathing down. Where New York was unfettered by any pretence to a federalist gloss and proud of its brutal competitive air, Washington seemed a smaller, more private kind of theatre, full of cautious collaborations and conspiracies.

Guttman walked east to the corner of Lexington, the *Daily News* tower looming ahead of him on 42nd Street. He turned south. The Manhattan Savings Association was located a block away, just below the corner with 41st Street. It occupied the ground floor of a dark, square-set building of a dozen storeys. Built of solid masonry, its façade was unornamented, as if to say no frills – the bank didn't want to waste your dough.

Guttman had called the day before, posing as a prospective customer to make an appointment with Sedgwick. Now a receptionist phoned through news of his arrival and led him through a steel door next to the teller cages. In a large low-ceilinged room half a dozen secretaries sat typing and the receptionist walked him past the probing eyes of this female inspectorate. They were chicly dressed with made-up faces and hair that had been shaped and teased and put in place. Less demure than their D.C. counterparts, they had none of their Southern softness and looked hard as nails.

The receptionist stopped at an office at the back of the building, knocked on the door and then opened it without waiting for a reply. Guttman walked through, as Roger Sedgwick stood up to greet him. He was a little man in an ill-fitting suit and a dull patterned tie. For a putative spy he seemed remarkably unprepossessing.

'Pleased to meet you, Mr Guttman,' said Sedgwick and they shook hands. He motioned Guttman to sit down across the desk from him. 'Now, what kind of loan are you interested in?'

'Actually, I'm not here for a loan. It's about a money transfer.'

Sedgwick looked surprised. He had straight blonde hair, which he pushed back impatiently with his hand. 'Gosh, the gal must have got it wrong. You'll need to see our currency officer, George Biederman. Let me give him a call and see if he's free.'

'It's you I want to see, Mr Sedgwick. On official business.' He placed his business card on the desk and turned it round so Sedgwick could read it. There was a grass stain near one of its corners and Guttman realised with dismay that it was the same card that Reilly had returned to him in Rock Creek Park.

125

'What's this about?' Sedgwick was staring at the card and didn't look up.

'I'm interested in a transfer of funds from this bank to a Japanese bank in Los Angeles. It was done for the Russians.'

'What Russians?'

'I assume they're with the consulate here. But you tell me; you did the transfer.'

Sedgwick shook his head emphatically. 'I've explained, Mr Guttman – I'm a loan officer. You've got the wrong guy.'

'I don't think so. My source was clear about that.'

'Tell your source he's got it wrong.' Sedgwick was swallowing so hard that his Adam's apple had swollen, as if he were feeding on too big a frog.

Guttman said, 'I wish I could, but you see, it was Thornton Palmer who told me.'

Sedgwick stopped swallowing long enough to say, 'I think I've heard the name.'

'I'm not surprised: Palmer seemed to know you well enough. You two had a lot in common. You both went to Yale, you were both Whiffenpoofs and you both enjoyed the favours of a woman named Kristin Pichel in Vienna.' He paused for a couple of beats, then added softly, 'Though Palmer was never a member of the Communist Party.'

'You're saying I was?' Sedgwick's mouth stayed open, like a caught fish squeezed by a fisherman's hands.

'Yes.'

'Who told you that?'

'Palmer did. Not that he's about to repeat the accusation – he was found shot dead in Rock Creek Park.' When Sedgwick didn't react to this, Guttman wasn't surprised – Palmer's death would have made the New York papers. 'That doesn't matter – you were already

126

in our files.' Since this was a lie, Guttman said it slowly to give it more weight.

And it worked: Sedgwick sat motionless for a moment, then suddenly buried his face in his hands. When he lifted his head up again he seemed to have made a decision. 'What do you want from me?' he asked.

'I want to know how often you've done errands for the Russians.'

'This was the first time,' he said so immediately that Guttman believed him. 'Other than setting up the account, and that was perfectly above board. It's not like the Germans or Japanese. The Government hasn't stopped the Russians from conducting normal financial activity. They have a checking account with another bank to pay their bills, and a savings account with us.'

'Who was your contact?'

'A man named Milnikov. But listen, I've never taken a dime from any of them.'

'You did it out of conviction?'

'Hardly,' Sedgwick said bitterly. My boss doesn't know I was in the Party – I wouldn't last five minutes if he found out. Milnikov said he'd tell him if I didn't play ball. So I did.' He looked defiantly at Guttman. 'It's not as if I was hurting anybody.'

There was a whine now in his voice that Guttman figured was only going to get worse. 'Tell me about this transfer.'

'I handled it for them about two months ago. I told Palmer about it because I wasn't happy doing it.'

'How much money got transferred?'

'Fifty thousand dollars.'

'Why did they have you do it? You said yourself, you're a loan officer.'

'A sum that large would draw the attention of a transfer officer and then get reported to the Feds.

Milnikov didn't want that. By having me handle it, it could get buried.'

'Who did it go to?'

'A Japanese-American bank in LA.' He reached for a pad. 'I'll write down the name for you.'

Sedgwick scribbled for a moment, then tore off the sheet and handed it across the desk to Guttman. He asked, 'I meant, to what individual? Can you look it up for me?'

'I don't need to. It was sent as a wire to a man named Lyakhov.'

'Is he a Soviet official?'

'I don't know who he is. There was no reason for me to know.'

'What about Milnikov? Has he been in touch since then?'

'No – he's gone back to Russia, thank God.'

There wasn't much else to ask about the money, Guttman decided. It was over to Nessheim now, to follow it up at his end. 'So when exactly did you join the Party? Our records don't say.'

'September 1936. I didn't stay in it for long. Less than a year.'

'That was after you met this Kristin woman in Vienna. Why did she go after you in the first place? Had you been politically active?'

'Not at all.' Sedgwick shrugged.

'What about members of your family?'

'Not likely. My father farms potatoes in Maine. Not the fancy bit of Maine, either; our place is miles from the coast. I'm not a Massachusetts Sedgwick,' he added, the whine returning to his voice. Guttman wanted to say that he wasn't a Philadelphia Guttman either.

'You see,' added Sedgwick, looking slightly sheepish, 'I was never a real believer.'

128

'Then why did you join the Party?'

'Kristin wanted me to,' he said quietly.

'And that was reason enough?'

Sedgwick nodded sadly. 'At the time it was.'

The poor sap, thought Guttman. You're neck deep in shit thanks to a golden-haired siren. Boy, did she take you for a ride, and Palmer too. But at least Sedgwick was still alive to contemplate his foolishness.

Sedgwick was eyeing him warily. 'Are you going to talk to my boss?'

'Not yet, and maybe never. But if you hear from these Russians again – any Russian – I want you to call me right away.'

'I will.'

'Good.' Guttman stood up, ready to go.

Then he remembered there was still another question to ask. 'One more thing, Mr Sedgwick. What do you think made the Russians put this Pichel woman on to Palmer? Our files don't show any left-wing activity on his part.'

'There wouldn't have been. His background was standard stuff: Yale, prep school and the Republican Party – he told me his old man was a banker, who hated Roosevelt with a passion. But the summer after his junior year he drove west across the country with a roommate from Yale.'

'He mentioned that,' said Guttman.

'He and the roommate got stranded in Oklahoma and ended up hitchhiking to Hollywood, along with a million Okies heading for California. I don't think Palmer had ever seen poverty first-hand before.

'In Hollywood they stayed with a cousin of Palmer's mother. This cousin was the black sheep of the family, and a Party member; he worked in one of the studios. Palmer had grown up knowing that bankers didn't think much of writers, but it was a revelation to learn that writers don't think much of bankers either. Palmer told me he'd been hoping to see Gloria Swanson or meet Louis B. Mayer, but instead he got lectures from his cousin on the virtues of the dictatorship of the prole-tariat. Some of it must have stuck, because after that Palmer was very left wing. He was obsessed about the rise of fascism.'

'If that was the case, why didn't he join the Party?'

'Simple. Kristin Pichel told him not to.'

'*What*?'

'Yes. And that's why you'll find he never signed anti-Franco petitions or marched for the downtrodden or subscribed to the *Daily Worker*. He was instructed not to.'

'By Kristin?' Guttman was trying not to show how surprised he was.

'Yes at first, and later it would have been Milnikov. Does it matter?'

'No.'

Sedgwick was smiling now for the first time. 'It's a killer, isn't it? I'm told I have to join the Party when it's the last thing I want to do. Palmer's desperate to join but gets ordered not to. Ironic, wouldn't you say?'

'Yeah, very,' said Guttman, but his thoughts were already moving forward. 'Tell me, when you saw Palmer did he tell you that the Russians had been in touch with him recently?'

'Yes, and he wasn't happy about it. They'd left him alone all the time he was in Argentina; I think he was hoping they wouldn't ever come back. Fat chance.'

'Did he say *why* they'd contacted him again?'

'No, he just said that he didn't want to help them in any way. I know he was sickened by the Moscow-Berlin pact.'

'Did he happen to mention what he was working on at the State Department?'

'Not really. He said he'd been moved to the Asian desk. He was supposed to specialise in Japan.'

Ten minutes before, Guttman had been ready to return home to Washington. Roger Sedgwick was not a Captain of Espionage. However you looked at it, he had been little more than a clerk in his dealings with Milnikov and company. Which meant Guttman could safely have left the whole business alone, returned his attention to Nazi influence from Guadalajara to Santiago, and known he was doing what J. Edgar Hoover had told him to do.

Then he'd gone and asked one more question, more out of mild curiosity than any pressing need to know. The answer had changed everything.

Thornton Palmer had lied to him. Yes, the Russians had approached him several years before, *but he hadn't said no*. Instead he'd followed their instructions and kept a low profile, never joining the Party – because 'Kristin Pichel told him not to.' It was only after the Berlin-Moscow pact that Palmer had turned against his Russian masters, and then come to Guttman for help when they wouldn't take no for an answer.

Guttman hesitated as he reached 42nd Street, heading towards Grand Central. He felt trapped in an impossible situation: he couldn't turn the case over to Tamm without getting fired for having pursued it; but there wouldn't have been a case to turn over if he hadn't pursued it.

He wasn't scared for himself, but Isabel was a different matter. If he lost his job how would he pay to have her cared for properly? What else could he do to make a living? Join a private security company or a department store where his largest responsibility would be catching shoplifters?

He kept walking, past Grand Central and then north on Madison Avenue, idly looking at the windows of Brooks Brothers. Isabel had bought him two shirts there years ago; he still had them both, lovingly cared for, their collars turned when they'd grown frayed. He wouldn't be buying any more shirts there once Hoover got through with him.

He crossed over to Fifth Avenue, onto its west side, for though his thoughts were churning, he knew where he was going. At the corner of 50th Street he stopped at a hot-dog cart, unmindful of the pedestrians who had to move around him. He bought one with the whole works, watching as the vendor forked steamed onions over the frankfurter and spooned on relish and mustard, before handing it over half-wrapped in a sheet of waxed paper. Guttman stood next to the trolley's sun umbrella to eat it.

If he was going to proceed, he needed an ally. Nessheim would be important to anything he did, since the only real lead they had was out west. But Guttman needed help closer to home, from someone powerful but independent, who would trust Guttman enough not to question why he was defying Hoover's orders.

He was still undecided enough to wish he could find guidance. For a stray moment he was even tempted to cross the street and enter St Patrick's. Someone had said that in the last difficult decade any man worried by the state of the world either converted to Catholicism or joined the Communist Party, and Guttman had never been tempted by the latter. Strange how he, a lapsed Jew, had a latent religiosity that drew him to the cathedral, whereas Isabel – raised by nuns – would not have dreamed of setting foot in the place.

He stayed on his side of the street, however, and walked towards the dozen buildings that formed the newly completed Rockefeller Center. Efforts had been made to soften the stark modernity of the skyscrapers: crab apples had been planted around the plaza and in the small gardens of the lower-level buildings, and beds full of red and yellow chrysanthemums were still in bloom. But unlike the brand-new colleges of Yale, which sedulously aped the historical features of their ancient counterparts across the Atlantic, here the buildings themselves, sleek and improbably tall, made no concession to the past.

Guttman crossed the little sunken plaza that doubled as a skating rink in winter. He could make out the gilded bronze statue of Prometheus at the near end. As he neared 30 Rockefeller Plaza, half a block in from Fifth Avenue, he craned his neck and looked up at its series of recessed mount backs, then brought his eyes down to ground level, where along the outer walls there ran a rich and dignified ribbon of granite. The buildings had reputedly cost $250 million to build – more than two bucks a head for every American, and all paid for by one man, who Guttman figured was entitled to name the place for himself.

He went through one of the revolving doors of the RCA Building and crossed the marble floor to the elevator banks, positioned in the centre of the lobby. They were unmanned, but he hesitated, then turned away. He walked around the ground floor for almost a quarter of an hour, barely taking in the lavish artwork on the walls, made notorious ever since the Diego Rivera murals, with their defiant head of Lenin, had been taken down and destroyed on the orders of young Nelson Rockefeller. They'd been replaced by a series of bafflingly abstract murals, full of inchoate messages about peace and progress and the importance of manufacturing to humanity in the twentieth century.

He found no comfort in this secular cathedral and wished he'd gone into St Patrick's instead. But he knew no parable existed to tell him what to do. If he was going to go after Palmer's killers, it wasn't going to be in defence of a religion, not even the religion of capital.

And when he weighed the odds of what he was pretty sure he was going to try and do, he found them wanting. If his New Haven junket were discovered, he could probably get away with it – he had only received Hoover's memo after he'd gone to Yale and he could claim that he had misunderstood Tolson's instructions. He might only get his knuckles rapped. This New York junket was trickier, but even there he could insist he had actually visited his mother, and had simply checked in at the Manhattan Savings Association to keep the appointment he'd made to see the Sedgwick man a week before. Thinner ice, but survivable.

But now he was at the point of no return, from which, if it were discovered, there would be no way back. He was risking his career, and for what? To avenge a dead man? No. He didn't give a damn for Thornton Palmer, now that he knew Palmer had lied to him. But he did care about the truth.

Guttman had always wanted to catch the bad guys – that was his mission, pure and simple. He knew that if he faltered now he would become a different kind of man. He was going to do this because he felt he owed it to the part of himself he wanted to admire.

11

THE DOOR ON Suite 3606, on the 36th floor of the International Building, had frosted glass with embossed black letters that said **British Passport Control Office.** Guttman would not have advised any applicant to use this office, for its title was a misleading but benign cover for the British Security Coordination force, known as the BSC. The American authorities (technically neutral but with a partisan President's okay) turned a blind eye to the BSC's activities, which were a mix of overt political lobbying, press propaganda and the much more furtive practice of espionage.

Guttman pressed the bell and a moment later the door buzzed and he went in. A pretty girl was sitting behind the receptionist's desk.

'I was hoping to see Bill Stephenson,' Guttman said.

'Do you have an appointment?' she asked. Her accent was faintly Southern.

'I don't, Katie. But if you could tell your uncle Harry Guttman is here, I think he might let me in.'

The girl was blushing as she stood up. 'I'll just go and check.'

He sat down and looked idly at the magazines on a little low table next to his chair. *Punch*, the *Spectator*, a week-old copy of *The Times*.

Katie came back. 'He's free, Mr Guttman. He said to go on in.'

Guttman walked through into a large room full of young men and women seated at desks, reading and typing on big Underwood machines. In one corner there was an enclosed office with its door open; inside

Stephenson was standing by the window. He turned around as Guttman came in and grinned as he advanced to shake hands.

He was a trim man, not very tall, though Guttman always thought of him as a six-footer – there was an air of command about him, perhaps a hangover from his days as an ace flyer in the Royal Air Corps. Although he'd been born and raised outside Winnipeg, his military service on the Great War had cemented his allegiance to Great Britain and he had become an enormously successful businessman there. Now he had Churchill's trust and (to Hoover's fury) FDR's confidence as well. As he'd come to know him, Guttman had gradually realised how efficient Stephenson was; like most self-made men he got things done, even if it meant doing them himself.

'Harry, it's good to see you, but you're lucky to catch me. I'm leaving for London in a couple of hours.'

'Which way are you travelling?'

'The hard way.'

Guttman nodded. That would mean a train north to Montreal, then a seat (more a space really, since the chair tended to consist of a wooden crate) in a stripped-down plane from the Ferry Command. A stop in Labrador, then Scotland, then south to London.

'Bermuda would be the softer option, but the Canada route's quicker – Masterman wants to see me asap.'

'Your Bermuda people have been very helpful,' Guttman said. Bermuda was the stopover for almost any post sent from South or Central America to Europe. The British SIS had proved highly adept at surreptitiously opening these letters; just the month before they had alerted Guttman's people in Rio de Janeiro to the recent arrival of a Nazi spymaster, who had unwisely written to his wife at home in Mannheim with news of his arrival.

Stephenson nodded. 'Glad to hear it. I'm trying to keep Katie from joining them. I wish she had thicker ankles.'

Guttman laughed. 'I heard about that.' It had been become part of BSC lore that girls with thin ankles proved better at opening letters undetected than girls with thicker pins. It sounded crazy, but Guttman had been assured it was true.

Stephenson peered at Guttman. 'Harry, have you been doing some painting?'

'Painting? No. Why?'

'You've got something yellow under your eye.'

Guttman daubed under one eye but Stephenson shook his head, so he wiped at the cheek, then looked at his fingers and sniffed. 'Mustard,' he declared. 'I stopped for a hot dog on the way over.'

Stephenson looked amused. 'I won't offer you a sandwich then.'

'I didn't know you ran to a canteen here.'

'We don't. Believe it or not, there are only fifteen of us in this suite, and they're mainly Canadians – you know we're not allowed to hire American nationals any more.'

Guttman nodded; he didn't mention that the Bureau had spotted the Help Wanted ads in the Toronto papers. He asked, 'And how many in the rest of the country?'

Stephenson shrugged. 'About a thousand if you must know. And twice as many in Canada and South America. All the more reason to keep this office inconspicuous. Being in New York has been a blessing: less attention from your Congress and, if I'm being honest, welcome distance from your Director. Mr Hoover wants to keep us at arm's length and I've found advantages in obliging him.'

They talked for a while about developments in South

America. 'It's not just the Nazis,' said Guttman. 'The Japs have been using Mexico as a base. But that's not really part of the FBI brief – Naval Intelligence are watching that on our side.' As far as he knew, R.B. Hood, the SAC in LA, was confining his counter-espionage efforts to making lists of Japanese-Americans who would be put behind bars if war broke out. The idea that most of them were probably loyal citizens didn't seem to trouble Hood.

Then there was a lull in the conversation, which Stephenson broke. 'Listen, it's always a pleasure to see you, and God knows, there's plenty to discuss. Yet something tells me you're not here just to talk about Caracas.'

Guttman smiled shyly. 'Can I speak in confidence?'

'Always,' Stephenson said immediately.

'Okay.' He tried to gather his thoughts and present his account coherently, beginning with the original meeting with Palmer, the man's claim that he had been approached and then, several years later, re-approached by the Russians, and the subsequent discovery of Palmer's corpse in Rock Creek Park. Yet it was a complicated story and Guttman found himself thinking how bizarre it must sound. As he talked, he wanted to know what Stephenson was thinking, yet Stephenson was listening in silence, which flustered Guttman. His spirits sank at the thought that, like Tolson, Stephenson might be finding the whole thing preposterous. He jumped ahead, truncating his description of his trip to Yale and the assistance he'd received from Vail, and was starting to explain that he was certain Palmer had been a spy when Stephenson suddenly interrupted.

'Let's go for a walk, Harry,' he said quietly.

They took a half-full elevator down to the lobby without speaking. Stephenson led the way, striding out the Fifth Avenue entrance like a man in a hurry, passing without a glance by the statue of Atlas holding the world in his arms. Directly across the street the Gothic pinnacles of St Patrick's resembled the bishops of a chessboard, out of place amidst the sharp box-like edges of the towers of midtown. Guttman caught up to Stephenson and they joined the sun-lit bustle of Fifth Avenue.

They were heading south when a voice called out. 'Harry? Harry Guttman?' Guttman turned slowly, dread swelling like phlegm in his throat. He smiled automatically, trying not to blink in the bright sun as he saw the man coming towards him, hand extended. His face was vaguely familiar.

He realised it was Powderman, the Deputy SAC in New York. They'd met two years before, when Guttman had led local agents in the arrest of a dozen German-American *Bund* members, caught attempting to hijack the arms stores of the Armory building on Park Avenue.

'Hello, Chris,' he said, swallowing hard. Stephenson had stopped, waiting to one side, but Guttman realised he should introduce him. 'Do you know Bill Stephenson?'

'I know *of* him, of course. But we've never met.' They shook hands and Powderman turned back to Guttman. 'What brings you to New York, Harry?'

What indeed? Guttman stared at Powderman and absolutely no excuse came to mind.

'It's my fault,' Stephenson interjected smoothly. 'I wanted to meet the Rockefeller people working on South America. I managed to strong-arm Harry into coming along – I thought I might get a better reception that way.'

It was done perfectly and Powderman nodded. Guttman resisted the temptation to offer further explanation. Powderman said jocularly, 'Last time I saw you, Harry, we were chasing Nazis a lot closer to home.'

'Couldn't have done it without you, Chris.' He reached out and pumped his hand again. 'Got to run, but good to see you again.'

As they moved off he said to Stephenson, 'You saved my bacon. I'm supposed to be visiting my mother.'

'I had the feeling yours was an unofficial visit.'

They kept walking, moving at a fair clip and Guttman finally asked, 'Are we headed somewhere, Bill, or did you just want some fresh air?'

Stephenson slowed down a little. 'Sorry,' he said. 'But if we stayed in the office I had a problem. I could have closed my office door and then everyone would have wanted to know who you were. Or I could have left it open and then we might have been overheard. So I thought we'd go somewhere more private.'

They'd reached 43rd Street by now and Stephenson turned west. They had walked a hundred feet or so when Stephenson stopped in front of a handsome Italianate mansion building of white stone.

'I thought we'd talk here,' said Stephenson, leading the way up the front steps.

Inside a porter in a uniform came out of his mahogany booth and nodded as they went up a central staircase to a mezzanine floor. There they faced a large dining room, but Stephenson led him to one side and into a small, book-lined room. It was empty and Stephenson motioned to a pair of padded leather chairs. 'Have a seat while I go rustle up some service. What'll you have, Harry? There's tea if you want it – I'm going to have a beer myself, the hour be damned.'

'I'll join you.'

While Stephenson went off for their drinks, Guttman sat wondering where he was. He'd seen the building before – three years selling jewellery on 47th Street meant he knew the neighbourhood by heart – but had always assumed it was a magnate's private mansion.

When Stephenson returned, he was followed by a black man in a white waiter's jacket, carrying a tray that held two large glasses of beer. He deposited the glasses carefully on a side table and withdrew.

Guttman asked, 'Is this another British veterans' club?' He was referring to a townhouse in Georgetown where Stephenson had established the BSC's first informal American headquarters, under the cover of a club for ex-British-servicemen.

Stephenson grinned. 'We haven't got that big for our boots. This is a real club. I don't know why they let me in, unless they thought I was English. You know, *"I say old chap, weren't you at Oxford with my cousin Cuthbert?"'* He sounded like a Limey out of central casting and Guttman laughed. Stephenson went on, 'If they'd known I was a hick from Manitoba we'd be sitting in the coffee shop down the street. But it's bloody useful when I need to have a private conversation.' He looked around the empty room. 'So you were saying . . . ?'

'I was about to tell you that I'm sure Palmer did spy for the Russians. The problem I'm having is that nobody else seems to think so – or at least, nobody else seems to care.'

'I suppose there must seem higher priorities right now. I mean, in three weeks' time there may not be a Russia any more.'

'Maybe, but that doesn't explain why they'd be spying here.'

'Of course not. And I've heard rumours in our neck of the woods too.'

This was reassuring, but also alarming. Guttman

continued: 'And I can't understand why the Russians sent money to a Japanese bank in LA.'

'Have you got any way of finding out?'

'Maybe. Do you remember Nessheim?' Guttman asked.

'How could I forget him? If it were up to me I'd give him a knighthood. I hope he's still working for you.'

'He is, in a manner of speaking.' He explained Nessheim's odd movie duties on the Coast.

'Lucky boy,' said Stephenson.

'Actually, he doesn't want to be there. I don't think he even wants to be in the Bureau.'

'That's entirely commendable,' said Stephenson with a grin.

'Anyway, I'm going to have him try and trace the money. He's got a Jap connection out in California.' He didn't mention that this Jap connection had gone missing.

'I don't know if I can help you there – the Japanese are pretty low on the British list. But informally at least, we might have some info on any Russian activity in California. Let me check, we have a few people there.'

'Agents?'

'Nothing that formal. But a lot of ex-pats, with access to the international community that's gathering in LA – Stravinsky, Chaplin, Thomas Mann, our own Christopher Isherwood.'

Guttman tried not to look blank, but Stephenson spotted this and laughed. 'Don't worry, Harry, I'd never heard of most of them either, until I read the reports. But the point is, most of these people are left-leaning and chummy with the Russians. Russia is Britain's ally now.'

'How do you investigate your own ally? I can't believe you'd get the okay for that.'

'I wouldn't,' he said cheerfully. 'So let's keep that between us too. But tell me, are you sure Palmer wasn't a suicide?'

'Well, let's just say I've never heard of anybody standing knee deep in running water in order to shoot themselves. And Palmer didn't put the gun against his heart or his head.' He put two fingers on his own nose. 'The bullet was fired right here.'

Stephenson grimaced. 'Awfully brutal. But why go so far as to murder him?'

'Maybe what he told me was true – he said he wouldn't work for them any more.'

'But the murder only served to call more attention to Palmer. It seems pointless.'

'Unless he knew something the Russians didn't want us to know.'

'What about?'

'Maybe this Japanese connection in California. Sedgwick told me that Palmer had recently been put on the Japan desk. Of course, that could be a coincidence—'

'I don't believe in coincidence, unless it's a happy one,' Stephenson said with a frown. 'The only Japanese connections I'm aware of are with the Nazis. We've tried to disrupt those, but it's all a bit late.' He looked slightly guilty about this, then brightened. 'But we do have a new source, someone Masterman wants Hoover to see. His name's Popov – ever heard of him?'

'No.'

'My people have given him the code name "Tricycle".'

'Tricycle?' Guttman said. He wondered why Stephenson was smiling. 'How did you come up with that?'

'It seems Popov is bit of a Lothario – with rather peculiar tastes in the boudoir. He likes two women at a time.'

'The more the merrier, I guess,' said Guttman. 'Though I'm not sure the Director would approve.'

'The thought's occurred to me. I haven't met Popov myself, but I know he's got information Masterman thinks Hoover would like to hear. Popov's going to Washington in ten days – right now he's in Canada. It might be useful if you were there when he saw Hoover.'

Guttman knew this was unlikely; Tamm would be there instead, doubtless backing Hoover, who would be sceptical of any source of information that came from the British.

Stephenson seemed to read his thoughts, for he said gently, 'Is it that bad, Harry? Hoover just won't forgive you for being right, will he? Christ, he'd be out on his can if you hadn't done what you did.' When Guttman shrugged, Stephenson said with cheerful cynicism, 'You know what they say: No good deed goes unpunished.'

Guttman laughed. 'I tell you what. If you think it will help if I saw this Popov character, have Masterman give him some titbit about South America to send ahead to Hoover. That should get me into the meeting.'

Stephenson nodded. 'I'll see what I can do – there's always the failed *putsch* in Colombia, I guess. In the meantime, I'll also find out what I can about the Russians in LA.' Stephenson finished his beer. 'I better be getting back, Harry. I've got a plane to catch in Montreal tomorrow morning.'

'One more thing before you go,' said Guttman. 'Are you on good terms with the Bureau here?'

'Surprisingly good, actually. It's Washington that's the problem. Why do you ask?'

Guttman pushed a creased slip of paper across the table. He had kept it in his wallet since the evening in Rock Creek Park. 'Could you run this by them and see what turns up? The car was parked near mine the night I met Palmer.'

If Stephenson was surprised he didn't show it. Maybe he was sparing Guttman the embarrassment of having to admit he couldn't use the FBI – his own organisation – in even this most pedestrian way. But Guttman didn't want to take the risk of having his own request for a plate trace get back to the Director's office in D.C.

'It's a local number plate?' asked Stephenson.

'That's right.'

Stephenson looked at him appreciatively. 'You are out on a limb, aren't you Harry?'

Guttman laughed at the starkness of this depiction. 'And I've just handed the pruning saw over to you.'

12

GUTTMAN WAS LATE getting back to Washington; someone had jumped in front of a train outside Philadelphia. By the time he parked in Arlington it was almost midnight and he was dreading Mrs Davis's reaction. He let himself in quietly, expecting to find her sitting angrily in the living room. Instead he found Annie Ryerson, quietly reading a book.

'What—?' he started to ask, but she put two fingers to her lips. She had changed from work and wore olive-green trousers and a white blouse. No make-up, as if she'd decided not to bother prettifying herself. A pity, he thought, for though she was striking rather than outright pretty (but with wonderful green-blue eyes), she was too young to stop caring how she looked.

'She's only just gone to sleep,' she said, gesturing towards the bedroom. 'I think she wanted to be awake when you got back.'

'What happened to Mrs Davis?'

'I sent her home. When I dropped by to see Isabel earlier on, Mrs Davis said she was worried about her mother.'

'She's always worried about her mother. Sometimes I wonder if her mother even exists.'

Annie smiled. 'Anyway, I sent her home. It seemed the easiest thing to do.'

Mrs Davis hadn't been worried, Guttman thought. She'd been complaining – to Isabel, no doubt, and to Annie.

'What about Jeff?'

'He's fine, Harry. I told him I'd be popping in here

once he fell asleep. And he sleeps like a log – all little boys do. Mrs Jupiter is in the house if there's any problem.'

He gave a small snort. 'She's even older than Mrs Davis's mother. Is Isabel okay?'

'She's fine. Just a little restless tonight. She'll be glad you're back.'

'She never likes it when I'm away.'

'Neither do you, Harry,' said Annie. 'You can call on me any time, especially if Mrs Davis kicks up again. We'll be gone at Christmas for a week, but otherwise we're here.'

'Just a week? I thought you were going to California.'

'No.' She didn't offer any explanation and the silence was awkward. Finally she spoke: 'I'll say goodnight now.' Before he could thank her properly or offer to pay her for looking after Isabel, she had closed the front door behind her.

It had been a long day and he was glad to be home. Annie was right about that. Guttman realised that she knew him better than he knew her. He wondered what had happened to her Christmas plans. Why wasn't she taking Jeff and going to California to visit Nessheim? Had he found himself another girl out there? The idiot. It was hard to believe he'd do better than Annie.

He pulled off his tie and unbuttoned his collar, then went and poured himself half an inch of Johnnie Walker from the bar he kept in the living room. The whisky was a gift from the Director, which seemed ironic, to use Sedgwick's word, given his situation right now.

He raised his glass to take a first sip, then stopped and held the glass up even higher in a small private toast. To what? To his mission, he supposed, now that he knew he had one.

*　　*　　*

This time there was no memo from Hoover when he returned to the office, just a message to call Kevin Reilly of the Metropolitan Police. He ignored Marie's question about his mother's health and dialled the number. Reilly answered after the first ring.

'Kevin, it's Harry Guttman. You get anywhere with the Palmer case?'

'No, and that's not why I called you. Tell me, do you know a guy named Tamm?'

'Yeah, if he's from the Bureau. Edward Tamm. He's almost as important as I am.'

'Hard to believe,' Reilly said. 'Anyway, he came to see me, said he wanted to talk about Thornton Palmer.'

'Oh yeah?' This seemed to show unprecedented initiative by Tamm. After his memo, Hoover wouldn't be happy to find Tamm pursuing this. Unless Hoover had told him to.

'Tamm wanted to know where things stood with the case. He asked if I thought it was a suicide and I said we were keeping an open mind. Not that there's much else to go on. Without any new leads this case is going cold fast.'

'Is that all he wanted to know?'

'No, and that's why I called you. He asked what your involvement was. I explained that we'd found your card near Palmer's body.'

'Right,' said Guttman neutrally.

'He asked how you'd explained that. I told him you said you had met with Palmer the week before to talk about Argentina.'

'Was he all right with that?'

'Yeah, he was.'

'Did he want to know why we met in Rock Creek Park?' Guttman asked tensely.

'No he didn't – but that's because I didn't tell him

148

you met Palmer there.' Reilly paused. 'I figured there was no reason for him to know.'

'Thanks, Kevin,' Guttman said quietly.

But Reilly wasn't interested in his thanks. 'The thing is, I didn't get the sense he was all that interested in Palmer. I mean normally, he would have pressed me – *Have you done this? Have you done that?* The usual crap you experts give us amateur gumshoes. But he didn't do that.'

'Well, you said yourself there aren't any leads.'

'That's not my point. Like I say, he didn't really give a shit about Thornton Palmer. The person he wanted to know about was you.'

Part Five

Los Angeles
Mid-October 1941

13

He was collecting Lolly at seven, so Nessheim left the studio early and went home. He drank a beer out in the backyard and tried hard to think of nothing other than the extraordinary fact that Ted Williams had managed to hit .400 over an entire season. Yet the Red Sox hadn't made the World Series, which the Yankees had won in a 'subway series' against Brooklyn. Until April there would be no more baseball to distract him, and though he had played football at the highest level, he didn't follow it except to check his old team Northwestern's progress. Anything more made him think of what might have been.

There was still no sign of Billy Osaka. Guttman had phoned Nessheim early that morning. He hadn't bothered with preliminaries, but plunged in right away: Guttman had learned that Russian money had been sent west from New York to a Japanese-American bank in LA and he wanted Nessheim to investigate the transaction. Guttman had provided the name of the bank in Little Tokyo and the name of its recipient. There was nothing illegal about the Russians moving some money around, but it seemed a peculiar choice of bank to receive it, since Russia and Japan remained bitter enemies.

Nessheim finished his beer by the persimmon tree, confirming that the spare key to the back door (which hung from a nail he'd hammered into the trunk of the tree) was still there. Reassured, he went inside and showered, then changed into a light-grey, birdseye suit – even in October the evenings were still warm. As he

153

left the bedroom he collected his gun and holster. He wouldn't normally take them for a social occasion, but since finding Mrs Oka dead in her bed, he didn't go many places without his gun.

Lolly lived on a little street in West Hollywood near Poinsettia Park, about two miles south and down the hill from his place. He liked her neighbourhood: quiet streets and trees he recognised, with little fenceless strips of grass in front. Lolly had told him she shared a house with two other girls; pulling up in front, Nessheim gave his horn a single gentle toot and got out of the car.

When Lolly appeared the two roommates came out as well. One was wearing shorts and had her hair up in curlers; the other was barefoot and wore an old terry-cloth bathrobe. They were both plain girls and good-natured as they stood on the porch, giving him the once-over.

'You look after our Lolly, you hear?' the one in curlers joked.

'Yeah,' her companion joined in. 'You better have her back by breakfast.'

'Charlene!' said Lolly reprovingly and Nessheim laughed.

As Lolly came down the porch's short flight of stairs the two roommates watched her with what looked like a mixture of pride and envy. Her sleeveless, pale-green taffeta gown swished as she walked; over one arm she carried a dark clutch coat. Red lipstick had replaced her usual peach lip gloss and she'd washed her hair and pinned it up in a sleek up-do. She didn't look so young now, thought Nessheim; she just looked great. He said as much and Lolly gave a tight-lipped smile, since she knew she did, especially if she didn't show her jumbled teeth. As they drove off the roommates called goodbye and waved from the porch. Lolly didn't even turn her head – Nessheim could see she was thinking of the evening ahead.

The benefit was in the Arabia Ball Room, a large shabby building of dark brick on Sunset Boulevard, a few blocks east of Vine. Nessheim had passed it often enough, but never paid it much attention, for it was overshadowed by its opulent near neighbour – the immense Hollywood Palladium, which had opened a year before with Tommy Dorsey and his Orchestra and become the most popular dance hall in town.

Cars lined both sides of Sunset and Nessheim had to park on a side street, but Lolly shooed away his suggestion that he drop her off. As they walked through the neighbourhood, the cicadas were singing and leaves from the sidewalk trees shimmered in the night's mild breeze. On Sunset they joined other couples walking in the same direction. Couples in cars cruised down Sunset slowly, sticking to the 20 mph limit. Then a yellow jalopy sped by at twice that speed, with two teenage boys in front and another in the back with his head out the window, hooting at the people on the sidewalk. Nessheim said, 'If he leans out much further he'll fall out and kill himself.'

'Hope so,' said Lolly vehemently and Nessheim laughed in surprise.

Inside the Arabia they checked their coats in the fading atrium, then went into the vast ballroom, which was rapidly filling up. At the far end of the room there was a raised stage flanked by a pair of matching wooden columns, each adorned with carved griffins and snakes and topped by the head of Cleopatra. On the wall behind the stage there was an enormous blank screen, which Nessheim figured must be a vestige of an earlier incarnation as a movie theatre. Above it there still remained faded painted scenes from *The Arabian Nights*.

Along the walls, red-and-white bunting had been taped, and in the middle of the ballroom a crimson banner had been stretched across the width of the room, hovering twenty feet up in the air. *Save Our Soviet Comrades!* it read in gold letters.

Nessheim and Lolly joined the crowd on the hardwood dance floor. There was half-repressed anticipation in the air – like a wake, the evening promised a good time behind a sombre purpose. A jazz band of a dozen players were on one half of the stage, but their music was muted and Nessheim could just make out the tune of Artie Shaw's 'Frenesi'. A bar had been set up on three trestle tables along one side of the room, and Nessheim fetched two highballs after Lolly assured him she didn't want a ginger ale.

They stood sipping their drinks, watching as the room continued to fill. Most of the women were dressed up in cocktail dresses or fancy frocks with butterfly sleeves and padded shoulders. A few (like Lolly) wore evening gowns. A lot of the men were in suits, though a more artistic slice of the audience wore colourful pants, smoking jackets and loud shirts – Nessheim saw purple, pink and yellow ones. A tiny minority had adopted proletarian costumes of rough jeans and work boots, presumably out of solidarity with their working-class comrades elsewhere. If most people had come for a party, Nessheim thought, a few had come for *the* Party.

Teitz appeared at Nessheim's elbow, wearing a bright yellow bow tie and a blue suit with thick chalk pinstripes. He looked like a bookie. 'You made it, G-Man,' he said cheerfully. 'Waverley thought you'd never show.'

'How could I miss this?' Nessheim parried.

Teitz looked at Lolly appreciatively. 'I'd say you made

the right call.' He surveyed the crowd. 'What a funny mix,' he declared. 'It's like New Year's Eve at a Polish workingmen's club. Tuxedos with kielbasa on paper plates.'

'Who's the band?' asked Lolly.

'Don't get your hopes up. They're a bunch of long-shoremen from San Francisco, Harry Bridges' boys. They read Marx better than they read music, though they're not too bad.' He looked at Nessheim. 'Say, did you ever find the kid?'

'Who's that?' asked Nessheim abstractly, for he'd seen a familiar face, only to realise it was familiar because it was famous – Fredric March stood about fifteen feet away.

'Billy, of course. You know, our Jap friend.'

'Nope. No luck.'

Teitz seemed unsurprised. 'He's probably holed up in a tourist court with some broad.'

'Why a tourist court? Billy has his own place.'

'Yeah,' said Teitz knowingly. 'That's the first place he'd look.'

'Who's he?' Nessheim asked shortly.

'An angry husband.' Teitz laughed. 'Billy's got a girl-friend, some Jap girl in Boyle Heights, but I've seen him with a white chick. Well, she looked older, broiler rather than chick.'

Others from the Ink Well joined them, including Grenebaum and Stuckey, which surprised Nessheim since he would not have figured Stuckey as a sympa-thiser. It was too early to dance, so they talked among themselves. Teitz said, 'It makes me positively nostalgic being back in this old dump. I used to come here years ago.'

'To see movies?' asked Nessheim.

'No, it didn't make the transition to talkies. They

used it for marathon dances in the early Thirties. People danced until they dropped – literally.'

'Did you take part?'

'What do you think?' asked Teitz, and suddenly he slumped his head on his shoulder and closed his eyes. His tongue slid out between his lips, and Lolly gave a little squeal.

Nessheim laughed. 'Come on, you're scaring the horses.' Teitz opened his eyes and made a show of coming to. Then he looked around him intently. 'Goddamnit, I forgot my glasses. I can't tell who's here. Stuckey, any of the big guys show up?'

'Lots of them. You got to hand it to Waverley – he's still got clout.' He pointed at a bunch of smartly dressed men, huddled together with drinks in their hands. They were laughing confidently as one of them told a story. Stuckey started giving them names: 'Young Schulberg's over there, and Ring Lardner Junior, and Hecht.'

'Are they famous?' asked Lolly, sounding puzzled.

'Not to you, young lady,' Teitz said, 'but in our neck of the woods they are. Put it like this: we eat a lousy lunch at Elsie's Diner; they dine in the swanky confines of Musso & Frank. We live in sweltering East Hollywood rat traps or south of Central; they "reside" in the elevated air of Beverly Hills or Santa Monica. We think we've got it made if we're paid two bills a week; they're content to have an extra zero at the end of that.' Speech over, he turned to Stuckey. 'Waverley said Hammett might be coming.'

Stuckey was unimpressed. 'The rudest son of a bitch I ever met. I introduced myself at a party and he said he'd be happy to talk once he'd heard of me.'

'I loved *The Thin Man*,' said Lolly. 'I heard they shot it in eighteen days. The same as *The Red Herring*,' she added.

Grenebaum said gently, 'That, my dear, is the only point of comparison,' and even Nessheim had to laugh.

Waverley was working the crowd and stopped to say hello to his workmates. He nodded at Nessheim. 'Special Agent, glad to see you're here.'

Trying to sound cordial, Nessheim said, 'You've got a good turnout tonight.'

'Would you like a list of attendees? You know, for your bosses at the Bureau.'

It was said coldly and Teitz tried to lighten things. 'You could ask Lolly to type it up.'

Waverley didn't laugh. 'I've been meaning to ask, Nessheim – why are you called a "special" agent?'

'Jim *is* special,' Lolly said fiercely.

Teitz rolled his eyes and said, 'Of course he is, my dear. Nothing humdrum about our very own G-Man.'

Waverley shook his head. 'I'll see you gentlemen later. I've got to round up our guest speaker.'

Stuckey had brought his wife, a tall gal with shoulder-length strawberry blonde hair who looked a good ten years younger than her husband. She started talking to Lolly and Nessheim went to get refills for their highballs. As he stood in line for the bar, he looked around and figured there must have been two hundred people in the ballroom. He was still standing in line when the band finished their number and a man walked onto the stage. It was Waverley.

'Good evening,' he said, tapping the oversized mike. 'Welcome to the benefit for our Soviet brothers. We had originally hoped to hold this event in the Hollywood Palladium, but for some reason Norman Chandler didn't want us there.'

People laughed. Everyone knew that Chandler owned the Palladium and his father was the owner of the *Los Angeles Times* and almost as ferociously anti-Communist as he was anti-union – the unions providing the more immediate threat. Waverley went on, 'But this place suits us just fine and we've got a big turnout tonight – I want to thank you all for coming. People from every corner of Hollywood – why, we've even got the FBI in attendance tonight.' People laughed again and Nessheim looked vacantly at a distant wall.

Waverley went on: 'Some of you may remember that five years ago we had a similar benefit event. That was to raise money for the Republican forces in Spain – at a time when they had their backs to the wall.

'But that was small beer compared to what's happening today, when the very fount of progressivism is under threat. Spain was a guinea pig, a test tube if you like, an experiment in building a world all men would be welcome in and all men can enjoy. We have always known that certain forces would do everything in their power to fight off such a pioneering development, but what even the most realistic of us could not foresee five years ago was how quickly the forces of reaction would mobilise.'

He paused to let this sink in, pursing his lips grimly. Then he said, lowering his voice, 'And now truly the barbarians are at the gate, putting in peril the greatest experiment the world has ever seen in equality and comradeship.'

Suddenly someone shouted: 'Some experiment. What about the show trials?'

Waverley turned and glared down at the crowd below the stage. Nessheim couldn't see who the heckler was. Waverley continued: 'Ladies and gentlemen, it is essential that we do everything we can to help our brothers in the Soviet Union.'

'Like they helped Trotsky?' the voice in the audience shouted out.

Waverley stopped. Nessheim could see the heckler now – he was a skinny young man in a dark cotton jacket, unremarkable looking. Waverley seemed to nod at the man, or perhaps it was at someone else, for suddenly there was a commotion on the floor. Two men had seized the heckler by the arms and were trying to force their way with him through the crowd. The heckler was shouting '*Get your fucking hands off me!*' and then a third man approached him from the front and punched him hard in the stomach. The heckler doubled over and the two men got him through the crowd and rapidly out an exit. As they went through the steel fire door Waverley began to speak again.

'I apologise for the interruption. You can see that counter-revolutionary elements are everywhere. But that should not distract us from our goal, and tonight that goal is to help our embattled brothers. I urge you to contribute what you can – and then some. Before we pass the hat, it is my great honour and privilege to welcome a representative of that brave nation here in this city. I know you'll join me in welcoming the Vice-Consul for the Soviet Socialist Republics, Mikhail Mukasei. I've asked him to say a few words to us – about the dangers his country and every right-thinking citizen of the world face today. Comrades, I give you Mikhail Mukasei.'

The applause that followed was muted; people seemed stunned by the violent ejection of the heckler. It was as if something bad had happened so quickly that it seemed unreal.

Then someone pushed against Nessheim, harder than an accidental brushing by. He turned and found a big man with a face pitted by acne scars right behind him. The man glanced at Nessheim, as if to acknowledge his presence, but not the push.

'Take it easy, bud,' Nessheim said, his words only half-audible since the polite applause continued. Behind the man a woman stood, elegantly dressed in a black bolero jacket over a black cocktail dress. She tugged at the sleeve of the man's jacket. 'Ivan,' she said loudly. 'Give the man some room.'

The big guy glared at Nessheim, but moved back a step or two. The woman quickly got between them. 'Forgive my friend,' she said in accented English.

'That's okay. Maybe he thinks I'm a counter-revolutionary too.' He studied the woman for a moment. She had a handsome rather than pretty face; her dark, curled hair was parted on one side and caught back in a silver slide. 'I know you,' he said. 'You knocked on my door at the studio.'

'Did I?'

'Yes, you were looking for Waverley.'

'Ah,' she said, 'I remember.' She smiled and was about to say something else when the Russian began to speak and they both turned to face the stage.

Mikhail Mukasei was smartly dressed in a double-breasted suit and a wide-striped vermilion tie, a far cry from the kulaks and commissars he had come to represent. His hair was slicked back, which emphasised his high forehead and aquiline nose. His English was strongly accented and Nessheim found it hard to understand him as Mukasei embarked on an account of what he called 'the situation'. Which was dire, though the audience didn't need this man to tell them that. The Nazis were moving across the grain fields of the Ukraine like scything machines. Mukasei was unsparing in his depiction of the desperation of his country's plight, and

Nessheim couldn't help wondering if the man really thought things could be turned around. Mukasei's voice grew imploring: 'We need money not because it's money, but because it will allow us to defend our country. It will buy our soldiers the ammunition and guns needed to repel the Nazi foes. It will provide tanks and cannon and airplanes – all to be used in the name of liberty and equality.'

He went on in this semi-incantatory vein and Nessheim found his thoughts straying. He looked over, but couldn't see Lolly. He hoped she didn't think he'd deserted her. Finally the Russian finished and the audience clapped, though without much enthusiasm in case it triggered an encore.

'Jesus,' Nessheim said, half to himself, 'he did go on.'

The woman at his side looked at him questioningly. Nessheim shrugged. 'Sorry. But it's not as if we're allies yet.'

'Maybe he's trying to speed things up.' There was a defensive note in her tone.

'Do you know this guy?'

'A little bit,' she said with a knowing smile. Her voice was low and husky, as if she'd been born with a smoker's cough. 'He's my husband.'

'Oh.' He resisted the temptation to apologise and raised his eyes towards the big ugly man on her other side. 'At least you're not married to Bruiser here.'

She smiled again, like a tolerant parent, then her expression grew serious. 'You are not an admirer of the Soviet Union, I take it.'

'I'm afraid not.'

'Why is that?'

'Politics. As always these days.'

She smiled and held out her hand. 'I am Elizaveta Mukasei.'

'Nessheim,' he said, taking her hand. 'You're Russian then?'

'Not my fault,' she said, and it was his turn to smile. 'But what is it you don't like about my government?'

'Where do I start? I guess it began with the way they acted in Spain.'

'You objected to their helping the Republicans?' She sounded mildly alarmed that a Francoist had snuck into the ballroom.

'Not at all. It was the kind of help they gave I didn't like the sound of. They seemed more intent on eliminating Trotskyites than defending the Republic.'

She shrugged, which annoyed him.

He said, 'And then there were the show trials. I'm not saying I have all the facts, but it didn't seem like justice to me. Don't misunderstand – I hate the Nazis. But I find it hard to defend the Soviets either.'

'You seem to know facts enough,' she said to his surprise. She was looking across the room. 'It would be interesting to talk with you some more. But I have to be polite to our hosts tonight.' She nodded in the direction of her husband, who was talking to Waverley and the other organisers. 'I hope we'll meet some other time. Excuse me now,' she said, and shook his hand again, before going to join the other Mukasei.

The band was playing again, only this time dance music, and when he rejoined the Ink Well bunch Lolly grabbed him by the hand and took him onto the dance floor. It had been a long time since he'd been dancing and he felt rusty, but Lolly was a terrific partner and soon he had his rhythm back. They danced the Big Apple in a circle with others and then the Lindy Hop. The brass section of the band was good and he found the grimness of the evening's start erased by the easy music washing over them.

Eventually breathless, they went and had a few more drinks, talking with Teitz and the Stuckeys. Stuckey said he'd only come because his wife had insisted – 'She's a bit pink, aren't you darling?' She nodded happily in agreement. 'And I've got two left feet – well, she'd say they were right feet,' he added.

So Nessheim danced with Mrs Stuckey, while Lolly did a jitterbug with Teitz that had people gathering round to watch. Then Mrs Stuckey ran out of gas as well and Nessheim took her back to her husband and went to find Lolly, who was done dancing now. She stood laughing with Teitz and Grenebaum and a couple of unknown admirers, a drink in her hand, which someone else had supplied. He could see she was enjoying herself.

'Hiya Nessheim,' said Teitz. His bow tie had loosened and turned down at a slant like an airplane making its descent. 'Would you like a drink?'

'You mean another drink. No thanks. I was thinking of heading home.' He looked at Lolly. 'Don't feel you've got to leave. I'm sure one of these reprobates will give you a ride.'

She shook her head heavily and he realised she'd had one too many. 'No, I want to go with you, Jim.'

'Nobody calls him Jim,' Teitz protested. 'He's Nessheim, the one and only Agent Nessheim.'

'He's Jim to me,' she said.

'Let's go then, Lolly.'

They said goodbye and moved across the dance floor, which was now filling up. In the distance he saw Waverley talking with the Russian woman Mukasei, and their eyes met. Nessheim waved cheerfully and Waverley half-heartedly raised a hand in return.

Outside it was much cooler now and Lolly shivered. 'You had a coat, didn't you?' he asked.

'I left it in your car,' she said, which pleased him, since it suggested she'd planned all along to leave with him. They walked along Sunset Boulevard, then turned down the quiet side street. Lolly put an arm through his, tottering a little in her heels.

As they got to his car she withdrew her arm and he started to reach for his keys. Suddenly she put a hand on his shoulder and leant towards him and kissed him firmly on the mouth. It was a good kiss and took him by surprise. Breaking away, she said, 'Thanks for taking me.'

'Would you like to see where I live?' he asked. He suddenly wanted her very much.

She smiled and he could just make out her crooked teeth in the dark. 'Tell me something, Jim. How well do you know the Count?'

It wasn't the response he'd hoped for. 'Well enough, I guess. Why?'

'He's looking to fill a part – one of the girls in the office told me. It's not a big part, but it's got a few lines. It would be a start.'

'I don't know if you want to be cast by the Count, Lolly. You know his reputation.' He didn't add that even if a girl put out for the Count there was no guarantee of a role in one of his movies. Teitz had said that the Count's secretary at Warners spent many an afternoon with her legs wrapped around the director's, yet she was still just his secretary.

'I can look after myself,' she said defiantly. This made her seem so young that Nessheim had to keep from laughing. 'What I want to know is if you'll put a word in for me.'

He hadn't expected this. It was the last thing he should do – he wasn't at AMP for this, and the Count was the last person he wanted to feel beholden to. His doubts must have shown, for Lolly said, 'Forget it. It doesn't matter.'

He didn't say anything, but unlocked her door, then went round and opened his. He got in and started the car, then looked at Lolly. She smiled at him and he felt relieved – she wasn't sulking. 'The thing is –' he started to explain.

'Don't worry about it, Jim.'

'I'm not sure it would do you any good.'

'It's okay. Honest. Listen, would you mind taking me home? I'd love to see your place, but maybe another time, okay?'

'Sure,' he said neutrally, masking his disappointment.

Lolly's house was only a mile away and Nessheim did his best not to sulk as he drove her there. Perhaps sensing this, she kept up a line of chatter about the party while he drove in silence. 'Waverley looked like he enjoys giving a speech,' she said.

'I guess he's used to it.'

'Since you showed up he can't say you're on the other side any more, now can he?'

'What do you mean?' Nessheim asked, suddenly alert.

'You know, you being German and all. Waverley claimed you're bound to sympathise with them.'

'What?' he demanded angrily.

'Oh, he doesn't think you're a Nazi, Jim, don't get me wrong. He just reckons you're like Lindbergh. He says you even went to hear him speak.'

He had, earlier in the summer in the Hollywood Bowl. But he went out of curiosity not belief, and had been appalled by Lindbergh's patent sympathy with the Third Reich. The press played down the flier's sympathies, Nessheim felt. You only had to pay attention to his speeches to realise that Lindbergh was less anti-war than pro-Nazi.

'I'm as American as Waverley,' he said now angrily, but Lolly didn't reply.

He parked outside her house, where lights were still on in the living room. 'I'd ask you in but –' Lolly began.

'Don't worry. I've got an early start tomorrow.'

'The Count?'

'No, something else. I'll be in by lunchtime.'

'I guess I'll say goodnight then.' She hesitated, then turned towards Nessheim. When he leaned towards her, she placed a hand behind his neck and brought him closer, then repeated the intimate kiss of a few minutes before. He felt everything start to stir, but she broke away and opened her door. Hopping out, she said, 'That was fun, Jim. Thanks for taking me.' And she gave a big wave and scooted along the pavement for home, just as the front door opened and the barefoot room-mate stood there, still in her terry-cloth robe, looking surprised at Lolly's return.

As he drove slowly up the east side of Laurel Canyon, Nessheim left the lights of the city behind him, and was glad for the strength of the full-beam lights on his car. It was late enough that few people were still awake in the houses that lined Laurel Canyon Drive, even fewer when he reached Mount Olympus Drive. A single light glowed in the distance as he steered along its ribbon-like curves, and as he neared his own house he thought it must come from Mrs Delaware's house. Surprising, since she usually went early to bed.

There was a final bend in the road just short of his house and here the yellow glow disappeared, then grew visible again as the road straightened – it was closer than he expected and he realised the glow was coming from his own house. Had he left a light on?

It was possible, but it seemed oddly placed – not in the living room in front or in his bedroom. It didn't make sense, a light coming from a part of his own house he didn't recognise. And then he understood: it was the spare room, the third bedroom he never used. He couldn't have left a light on in a room he hadn't set foot in for months.

Suddenly alert, he drove past his house and parked on the edge of the road just past Mrs Delaware's, then extinguished his lights and turned off the engine. Getting out, he closed the door quietly, letting the lock click faintly. This high up a light breeze with a faint aroma of wild sage wafted in from the nearby Santa Monica Mountains. He stood motionless for a moment, letting his eyes adjust to the darkness and his ears adapt to the sound of the wind. Something slithered in the brush across the street – a snake maybe or a chipmunk. There were deer around too, hiding in the remaining chaparral which had once covered the entire mountainside.

He drew the Smith & Wesson .38 from its holster and held it by his side as he crossed the front lawn of the Delaware house, walking at an angle that took him to the edge of his own backyard. He had used the weapon in his line of work once before, but he had not expected the need to arise ever again. What had Guttman said of his sedentary duties? *A desk job can still be interesting. Mine is.*

Mrs Delaware had planted a low hedge of rock plants to demarcate the border of their properties, and they sat slightly higher up the hill. He jumped them and landed softly on his lawn, then slowly swept the yard with his gun. A trio of pepper trees in one corner would provide cover for anyone waiting to pick him off.

To hell with it: he cut across the grass and came to the back door. Pausing there, he kept the gun in one hand and fished his keys out of his pocket. But when he started to put the key into the lock he found the door was unlocked. Someone had got into the house. Were they still there?

He pushed the door and let it swing open, his gun up. Kicking off his shoes, he stepped silently onto the linoleum floor of his kitchen. The door straight ahead was open – it led to the living room, which was completely dark. To his right another door opened onto the corridor stretching the length of the house, with three doors on its far side, one for each bedroom. He could see secondary light in the hall, coming from the unused room, which was closest to the kitchen.

He didn't go there first. In his stocking feet he crossed the kitchen and entered the living room. It was a wide room with a picture window facing the street and a dining nook at the far end. As he reached for the light switch on the wall with his free hand, he felt a tension he didn't want to release – in case he got shot as a result. As the light came on his gun was ready. There was no one there.

He walked over to the hall, then checked each of the first two bedrooms, flicking the light on and searching them carefully, even looking under the bed in his own room. On to the bathroom, where he stood for a moment, then pushed the shower curtain back across the tub in one motion. Nothing.

At last he came to the unused spare room at the end of the hallway. The door he always kept shut was half-open and light came out in a tapered shaft from the overhead bulb in the middle of the room. He kicked the door from an angle and it swung wide open: no one was standing behind it, and as he went in he saw only two boxes of books he hadn't unpacked, and a spare desk his landlady had never removed. He came to the last possible hiding place and opened the closet door with his gun ready. It held only the winter overcoat he'd put away when he'd first arrived in LA and never looked at since.

Then he saw the piece of paper, pinned to the surface of the desk with a hunting knife he had never seen before. It had a dark bone handle, freckled by amber-coloured spots, and it had been stuck through the paper and deep into the cheap pine top.

He looked down at it and read:

Billy Osaka
RIP

On the bottom of the page someone had placed the key from the persimmon tree.

14

IF YOU'RE A banker, thought Nessheim as he watched
Mr Satake lift his long grocer's apron over his head,
then I'm Felix Frankfurter. But when the Japanese man
put on a pinstriped suit jacket that matched his trousers
and did up his tie, the transformation from grocer to
man of finance was miraculously effected.

Mr Satake led Nessheim the length of the store,
through the grocery department, then past a long
counter to one side which had three Japanese women
standing behind it. At the very back he opened a door
into a small office. Here he motioned Nessheim in and
walked behind a desk, where he sat down and swept
back his straight grey hair with both hands. As Nessheim
took the chair facing him, Mr Satake beamed in
welcome. Under his chin a canary-coloured tie bulged
like a gorged snake.

It had taken Nessheim twenty minutes to find this
'bank'. Its location in Little Tokyo was obscure – it sat
on Woodward Court, directly behind First Street where
Nessheim initially went, and where he found half a
dozen stores and, confusingly, two other banks. A
friendly guy in the Seiko Watch Company, English-
speaking, had explained that the bank Nessheim was
looking for was part grocery store and part bank. This
was confirmed when he went around the corner and
found a sign, in Japanese and English, which said 'Satake
Groceries'.

When Nessheim had entered the premises he'd found
bushel baskets full of produce in the middle of the room
– eggplants, green and red peppers, zucchinis with their

flowers attached, heaps of green beans and some odder-looking vegetables he'd never seen before. The place was full of customers, all Japanese women, but otherwise the setting could have been his father's old general store in Wisconsin.

A shop girl in a smock had come towards him hesitantly, as if he must be lost. When he'd asked for Mr Satake, she had led him to an older man in an apron, who was spooning cane sugar out of a metal canister for a customer.

Nessheim now looked around at the office, which seemed to double as a storeroom: ranged against one wall was a row of burlap sacks – one was open, revealing a measuring cup tilted on a mountain of polished rice. Higher up the wall two shelves held lines of dark bottles, three deep, labelled in brightly coloured Japanese characters. Soy sauce, Nessheim decided.

He stifled a yawn, inevitable after his sleepless night. He'd jammed a kitchen chair under the brass knob of the back door and slept with his .38 next to his pillow. He hadn't expected his intruder to come back, but wasn't going to take any chances. A locksmith was due out that evening, though he doubted if his intruders would have had time the night before to make a copy of the key from the persimmon tree. It must have been a close-run thing: they would have gone into his house after it was dark, since otherwise the risk of being spotted by Mrs Delaware would have been too great. But how did they know Nessheim would be gone all evening?

And was Billy dead? *RIP*? Or did they want Nessheim to think that so he would stop looking for him?

In which case, Osaka was alive.

Now he pushed his card across the desk. 'I'm from the FBI. I've come to ask about money that was

173

transferred here recently from the Manhattan Savings Association.'

Mr Satake beamed some more, but did not reply. Nessheim tried again. 'I am here to enquire about a transfer of monies from a New York bank. Can you help me with this, please?'

Mr Satake beamed a third time – yet he seemed to recognise the impasse, for he opened a drawer. Extracting some slips of paper, he peered at them, then pushed two across the desk to Nessheim.

Both had Japanese writing on them and Nessheim was at first none the wiser. He looked at Mr Satake beseechingly, but the Japanese man only offered another smile – like a cook in a diner, waiting to hear what the order would be. Nessheim looked down again at the two slips. They had blanks prefaced by dollar signs and except for the Japanese characters at the top they looked just like the slips in their counterpart American banks – for deposits and withdrawals respectively, he realised. Presumably, Mr Satake was waiting for him to say which he wanted to make.

Something would have to give. Nessheim stood up, holding out a stiff palm like a traffic cop to tell Mr Satake he should stay put. He went and opened the door, then looked out at the nearby bank end of the store. Three rough tills had been created by the insertion of wooden dividers along a giant slab of mahogany. There were no security grilles, not even a pane of glass between the tellers and the customers. And no sign of any guards. Maybe Little Tokyo was immune to the bank robberies that even seven years after John Dillinger's death were still plaguing the rest of America.

The three young Japanese women were standing behind the mahogany counter. An aged Japanese man took a slip from one of them and moved towards the front of the store. The two girls nearest him looked at Nessheim curiously.

'Can you help me please?' he said, stepping out from the office. His voice sounded loud in this empty part of the store.

The two girls nearest to him looked up and smiled. Both wore white blouses, buttoned up to the neck, and dark skirts. The third girl, furthest away from Nessheim, was dressed differently, in a grey kind of smock with padded shoulders and long sleeves. She was counting a stack of bills and hadn't looked up when Nessheim asked his question.

'Do you speak English?' Nessheim asked.

The first girl gave the same unilluminating smile as Mr Satake. Nessheim looked at the girl next to her; she just shook her head. The third girl was still counting, concentrating as she peeled off individual bills from a diminishing stack of greenbacks.

'How about you, miss?' Nessheim asked.

He could see her lips moving. When she'd counted the last bill she exhaled with relief and scribbled down a number. Without looking at Nessheim she said curtly, 'What do you need?'

'A translator, I guess. I was supposed to have one, but he couldn't make it. Mr Satake doesn't seem to speak English.'

The woman sighed and came out from behind the counter. She was taller than the other girls, who were tiny, and walked with an energetic spring to her step that made her seem taller still. She had good legs under the smock she wore and her black hair was cut nicely with a straight fringe. Hers was a pretty face: a sharp chin, lips the shape of a cupid's bow and expressive eyes. For a split second Nessheim thought he recognised her, but couldn't quite place from where.

She moved towards the office, moving by Nessheim without a glance, and he followed her in. She spoke briefly in Japanese to Satake, then sat down beside the desk with her legs uncrossed and knees together.

Satake handed over the card Nessheim had given him and as she read it her eyes widened slightly. She spoke sharply to Satake and he too looked surprised.

'So, Mr Special Agent Nessheim,' she said as he returned to his seat, 'how can we be of service?'

'I'm here to ask about a wire transfer of funds. It came from New York.'

'We have many such transfers, you know. Most come from Japan, but some are within the domestic US of A.'

He stared at her. Her English was accentless, the voice soprano but stern. She was clearly born here – *Nisei*, he remembered from Billy Osaka's brief tutorial. He said bluntly, 'This transfer was for fifty thousand dollars.'

She swallowed and he realised that her air of confidence was as fragile as it was determined.

'Could you please ask Mr Satake if he remembers this transfer?'

She turned and spoke to the banker in a torrent of Japanese. As she spoke, the man was nodding, but when she'd finished he gave an emphatic shake of his head. She turned to Nessheim, 'No, he doesn't,' she explained unnecessarily.

'Ask him to have another think, please. It came here in August or possibly July.'

The girl looked at him stonily, then shrugged as if to say *more fool you*, and turned back to speak to Mr Satake. This time the banker seemed to be pondering his answer. After a moment, when he still didn't speak, Nessheim said firmly, 'I can, of course, get the transfer-wire number, if that would help. It would take a day or two and frankly the Bureau has better things to do.'

The girl stared hard at Nessheim, then almost casually she spoke to Mr Satake. Whatever she said struck home, for Mr Satake replied at length in a high-pitched voice that sounded like the clack of typewriters in Ink Well Alley.

'What did he say?' asked Nessheim impatiently.

'Mr Satake was away for much of the summer, visiting his family in Japan. But he says that naturally there would be a full record of the transaction, especially since such a large sum was involved.'

'I'm glad to hear that. I'd like to see the record, please.'

'Do you read Japanese, Mr Nessheim?'

'No, but you do, miss.' He let this sink in, then asked, 'What's your name?'

'Hanako.'

'Hanako what?'

'Hanako Yukuri. Do you want my middle name too?'

'Not yet,' said Nessheim. 'What do you do here, Hanako?'

'I'm the head teller. And Mr Satake's secretary – I have shorthand.'

'Do you remember this wire transfer?'

'I wasn't the head teller then. Miss Waganaba was.'

He sighed. 'I don't suppose I could have a word with Miss . . . Waganaba?'

'Not easily,' Hanako said cheerfully. 'She retired and went back to live in Japan.'

'What about you? I suppose you were in Japan this summer too?' he asked with a hint of sarcasm.

The girl gave a shadow of a smile. 'No, I was here.'

'Well, that's good news.'

She didn't reply, but stood up and headed for the door.

'I hope you're coming back,' he said, alarmed at the prospect of being alone with Mr Satake again.

The girl laughed. 'If you're good I might,' she said. There was nothing meek or mouse-like about this girl, thought Nessheim, who had a soft spot for a smart alec.

When she came back it was with a typed slip – in Japanese. 'Looks like Greek to me,' said Nessheim lightly.

She didn't smile this time. 'Money came from New York on August 5th in the sum of twenty-five thousand dollars. It was sent on behalf of a Mr Milnikov on behalf of the Russian Consulate in New York City and was received here by a Mr Lyakhov.'

'Who's he?'

'You would have to tell me, Mr Nessheim,' she said coolly.

'Wouldn't he need to have an account to receive that large a sum of money?' Especially since he wasn't Japanese.

'Not necessarily. But I checked and in fact Mr Lyakhov did have an account here, which he opened on August 1st.'

'Interesting. You said Mr Lyakhov "did have" an account – has he closed it?'

'Yes, on August 19th.'

'That's quick. Would Mr Lyakhov have to establish his credentials to open an account?'

'He would have had to show identification.'

'So you have an address?'

'As a matter of fact we do. A driver's licence was used as identification and Rose – that's Miss Waganaba – wrote down the address.' She handed over another slip of paper. Nessheim looked at it – 301 Longworth Drive.

'Where is this?'

She seemed amused. 'I think you'll find it's in Palisade Heights.'

'You said twenty-five thousand dollars. I was informed it was fifty.'

'No.' She was emphatic. 'We wouldn't make a mistake over that kind of amount. We handle larger sums than our surroundings might suggest, Agent Nessheim. But that's a lot of money by any standard.'

'I know it is,' he said, trying not to show his puzzlement. 'But could it have come twice – I mean, two twenty-fives . . .'

'Make fifty, Agent Nessheim. We may not speak your language perfectly, but even Mr Satake is numerate.'

'I wasn't suggesting—'

'Is there anything else you need?' she asked.

Mr Satake was beaming again.

'No,' said Nessheim getting up. 'Other than Mr Lyakhov.'

15

'*Nessheim!*'

He was putting back the Osaka file when the SAC called out. Damn: another ten seconds and Nessheim would have been out of there, unnoticed.

He went and stood in the doorway of Hood's office.

'Here I am,' he said.

The SAC was standing by the window. Behind him a warm and hazy sky blurred the view of the mountains. There was often a murky quality to the air downtown. Teitz said it was due to the exhaust fumes of the growing number of cars, but some days the sky was clear as gin without any noticeable reduction in traffic.

'I've had a complaint about you,' said Hood.

He was dressed in a khaki-coloured suit with a buttoned vest that was a darker shade of tan and light brown brogues. He looked like a dandified country sheriff, dressed up for a visit to the big city.

'Who from?'

'The LAPD. They found the dead body of an old Japanese lady in Little Tokyo. Apparently they found you there too.'

'I'm the one who called them.'

'They seem to think you were messing up the crime scene.'

'Like hell I was,' Nessheim said. He explained about the money he'd found.

Hood said, 'What were you doing there anyway?'

'I was looking for Osaka. The old lady was his grandmother.'

'I thought I told you not to waste your time on the

guy. I understand you've been in touch with the field Office in Hawaii. Shivers, the SAC out there, answered your telex personally.'

'I was only asking for a Scoop search,' said Nessheim, slightly appalled by the level of the response.

'Just a Scoop search?' Nessheim could see Hood was getting annoyed. 'Listen, you know I'm not happy about this whole set-up. I don't know why Harry Guttman wants you under his wing and I don't care, provided you keep your nose clean and stay out of my hair. But when I have a SAC asking me who you are and the local cops complaining, I don't like it one bit. Now I want you to stay in that studio and make sure they make us look good, and once a month tell me who the Reds are under Hollywood's bed. You're not in Investigations any more – I don't know if you ever really were – and that means you're not to investigate, except to point the way to Communists, got it? As far as Osaka is concerned you should consider the kid dead and buried.'

Nessheim flinched at Hood's choice of words and Hood stared at him. 'Listen, if this Jap kid killed his grandmother, then he *is* dead and buried. He'll get the chair for that.'

'If he killed her why would he leave five hundred bucks on her dresser?'

'Why would anyone?' Hood said sharply. 'Like I say, leave it alone. I want his file given the deep six, right?'

Nessheim nodded and Hood said, 'Now, did you go to the Reds' rumpus last night?'

'I did. The usual suspects – and a lot of writers from the studios.'

'Who organised it?'

'A guy named Waverley. He's a Party member.'

'I know who he is. Did he speak?'

'Yeah. The standard stuff about our brothers in red. A Russian gave a speech too – the Vice-Consul in LA.'

But Hood wasn't interested in this. He asked, 'How many people were there?'

'I'd say between two and three hundred.'

'How much money did they raise?'

'I can tell you that,' said Nessheim, trying to think of a plausible figure. 'It was a little more than five grand. I've got a friend at the studio who does typing for Waverley on the side.'

'What's the name of your friend?'

'Her friends call her Fifi,' said Nessheim, picking the name out of a mental hat. Anything to keep Hood off his back. 'She's not a Red, though. Waverley pays her for the typing.'

'Fifi, huh?' Hood shook his head and Nessheim remembered that Guttman had called him a Puritan, and not in an admiring way. Hood said, 'I worry about the company you keep, Nessheim.'

Nessheim went down to the typing pool, where he asked for the reply from the Hawaii Field Office. The head typist rummaged in the papers in a wire tray at one end of her desk, then handed over a sheet of telex paper. It was from the Hawaii SAC:

```
In answer to your query:

William Osaka attended Grade School at
PS 5 in Honolulu from 1922 to 1928.

Last known address was 15 Maypole Avenue
in Honolulu, Oahu. Father reported
deceased Honolulu May 1924. Mother
deceased Honolulu June 1935.
```

```
No felony convictions in the Island
Territory jurisdiction, and no record of
misdemeanours with police authorities.

No Territory driver's license issued in
his name.

Details of High School education were
unavailable.

Robert Shivers

SAC Honolulu
```

Both Osaka parents were dead, which Billy had not noted on his application form to the Bureau here in LA. Why not? It seemed curious, as did the absence of any high-school records. He must have gone to high school, otherwise he wouldn't have got into UCLA.

Nessheim walked back to the elevators. When one came it was empty and he breathed a sigh of relief as the door started to close, glad to get out of Hood's bailiwick. But an arm protruded between the closing doors and whacked them open – revealing Cohan, the Deputy SAC.

'Just the man I want to see,' he said, entering the elevator. His drawn features looked like the air had been sucked out of his cheeks.

'Really?' said Nessheim with foreboding. It was bad enough getting chewed out by Hood. He didn't need a second round with the SAC's chief sucker-upper.

'I want a favour,' said Cohan, sounding confident he was going to get one.

Nessheim turned his head and looked at him blankly.

'You know Harry Dedway?'

Nessheim laughed. 'Special Agent Parker?' The leading

man in *The Red Herring*; the former cowboy picture star who looked lost without his horse.

'That's the one,' said Cohan. 'The thing is,' he said, and Nessheim realised he was embarrassed, 'my wife's a big fan. Don't ask me why.' He shrugged meaningfully, as if to say, Women! 'Anyhow, I was wondering if you could get Louise an autograph.'

'Well,' said Nessheim, unused to a beseeching Cohan. 'Dedway's kind of a prima donna. But we get on okay, so sure, I can get an autograph for your wife.'

'That'd be great.' The doors opened on the ground floor and Cohan strode out.

'Hang on a sec,' Nessheim called out and Cohan stopped, surprised. Nessheim took two steps closer on the lobby's polished marble floor. 'Could you check something for me? I need a line on a guy.'

'This on the job?'

'Of course.'

'Does the SAC know?'

It was Nessheim's turn to shrug. 'No. And he wouldn't be happy about it if he did. Hood's already sore that I report to D.C. But I don't even need to see the file. I just want to know if there is one, and the gist of what's in it. Shouldn't take more than a minute or two.'

'That's a lot to ask for just one autograph,' Cohan said with a shake of his head, starting to edge away.

'Fair enough,' said Nessheim placidly. He could hear the empty elevator close behind him, and he said just loud enough for Cohan to hear, 'Would your wife like a tour of the studio? Maybe meet some of the actors?'

Cohan stopped moving. 'She'd get to meet Dedway?'

'Absolutely,' said Nessheim, wondering how he was going to bring this about. He hadn't exchanged more than fifteen words with the actor, who only took instruction from the Count.

'Could you really arrange that? I'd come too, just so she feels comfortable.'

Nessheim laughed. 'You better. I wouldn't want my wife to spend time alone with Harry Dedway.'

'I can trust my wife,' Cohan said haughtily.

'Of course you can. Anyway, I can get her a tour all right, and she can meet Harry Dedway. I'll be there, you can be there. Hell, there's a pet donkey in Studio Two that can be there too. All I want in return is a quick sweep of the files. I don't need anything written down and I promise you it's Bureau business you'll be assisting, whatever Hood would say.'

At last Cohan gave a small resigned sigh. 'Name?'

'Dubin, Mo Dubin. And any mention of an associate named Ike. I don't know his last name. Both are originally from Cleveland.'

'I got to phone the field office there?'

'Nah. Dubin's been in LA a while, I think. If mud stuck in Ohio, some of it would make the file out here. If he has a file.'

'When's the tour?' asked Cohan, happier to discuss Nessheim's end of the bargain.

'Gimme a week or two. Dedway's between pictures – they wrapped on *The Red Herring* this morning. But I know he's on the lot later this year, so I'll arrange a tour for then.'

'Good. Let me know.' Now it was Nessheim's turn to walk away and this time Cohan called out, 'Hey, Nessheim!'

'Yeah?'

'No Dubin if there's no Dedway.'

He stopped for a grilled cheese and Coke on North Broadway. Between diner food and the meals he made for himself, he was getting awfully sick of sandwiches.

That had been one good thing, perhaps the only good thing, about the boarding-house life he'd led in Chicago and D.C. – hot meals cooked by someone else.

It took half a mile for him to spot that he was being followed. The tail was clever; it was a cab not a car and Nessheim might never have noticed if the driver hadn't made a mistake. Nessheim was approaching MacArthur Park on Wilshire and he crossed Alvarado as the light turned red. Seconds later he heard a horn blast and looking in his mirror saw a taxi had sped up to cross the light too, just avoiding a collision with a Plymouth coming on from Alvarado. There was no fare sitting in the cab, so what was the driver's rush?

When Nessheim came out of the park he turned right onto Vermont Avenue without signalling and the cab cut across a lane in order to turn as well. Now he knew.

He didn't want company where he was going next. When he came to Sunset he turned left, wondering how to shake the tail. He pulled over by the kerb outside Albert's Barber Shop, watching in his side-view mirror as the taxi kept coming, and took a deep breath waiting for it to pass. When it did the driver had his hand up against his ear, shielding his face. It was a man; that was about all Nessheim could tell.

He got out of his car and walked until he came to the spinning barber pole and then slipped into Albert's Barber Shop. He found Albert at the first chair, working with clippers on the neck of an old boy. He did a double take when he saw Nessheim. 'Don't tell me you're here for another haircut,' he said. 'If you're enlisting, the army cuts your hair for free.'

'I need a shine,' said Nessheim, walking through to the back. There Arthur put down his newspaper and stood as Nessheim hopped onto the chair and put his feet up on the two brass supports. His Florsheims

were almost brand new and didn't need a shine, but
he had a bird's-eye view of the sidewalk. He turned
down Arthur's offer of the paper and kept his eyes
peeled on the front door as the old black man worked
polish with a rag into his shoes.

'I told you Williams was going to hit .400,' Albert
called out.

'Sure you did,' said Nessheim vaguely, his eyes intent
on the street. Traffic was light and the cars were going
by at a good clip. But he managed to spot the taxi,
which had turned around and was heading back east
on the far side of the street. This time the driver had
his hand down and his head swivelled towards the
barber shop. Nessheim tried focusing on the face, but
the cab was going too fast to get a fix on anything.

Arthur finished by buffing with a chamois rag until
Nessheim's shoes had a high shine. Nessheim paid him
two bits and said goodbye to Albert, then moved quietly
out the barber shop door. Standing on Sunset, he looked
casually each way. Another cab came by, but it had a
fare – an old lady with shopping piled on the back seat.

He wondered if he was being spooked by the intruder
in his house and the note he'd left behind. Let's not get
a persecution complex, he told himself. After all, he
didn't believe anyone other than Guttman cared that
the Russian Mission in New York had wired money to
somebody here in LA. But Osaka had attracted some
other people's interest – Ike, for one. Nessheim decided
he'd tend to Guttman's concern later on; for now, he
was following his own instincts.

16

H<small>E</small> <small>DROVE WEST</small> on Sunset Boulevard, limning the
bottom of the northern hills, passing the green sign for
the Beverly Hills Hotel at the intersection with Crescent
Drive, where he had turned to go to Buddy Pearl's house.
Parking on the eastern edge of the UCLA campus, he
walked across a long new bridge with three Romanesque
arches that were sunk deep into one of the regional
arroyos, gulches which filled with racing water when
the rains came late in the year, but were otherwise desert
dry. Two logging trucks passed him, spewing dust, and
ahead he could see construction workers laying the
foundations for another university building. One day
the campus would be stunning, he thought, perched on
an elevated small plateau west of Beverly Hills with
distant views of downtown LA.

Royce Hall was at the hub of the projected campus
and had the merit of being finished – a handsome
ornate building with two high campaniles that looked
like they belonged to an Italian church. Entering it he
found the registrar's office and got directions to the
Political Science faculty, which was housed further
along a large plaza of chewed-up, muddy grass that
would presumably one day be lawn. Nessheim almost
broke an ankle angling across it, then made it to the
safety of some duckboards that led to a new brick
building.

He knocked at an obvious door in the corridor
running off the building's atrium and found a trio of
giggling typists drinking coffee inside. They pointed him
upstairs, resuming their giggling as he left. He followed

students up the stairwell to the second floor, then found himself alone reaching the third, where a long corridor ran either way from the central landing. He picked a side and walked slowly, examining the little cards taped to each doorway. Four doors down he found the name he was looking for and knocked.

'Come in,' said a high-pitched voice. When Nessheim opened the door he was surprised to find a man his own age; he'd expected someone weighed down by wisdom and years. The man stood up from behind his desk: he was as tall as Nessheim, but skinnier, the gauntness of his frame evident even under his jacket, which he wore with a check plaid shirt and a brown tie. He looked like a lumber thinner who read books.

'Professor Larson?' Nessheim asked, somewhat surprised. It was what the card taped to the door had said.

'Do you have an appointment?' The man looked a little nervous.

'No, I don't.'

'Are you taking 103?' the man asked, flicking back his hair. It was sandy-coloured and ran over his ears. Nessheim figured Albert could do a lot for the guy.

'I'm not a student,' he said. 'I'm with the FBI.'

Larson sat down again. On the wall behind him hung a framed daguerreotype of a man in a frock coat and black bow tie. He had a moustache and long beard that dated him by at least half a century, never mind the black and white grain of the print.

Larson said, 'Usually you guys call ahead.'

'Usually?'

'This isn't the first time someone from the Bureau's come to see me.'

'If you help me out, Professor, maybe it can be the last.'

'I told your colleague everything he wanted to know. I've got nothing more to say about my time in Berkeley, and I won't talk about other people there. And if there are complaints about my teaching, raise them with the Dean.'

'I'm not here about any complaints,' said Nessheim calmly. He pointed at the daguerreotype. 'Nice picture.'

'Some people think it must be one of my ancestors. Your colleague did.'

'I doubt that you're descended from Engels.'

Larson looked impressed. 'Is that part of your training at the FBI – you know, spot the Red?'

'Nah,' said Nessheim, shaking his head. 'I'm from Wisconsin. We had a socialist governor.'

'Hah.' Larson laughed despite himself. 'I'm from Minnesota myself. Where'd you go to college?'

'Northwestern.'

'What did you major in, Accounting?' His smile only reinforced his patronising tone.

'Political Science.'

Larson looked at him more closely. 'Did you know Professor Harrison?'

'I wouldn't say "know", but I took his course on political philosophers.' Pol Sci 330. Harrison had been brilliant. If Nessheim had ever had any latent disposition to political extremes – right or left – a semester of Harrison's withering analysis had quashed it for good.

'Really?' asked Larson. 'Then why are you persecuting the likes of me?'

'Because I didn't graduate.'

Larson chuckled. 'I was Harrison's student at Berkeley. He didn't approve of my politics, but he taught me a lot. God knows why he moved to Northwestern.'

'Maybe he wanted a milder climate.'

Larson laughed again. 'Okay, so what do you want?'

'I'd like some information about one of your former students.'

'Don't get your hopes up – I teach two hundred of them a year.'

'It's a guy named Osaka. Billy Osaka. I don't know what course of yours he took.'

Larson looked at him stonily and Nessheim saw this was one student the teacher remembered. But then, as Teitz has said, everybody knew Billy Osaka.

Nessheim added, 'He listed you as a reference on an application.'

'He did? He never asked me,' Larson said crossly.

'So you do remember him.'

'What was he applying for?'

Nessheim paused, savouring the moment. 'A part-time job with the Bureau.' If Osaka was dead, letting this out wasn't going to matter; if Billy were alive, Hood had made it clear he wasn't going to be working for the Bureau again.

'So what do you want to know?'

'What was he like? Was he a good student?'

'Yes,' Larson replied simply. For a minute Nessheim thought that was all the man was going to say, but Larson went on: 'He came to me in his sophomore year and asked if he could take a seminar I teach. It's called "Democracy in America", though personally I'd rather call it "The Lack Thereof". Normally it's limited to majors – that would be juniors and seniors – but I was impressed by his eagerness, so I let him enrol.'

'Did he do well?'

'Not at first. He struggled with the written work. It was okay, but he talked a lot smarter than he wrote. So we met once a week to go over his writing.'

'Did it improve?'

191

'Yes, a bit. He worked pretty hard, but he was always busy doing other things.'

'What kind of things?'

'He worked part-time on an English-language paper in Little Tokyo. He did shifts at various factories; those that would have Japanese workers anyway.'

'Maybe he needed the money.'

'Maybe. But he also played in a softball league and taught Japanese kids to swim. Anything but hit his books.'

'What about politics? He must have been interested or he wouldn't have taken your course.'

'He was interested in a classic immigrant's way. He wrote his thesis on Japanese arrivals here and their Americanisation.'

'That seems normal enough.'

Larson grew impatient. 'Don't you know the laws we have about the Japanese? They can't own property any more, they can't bring brides over from Japan, they're subject to every kind of exploitation, and other than agriculture and fishing, most industries won't employ them. It will take a lot more than efforts to assimilate for them to get their full rights.'

'But Billy's only half-Japanese.'

'That's more than enough. Look, Billy's a charming guy and he seems to think that charm is enough. But it's not. I told him he might do better going back to Hawaii. Most of the population is Japanese, so they can't be kept out of professions the way they are here. He could have been whatever he wanted out there – maybe even a lawyer. But he wasn't having any of it – it was the only time I ever saw him angry.' Larson shook his head; he seemed exasperated on behalf of his former student.

'So he wanted to stay here.'

'Yes. He had a misplaced belief in the American Dream.'

'When in fact a revolution is required?'

'Mock me if you like.'

Nessheim decided to leave ideology alone. 'Did Billy ever talk about his family?'

'Not much. He grew up in Hawaii. I know his father died when he was little. When his mother died he came over here. His grandmother was already in LA, I think.'

Nessheim tried to sound wistful: 'What I don't get is why he left Hawaii. Like you say, life's a lot better for the Japanese there.'

Larson said, 'I think he had a cousin – some guy who was like an older brother to him when they were growing up. The cousin came over here and he persuaded Billy to follow.'

'Was this cousin called Osaka too?'

'I haven't the faintest idea.'

'Did Billy ever talk about his girlfriends?'

'Not much. There was one I remember, though. One he seemed to care about.'

'Do you know this girlfriend's name?'

'Nope. She was *Nisei*, I know that, and she worked for a bank. And, Special Agent, that's really all I have to say.'

17

CERTAIN LA MYSTERIES unravelled the longer Nessheim lived in the city. He had not realised for a long time that Sunset Boulevard traversed virtually the length of the city, ending up near Santa Monica, facing the ocean and, inevitably, the setting sun. He followed it down from UCLA, and although traffic was light the road itself was full of twists and turns and badly surfaced, so it took him an hour to reach Pacific Palisades. There he spent another futile twenty minutes trying to locate the address that Hanako Yukuri from the Satake Bank had supplied for the mysterious Mr Lyakhov, recipient of $25,000 from the Manhattan Savings Association.

He finally found where Mr Lyakhov's address might have been – 'might have been' being the operative phrase, since as near as Nessheim could make out it would have been sited, give or take a nine-iron, halfway along the 2nd fairway of the Riviera Country Club. So the address given to the Satake Bank was phoney.

By now it was after three o'clock. Traffic was bad and it took almost until four for Nessheim to return to the studio. There he found the Ink Well near-deserted and quiet. In his little office Teitz was alone and sat with his head on his desk, moaning gently.

'I see you kept going last night,' Nessheim said.

Like a pond-bound frog, Teitz opened one eye. 'It's all Grenebaum's fault. He told me he'd made a great find in West Hollywood. He didn't tell me it was three different bars.'

Hoping to see Lolly, Nessheim went along the corridor and peered in her office, but she wasn't there. In his own office he shut the door. He needed to telegraph Guttman about the disparity between the fifty grand and the twenty-five grand acknowledged by the Satake Bank. It was too large a sum for a misunderstanding. But he also needed to sit and think.

There was a tap on his door and Lolly came in. He stared at her, for something had changed. Then he saw that she was heavily made-up, with eyeliner and mascara and powder on her cheeks. Gone was the youthful farm girl look.

'You're back,' she said cheerfully.

'Yeah, I stuck my head in but you were nowhere to be seen.'

'I was over in Studio Two,' she said. He gave her a look and she laughed. 'I was just watching a rehearsal for a minute, and then I saw my friend in Make-Up. Can't you tell?'

'I'd never have guessed.'

She gave a snort. 'Have you seen Teitz?'

He nodded and Lolly said, 'Looking at him makes me glad I got an early night.'

He didn't reply, for he wasn't glad at all. Lolly said, 'There was a phone call for you about an hour ago.'

'Who was it?'

'Don't know. I told her to try your office at the Bureau. She sounded kind of foreign to me.'

Lolly seemed more interested than jealous. The odds of getting her out to his place seemed to be receding; Nessheim decided to bide his time.

Suddenly the door to his office opened and Pearl strode in. His entrance seemed characteristic – this was a no-knock kind of guy. But as Pearl would have been the first to say, he owned the room.

'Agent Nessheim,' he said loudly, as if he wanted to confirm what he was looking at. But he seemed cheerful.

'Mr Pearl,' acknowledged Nessheim. 'This is Lolly,' he added, gesturing at the girl.

'Great. Listen, doll, let me have a minute alone with Mr G-Man, okay?'

'Yes, Mr Pearl,' she said obediently and closed the door behind her as she left the room.

Pearl stood by the big side window in a dark chocolate suit with thick stripes the colour of tailors' chalk. As he looked at Studio Two he whistled tunelessly, clasping his hands behind his back and wiggling his sausage-like fingers. On his left pinkie he wore a thick gold ring, which had a centred ruby that glowed like a hungover eye.

Nessheim broke the silence. 'Thanks for having me out on Sunday,' he said.

'Sure,' said Pearl, his back still to Nessheim as he continued to stare out the window. The Count was standing outside Studio Two now and to Nessheim's consternation he saw Lolly approaching him. No, he was wrong; she was going back to Studio Two, though as she passed the Count he looked at her appreciatively and said something. Lolly laughed, but kept going. Good girl, thought Nessheim.

To break the silence, Nessheim said, 'I enjoyed meeting one of your friends.'

'Who was that?' asked Pearl dubiously, as if no one in his right mind would call his Sunday guests his friends.

'Mo Dubin.'

Pearl's fingers stopped wriggling. He did a half-turn and eyed Nessheim, who added, 'He said he was from Cleveland.'

'That's right.'

'He said you used to be partners there.'

'Partners? Me and Mo?' Pearl looked incredulous. 'You got to be kidding.'

'That's what he said.'

Pearl shrugged. 'You know how it is,' he said confidingly, accompanied by an undertone of demand. 'Sometimes you have an old friend who's on his uppers and you do your best to help him out. Between you and me and the lamp post, Mo got himself into a little hot water with the folks at Alcohol, Tobacco and Firearms. Not with the Bureau, I hasten to add,' he said with a chuckle. Pearl waited for Nessheim to laugh too. He didn't.

Pearl turned around. He had unclenched his hands and his palms were up in mock surrender. He pointed a finger right at Nessheim, jabbing the air as he spoke. 'Agent Nessheim,' he said, and though he was smiling there was nothing ingratiating in his voice. 'You're a bit of a dark horse.'

Nessheim didn't say anything, but Pearl didn't seem to notice his silence and continued: 'I checked you out. Tolson said you played ball.'

'I told you that on Sunday.'

'You didn't mention you were an all-American.' Pearl sounded as if he were offended by this omission.

'I was only second team.'

'Who cares?' Pearl had raised his voice. 'I heard you didn't play your senior year. Did you just go off the boil or something?'

'I got hurt,' said Nessheim. He resented having to say this. It triggered a memory he could do without: jumping high as a gazelle, catching the ball with his outstretched fingertips, then the next thing he knew he was coming round on the locker-room table, a vial of ammonia spirit shoved under his nose.

Pearl took two steps closer. 'You know my boy TD, he's a pretty good ballplayer too.'

'So I heard.' From Junior himself. 'Did you play football, Mr Pearl?'

'Me?' Pearl said with disbelief. 'I played stickball, Nessheim, not football. And that was only in a Bronx alley while I waited for the groceries that I had to deliver. I worked every day after school since I was twelve years old.' There would have been something endearing about this, had Pearl not seemed so impressed by it himself. 'Anyway, USC is nothing to sneeze at,' he said, as if Nessheim had just gone *kerchoo*. 'You should help my boy – you know, give him some tips.'

Nessheim said, 'USC is top of the heap. He'll get the best coaching in the country – there's nothing I could teach him that they couldn't teach him a million times better.' Except how to be nice to the Mexican help, he thought.

Pearl said, 'They don't seem to appreciate the talent my kid's got.'

'They will,' said Nessheim earnestly. 'They will.'

Pearl nodded and Nessheim hoped their little talk was over. But then the mogul started to pace, first back to the window where he barely looked out, then over to the desk, then finally to the middle of the room, where he seemed to make a decision to stand still. 'Have you heard from Mr Hoover lately?' he asked abruptly.

There seemed no point explaining that he never heard from Mr Hoover. 'No,' Nessheim said simply.

'He's supposed to be coming out here this Fall. Did you know that?'

Nessheim tried to look benign. 'There has been rumour of it. But the Director's plans have been known to change.'

'Rumour.' Pearl lifted his head and eyeballed Nessheim as if he were a plucked bird, and he was trying to decide which end to shove in the oven first. 'Tolson says they'll be coming. I hope so, because I got something to discuss with them.'

Nessheim knew that people didn't announce they wanted to talk about something unless they wanted to say what that something was. He waited and eventually Pearl explained. 'The thing is, the FBI pics so far have done okay, but they haven't changed the way that AMP is seen.'

'By the other studios, you mean?'

'The other studios can go fuck themselves. They owe me, pal, in ways I don't even want to discuss. But that's not why I'm here. I've had an idea.'

For all his vulgarity, Pearl wasn't stupid – that much Nessheim knew, so he was paying close attention. 'You see, this series you've been helping on only goes so far. Yeah, they're cheap to make and easy to sell, but only to the B theatres. If AMP is going to break into the big time, it's going to have to have bigger productions.'

That means money, thought Nessheim. Colour film sometimes and bigger stars than the likes of Dedway or other deadbeats borrowed from the bigger studios.

'With all the dough in the world you can't make people buy something that's no good. If we're going to make the big time we need something special.'

'What do you have in mind?' asked Nessheim, trying to sound patient.

'An FBI picture.' He raised a hand to stave off objections Nessheim was not about to make. 'But not the kind of *schmaltz* low-budget dogshit our esteemed Mr Dedway has been starring in.'

'Right,' said Nessheim tentatively.

'This would be the FBI flick to end all FBI flicks. It'll have an agent – but not just any agent. It will be *the* Agent.' Pearl was now staring at him so intently that for an awful moment Nessheim wondered if *the* Agent might be himself. Pearl continued, 'The Bureau was made by Hoover, Hoover *is* the Bureau, and that's your movie right there: *The Life and Times of the Man Who Made the FBI*. What do ya think?'

'It seems a natural idea,' he managed to say.

'That's what I believe.' Yet Pearl's face was troubled. 'There's just one thing. I've got to persuade your Director to let me do it.'

This didn't seem the problem to Nessheim. He knew, part by reputation, part from his own experience, that Hoover in his own eyes was synonymous with his agency. Woe betide anyone else who tried to share the limelight. Sometimes it seemed Hoover begrudged the Bureau itself when it got publicity; as Guttman once remarked, it was as if Dr Frankenstein himself had run amok. Hoover hadn't created a monster – his creation had turned him into one.

Nessheim said carefully, 'I think the Director would be very flattered.'

'Oh, he's tickled pink by the idea. It's just whether AMP's the one to make the picture. A lot of people would say Warners was the obvious choice, and I know Mayer or Zanuck would do it given half a chance. So I need all the help I can get.' Pearl looked meaningfully at Nessheim. 'The Director says he and Clyde Tolson are coming to LA this Fall and he'll be happy to talk about my idea then. I said I'd show him the town and he seemed to think that was a swell idea. I know he likes the nightlife and the track – I got friends at Santa Anita, so that won't be a problem. I can show him and his buddy Clyde a good time all right, but that may not be enough. He's got to be persuaded that we can do the job.'

Nessheim could see the problem now. Hoover must like Pearl – why else encourage the studio to make the quickie pictures Nessheim advised on? But there would only be one shot at this big idea – with bad consequences for the studio if it got it wrong, and even worse ones for Hoover and the Bureau.

'I am sure you can make a good case to the Director,' he said stolidly.

'Sure, but anything I say he's gotta take with a pinch of salt. What he'll want is an objective opinion from someone he can trust.' Again he gave Nessheim a look.

Nessheim said nothing and suddenly Pearl took a different tack. 'Tell me Nessheim, you got a girlfriend?'

'Not any more.'

'I wouldn't waste much time worrying about it. You're still a young fella and LA's full of girls. Half of them want to be in the pictures, and the other half want to hump the guys who already are. You've got a good position here if you're feeling lonely. I could help some, you know. Not a day goes by that I don't have something special in my waiting room, and if I was to say the word they'd be happy enough to pay you a visit too.'

'Thanks,' said Nessheim without enthusiasm.

Pearl must have sensed Nessheim's lack of interest, for he went on. 'Maybe you like the track too, just like the Director. I got a box there. You're welcome to use it any time. Take a girl along, meet the jockeys and some of the other owners. I can even give you a tip or two,' he added slyly.

The silence that followed was awkward. Pearl grew exasperated. 'What do you like then, buddy? There's got to be something. Cars? A vacation in Tijuana you'll never forget? Everybody wants something.'

'There is one thing. I'm looking for somebody.'

'Is that right?' Pearl said without apparent interest.

'His name's Osaka.'

He stared at Nessheim. 'A Jap?'

201

'He's half-Japanese, half-Irish. And I'm not the only one looking for him.'

Pearl's lips pursed. 'What's he done, this guy?'

'Disappeared.'

'That's all?'

'As far as I'm concerned. The other people looking for him may think different.'

'Yeah, and they may think you're in the way.' He put a finger up to his face and scratched one cheek absent-mindedly, then pointed a finger at Nessheim. 'You don't want to be sticking your nose into something that doesn't involve you, young man.'

He was trying to sound avuncular, but there was a coercive timbre in his voice which Nessheim resented. He said firmly, 'I'll have to be the judge of that.'

Pearl didn't like this; his eyes flared angrily, then just as suddenly relaxed, slipping into neutral. Pearl tried to smile. 'Take it easy, okay? Tell me the guy's name again and I'll see what I can do. I'll scratch your back and when Hoover's here you scratch mine.'

Nessheim nodded, figuring he had nothing to lose. 'His name's Osaka,' he said, 'Billy Osaka.' But Pearl was already halfway out the door, figuring his side of the deal was set.

18

HE SAT IN his Dodge with the radio on and watched until the girl came out of Woodward Court and walked along First Street, then caught the yellow LARy streetcar that would take her east. Once she got on, Nessheim set off himself, though he couldn't keep up with the tram despite its frequent stops, since traffic was heavy heading out of downtown. He'd read that one in three Angelenos owned a car and all of them seemed to be heading east this evening.

After he'd crossed the bridge and followed First Street he spotted her turning towards the address he'd found in the phone book, half a mile north of Billy Osaka's apartment. This part of Boyle Heights was tidy if poor: the streets were smoothly paved, the sidewalks laid to square and the lawns, though tiny, carefully mown, with trimmed ornamental bushes and flowering plants in neatly tended beds. The bungalows and two-storey houses were undivided. This was a neighbourhood of families, all of them Japanese in these half dozen streets, less than a mile east of the Los Angeles River.

He did a circle of two blocks and pulled up a hundred yards ahead of her on Concord Street. Making a U-turn he parked so that the passenger door was next to the curb. Looking in the side mirror he timed his wait, then opened his door and got out, standing with his forearms crossed on the top of the car. The woman was almost even with him now and looked over at Nessheim, first with curiosity, then with dismay. He was sure now – it was the same unhappy expression on her face that he'd seen on the porch of Billy Osaka's house, though this time there were no tears.

'Got a minute, Miss Yukuri?' he said.

'No, I don't,' she said firmly.

'You sure?' he said. 'I don't want to have to make this more formal.'

'Formal?'

'Yeah, I could drive you downtown and we could talk there.'

'You've been watching too many movies.'

He'd forgotten the discrepancy between her sweetie-pie appearance and sharp tongue. 'It wouldn't look too good, now would it? What would people think?'

'People would wonder why some plain-clothes cop was harassing me. It would be a lot worse if I got in the car. If they saw me sitting alone with a white man, people would really talk.'

'I tell you what. I'll drive up and park in the alley. We can talk there and no one will see us. How's that sound?'

She didn't answer, so he got in the car and started up, then drove about a hundred feet before turning right into a little alley that intersected the otherwise continuous line of tidy houses. In his rear-view mirror he saw her come to the corner, hesitate, then finally walk his way.

She opened the passenger side door and slid into the front seat, leaving the door open. She winced at the heat of the leather seat and tucked her skirt under her stockinged thighs.

'What's this about?' she asked. 'I thought we'd done all our business at the bank.'

'Not quite. I'd like to know where the extra twenty-five thousand went.'

She made a show of sighing. 'I told you, we only received twenty-five thousand. I double-checked.'

'So where's the rest?'

'It was probably some clerical error in New York.' She moved over the 'r's in her words like a pianist skimming scales – too quick to make the error identifiable, but with something sounding not quite right. When he kept looking at her, she said sharply, 'It didn't make it to LA. You need to talk to the people back East.'

'Oh we will, don't you worry about that.'

They sat in silence for a moment, and then she said brightly, 'Okay mister? I need to get home.'

'There's another thing.'

'What's that?'

'Billy Osaka.'

'Who?' she said, but her voice quavered.

'He has a message for you.'

Without thinking she said, 'You've heard from him?'

Realising her mistake, she made to get out of the car, but he grabbed her arm, roughly enough that she wasn't going to get away without a struggle. When she sat back again, he let go.

He said, 'Now that we've established you know him, the honest answer is no. I'm trying to find him and it sounds like you want to know where he is, too.'

She gave a thin laugh. 'If you know Billy at all, you know he never stays put for long.'

'I know that, but I'm worried about him. He's never let me down before.'

'Let *you* down?' she asked.

'He called and said he had something urgent to tell me. Do you know what that could be?'

'No.'

'Anything about the bank?'

'Why would it be about the bank?'

Because the coincidence of Guttman's instructions and

Billy's links to this girl troubled him. He said, 'Is he in trouble?'

She exhaled, and said, 'Billy is always in trouble. And no, I don't know where he is. Can I go now?'

'Did you know his grandmother?'

'Mrs Oka?'

'That's right.' There was no point holding back. 'She's dead.'

Her lips opened for the briefest moment, like a clam trying a taste of air before saying no thanks. She lowered her head and said quietly, 'I'm sorry, but not surprised. She was very old. When did she die?'

'At the weekend. She was murdered.'

'No! Who would do that?' Her horrified expression seemed genuine.

'The police think Billy did.'

'You can't be serious. He loved his grandmother. He was devoted to her.'

'I went to see an old teacher of his, a man named Larson.' When Hanako frowned he said, 'You know him?'

'I never met the man.'

'Well, Professor Larson said Billy came to California because he had a cousin here. Do you know who that is?'

She hesitated. He could see she was trying to decide what to tell him. He said, 'Listen, Hanako: the cops are looking for Billy, and so are some other people – not nice people. You don't want them finding Billy before I do, you understand? You've got to trust me.'

'Why should I?'

'Because you haven't got any choice. And because I know he didn't kill his grandmother, and I'm not just saying that. I can prove it.'

'How?' she asked, sounding as if she wanted to believe him.

He brought the envelope out of his side pocket. 'Recognise the handwriting?'

'Where did you find this?'

'It was on the dresser in Mrs Oka's bedroom. It had five hundred dollars in it – that's with the LAPD now. I kept the envelope.'

'Do you know what it says?'

'"Grandmother". He wouldn't have left Mrs Oka five hundred dollars if he'd just murdered her.'

Hanako Yukuri sat silently for a moment. Down the alley two Japanese boys were playing on bicycles, circling around each other slowly and talking animatedly.

'Did she suffer very much?' asked Hanako.

'I'm afraid she did.'

Hanako shook her head. 'I don't know why anyone would want to harm her.'

'It had to do with Billy. They were warning him.'

'Warning him, how?'

'I was hoping you could tell me that. All I've managed to find out is that Billy liked to gamble. I think he had debts.'

'He liked to play cards, but he only told me about the times he won.' She looked suddenly disheartened.

He said more gently, 'That's what most people do.'

'I wouldn't know,' she said flatly. 'I'm a good girl, from good hard-working parents. They raised me as a Baptist and raised me as an American – it's other people who seem to have a problem with that. And I never put a foot wrong – until I met Billy.'

'Your parents don't approve of him.'

She shook her head. 'They were polite, but I could tell they didn't like him. He was doing his best to be humble and respectful, but they could see he isn't really that way. They thought he was *yogone*.'

'What's that?'

'A roughneck.'

He nodded. 'Did you ever go with Billy to the Sierra?'

'What do you know about that?' Her eyes widened questioningly.

He shrugged. 'Billy mentioned it.'

'He promised to take me there this summer. I arranged everything. I told my parents I was going with old school friends. Then he cancelled at the last minute.'

'Why was that?'

'He went to Hawaii instead.'

'Hawaii?' He thought back to Billy's absence. It couldn't have been more than ten days. Had he lied about this to Hanako too?

'Yes, he flew there. Don't ask me where he got the money. It costs more than six hundred dollars to go that way.'

What a layer of lies – telling Nessheim he was helping a relative in Oregon, then 'admitting' he'd gone to the Sierra, when in fact he'd gone to Hawaii. 'Was this a vacation?'

'He claimed it was family business,' Hanako said crossly. 'Since both his parents are dead, I don't know what family he had in mind.' She gave a sour laugh, and added, 'He was only gone a week.'

'What about this cousin of his, did you ever meet him?'

'No.'

'Where does he live?'

'On Terminal Island, off San Pedro. There's a Japanese community there. He's one of the fishermen. They sell their catch to the canneries on the island.'

'Have you been there?'

'No. Talk about *yogone* – Billy says the people there are very coarse.'

'Does his cousin look like Billy?'

'No. By Japanese standards he's tall – but not as tall as Billy. I saw a picture of him once at Mrs Oka's. He has a harsh face and when he's out at sea he doesn't shave.'

That will help me find him, thought Nessheim. 'Did you ever meet him?'

Hanako shook her head. 'Billy said since he'd met my family I should meet his, and I was always happy to see Mrs Oka. She was a sweet old lady. But I drew the line at Akiro.'

Nessheim noted the name. 'Why's that?'

'He is not a good influence on Billy. For one thing, he started him gambling. And I know he doesn't think Billy should be courting me.' Hanako said irritably, 'Billy told me Akiro called me a *gaijin* wannabe.'

'What?'

'It means I'm loyal to America more than Japan. Which I am, Mr Agent Nessheim. I was born here, I work here, I have a home here. I have as many rights as you do.'

'I'm not arguing with that,' he said mildly.

She was still cross. 'I just want to be American – if I'm allowed.' She added with a shake of her head. 'You wouldn't understand.'

'Yes I would,' he said quietly. Nessheim thought of his father, hounded during the last war for his ancestry – a mob had made him get on his knees and kiss the American flag. 'But Akiro doesn't want that for himself?'

'No,' she said emphatically. 'He believes in Japan. He likes to look backward rather than forward.'

'Was Billy like that?' It seemed hard to believe, after Larson's portrait of Billy as so eager to be American that he turned a blind eye to the prejudice blocking his way.

Hanako hesitated, but when she spoke it was emphatic: 'No.'

'If you never met Akiro, how do you know? Did Billy tell you?'

'He knew I disapproved of him so he didn't talk about him much. But you only have to know the kinds of people Akiro hangs out with. Gamblers, hoodlums.'

'The Tokyo Club,' he said.

'For sure,' she said vigorously.

'You know much about them?'

'More than enough.'

'How's that?' asked Nessheim.

Hanako sighed. 'You remember Mr Satake?

'Of course.'

'He's a very good grocer.'

'Yes, and president of the bank.'

'He doesn't own the bank.'

Nessheim could see she wanted him to ask. 'So who does?'

'The Tokyo Club.'

19

HOOD WAS ON vacation and Cohan was acting SAC. He'd taken over Hood's corner office and made a point of calling people in to see him. When it was Nessheim's turn he found Cohan gazing out the window towards the San Gabriel Mountains, which were picture-sharp this morning and snow-peaked. He swivelled in his chair and Nessheim saw that Cohan had his suit jacket buttoned and his tie pulled up tight in a Windsor knot. He looked like he was going to a funeral, or about to conduct one.

But he spoke cheerfully enough, saying, 'You had a phone call earlier today. One of the girls took the message – I got it somewhere here.' He fumbled with the papers on his desk, then handed a pink phone slip to Nessheim. It had a number and the Please Call box was ticked. The caller's name was written down as *Mrs M.*

Cohan said, 'So how are we doing on the visit to the studio?'

'I spoke to Dedway – no problem there. Let me talk to Pearl. I know he'll want you to have the VIP tour.'

Cohan seemed satisfied by this. 'Well, I checked out your friend Mo. There's nothing in the file.'

'Really?'

'He's clean,' said Cohan emphatically. 'I even called Cleveland for you. Nothing there.'

'Cleveland have never heard of him?'

'Oh they've heard of him – he was a big shot there until he came West. But the businesses were all legit.'

'I thought he was in booze.'

'He was for a while, after Prohibition. He had a little trouble at one point with the Alcohol, Tobacco and Firearms folks, but they never charged him with anything. And while nobody's saying this guy's a fairy godmother, he's white as far as the Bureau's concerned.'

Cohan looked down at the papers on his desk to indicate that they were through. But there was another question Nessheim wanted to ask. 'Tell me something. You know this guy I was using, Osaka?'

'What about him?' Cohan said warily.

'What does Hood have against him?'

Cohan shrugged. 'Osaka was supposed to help us with our list of who's who among the Nips in LA. That way if war breaks out, we'll be ready to nab the important ones right away. Though if it was up to me,' he added, making Nessheim grateful it wasn't, 'I'd round them all up.'

'So what happened?'

'Osaka kept making excuses and not giving us any names. Finally Hood got fed up and took his retainer away. I don't think Osaka was ever going to help us.'

'Maybe he didn't want to be a pigeon for his own people.'

Cohan looked at him scornfully. 'When you start thinking that way you're no use to the Bureau.'

Nessheim took the cue this time and left.

His desk didn't have a phone, but the agent sitting closest to him was away so he used his. He tried Guttman first and got his secretary Marie, who explained he was out of the office – Nessheim was leery of leaving a message. There was a telex in the field office, but he distrusted it – a copy of what he sent would be retained and could be read. On the drive home he could stop at Western Union in Hollywood and send a wire instead.

Then he looked at the slip Cohan had given him and dialled the number.

After three rings a woman answered.

'Hello, I had a message to call a Mrs M,' he said.

'Is that Mr Nessheim?' The voice was mildly familiar.

'Yes. Who's that?'

'It's Elizaveta Mukasei.'

It sounded like a garble of consonants. 'Yes,' he said tentatively.

'You know, the lady standing next to "Bruiser" at the benefit the other night?'

He laughed. 'Otherwise known as the wife of the Soviet Vice-Consul.'

'I believe you found my husband a little verbose.' Her English was excellent – accented to be sure and with the elocution of someone taught the language, but surprisingly idiomatic.

'Don't mind me: I was just itching for a drink.'

A chuckle came over the phone. 'You amuse me, Agent Nessheim. I enjoyed our little talk. It would be nice to meet up with you some time.'

'Well sure,' he said, taken by surprise. 'I'm a little busy right now, but I could meet for a coffee maybe,' he added, feeling slightly awkward.

'I had something more formal to offer.'

'Right,' he said neutrally.

'Show some enthusiasm, Agent Nessheim,' she said, struggling with the 'th' – it came out as 'entusiasm'.

'Okay, I'll do my best.' What did this woman want?

'My husband and I are hosting a weekend at a ranch near Santa Barbara. Have you been there?'

'Never.' He found himself wondering how the workers of the world could run to a Santa Barbara ranch.

'Before you say anything, you should know that it doesn't belong to us. It belongs to a friend of our

213

country, and he's lent it to us. The weekend after next I would like you to come.'

'Me?'

'Yes, along with other friends from LA. Before you politely say no, let me explain. You see, there's something in it for both of us. It will let me try and convince you that America is a natural ally for the Soviet Union. And in turn you can see the kind of company the Russians are keeping in Los Angeles.'

'What do you mean?'

She gave another low chuckle. 'I know something about the FBI, Mr Nessheim. Your Mr Hoover is no friend of ours. But I am sure he believes in that old saying "know your enemy". I am coming to you as a friend, but if I have to entertain you as an enemy, that's all right too. You will be able to tell your superiors all about the Soviet plans for world domination, even if the presence of the German army in my country would suggest the foolishness of that view.' This time she gave a full-throated laugh.

'That's kind of you, but I'm not sure how I'm fixed that weekend. I may be working.'

'At the weekend? Some of our guests are coming out Friday evening, but if you prefer come Saturday. Bring trunks and some warm clothes – it gets cold up in the hills when the sun goes down. And you'll want to spend the night I hope. It's a long drive after all. Believe me, I know you would not find it a waste of time. And I think you would enjoy yourself.'

'I'm sure I would,' he said mechanically.

'So you will do your best to come? I think we have a lot to talk about, Agent Nessheim. You might be surprised.'

'Okay, I'll let you know,' he said.

'I'll send you directions. *Do svidaniya,*' she said and hung up.

He sat for a minute, puzzled by the call. Hadn't the Russians better things to do right now, with their backs against the wall? It wasn't as if Nessheim was looking for company – at least not the artsy Communist sort. If Hood didn't like Nessheim's imaginary source Fifi, God knows what he would make of the real Red thing.

20

HE WAS TIRED and hot when he reached San Pedro after his drive south the following morning. It was only twenty miles from downtown Los Angeles, but Figueroa was a jammed road, full of trucks coming back and forth from the port of Los Angeles, rather than any kind of free-flowing highway. It took him an hour, driving at a speed where the air blown through his open windows didn't cool him down at all – it was over eighty degrees and he yearned for the crispness that was October in Wisconsin.

As he came down out of the foothills he could see the town's harbour, a messy assemblage of docked freighters, warehouses and factories. A thin line of blue divided the mainland from a right-angled piece of land that must be Terminal Island. When both Figueroa and the Highway ended he took Gaffey Street into San Pedro itself. It was a wide avenue of wooden houses that turned to stores as he neared the water. Pulling over, he went into a coffee shop, where a big and long-jawed blonde was cleaning away dishes from the tables.

She looked up as Nessheim came in and said, 'You're kind of late for breakfast. I could do eggs, but that's about it.'

'I'm just looking for directions. How do I get to Terminal Island?'

She pointed. 'Water's three blocks that-a-way. The island's on the other side of it.'

'Is there a bridge across?'

'At the northern end. But a ferry's opened at Sixth Street. You'd be quicker taking that.'

'What street is this?'

'Ninth, though people called it Croatia. You know your way around the island?'

'No. I'm trying to find somebody who lives there.'

'Lives there?' She looked at him, rag in her hand. 'Only folks live out there are Japs.'

'Guy I'm looking for is one of them.'

She shook her head and frowned. 'They don't like strangers much. Especially white ones.'

'I'm not sure where to start.'

'There's a community centre in Fishermen's Hall on Terminal Way. They might be able to give you a steer.'

'Thanks. But why do all the Japs live out there?'

She gave a short laugh. ''Cause nobody wants them over here.'

'Is that right?'

She finished wiping the last table and stood upright, looking at Nessheim. 'We got all sorts here – Croats like me, and lots of Italians. Then there's the Norwegians – look for a beard, they used to say, and you got yourself a Viking. Lately there's even been a few Mexicans. But not the Japanese. They're just not welcome.'

'That bad, are they?'

'I didn't say so. But they stick together and don't mix in. People worry that if war comes they'll cross the water and knife us in our beds.' She gave a rich laugh. 'As far as I can tell, they're pretty quiet folks, which is more than you can say about half the white sailors show up in this town. But they don't like strangers, I do know that.'

'I'll bear that in mind.'

'You better do more than that, mister. Take care out there.'

*　　*　　*

The ferry wouldn't go for another half hour, so he parked on the street in front of the new ferry building, a squat concrete block that had a central tower four storeys high and an enormous black numbered clock on the side facing town. Getting out of his car he could smell fish and a salt tang in the air, as well as the faintly nauseating smell of diesel. He walked around to kill time, admiring a new post office and a new courthouse, both of which he figured came courtesy of FDR. The adjacent park was almost deserted, except for an old man in a captain's cap, walking a dachshund, and a pair of old biddies in calico dresses, who sat on a bench crocheting. Along the waterfront's line of old brick buildings he passed a store selling nautical stuff (everything from rope to pea jackets), two tattoo parlours, a union hall, and bar after bar with exotic names – Shanghai Red's, the Scuttle Butt Inn. He peered into another one, a joint with Chinese murals called The Silver Dollar, where he saw a solitary customer nursing a beer.

It seemed a pleasant, sleepy kind of town, but he knew the impression was deceptive. The fishermen would still be at sea or unloading their catch; the other men would be working the docks or doing a shift in the canneries. In four hours' time this part of town would start to come alive; it would be another twelve before it went to sleep again, after too much of what Morgan, his former SAC in San Francisco, had called the *Double F* of every port in the world – fucking and fighting.

The ferry cost him thirty cents – a quarter for the car and a nickel for its driver – and the ride lasted less than ten minutes: only a thousand feet of listless channel divided the island from the shore. He found Fishermen's Hall on Terminal Way and parked outside. It was a modest building of dingy brick that resembled a non-conformist chapel – one sharp gable and a few narrow windows on its ground floor. Inside, half of the building consisted of one large room the size of a high-school gym, but without the basketball backboards. The posters on the walls were in Japanese and a small exhibition of photographs showed local Japanese fishermen unloading tuna out of large fishing boats, the bows riding heavy and high, the sterns cut low to help bring the full nets on board.

Crossing to the other side he found a stout Japanese woman with pink coral earrings, sitting behind a thin, warped sheet of stud partition halfway along a narrow corridor. A pine slab perched on two empty barrels served as her desk, and held a phone and an empty coffee cup. When Nessheim tapped politely on her open door, she showed little interest. 'Yes,' she said eventually. She didn't ask him to come in.

'I'm looking for someone who lives on the island.'

'This is not a Missing Persons Bureau for debt collectors.'

'Do I look like a debt collector?'

She turned her head and eyeballed him. He was wearing a khaki suit he'd bought at Bullock's department store, but it fitted him well, and his shirt was starched, his tie straight and his hat was a good one. She said flatly, 'Debt collectors come in all shapes and sizes.'

He showed his badge. 'I'm from the Federal Bureau of Investigation. I need to find a man named Akiro and I am sure you don't want to obstruct me.'

She stood up and went to a filing cabinet in the corner. 'If he lives here he must be a fisherman.'

'That's what I was told.'

'He's probably ten miles the other side of Catalina

looking for albacore.' But she took out a stapled sheaf of mimeographed papers in her hand and began flipping the pages. 'Here he is. Try Dock Six. It's next to the Makovich Cannery – he must sell his fish to them.'

'Any chance you can point me in the right direction?'

'Right out the door, third left down, then head for the water.' She wouldn't look at him.

'Thanks,' he said.

He drove for a minute or two, past rows of barrack-like frame houses with low wide roofs. They were crammed into small lots – between the little parallel streets as many as four houses sat back to back where two would have been placed anywhere else. He passed a Baptist Mission and a Grammar school, then turned onto Tuna Street, which was lined by small shops with Japanese signs in front. When he reached the edge of the water he found the Makovich Cannery tucked in the shadow of its immense neighbour, the French Tuna Company.

He walked around behind the cannery, but the loading dock was deserted and no boats berthed. He went back to the building's entrance and went inside, into a small atrium that had time clocks on the wall where the workers punched in. Opening another internal door he stepped into a vast room with whitewashed walls. About two dozen Japanese women, dressed like nurses in white uniforms and wearing hairnets, were working on an assembly line which consisted of a single steel conveyor belt. It came out an open door at the rear, then twisted and turned through the room like a snakes and ladders game. He could see in the back the big tuna emerging, silver skins gleaming in individual wire trays.

'What are you doing?'

It was a gruff voice, and turning around Nessheim faced a man with a moustache thick as a hairbrush.

Five foot ten or so and built like a pulling guard. He wore a long white coat, like a hospital doctor, though there was too much blood spattered on its sleeves to make any patient feel comfortable.

'My name's Nessheim.' He showed his badge. 'Who are you?'

'I'm Makovich. People call me Mac. What can I do for you?'

'I'm looking for a fisherman, but didn't have much luck out back.'

'You wouldn't even if the boats were back. Hardly any of the fishermen speak English.'

'*Issei?*'

'You've done your homework. The few that do speak our lingo wouldn't want to talk with a stranger. It's a bit clannish round these parts.'

'But they work for you?'

'Sure they do. They'll take anybody's money.'

'The guy I want is named Akiro. I was told he fished for you.'

'He used to. But he hasn't been here for a while.'

'Where'd he go?'

'I don't know. The boats come in, the boats go out – I don't ask who's on board. Somebody mentioned he'd left the island, but I couldn't tell you when that was. Maybe he's gone back to Japan – he was *Kibei* after all.'

'What's that?'

'He was educated in Japan. Lots of the Japs send their kids back to go to school there.'

'I thought he was from Hawaii.'

'He is. They have *Kibei* there too. It's a way of keeping ties with the old country, I guess, especially if you don't trust Western education. But why's everyone so interested in Akiro anyway?'

221

'Who's everyone?'

'You're not the first guy looking for him.'

'Who else was asking?' He tried to sound matter of fact.

'I wasn't around. I think they spoke to his wife.'

Nessheim hadn't pictured Akiro as a family man. 'Where would I find her?'

'His wife works in this cannery.'

'She does?' He looked out at the factory floor.

'She's on the cutter out back. Once the fish get unloaded, the first thing we do is chop off the heads and tails. Akiro's wife does that with the guillotine machine. She was off sick, but I think she's back now. Let me send someone to get her.'

He stepped towards the women closest to them, who were running small tins of tuna through a labelling machine. He barked a series of orders that sounded only half-English. One of the women hurried off towards the back of the vast room, then went through the door that led to the loading docks.

Mac turned back to Nessheim, who asked, 'Was that Japanese you were speaking?'

Mac shook his head. 'Nah. They talk a funny kind of dialect here – it's half-Jap, half-English. I've picked up enough to communicate.'

'So do you know this man Akiro?'

'Not really. He was well-known among his people though. You might even say notorious.'

'How so?'

'Ah so?' said Mac in a passable imitation of a Japanese houseboy, and he laughed. Then he said, 'He liked to gamble and out here that's frowned upon. So's drinking and Akiro drank, down on the waterfront across the channel. I know some of the bar owners and they said he also liked to fight. Once he almost beat two ensigns half to death – the only reason he wasn't arrested is because they started it.' Mac looked at his watch. 'Where's that girl got to?'

It was just as he said this that the scream cut through the low hum of the room. At the far end of the line a woman turned, gesturing frantically. Next to her a colleague put her hand over mouth, trying futilely to hold back the vomit spilling through her fingers. Someone hit a switch and the long continuous conveyor stopped with a jerk. The vast room went silent, the only sound that of the butchers at the big block tables, putting down their knives.

Mac moved quickly, Nessheim just behind him. The two women were standing by the conveyor belt that was bringing out the decapitated and tailed fish from the back. The tuna sat in individual trays; spaced about a yard apart, massive tapered wedges, some must have weighed eighty pounds and were so wide that they lapped over the thin edges of their trays. They were still silver, but dulling rapidly from their exposure to the air.

The woman who had gestured pointed at the belt behind her, where one of the trays on the belt held something different from the other trays. It was the size and shape of a spring leg of lamb, and much smaller than the hefty tuna on either side. Nessheim stared at the fawn-sized limb; brown as worn leather, it had stringy tendons and skin which looked dry from too much sun and too much heat, and he knew at once that it wasn't any kind of fish. From the wider part of the thigh, blood oozed where the limb had been severed.

The smell of vomit was now vying with the oily smell of fish. The girl Makovich had sent to look for Akiro's wife came through the open door from the back. She stopped with a jerk when she saw the leg in its wire basket. She said, 'I can't find her anywhere, Mr Mac.'

Mac tried without success to speak. Nessheim saw that he was in shock, so he answered the girl. 'Thanks anyway, but I think we've found her.'

It was almost sunset when he swung onto Mount Olympus Drive. He had spent the afternoon with the San Pedro police, answering their questions about what he'd been doing on Terminal Island, knowing it was only a matter of time before his presence at the cannery was reported back to Dickerson at the LAPD and then to Hood.

The cops had been polite, then gradually deferential, and by three o'clock the questioning had become a conversation over coffee. The local police knew all about Akiro and were even able to show Nessheim a mugshot – Akiro had done thirty days in the local pokey a couple of times. Hanako had been right: it was a harsh-looking face, which stared at the camera with a coldness that knew no fear. The cops had plenty of theories about where Akiro might have gone, ranging from Japan (this more out of xenophobic principle than any knowledge) to a cement burial at the hands of Tokyo Club gangsters in LA.

Then a desk sergeant walked into the room and announced, 'I think we've found the rest of her.'

At the eastern end of Terminal Island, a grade-school kid walking along the shore had stumbled upon the head and torso of a Japanese woman, soon identified by Makovich as Akiro's wife. Her other leg was missing, apparently also severed by the same guillotine blade which the woman had operated in the cannery, topping and tailing hundreds of fish, some as big as she was. She would have bled to death, unless she'd drowned first.

Now as Nessheim came up the hill on Mount Olympus Drive and took the bend, he saw a car parked in front of his house. A two-tone grey Chrysler, with whitewall tyres and hubcaps that gleamed in the dwindling rays of sun. There was no one sitting in the car.

He pulled into the little drive in front of the garage and sat for a minute, hand inside his jacket on the butt of his gun, his eyes on his rear-view mirror for any movement behind him. As he got out he thought of going in the back door with his new key, but decided a burglar – or worse – wasn't going to leave a car parked in front of their intended victim's house.

He got out and checked that his gun was loose and easily retrievable in its holster, then kept his jacket unbuttoned and walked carefully around the bib of box hedge that ran beneath the front windows and jutted out to form an L at the point where the garage met the house. As he came out in the open he saw two men in suits and hats standing on his front steps, a few feet above sidewalk level. One wore brown shoes and had a face like a pig – little eyes and a snout for a mouth. The other was dark, with skin the colour of mahogany and black slicked-back hair. Neither was very big, but if there was trouble Nessheim didn't think either one would be using his fists.

As he stepped further away from the house he saw a third man, sitting in the folding chair which Nessheim's landlady kept stored in the garage. It was Ike from the casino, dressed in a light houndstooth suit with a pale-blue shirt and a burnt-orange tie. One of the men standing next to him murmured something, and Ike turned his head and looked at Nessheim, then smiled benevolently, like a local patriarch watching the neighbourhood parade.

As Nessheim drew near, one of the two henchmen

started to put a hand inside his jacket. Nessheim stopped moving and did the same.

'Jake,' Ike said in a commanding voice, 'keep your hands where our friend can see them.'

Nessheim didn't go any closer. He had also taken his hand out of his jacket, but he was ready to move it there again at speed. He said, 'What are you doing here?'

'Waiting for you,' said Ike. In the dwindling light the birthmark on his cheek was darker, the colour of scorched cherries.

'Hope you're comfortable,' said Nessheim, gesturing at the chair with his left hand.

'I knew you wouldn't mind. I figured you might be a while.'

'You should have got your friends a seat too.'

Ike shrugged. 'I don't pay them to sit.'

'I'd ask you in, but I got some hoodlums blocking my front door. So we'll have to talk out here.'

He figured if they got tough he'd rather be outside, giving him half a chance and maybe a witness or two. But it was hard to read: if they were here to take him out, they shouldn't be sitting on his front steps.

Ike said, 'I hadn't heard from you, so I wanted to see what was up.'

'I didn't think I was employed by you,' Nessheim said flatly.

'Take it easy. I just wondered if you were making progress.'

'Looking for Osaka?'

Ike nodded and Nessheim said, 'None at all.'

Ike didn't seem disappointed; he looked relieved in fact. 'That's okay. I came to tell you our deal was off.'

'What, no grand if I find him?'

'That's right.'

'Why is that?'

Ike just shrugged, then said, 'I thought it only polite to let you know that even if you find him there isn't going to be a grand in it for you. Simple as that, fella.'

'What if I keep looking?'

'That's up to you,' said Ike, and he seemed indifferent. 'But our deal's off. Got it?'

'Sure.'

Ike rose and wiped his hands like a man at the beach getting rid of sand. He motioned to the other two and the pig-faced man started to reach for the chair.

Nessheim called out, 'Leave it.'

Pig-face looked at Ike, who motioned him to leave the chair alone. Ike started down the stairs and his consorts followed him as he headed for the Chrysler.

Nessheim wasn't finished yet. He called out, 'How did you find me?'

'We can find anybody,' Ike said without turning around. He didn't sound boastful.

'Anybody? What about Billy Osaka?'

Ike had almost reached the car and the dark-haired henchman hurried ahead to open the back door for him. As he ducked down to get in, Ike stopped and turned his head to look at Nessheim. He said, 'We're not trying any more.'

Part Six

Washington, D.C.
Early November 1941

21

GUTTMAN HAD THREE agents in Bogota who were trying to stop the Germans from sending platinum out of Colombia to their arms industries at home. A crooked local cop had arrested one of these agents and the US ambassador had proved feeble about getting him released. It had taken Guttman most of the weekend and an extraordinary phone call (he had never before told an ambassador how to do his job), but the agent had been sprung, the platinum shipments interdicted and relations with Colombian law officials smoothed over. The Brits had been involved at the beginning and he would need to tell Stephenson what had happened, but the Canadian was still away in London.

Guttman had heard nothing from him since they'd met at his club in New York. A meeting with the double agent Popov had been scheduled in two days' time, and Guttman had been asked to attend by Hoover. Guttman had plenty else on his plate, including the telegram that had arrived on Friday from the Coast. TWENTY-FIVE GRAND RECEIVED THIS END it began – and as if to pre-empt Guttman's query, had gone on: REPEAT TWENTY-FIVE, NOT FIFTY.

Marie came in, with a mug of coffee in one hand and a slip of paper in the other. She put down both on the desk. 'Just one sugar, like the doctor ordered.'

'Since when?' asked Guttman irritably.

'Since yesterday. That's when your diet started.'

'Like hell it did.' He looked defiantly at the French Canadian divorcée he'd plucked out of the typing pool.

He had never regretted it – except when she tried to mother him.

'I meant to say that's how long your diet's lasted,' she said tartly, looking at the Danish that lay on his desk. 'At least it's an easy vice to hide. Nobody ever went home at night stinking of sugar. The name you wanted is on that paper.'

'Thanks,' he said grudgingly, but she was already out the door.

He looked down at the slip and the name Marie had written on it – Ogden Pierce IV. Where do they get these guys? Guttman thought. Probably a Yale alum happy to give a fellow Yalie and fellow Yankee a hand up. The one good thing about a war, thought Guttman, would be that this kind of scratch-your-back social stuff would not be able to survive.

He reached for his phone and got the switchboard, then gave a number to the operator and waited. When the call went through a woman answered, announcing he'd reached the office of the Loans Vice-President. Guttman said, 'Is he there?' When the woman said yes, he did his best to leave New York out of his voice, saying, 'Tell him it's Sam Peabody. We knew each other at Yale.'

He didn't have long to wait. 'Hello,' said a male voice uncertainly.

'Mr Sedgwick, it's Harry Guttman from the FBI. Sorry for the subterfuge, but I didn't think you'd want the world to know I was calling. Here's the thing: you told me fifty thousand dollars got sent to this Japanese-American bank in LA. But we checked it out and the people there swear only twenty-five grand was received.'

'Excuse me?'

'Yes, that's right, twenty-five. Can you explain the discrepancy?'

'No I can't, and I don't understand why you're bothering me again. I've told you everything I know. I cooperated. Now leave me alone.'

'I'm sorry, Mr Sedgwick, but I can't do that until we've cleared up this business of a missing twenty-five thousand dollars.'

'Why?' It was a rhetorical question, since Sedgwick wasn't waiting for an answer. 'What do you care if it's twenty-five grand? Or fifty? Or three hundred and ten? What does it matter? It wasn't your money. I wired it for the Russian Mission – I admitted that, and it was fifty thousand dollars. I don't care what your Jap friends out there say. I know because I did it myself.'

'I need you to confirm the telex trace, Mr Sedgwick. Then I'd like you to phone me with the confirmation code. Okay?'

'And then will you leave me alone?'

Guttman hesitated. There was no point misleading the man; it would only make things more difficult later on. 'That depends. Have you heard from our Russian friends again?'

There was a slight pause. 'No.'

Guttman knew he was lying. 'I'd like another conversation, face to face. I'll come up to New York next week – you tell me when's convenient. Don't worry, we don't have to meet in your office.'

'What's there to talk about?'

'I'd like to talk some more about Thornton Palmer. You may know more than you realise. And also we need to agree what you should do if you hear from Milnikov again.'

'If I see you, what's to keep you from insisting on another meeting after that? And another?' There was a heavy pause. 'I won't do it.'

Again, Guttman weighed which way to go. He decided

soft cop would lead to a greater sense of betrayal if he needed Sedgwick in future. So he said tersely, 'You've got no alternative.' He picked up the slip Marie had given him. 'Otherwise, I'll call Murray Hill 347.'

'Who's that? The police?' Sedgwick sounded oddly defiant.

'It's the home number of your bank's president, Ogden Pierce. Excuse me,' he added, unable to resist, 'Ogden Pierce the Fourth.'

There was a momentary silence at the other end of the line. 'Go ahead and call him, you bastard.' And Sedgwick slammed down the phone.

Guttman had been called worse, but he was still surprised. When they'd met in New York, Sedgwick had seemed terrified that his boss would learn about his former membership of the CP. What had changed? Had the Russians scared him more than Guttman had?

That night Nessheim telephoned just before nine. Guttman was listening to Jack Benny with Isabel, having cooked supper and washed and dried the dishes. The half-hour programme was his one chance to relax before the end of evening chores: when he would help Isabel to the bedroom, then help her undress and dress for the night; when he'd help her go to the bathroom and help her brush her teeth, then help her get into bed and tuck her in (for safety's sake, as well as comfort). Finally – it would be almost ten o'clock – he'd go through whatever papers he'd brought home from work before he locked up the house and went to bed himself.

On the phone the younger agent sounded agitated, which was a little alarming, for although Nessheim was not unflappable, he was never melodramatic. It had to be important, thought Guttman, and his irritation at having his evening interrupted dissolved.

Nessheim said, 'I need to go to Hawaii.'

You and me both, thought Guttman. He could almost taste the cool punch sipped out of hollowed-out pine-apples as he lay in a hammock underneath a pair of palm trees. When he looked towards the backyard and saw only the kitchen window's reflection of a tired-looking, heavy-set man talking on the telephone, he found it impossible not to laugh. 'You taking someone with you?' he joked.

But Nessheim didn't laugh back. He said he'd been trying to find the missing money from the bank transfer, and trying to find Osaka as well. But there was no trace of the money and no trace of the informant. The only real leads he'd come up with pointed to Hawaii. Where Osaka had been born, where he'd gone earlier that year, and where his cousin might have returned some months ago.

As Nessheim explained, Guttman did his best to follow, though the account of Nessheim's investigations unfurled like fishing line from a loose spool. An old Japanese lady murdered in her bed; a pair of hoods named Ike and Mo, who sounded like the kind of guys who had gone to school with Guttman on the Lower East Side and now lived in penitentiaries; the funny little Jap bank and the girl there who turned out to have been the missing Osaka's girlfriend. Also a grue-some description of what Nessheim had found at Terminal Island.

Finally Nessheim finished. Guttman said mildly, 'I understand a lot has happened, but what's any of it got to do with the money the Russians sent?'

'Maybe nothing,' Nessheim conceded with a sigh, 'but I'm starting to run into too many coincidences. First, this guy Ike is looking for Osaka too, and then I see Ike at Pearl's house. Billy's girlfriend works at a bank

– the same bank that received this money from New York. And the same bank Billy was supposed to visit with me.'

'Do you think the bank is connected with his disappearance?'

'I don't know. But it seems strange that Akiro has also gone missing. Nobody knows where he is either, and his wife, God help her, isn't talking any more.'

Guttman shuddered at the thought. He had seen ample violence in his life – as a boy on the tenement streets of New York, and as an officer of the law. But knives had always bothered him. His uncle Saul had been a butcher just off Hester Street; as a little boy Guttman had hated going with his mother to buy meat there. Cleavers and boning knives, all the razor-sharp blades, honed on steel until they were sharp enough for Saul's parlour trick – which was to slice off the hairs on the back of his hands.

Guttman asked sharply, 'What exactly would you do out there?'

And Nessheim hemmed and hawed and stammered, then finally admitted that he wasn't sure. He'd try to find this cousin, Akiro, and he'd dig into Osaka's past. Guttman sensed that Nessheim was still shook up by the severed leg he'd seen at Terminal Island.

So he said no to Hawaii, gently, but without hesitation. Maybe he had been wrong to involve Nessheim in this at all. Palmer's confession had opened a can of worms that seemed to have gone west – literally – and there taken on an unrelated life of its own as Nessheim pursued his lost informant.

'Will you at least consider it?' asked Nessheim.

'Sure I will,' said Guttman, thinking nothing of the sort. 'But now's not a good time to be away. The Director's coming out to your part of the world.'

'Pearl said as much. Do you know when?'

'Next month, I think. I know he'll want you around when he visits the studio, and maybe more than that. Sometimes Mr Hoover likes to relax on these trips.' An understatement. 'If he takes a shine to you, he'll expect you to go along for the ride.'

'Pearl has this notion of doing a picture about Mr Hoover. Sort of a history of the FBI.'

'As seen through the Director's eyes,' Guttman said, unable to keep a sandpaper edge out of his voice.

Nessheim said, 'I don't think it would be a good move, you know. For the Bureau or for Mr Hoover.'

'Why?'

'Pearl's not on the level.'

'Have you got something on him?'

'He came out from Cleveland a few years ago. He's got a lot of past history he wants buried, I think.'

'What kind of past are we talking about?'

'Will murky do?'

'You got any evidence?' he asked.

'Not yet. I had a check run on one of his associates here, but there's no file here in LA and the Cleveland Field Office says he's clean. I don't believe it.'

Guttman gave a small sigh. Hoover had never been interested in anyone's beliefs, unless they were subversive. Still, the kid shouldn't just be dismissed. 'Did you speak to Cleveland yourself?'

'I had somebody in the Bureau call on my behalf.'

'Well, unless you learn something you'd better leave it alone. Now listen, I'm double-checking the wire transfer from the bank here. I'd like you to do the same – ask to see the testing telex and their numbers. I'm kind of surprised this little Jap bank would have code privileges with a Manhattan bank.'

'Let me look into it.'

237

'Okay. Anything else?'

Nessheim paused momentarily. 'There is one thing. I went to a benefit for the Russians the other night – Hood wanted me to go. Someone from the Russian Consulate gave a speech, and I met his wife.'

'Yeah,' said Guttman perfunctorily. He wanted to get Isabel to bed.

'Well, the wife called me and asked me to go to some ranch near Santa Barbara where she and her husband are giving a party. I've ducked it for now, but figure I'd better say no.'

Guttman was alert now. 'You mean you'd better say yes. I want you to go. The money that went to LA came from the Russian Mission in New York. I don't know if there's any connection with the Russians out there, but I wouldn't be surprised.'

'I don't think I'm going to be able to find that out,' said Nessheim warily. 'This woman's kind of strange.'

'Do your best,' said Guttman. 'Use your charm. Pretend the ranch is in Hawaii.'

22

ON WEDNESDAY GUTTMAN drove to work early. It was raining and he was old enough not to like the wet – a faint arthritic twinge surfaced in his knees whenever the rain lasted more than a couple of hours. He felt fluey, too, but he couldn't complain, not when Isabel was feeling so rotten.

He was worried about her. His wife's mobility was worse now and the decline seemed to be accelerating. Isabel could no longer stand without either her walker or crutches, and had finally given up trying – her last attempts would have been disastrous had Guttman not been there to catch her when she fell.

She was uncomplaining as ever, but had started saying the damndest things. 'You don't have to like Mr Hoover, you know,' she'd declared out of the blue one evening, leaving Guttman uncertain how to respond. Then later, when he'd come to bed she'd moved her arm to show she was still awake. 'Harry,' she'd whispered, once he'd settled, his head on the pillow. 'There was a man out back in the yard this afternoon.'

'What sort of man?'

'Just a man,' she said.

'Did you tell Mrs Davis?'

'He was gone by the time she came to look.'

He had heard nothing from Sedgwick. Guttman was planning to go to New York on the following Tuesday, but had expected to hear from Sedgwick first, with the transfer codes for the wired money. He'd called, but Sedgwick's secretary had said he was in a meeting and would call him back. He hadn't.

Now when Marie came in he had her place another call and was annoyed when she came through a few minutes later to say, 'Mr Sedgwick's not in yet, Harry. Banks don't open till ten.'

'I bet the rest of the staff's there by now.'

He had her try again just before the bank opened. This time Marie shrugged as she reported: 'His secretary says he's off sick. And you'd better be off sick if you don't get upstairs.'

'Why's that?' he asked, still wondering what game Sedgwick was playing at.

'Because Executive Conference is about to begin.'

He took the stairs two at a time, which made him huff and puff, even though it was only one floor. He wasn't late for the meeting according to the round wall clock, but everybody else was already there, and Tolson, sitting at the head of the table, frowned. 'Okay, Guttman's decided to join us, so let's get started.'

They were meeting every week now, out of recognition that if the war in Europe hadn't directly affected the United States yet, it was going to. Hoover liked to be prepared. The number of agents and support staff had tripled in the past two years, as a result of Hoover's insistence that the Bureau be ready for wartime and his canny manipulation of Congress. Congress didn't want a war, as Roosevelt, despite his best efforts to get the country into one, had discovered. But by publicising foreign efforts at sabotage, Hoover had inflamed Congress's fears of alien enemies within, while demonstrating the Bureau's ability to counter them. There had been little Congressional resistance to his requests for more manpower.

Now the Bureau had ten divisions, over a dozen new field offices, and an extraordinary number of green recruits. Inevitably there had been growing pains and this morning's meeting concentrated on administrative issues. These were in Louis B. Nichols' bailiwick, and as a man who liked the sound of his own voice it gave him free rein to go on about them. Doubtless important, thought Guttman, but not very interesting. He looked at his successor, Tamm, whose handsome stolid face usually hid any emotion, and was gratified to find him suppressing a yawn.

At last the agenda moved on to investigation. Guttman was called first and he related recent events in Bogota, then talked a bit about Brazil, where they had entrapped three German businessmen who were bribing politicians. People listened politely, but without obvious interest. Tolson asked a pointed question about Mexico, but Guttman countered that oversight of German activity there had been ceded to the Office of Naval Intelligence.

It was Tamm's turn next then, and the meeting perked up as he described how an embezzlement ring in the Midwest had been rounded up by the Chicago Field Office. Nichols in his PR capacity passed round copies of the wire service coverage of the arrests. Turning to espionage, Tamm said they were still pursuing a few leads left over from the Duquesne case, though he didn't expect more than one or two further arrests.

Just before the meeting broke up, Tolson decided it was time for a small homily. He gave one every two or three meetings, like a benediction held back as a treat. Today's was about the need to keep standards high and not let the growth in staff affect the calibre of agents employed by the Bureau. Everyone nodded dutifully, but then Nichols asked what was likely to happen with recruitment if war broke out. Wouldn't it be difficult to enlist new agents if the draft continued?

'Let's worry about that when we have to,' said Tolson. Guttman could see he was eager to end the meeting.

To Guttman's surprise, Tamm spoke up. 'Recruiting more agents is one thing, but what about losing the ones we already have? A lot of my people are going to want to join up if war breaks out.'

Tolson looked startled before he reassumed command. 'Agents will be exempt from the Selective Service. The Boss's view is clear: an agent's loyalty should be to the Bureau.'

'What if they want to fight? Plenty of my people do.'

Guttman saw that Tamm had made a tactical mistake. Tolson could be reasonable, Tolson could brook arguments he didn't agree with, Tolson could preside over a meeting without trying to bend it to his will. But not when Hoover had staked out a position. Then there was to be no dissent.

'The Director's view,' Tolson said, pausing ominously. 'I repeat, the Director's view, is that an agent's priority has to be to serve the Bureau, in peacetime and war. Any other decision is a selfish one, without the best interests of the country at heart.'

Guttman watched Tamm struggle with the logic of this – it was selfish to volunteer to die for one's country? Tamm wondered aloud, 'What happens if my agents decide to be selfish?'

Tolson's discomfort metamorphosed into anger and he said, 'We don't prosecute people for selfishness in this country.' He looked as if he wished he could. 'But if any agent enlists in the Forces they will have no future with the Bureau. They can win the Medal of Honor for all we care, but they'll never be a Special Agent again.'

The meeting adjourned, but before Guttman could get out of the room, Tolson called out his name, gesturing for him to stay behind. Guttman waited. Tolson had stood up, but was leaning over to gather his papers. The man's hair was going, Guttman noticed happily, and Tolson's once-sharp nose was growing bulbous. Too many drinks on the house at the '21' Club.

'The meeting this afternoon's been called off,' Tolson said. 'I've told Tamm already.'

'What, no visiting fireman?' asked Guttman. If you were chipper with Tolson, but showed an edge, you could sometimes get something out of him – he seemed to like the occasional sparky exception to the fawning guff he got from everybody else. A secret gossip lurked within the soul of Clyde Tolson, but it took delicate handling to disinter it – any remark too acid and Tolson would bristle, remembering his position; any too bland and he would speak officiously himself.

Tolson said, 'The Director's already seen this guy Popov up in New York.'

'Did they talk about Latin America?' asked Guttman, though he could not have cared less. Stephenson had said Popov's important information was about spies operating in the United States.

'Not that I know of.' He added, 'It wasn't a very long conversation.'

'Oh?' asked Guttman.

'This guy's a real lulu. Do you know what the Brits call him? *Tricycle*.'

'I don't get it.' He hoped he appeared as innocent as he was trying to seem.

'You're married, so you wouldn't know,' he said archly, 'but girls with round heels are called "bicycles" these days. Well, Popov likes to enjoy two broads at a time. So they call him *Tri*-cycle.' He gave a small guffaw. For a partner in a prudish alliance, Tolson always seemed fascinated by sex.

'The Director wouldn't have been impressed,' said Guttman.

'You can say that again. He's never liked double agents

anyway. No loyalty: there's nothing to stop them from flipping back to the other side.'

'Did this Popov character have any useful information?'

'No. He was full of promises rather than facts. We were supposed to be impressed by all the swells he knew in New York. There was one thing, though. Ever heard of microdots?' Guttman shook his head. 'It's like micro-film, but the image gets reduced to the size of a dot. Popov gave us a letter which looked perfectly normal. But one of the periods could be peeled off, and when you look at it under a microscope it's got pages of information on it – all on one tiny dot.'

'Amazing.' He waited the length of a drumbeat. 'What was on Popov's dot?'

'Who knows?' said Tolson blithely. 'I don't think the Boss believed any of it. All sorts of stuff this Popov guy was supposed to do for the *Abwehr*. Most of it involving first-class travel.' He gave a small, high-pitched giggle. 'The guy's already got a penthouse in New York and more broads than you can shake a stick at. He's always short of dough, apparently, and the boss decided he'd say anything to get on our payroll. Still, this dots business could be very useful – it's with the lab boys right now.'

'What's going to happen to him?'

'That's up to the Brits – but he can't stay here, at least not under our aegis. He claims the Germans are waiting for him to send them back all sorts of info; he told them he was running an entire network along the East Coast. We're supposed to help make up stuff he can feed back to Berlin.' He shook his head. 'It ain't going to happen. And I don't think the Brits will want to keep subsidising him here – I imagine they'll send him back to Europe. Good riddance.'

*　　*　　*

At home Guttman found Mrs Davis long gone and Annie talking with Isabel in the bedroom. His wife was still in her nightgown and under the covers. 'You're not up?' he said, entering the room.

Annie spoke. 'She's got a cold. Apparently she got it from you.'

'So go easy on me,' said Isabel, and they all laughed.

When Annie went home a few minutes later, she left before he could thank her. He sat in the living room with the radio on and drank a weak highball. When he got up and peeked at Isabel, she was dozing, so he went and found his diary from his phone nook. Taking it to the kitchen he dialled the number he had written down that afternoon after calling Westchester County information.

A woman answered the phone and he asked for Sedgwick.

'Who's calling?'

'Harry Guttman.'

'Just a moment and I'll see if I can find him.' Guttman's name seemed to mean nothing to her.

She didn't return for several minutes, and when she did she said, 'Mr Guttman, he asks if you could call back later. He's writing a letter and he says he needs to finish it.'

'I'll call back in an hour if that's okay,' he said. 'It's kind of important or I wouldn't be troubling him at home.'

When he hung up he decided that writing a letter was such a bad excuse for ducking a phone call that maybe it was the truth.

He killed the hour making supper. As he boiled potatoes and cabbage and baked a large piece of ham, he went into the bedroom and woke Isabel gently. When he'd established that she didn't want a tray, he wrapped a wool robe around her and wheeled her out in her chair to the kitchen table, where she sat reading the evening paper. She read the society columns aloud and they laughed at the description of Eleanor Roosevelt's tea party for the members of the American Legion. Then she played Patience while he carved the ham, and he noticed she could no longer adequately shuffle the cards between games.

They ate in the kitchen, and after supper Isabel sat in the living room listening to the radio while he did the dishes and put them away. Then he called the Sedgwick house again, but this time there was no answer at all.

He joined Isabel and stretched out on their comfortable old green sofa, while they listened to Red Skelton on the Raleigh Cigarettes programme on NBC. It was good to hear her laugh. When the programme ended, he asked if she wanted to be put to bed. 'Not yet,' she said. 'I like to pretend the short days haven't set in.'

'Okay. I've got to make another call. You stay put.'

She laughed, since they both knew she wasn't going anywhere. As he stood up to go to the kitchen, Isabel said, 'Is this a good guy or a bad guy?'

Guttman's smile was bittersweet. 'He's a guy who got mixed up in something he didn't understand, and it's come back to haunt him.'

This time a man answered the phone. But the voice was unfamiliar. 'Is Roger Sedgwick there?' asked Guttman.

'Who is that?' the voice asked bluntly.

'Harry Guttman.'

'Are you a friend of Mr Sedgwick, sir?'

The 'sir' worried him. 'Not really.'

'Was he expecting your call?'

'I called before, but his wife said he was busy.'

'What's your relation to Mr Sedgwick, Mr Guttman?'

Enough was enough. 'I'm an Assistant Director with the FBI.'

There was a pause. 'Sir, this is Sergeant Duval of the Brewster Police. There's been an accident.'

'What's happened, officer?'

'Roger Sedgwick's dead. He shot himself.'

'Jesus Christ. When did he do that?'

'About an hour ago.'

Guttman thought of his second phone call, the sound of the phone ringing, unavailingly, like a siren summoning help too late. Guttman would need to tread carefully; the last thing he needed was for this to reach the ears of other members of the Bureau. 'What happened exactly?' he asked.

Duval said, 'His wife says he left the house earlier this evening to post a letter. There's a mailbox three or four blocks down the street which has an evening pick-up. She was making supper and he said he'd be right back. When he hadn't returned after half an hour, she went out looking for him. She found him slumped on a bench halfway down the block with a bullet in his head. The gun was on the ground by the bench.'

'Any note?'

'Nope. Not by the body and not in his study. We haven't been through the rest of the house yet.'

'What kind of gun was it?'

'Some foreign model. One of my men said it must have come from Europe.'

'Why'd he think that?'

'His dad fought in the last war and brought back some pistols from overseas. My guy said Sedgwick's gun looked like one in his father's collection.'

'Can you try to confirm the make of weapon, please?'

'Sure.'

'Did Sedgwick say anything at all before he went out?'

'Just that he was going to mail this letter. If the wife calms down I'll try to have another word. The doctor's with her now.'

'Let me give you my number. If she has anything to say about why he did this I'd like to know. Her husband was assisting me with an investigation.'

'Could that have anything to do with this?'

'Don't think so. He was just providing information about some bank transactions.' The last thing Guttman wanted was local cops asking him questions instead of the other way round. 'Listen, could you do something for me? Can you check the mailbox? You know, for the letter he went out to send.'

'I thought of that already,' said the sergeant, sounding proud of his astuteness. 'But they'd already collected from that box.'

'What about at the post office? Any chance of catching up to them there?'

'We may be a small town, Mr Guttman, but there's more than one mailbox here.'

'Of course,' said Guttman. There was no point trying to bully the sergeant – if the cop resisted, Guttman would have to get a court order to search the mail, and given Hoover's proscription this was the last thing he was about to do. 'Is there any chance you could have a word with the postmaster – you know, informal-like, and see if someone could have a look? Maybe Sedgwick put a return address on the envelope.'

'I guess I could ask,' the cop said hesitantly. 'If it's that important.'

'It is,' said Guttman firmly, though he didn't have any idea himself. Sedgwick might have been writing farewell to his mistress for all he knew, or cancelling

248

his membership at the country club. On the other hand, he might have been writing to his controller at the Russian Mission. It seemed worth the trouble to try to find out.

23

THE RAIN HAD stopped and the sun was out in the morning, though its light seemed weaker now, autumnal, casting a honey-coloured glow on the trees as he crossed the bridge and drove through Georgetown. He was feeling foolish since he had a small square of toilet paper pasted to the shaving cut on his chin. By the time he parked at the Justice Department Building the blood would have dried, and if he were careful peeling the little tab of paper off he'd have only a small scab left where he'd done a dipsy doodle with his razor. If he weren't careful he'd start bleeding again, until he took the elevators up to the fourth floor, where he could get more toilet paper from the men's room and start the process all over again.

He hadn't heard from Duval and he wondered if the cop knew what he was doing. It sounded like a suicide all right, but sometimes policemen jumped to that judgement too easily – Palmer's death hadn't looked like a suicide at all, but that was how it had been treated, and why it had been forgotten.

When he came into the office Marie was already there. She wore a green blouse that set off her bright red hair.

'Coffee?' she asked brightly and he nodded. Then she pointed to his chin. He had forgotten all about the razor cut. By the time Marie came through with his coffee he had got the bit of paper off without disaster, and he asked her to put a call through to Yale University.

'You going back to school?' she said.

'Nah. They want me to go teach there.' This shut her up. She went out looking unsure of what to believe.

Moments later, Guttman waited with the phone to his ear until he heard the authentic voice of New England say hello. He replied, 'Mr Vail, It's Harry Guttman of the FBI.'

'Call me Franklin. How can I help this time, Agent Guttman?'

'You remember Thornton Palmer?'

'How could I forget him? Did those names I gave you prove of any help?'

'They were very helpful. I wanted another favour, though, if it's not too much to ask.'

'Fire away,' said Vail cheerfully.

'One of Palmer's associates said he had a cousin in Hollywood. Palmer visited him one summer and that seemed to be instrumental in making him a radical. But this associate didn't know who this cousin was.'

'You want me to try and find out?'

'If it's not too much trouble.'

'Happy to help.'

There was no longer any pretence it was a club, though the butler named Jason still opened the door, dressed in a white jacket and wearing white cotton gloves. He led Guttman into the main sitting room, where four men were sitting at the back around a chestnut table stacked with files. They glanced idly at Guttman as he sat down in one of the deep leather armchairs, then resumed their conversation. He could only hear snippets – *Lend Lease isn't so popular out West* and *one of the Labour ministers may be coming over* – as he found the softness of their English accents made them hard to understand.

'Mr Guttman.'

He looked up into the face of the pretty young woman. 'Katie,' he said. 'What are you doing here? Has your uncle had you transferred from New York?'

She gave a small giggle. 'Goodness no. He brought me down on the train so he could work during the trip – he had a lot of dictation.' Guttman stood up, assuming she would take him upstairs, where Stephenson had a little office room of his own.

Katie frowned. 'I'm sorry, but Uncle Bill's not here. He asked me to send his apologies. He's been called to the White House. He asked if there was any chance he could meet you later on – he suggested six o'clock. He said he can't be sure he'll be free until then.'

Guttman wondered what he was going to tell Mrs Davis. But this was important. Stephenson had called Marie twice to make sure Guttman would have time to see him on his flying visit to the capital.

'Okay,' he said. They were out in the hallway now. Jason was nowhere to be seen, but Guttman figured he could manage the door himself. He was about to say goodbye when Katie whispered, 'My uncle also asked if he could meet you somewhere else.'

'Oh,' said Guttman, equally hushed.

'It gets a little crowded here later on,' Katie explained.

He sensed that wasn't the real reason. 'Why doesn't he meet me at my club? Let me give you directions; your uncle will need them.'

When he got back to his office it was already 4.30. Never helpful at the best of times, Mrs Davis had lately been downright cranky, and he dreaded her reaction now if he called. He thought for a minute, then picked up the phone and dialled another number.

Pray God Mrs Jupiter didn't pick up the phone. When it suited her she was deaf as a post, but when the phone rang she liked to get there first. Fortunately, Annie answered.

'It's Harry,' he said, then stopped, uncertain how to ask his favour. 'I was worried I'd get Mrs Jupiter.'

Annie laughed. 'I try to beat her to it. Otherwise after three or four "I can't hear you's" people hang up. But is there a problem at home, Harry? I can go over there.'

'No, Isabel's fine. It's later on I'm worried about. I've been called to a meeting at the end of the day. Mrs Davis has been taking a tough line lately, and I wondered—'

'I'll go over at five-thirty. Don't worry – Mrs Davis can leave at her normal time.'

'Thank you, Annie –' he started to say.

'I think we should put this on a regular basis.'

'Of course,' he said, a little taken aback. 'What's the going rate for this kind of thing?'

'I don't mean money, Harry,' Annie said sharply. 'I'm happy to help. I just think it might smooth things with Mrs Davis if she knew I was coming on certain days.'

'I couldn't ask you to do that, Annie. Not without paying you, anyway.'

'We can settle that later. I give Mrs Jupiter her dinner very early – she likes to eat at five o'clock. After that I'm free. Though there's one condition.'

'Okay,' he said, hoping he was right to agree to it in advance.

'That Jeff can play in your backyard. Mrs Jupiter hasn't really got one, and if he throws the ball against the shed she complains about the noise. That lady hears exactly what she wants to hear.'

The nickel-sized wart on the man behind the bar at Steamer's had grown, thought Guttman as he ordered a bottle of beer and sat down to wait. The owner's blonde wife was heating oil in the fryer to fry fish for the evening customers, and a couple of hamburgers sizzled on the grill. But Guttman resisted temptation. He'd eat when he got home and tried to remember what there was in the icebox that he could fix for Isabel and himself.

The door to the shack swung open, giving a glimpse of the Potomac a hundred yards away, choppy today in the wind, its waves a succession of grey shark fins. A short, trim man walked in and stood tentatively, his eyes adjusting to the gloom of the room. Guttman gave a little wave and Stephenson came towards him.

'It's not quite as ritzy as your club,' said Guttman, 'but you asked for discreet. I don't think you'll get many diplomats crossing the threshold.'

The man with the wart waddled over behind the bar and Stephenson pointed at Guttman's bottle of Gunther. 'I'll have one of those.'

When the man came back with the beer, Guttman got down from his stool. 'There's a garden in the back. Why don't we talk out there?'

It wasn't really a garden, more a small yard with concrete paving near the building and unmown grass behind that. A solitary picnic table sat halfway back and Guttman led the way, walking across fallen leaves, which crunched underfoot like peanut shells in a ball park's bleachers.

He went and sat at the far end of the picnic table, facing the rear door of the bar. Stephenson looked around before he joined him. He was elegantly dressed in a sage-coloured wool jacket and grey flannels, and he seemed subdued, his face pinched. 'I'm sorry about this afternoon,' Stephenson said.

'Katie explained you were at the White House.'

'I had to deliver a letter to Mr Roosevelt, but I was

really there to see Harry Hopkins. We're hoping he'll come over after Christmas and see how things are for himself.'

'And how *are* things?'

'Better than you might imagine,' said Stephenson, though he looked exhausted. 'The bombing's been every bit as bad as reports say. But morale's held up astonishingly well. It helps that we're hitting them back. We bombed Berlin, you know, which Goering said we couldn't do.'

'What do you think the Germans are planning next?'

'Well, Hitler's given up on the idea of invading Britain, for now at least. If you ask me, he had his chance the summer before last and missed it.'

'What happens if Moscow falls?'

'It won't help, that's for sure. But it may not happen; the snow's already starting and the Germans aren't prepared. Talk about *hubris*: Hitler never thought his soldiers would need winter clothes. The telltale will be if Stalin flees Moscow – if he stays there's every chance the Russians will hold the city.'

Guttman took a long pull of his beer, then put the bottle down on the table. 'I didn't get to meet Popov.'

'That's why I wanted to see you. Do you know what happened? I only have Popov's side of things and even that's second hand. Masterman has been running him directly.'

'Hoover saw him in New York. The Director spends a lot of time there.'

'So I gather,' said Stephenson dryly. 'Winchell has your boss in his column at least once a month.'

'The problem was that Popov's reputation preceded him, and Hoover's a Puritan about that sort of thing. He also felt Popov was trying to take us for a ride. Popov asked him for money.'

Stephenson nodded. 'Popov's been under a great deal of pressure. Since Hoover doesn't want to use him, we have to decide whether to move him to Latin America and work him there, or send him back to Lisbon.'

'What would he do in Lisbon?'

'What he did before. The Nazis think he's running an extensive ring of spies in Britain – it's an entirely fictitious network we helped him "set up", but the Germans believe it's real. Popov travels back and forth between London and Lisbon – he meets with the Germans there because it's neutral.'

'That sounds more useful than sending him to Latin America.'

'It is, but it's a lot riskier too. The Germans know he's not made much progress here and they're not happy. I don't know how Popov's going to feel about walking back into the lion's den. Until he met with Hoover I think he thought he'd spend the war years here, living high on the hog. He even planned to visit Hawaii.'

Guttman couldn't help but look startled.

'What did I say, Harry?'

Guttman said, 'I've just had Nessheim telling me he needs to go to Hawaii too. One of his informants is missing – and Nessheim thinks he might be hiding out there. He said this informant may know why the Russians sent that money to a Jap bank in LA. But why did Popov want to go there? Native girls?'

Stephenson smiled. 'For a change, no. The Germans were sending him to see the Japanese. I don't know why they were meeting in Hawaii, but Popov said his German masters attached great importance to it. It's not going to happen now though, unless . . .' He looked around them, but there was no one else in the yard and the back door hadn't opened since they'd come out.

'Unless what?' asked Guttman.

Stephenson stared at his bottle of beer. 'Unless Popov suggested to the Germans that he send someone else. It will be happening pretty late – Popov was supposed to get to the Islands in August. Still, I like his idea: it may tell us more about the Japs' plans. Though without help from Hoover we haven't got anyone to send.'

Stephenson kept his gaze firmly on his beer while Guttman took this in. Then Guttman asked tentatively, 'You'd need a German speaker?'

'Not necessarily, as long as he was a German sympathiser – or able to pose as one.' Stephenson's face was expressionless.

'Ah,' said Guttman as a knowing smile spread across his face. 'That sounds familiar.'

Stephenson gave a short laugh. 'I thought I was being wily.'

'James Rossbach, former member of the German-American *Bund*. We used that identity before to good effect. Maybe it could be resurrected.'

'Same actor in the role?' asked Stephenson and Guttman nodded. Stephenson said, 'Would he be willing? It could be bloody dangerous. We don't even know what we're hoping to learn from the Japanese.'

Guttman grunted. 'I can get our guy to Hawaii legitimately and he can have a look around for his missing informant. But after that you'd have to help me to arrange the rendezvous with the Japs Popov was supposed to see.'

'That won't be a problem,' said Stephenson. 'Back in a minute,' he added and went into the bar.

When Stephenson returned he was carrying two more bottles of beer. 'You look a million miles away, Harry.'

'I was thinking about our last conversation. The banker who Palmer told me about went and shot himself. At least it looks that way. It happened after I pressed him about the money he wired for the Russians.'

He explained about Nessheim's discovery of the discrepancy in LA.

Stephenson shook his head. 'It doesn't sound like a clerical error to me.'

'Not for that much money.' Harry scratched the bristles on his jaw with the flat of his hand; this late in the day, they were rough as filings. 'Anyway, it's not as if we haven't got more pressing things to worry about with the Nazis and the Japanese.'

It was Stephenson's turn to look worried.

Guttman said, 'Is something wrong?'

'How popular is this club of yours?'

'You mean this place? Steamer's?' He laughed. 'I stumbled upon it by accident. I was taking a walk along the Potomac when I saw the sign, so I stopped and had a beer. It's usually deserted in the afternoon, until the factory shift next door gets out. I met Nessheim here a couple of times after he was done infiltrating the *Bund*. Why?'

'It's probably a coincidence,' Stephenson said, and he and Guttman exchanged looks. 'But when I just went in there was a fellow inside who works at the other club – *my* club.'

'In Intelligence?'

Stephenson shook his head. 'No, he's just a gopher – delivers things, collects the mail. His name is Williams and he's from California and fresh out of college – just biding time until he gets drafted, I suppose. It seems a little odd that he should be here tonight.'

'We're pretty far off the beaten track. I don't know anyone who lives down here. What do you know about this kid, though?'

'Not much, but that doesn't seem to bother anybody.

He could be a card-carrying Communist and none of my lot would care. The Soviets are allies now. Sometimes I feel that half the BSC are as concerned about the fate of Moscow as they are about Coventry or Manchester.'

'That bad, huh?'

'Most of it's just naive – our enemy's enemy must be our friend. But there's a hard core of Reds in our ranks.'

'Is that why you didn't want to meet at the Club?'

When Stephenson nodded, Guttman remembered how they had hightailed it out of the Rockefeller Center offices in New York.

'It's very difficult,' said Stephenson, and he seemed uncertain how much to say. 'Proof's hard to find, and even when you have it you can't be sure who you're showing it to.'

'It's that high up?' Guttman was surprised. 'Look,' he said, 'I can't very easily run a check on Williams—'

'I know. I'm not asking you to. Speaking of which, we asked the Bureau in New York to run a check on the licence plate number you gave me.'

'Any luck?'

'I don't know if you'll consider it luck, but yes, they found the original owner. It's not who we were thinking. It was a German-American named Schultz.'

'Schultz?' Don't get excited, Guttman told himself. It was a common name. 'From New York?'

'That's right, Max Schultz, from Yorkville. His wife still lives there. He was a major figure in the German-American *Bund*, apparently.'

Guttman's heart was pounding. 'He's in Sing Sing, doing fifteen years.'

'He was, Harry. We checked and he died in June. Of natural causes it seems.'

'And you say the plates were his?'

'They used to be. His wife doesn't drive, so after his

death she sold the car. She claims she did it for cash and doesn't even know the name of the man who bought it. I don't know if she's telling the truth.'

Guttman was thinking hard. 'If the *Bund* were still using the car, why would they want to kill Palmer? Because he was a Communist agent? How the hell did they know that? It doesn't make any sense.'

Stephenson sat there, looking unhappy. He said at last, 'There's something about this Palmer business of yours which is bugging me. Probably more than it should.'

'Funny you should say that. I feel the same way. Yet it's not as if I don't have clear enemies in view. God knows you do too – you're at war.'

'Perhaps it's because for once the enemy *isn't* in plain view.'

24

NOTHING FROM DUVAL in Brewster, and nothing from Vail in New Haven. When Marie opened their connecting door Guttman looked up hopefully, but she shook her head. 'Do you want to speak with a Mr Larrabee?' she asked. She looked especially good today; she was wearing a charcoal pencil skirt and an ivory blouse.

'Do I know him?'

'He says he works at State.'

He looked at Marie, but her face was emotionless. It was never clear to him how much she knew; she was so discreet about his activities that she didn't even discuss them with him. But she'd proved her loyalty more than once and had even risked her job for him. She ought to find someone, he thought, not for the first time, then realised she was waiting for his answer.

'Put His Excellency through,' he said, and she nodded before turning on her high heels.

When his phone buzzed – until last year it had used to ring; he missed that – he answered cautiously. He was accustomed to having to make the running with State, unsurprising since Hoover made little secret of his disdain for the denizens of Foggy Bottom. 'Hand-holders for foreigners' he had once said.

'Mr Guttman?' When Guttman grunted affirmatively the voice said, 'My name is Braddock Larrabee. I'm with the State Department. I'm based in Washington right now, but my last posting was Vienna.'

So? he wanted to say, but something was niggling at him. 'What can I do for you, Mr Larrabee?'

'I was hoping my name would be familiar to you. I take it that it's not.'

'Not' was pronounced 'nought' in an East Coast drawl.

'Sorry Mr Larrabee, but I meet an awful lot of people in my job—'

'I thought my colleague Thornton Palmer might have mentioned me.'

Guttman decided to remain silent.

'As I said, I was stationed in Vienna. Mr Palmer was there, too.'

'Was he also working at State?' Guttman asked.

'No, it was before he joined.' There was a pause. 'I think you know that.'

'So how can I help you?' Guttman asked.

'I'd like to have a meeting with you. It would need to be discreet.' Larrabee added, 'I think I have information that will be of interest.'

'What about?' asked Guttman, confident a certain bluntness would speed things along.

'Let's just say I have affiliations in my past similar to those of Mr Palmer.'

'Are these affiliations ongoing?'

'Certain people want them to be. As they did with Mr Palmer.'

He didn't hesitate further. 'All right. When and where?'

There was a pause; perhaps Larrabee had expected Guttman to prove a harder sell. He said, 'Let me be in touch. I'll send you a note with a time and a place. Are you in D.C. for the time being?'

'Yeah. But what if I can't make it?'

'Then I'll send you another note, Mr Guttman.'

* * *

Guttman didn't know why he felt so jumpy, but the sooner he could get Stephenson's instructions typed up by Marie and sent to Nessheim, the better.

He was just about finished transcribing them when Marie came in. He looked at her vaguely, noticing her snail-shaped metal earrings, and said, 'No more coffee please or I'll be dancing on my desk.'

'I'd give a lot to see that,' said Marie, her lip curling. 'Though you may be doing that anyway, only on a bed of hot coals. Miss Gandy's just called. The Director wants to see you right away.'

He stared at her. 'Did she say why?'

Marie shook her head. 'But it wasn't five minutes from now or later on or in two weeks' time. It was Now with a capital N.'

Guttman groaned and looked down at the legal pad where he'd been transcribing the notes he had taken in the unique brand of shorthand which Marie called Guttmanese. It was not something she could read – hence the legal pad. 'I just need a minute more,' he said plaintively.

'Mr Hoover waits for no man.'

Guttman threw down his pen. 'Okay. Type these up, will ya?' He looked at his watch. 'Tomorrow morning will be fine, but lock them up before you go home.'

'Like that, is it?'

He grimaced.

'Okay.' Marie scooped up the pad and the pages filled with writing which he'd torn off. 'Do your tie up, Harry, and button your jacket for once.'

A few years before, an anonymous letter had been sent to the Director of the FBI, claiming a sniper was going to shoot him from across Connecticut Avenue. For a while the drapes had been drawn on the fourth-floor office accordingly. No threat had ever materialised and eventually the drapes had been opened again, though only after Hoover had had his desk moved out of the sight line of the window.

Now as Guttman entered, the Director sat behind the walnut, U-shaped desk, with two standing American flags on either side. He wore a smoke-coloured suit, beautifully tailored, a shirt the colour of unsalted butter and a tie of dull gold. Tolson sat in one of the two chairs in front of the desk and the two men were laughing when Guttman came in. From the way Hoover cut off his smile, Guttman sensed there was trouble ahead.

'Have a seat, Harry,' he said. At least it wasn't 'Mr Guttman', which was a certain weathervane of storms.

Guttman sat down and glanced at Tolson. His face was expressionless, which meant he was leaving this one to the boss.

'Thornton Palmer,' Hoover said without preamble. 'Tell me about it.'

'Yes, I reported to Clyde about my meeting with him and I then had your memo saying to leave it alone. Ed Tamm has the file.'

'The D.C. police have closed the case.'

'Yes,' said Guttman. But he didn't think Palmer was the issue.

'And you've left it alone?'

'That's right. The information is with Tamm.'

Hoover was nodding benignly; Guttman noticed Tolson was no longer looking his way. Suddenly Hoover said, 'Then can you explain this? I received it this morning.'

He pushed a sheet of paper across the desk. Guttman was sitting too far back to reach, and he had to stand and take a step forward to collect it. When he saw the letterhead he didn't feel like sitting down again:

43 Wells Street, Brewster, New York

J. E. Hoover
Director Federal Bureau of Investigation
The Justice Department Building
Washington, D.C.

Dear Mr Hoover,
    There won't be any need to reply to this letter because by the time you do I will not be around to read it. I never thought a citizen of this country could be hounded by his own government, but thanks to your agent Guttman I have been disabused. I made a youthful mistake which many others also have made.
    Please assure Mr Guttman that contrary to what he thinks I have told him the complete truth in response to his recent investigation into the late Thornton Palmer. That makes my position doubly hard – and to threaten my exposure when I have given my full cooperation seems unjust to say the least. I am truly damned whatever I do and have nowhere to turn. I hope you are proud of your agency's efforts.

Yours sincerely,
Roger Sedgwick
Vice-President of the Manhattan Savings Association

'What do you make of this, Mr Guttman? I gather Mr Sedgwick took his own life just after writing this letter.'

Guttman looked up at the square, almost encephalic Hoover head and found the dark eyes demanding a reply. He threw up his hands. 'I don't know what to say. I'm astonished.'

Hoover made a face. 'Let's start with the basics. Did you know Mr Sedgwick?'

Guttman's instinct was to give a narrative, try to describe the strained meeting with the man, the mixture of guilt and guile and simple facts – fifty grand to a Mr Lyakhov – that had made their conversation so strange. But Hoover didn't like stories.

Guttman looked across the room to the large framed photograph of the Justice Building, the building in which they now sat. He said, 'Palmer told me about Sedgwick. When he said the Russians had asked him to spy for them, I asked if there were others they'd recruited. He answered in the affirmative; when I was doubtful he cited Sedgwick as an example.' Palmer hadn't named Sedgwick, of course, but the last thing Guttman was going to do was explain how hard he'd worked to find the banker.

'So you went to see him? Even though I had expressly told you to drop it.'

'I took your memo to mean I should leave the Palmer case alone. I did that. You can check with Reilly of the Metropolitan Police – he was in charge of the case.' Tamm had done just that, he thought.

'I also told you to leave it alone,' said Tolson, speaking for the first time.

'And I have,' said Guttman, adding a perplexed note to his voice. It would be suicide to act guilty; far better to sound aggrieved.

'Then why did you go and see this banker?' demanded Hoover. Never a relaxed man, he was sitting particularly rigidly.

'Because Palmer told me this man Sedgwick had sent money for the Russians to a Japanese bank.'

'Had he?'

'Yes.'

'It doesn't prove anything much now does it? The Russians are hardly likely to be funding the Japanese.'

'Agreed. They were sending the money to a fellow Russian, I think.'

Tolson piped up. 'No law against that.'

'Yes, but Sedgwick admitted that he'd been recruited by them.'

Hoover grew impatient, signalled by a quick stuttering movement of his lower lip. When he was angry his jaw jutted, but it hadn't reached that point yet. 'You say that, but he wasn't spying for them, was he? Sending money for a client doesn't constitute espionage.'

'Yes, but I had both Palmer and Sedgwick telling me the same story. They were suggesting a pattern of subversion I felt I had to explore.'

Hoover shook his head. 'In neither case could they provide any real evidence of anything illegal they'd done for the Russians. That's not all they shared – both were obviously unstable. Both killed themselves.'

Guttman tried not to look sceptical, but failed, and Hoover's teeth were tight as he spoke. 'I have fought the Communists for over twenty years, so I don't need lectures from you about the dangers of subversion. Especially since you can't provide proof of anything.' He was hitting his stride now and Guttman was struck yet again by how Hoover's anger could co-exist with such pompous fluency. 'You've been on a wild goose chase, Guttman, and I'm baffled as to why. Anyone would think you were a rookie. Or that you had some other agenda we don't know about. I have to wonder if you may have an undeclared interest in this.'

'What sort of interest?' He tried not to sound annoyed.

'I know your spouse isn't well, but she used to keep some pretty dubious company.'

Guttman bristled. 'That was years ago. She was young, just a student. And she was never a Party member.'

Hoover shrugged. 'Either way,' he said, then paused.

Guttman waited for the coup de grâce and found himself grinning despite himself.

Hoover mistook his smile for smugness. He barked, 'I don't find this amusing, Assistant Director. You have some friends in high places, as we're both well aware, but believe me, I am not one of them. You have done good work on occasion, but I think you overestimate your importance to the Bureau. Be that as it may, I am not going to fire you or suspend you.'

Then Hoover said, 'But I want you well away from this office and from opportunities for further trouble-making.'

Guttman's puzzlement must have shown.

Hoover continued: 'I'm sure we're in agreement about the need for you to focus on your duties as head of SIS. Being closer to those operations will only help you serve the Bureau, and your country. I have spoken with the Director of Naval Intelligence. Rear Admiral Anderson agrees that an augmented Bureau presence in Mexico would be valuable to their own counter-intelligence efforts there. So you are to transfer to Mexico City as soon as possible, and not more than ten days from now.'

This was a high-level equivalent of 'being sent to Butte', long the graveyard for agents Hoover had no reason to fire, but wanted to get rid of anyway. Guttman knew that if he refused he *would* be fired, and without the benefit of anything that might help build a future – no final pay-off, no guarantee of decent references.

He said quickly, 'I understand.' He was thinking on his feet. 'If I could have a little more than ten days I'd be grateful. I'll have to make arrangements for my wife.' What could they be? he wondered. Life for Isabel was grim in Arlington, but manageable. Mexico City would be impossible. It was starting to sink in that he was effectively being fired after all.

Hoover gave a curt nod. 'Very well. Mr Tolson and I are planning a visit to California next month. When we return I'll expect you to be in Mexico. Now,' he said, as if strictly ordinary business had been conducted, 'anything else?'

Guttman must have shaken his head, but he was not even aware of it.

'Good,' said Hoover. He reached for his phone, adding in a final aside, 'You'll still be reporting to Clyde.'

'And my reports?' Guttman asked quickly, before Hoover could be diverted by Helen Gandy.

Hoover held the phone in mid-air. 'They'll stay the same. Only now you'll be closer to them.'

'Especially your football player,' added Tolson with a smirk.

25

REACHING HOME, STILL reeling, Guttman suddenly remembered that it wasn't one of Annie's nights. He was disappointed. Mrs Davis had never been much of a conversationalist and Annie had been a welcome contrast. He could use a distraction right now.

Mrs Davis had already left and he found Isabel in the living room in her wheelchair, a blanket over her legs. He brought her through to the kitchen and made supper while she read the paper, mainly in silence. He browned some floured pieces of stewing steak in a skillet, softened onions in a pot, then added the beef and chunks of carrot and potatoes along with a pint of water and a bay leaf. His mother had made it often enough when he was a boy, though there had been no bay leaves on Delancey Street.

'That smells good,' she said as the stew started to bubble on the burner. 'You haven't told me about your day.'

He tried to shrug. Lately he'd taken to talking about his work in more detail than before. He didn't know why. Maybe it was to share as much as he could before she wasn't there to share it with.

Now his side of the exchange was going kaput as well, though he decided not to tell her about Mexico. The bad news could wait, until he had some good news to balance it. Like what? A department store post as Head of Security?

He told her, elliptically, about the Russians instead. No mention of Sedgwick, none of Palmer's fate – why burden her with the violence of that? Instead he explained his own view that the Russians, far from being allies, were actively spying in the United States, and he wondered to himself when he would hear from this latest confessor, Braddock Larrabee.

When he'd finished, she smiled knowingly. 'You were never very practical, Harry.'

'Why's that?' he asked.

'The Russians aren't our enemy right now – no wonder Mr Hoover can't get worked up about all this. Does anyone else agree with you at work?'

He shook his head regretfully. 'Tamm doesn't seem to care. They're all busy chasing Nazis. Nothing wrong with that. I'm doing it myself in Latin America.'

'But you're really after the Reds instead. It's a good thing we got married or you'd be hunting me down.' Her breathing was forced.

'That's not fair, Isabel. In your heart, you were always on the right side,' he said. She'd never had any illusions about Stalin. He thought she was dreaming when she claimed that Trotsky would have been a more democratic leader, but at least she hadn't ever fallen for the avalanche of propaganda coming out of the Soviet Union during the Thirties. The Popular Front in the US had fallen apart when the CP had refused to criticise the Soviets' treaty with the Nazis in 1939, and Isabel had been able to say *I told you so*. Not that there had been anyone but Guttman to tell, confined as she was.

She said, 'I think you mean I was on the right part of the wrong side.'

Guttman pretended to growl, then said, 'I just don't like what Moscow seems to be up to. They must think we're all naive – and dupes. Maybe they're right: nobody else at the Bureau seems to see it.'

She laughed now. He was pleased.

'Harry, Harry,' she said, 'it's how you've always been.

You never bother to get anyone on your side when you're sure you're right.'

'Well, I'm sorry about that,' he said stiffly.

'Don't get shirty. I wouldn't have you any other way.' She stared at Guttman's tie. 'Though that's got to go to the cleaners – you've put a stain there while you were cooking.'

'So how was your day?' he asked, not wanting to talk about work any more.

'Fine, Harry. Nothing unusual, but nothing bad either. I saw the man in the yard again.'

'Oh,' he said. She had been making perfect sense until now. 'What time was that?'

'A little before you got home. Mrs Davis had already left or I would have called her.'

'What did this man look like?' Better to humour her, he thought.

'Tall. He was over at the side of the fence. I don't think he saw me looking out.' She seemed proud of this, though equally she sounded unalarmed.

'I'll have a look after supper,' he said and got up to check the stew.

After their meal he helped Isabel to the living room to listen to the radio while he washed the dishes, then picked up the big paper bag of trash from under the sink. Collection was the following day, and he'd lug the garbage cans in the garage out to the front sidewalk so he wouldn't have to do it in the morning.

But when he opened the back door and stepped onto the flat unbalustraded porch, he set the bag down. Was Isabel imagining this man she'd now seen twice? She must be, he thought, since what would he be doing there, snooping around? No burglar he knew of cased a place so obviously. If this man were not a phantom

– Guttman remain convinced he was – then wouldn't he come to the front door, ring the bell and state his business?

He decided to play it carefully nonetheless. He walked slowly to the fence at the end of his backyard. Lights were on in the house behind, casting a faint luminescent line across the boundary. When he turned back he realised his own house threw out even less light, and he vowed again to install an outdoor bulb by the kitchen back door.

He had moved past the small circle of turf where he had planted the ill-fated maple, when he heard something moving by the back of the garage. He stopped, listening hard. There it was again – a rustling, scratching sound. He wished he had his gun, but he'd taken off his jacket and in shirtsleeves would have had to go outside with a weapon in his hand.

'Someone there?' he called out, trying to sound resolute. He waited as the faint echo of his words receded, but heard nothing.

He took a few steps closer to the garage. 'Who's there?' he demanded, half-convinced that no one was.

There was no reply. It was probably nothing, he thought, or else just rats or a raccoon. But he was sufficiently on edge that he decided to go back into the house and get his gun before taking the garbage out. It seemed ridiculous, but he didn't care – he was scared.

'Harry, where are you?'

It was Isabel at the back door. How on earth had she managed to get there?

'Just coming,' he said, worried she had somehow stood up and now would fall. Then he heard the scratching again. As he started to turn around to look back at the garage something hit him from behind. Like a hard punch, Guttman thought as he stumbled forward, his shoulder feeling leaden and heavy. The impact coincided with a dull flat crack that was like – like what? *Silencer*, he suddenly thought just as he heard the flat noise again.

The side of his head felt on fire. This time he didn't merely stumble, but fell forward, just as Isabel shouted again from the back door. She's still got lungs, thought Guttman proudly, as he landed on the grass, breaking his fall with his arm. His last thought was to wonder if the shooter was going to come closer and finish him off.

Part Seven

Santa Barbara and Los Angeles
Mid-November 1941

26

IT TOOK ALL morning to reach the ranch. When Nessheim had started from home it had already been humid and warm, but the coastal highway was much cooler. It wriggled along the edge of the Pacific, so close that spray from the waves splattered his windshield. The road was a remarkable feat of engineering, he realised, since it rarely climbed or twisted through the adjacent hills, but stuck like a limpet against their base, just above the incoming tide.

He stopped halfway at a lay-by of landfill pushed out like a pie which the diggers had excavated from the hillside. He got out of the car to stare at the ocean, where the waves were throwing enormous white-topped curls against the shoreline rocks, like a glamorous woman tossing her hair.

In Santa Barbara he stopped again, filling up with gas and checking his oil and water. He'd skipped breakfast at home after discovering the milk had gone off and he'd run out of bread, so now he ambled over to a neighbouring roadside stand next door where a Mexican sold him a tortilla filled with chopped hamburger meat, chillies and onions. Tacos, the Mexicans in LA called them, and Nessheim wolfed his down, taking pains not to stain his suit. He'd brought a clean shirt for dinner and a hat – a panama he'd got in San Francisco, but he didn't like to wear it when he was driving.

He moved east now, on a new highway called 154, climbing sharply almost as soon as he left town. In the lower parts he passed groves of shaggy avocado trees, the long thin leaves flecked with crimson. There were pastures, yellowed from a summer of sun and dotted with cattle and horses. Then the road steepened; he followed directions and turned off on to El Cielo, then drove onto on a track of packed, dusty sand that gently traversed the mountain, back and forth in an almost imperceptible ascent. The terrain up here was more barren and the mix of trees that lined the meadows below – conifers and peeling red madrone and bay laurel – gave way to stand-alone specimens, mainly oaks. The papers said more people were migrating to California than the rest of the states of the Union combined, but out here Nessheim could only think there was plenty of room. Especially if most of the migrants were hell bent on Hollywood and dreams of a movie career.

The track itself suddenly climbed sharply and, as he came to the top of a ninety-degree bend, dipped down into a small valley which sat like the folded underbelly of the mountain. There were trees here, too, including a large stand of jack pine the track cut through, and as he emerged out of its cooling shade into the glare of a now overhead sun, he could just make out a collection of low-level buildings a quarter mile ahead. As he drove closer he saw that one of them was larger than the rest, and must be the ranch house; the others were a mix of low hay barns and sheds, without the shade that a little copse of taller oaks provided the main residence. At one side a pond not much bigger than a football field sat like a spilt pool of black ink, glittering in the sun.

There were two cars parked in the shade by the house, and he drew up next to them. He got out, wondering if the other guests had yet to arrive and wondering why he had been asked. At the front door of the long, adobe-faced house he raised its heavy brass knocker and banged it hard against the dark panels of the door. He waited but no one came and he looked around. From one of the sheds a door opened and someone came out. He was a short Chinese man, wearing black trousers and a short-sleeved white shirt. Nessheim reckoned it was ninety degrees in the shade, and even this high there was no breeze.

As the Chinese man approached, Nessheim said, 'I'm looking for Mrs Mukasei.'

'You are who?' the man asked.

'Nessheim.'

'The others gone to town. But Mrs M say you come join her.' The Chinese man pointed down past the sheds and Nessheim could see a row of whitewashed stables and a dirt-packed corral.

'Mrs M say you riding. You better give me jacket.'

Thankfully he hadn't brought his holster and .38. Nessheim took his suit jacket and handed it over. As the Chinese servant headed back to the house, Nessheim set off towards the barn, trying to think when he had last ridden a horse. It had to be fifteen years, he reckoned, when the Karlbergs, his parents' nearest neighbours, had briefly kept two mares.

He found Mrs Mukasei inside the barn, dressed in Western jeans, a man's shirt she had tucked into her pants, and no make-up as far as he could see. It didn't matter: he found her face attractive precisely because it was so frankly unadorned. It wasn't a hardened set of features – those were for Hollywood's aspirant actresses, once they'd learned that advancement had less to do with talent than with the casting couch – but you felt nonetheless that this woman had seen a lot.

She was saddling the second of two horses, an Appaloosa. The other was a grey. 'Agent Nessheim!' she exclaimed when she heard his footfall. 'You have made it.'

'I hope I'm not late. And I hope you won't keep calling me Agent Nessheim.'

'You are Chimmy then?' Her face was handsome rather than pretty, but Nessheim found her attractive.

'Most people just call me Nessheim.'

'I hope you don't mind, but everyone has gone to lunch in Santa Ynez. It's that way,' she said, pointing north. 'We can join them if you wish, but I thought you might enjoy a ride.'

'I'd like that,' he said. It would not have been his first choice on such a hot day, but she'd saddled the horses already. 'I'm a little rusty.'

'So am I. I did not learn to ride with a saddle. You had better take the grey. The Appaloosa seems to be in love with me.'

They rode out slowly, heading north through the little valley where the ranch was situated, then up a trail that climbed gently through a stand of tanbark oaks and pines. Elizaveta sat easy in the saddle and had a natural seat; Nessheim, used to his Wisconsin neighbour's ancient mare, found the grey tricky, fighting the bit each time he pulled the reins.

When they emerged from the trees side by side they faced a stretch of meadow grass before the terrain climbed to a high ridge. It looked like rich grazing land, but didn't hold a hint of green. Most grasslands in California were yellow eleven months of the year, but after the lush greenness of Wisconsin it was still a startling sight.

Elizaveta looked at Nessheim. 'I will race you,' she said, and slapped the Appaloosa's mane with the doubled-up reins. He watched as her horse took off, then he broke the grey into a canter which with a bit of urging turned into a steady gallop. But the Appaloosa wasn't going to be caught, and when he reached the bottom of the trail on the far side of the meadow, breathing hard, Elizaveta was waiting, looking triumphant and cool. She grinned at him. 'For a rusty rider you are doing well.'

They climbed the ridge single file, working back and forth against its steep side. The trail was narrow and rocky, and Nessheim paid attention, since to stumble here would be no joke. As they rose, the grassland gave way to sage scrub and the dry mix of chaparral. The odd madrone tree grew out of the sandy soil, and twice the path meandered around sandstone boulders that must have been too big to move.

Just as Nessheim was wondering when the climb would end, they turned a last bend and reached the top of the ridge. Elizaveta pointed behind them. He turned and saw the Pacific in the distance, sky blue in the blistering sun. Down below, nestled between the shore and the first sharp rise of hill, lay dotted little dice-like cubes he recognised as houses. 'Santa Barbara,' said Elizaveta.

She turned her horse and he did likewise. To the north, a long wide valley stretched for miles below them, punctuated by small rises and dotted by large stands of trees. Far away an even higher mountain range ran at an angle, its peaks like jagged teeth.

They sat for a moment just looking. 'So tell me about yourself, Jimmy.' She said it matter-of-factly, as if the time for small talk was over and they had to get down to business. Inwardly he groaned.

'You know what I do for a living,' he said hesitantly.

She flapped a dismissive hand. 'I don't mean your work. I mean you – the person. How did you get here?'

He knew she wasn't asking if he'd come by Highway 154 or Route One, but he was uncomfortable with anything more. Yet her manner was such a mix of insistence and seemingly authentic interest that he felt obliged to try. So he started, awkwardly, explaining that he'd grown up on a farm.

'Your own?' She seemed surprised.

'Well my father's, though he rented some of it out. He also owned a store in town. He lost them both.'

'Ah, were they seized by the Government?'

Nessheim shook his head. 'No – they just went bust. The bank took them, not the Government.'

'Did it happen to other farms where you lived?'

'Lots.'

'Did the owners starve?'

'Starve? No, I don't know anybody that actually starved.'

'Are you sure?' she challenged.

'I'm sure. Why?'

'One heard tales of hunger,' she said.

'That was true enough. But not starvation.'

'I thought perhaps it was your form of propaganda. In the Soviet Union sometimes the papers were allowed to say of a place, "people have been hungry". That meant corpses were stacked like firewood in the fields.' She laughed bitterly and looked at Nessheim intently. 'I think I have still a lot to learn about your country. But I like it, even though there are so many lies. "Buy a Packard and be happy,"' she said, lifting her voice to a radio ad's pitch. 'Such nonsense. But at least you don't have to believe it. No one goes to prison if they don't. I like that. Though no true Communist could like Los Angeles.'

'And you do?'

'Absolutely.' She put a finger to her lips to indicate it was a secret, then laughed. 'Don't you?'

'Not much.' He thought of his beautiful drive that morning, thought too of San Francisco, where he had lived very happily if impatiently (he had been waiting for a special assignment) for two years. 'I do like California.'

'So we are not so far apart.'

'What about you? Are you a farm girl?'

She shook her head. 'City girl. But very poor. We had to move to Tashkent in order not to starve.' She laughed at the thought. 'If you knew Tashkent, you would know how bad off we were – no one would go there out of choice. But come, I have something to show you.'

They rode along the ridge for half a mile or so, then followed a trail down the north side, trotting now, down and up until they came through a stand of pine and there, in front of them, were the ruins of a colossal house. More than one house – Nessheim counted seven buildings, or what had once been buildings since all that remained were foundations and a few half-walls made of sandstone, charred black by fire.

'What was it?' asked Nessheim.

'A rich man's mansion. Then a nice lady bought it for her friend, only it burned down five weeks later. Very sad,' she said, for the first time with a false note. 'Her friend was a woman friend,' she added meaningfully. 'She is an opera singer – have you heard of Lotte Lehmann?'

'I've even heard her sing.'

'You are a lover of opera?'

'Can't bear it,' he said.

She laughed. 'So why have you heard this woman sing?'

'A girlfriend took me.' Stacey Madison's rich parents had a box at the Lyric Opera House in Chicago. Nessheim had gone once; he'd had to rent a penguin suit and make polite conversation with Stacey's mother, who seemed happy to discover that her daughter had at least one friend who wasn't a Communist. At

intermission Mr Madison had bought him a weak highball and admitted that he couldn't stand opera either.

'You must have been in love,' Elizaveta said teasingly.
'Or was it lust?'

'A bit of both,' he admitted.

'I think you are something of a lady's man, Agent
Nessheim.' And she looked delighted when he blushed.

They dismounted and she took off a large saddle bag
while he tied up her horse to a thick bay laurel. They
walked over to the ruin of the big house. Enough of
the ground-floor walls remained to indicate the different
rooms. It had been a big place and the largest room
– which must have been the living room – was a good
forty feet long. It sat in the north-west corner of the
site and had the best view of the Santa Ynez Valley to
the north. Elizaveta sat down on the low remaining part
of the outer wall and took out parcels wrapped in brown
paper, two tin plates and two tin mugs, and a bottle of
California wine. 'I hope you are hungry.'

She handed him a sandwich – pork loin between slices
of rye bread studded with caraway seeds and slathered
with a sour mustard. She set down some garlicky pickles
and small roasted beets with their stems still attached
so they could be eaten by hand. She poured red wine
from the bottle, after handing it to him so he could pull
out the cork, which she'd partly pulled out before. 'Is
it okay?' she asked as he took a sip, and he nodded.
She said, 'I like wine, but there isn't much of it in Russia.
Just vodka.'

'Where I'm from everybody drinks beer.'

They ate in silence until she sat back against the remains
of a sandstone pier, looking out over the long valley of
golden-coloured grass speckled with green by the occasional stand of trees. She said, 'It is hard to believe that
at this very moment Russia is covered with snow.'

'They say it should help your side.'

'I hope so. But it can't be easy being a soldier there, whatever your side. My husband is itching to get back and fight, but the authorities say what he's doing here is more important.'

'Do you want to go back, too?'

She lowered her chin shyly onto the front of her shirt. 'Would you think less of me if I said no?' Before he could reply, she added, 'I hate the Nazis as much as anyone – I hate them as much as the Jews do.' Her voice was protesting and Nessheim felt the urge to reassure her, but reassure her about what?

'But . . . ?' he asked encouragingly.

'I am not a counter-revolutionary, Agent Nessheim,' and she smiled. 'But I am not a great believer in Comrade Stalin either. I know too many people he has wronged – too many sent to camps, too many even executed for not believing enough. Yet it is amazing how many still believe.'

'Like your husband?'

She started to speak, then bit her lip and nodded grimly.

'What exactly does he do here?' He looked determinedly into the distance, miles away where the valley gave way to the towering San Rafael Mountains.

'As you know, he is the Vice-Consul,' she said. She added with a deliberately thick accent, 'Is important job, no?'

'*Da*,' he said.

'Good pronunciation.'

'It's the only Russian word I know.'

She pointed at the remaining food. 'If you do not eat that pickle, Nessheim, I will.'

When they returned to the ranch the Santa Ynez party was back – there were half a dozen cars by the house.

Nessheim helped Elizaveta untack the horses and then walked up towards the pond and the other buildings. Elizaveta said, 'Let me show you where you are staying tonight. I hope you do not mind it is not in the main house – there are not so many bedrooms.'

He got his bag from the car while she waited, then she led him along the edge of the pond towards a group of mixed oaks and pines. Nestled in a break in the trees was a small clapboard cabin with a sharply pitched roof.

'Mrs Willems says this is for bachelor guests. But I hope you will be comfortable. There's a bath inside, but if you want a shower there's one outside, behind the cabin. Or have a swim in the pond – the water is warm. I'll leave you now – I want to make sure everyone else is settled in. Drinks are at five thirty, but do please arrive when you like.'

His cabin was simple but well appointed, with a desk and chair, a big dresser and watercolours of the Santa Ynez Mountains on the walls. The bed was cedar-boarded and stretched under the window, which was hooked open with a screen to keep out mosquitoes. The Chinese man had left Nessheim's khaki suit jacket draped over the pillows.

A door in the rear led to a bathroom, which had a big tub with claw feet and brass taps. From a rickety basin Nessheim drew and drank a tin cup of the water, which must arrive straight from the mountains.

He stripped off and rubbed the long scar that ran down the right side of his chest. It was itching, as it was wont to do in the humid heat. Taking a towel from the bathroom he found the shower, a rudimentary affair with water running from a pipe that came out of the cabin. There was no soap, but he washed himself clean in the cool water that fell in unsteady streams from the rusty head. He was tired from the riding and stiff, so after drying off he went and lay down in his cabin, wearing just his boxer shorts, since the day was still warm. He read some more of Hemingway's *To Have and Have Not*, finding it oddly dissatisfying. There was something phoney about the novel's adventures, as if Hemingway's hero actively wanted trouble. Having seen more than his share, Nessheim no longer thought it was something worth looking for.

Drinks and dinner were in the main house, which had a long comfortable living room with views of the pond. At the room's far end the Chinese man stood in a waiter's coat by a makeshift bar. As Nessheim entered, Elizaveta came over, followed by Mikhail. She introduced them and the two men shook hands as Elizaveta went to talk with the other guests. The Russian was as tall as Nessheim and dressed in a thin grey corduroy suit with a white dress shirt and polished black ankle boots. He had a hawk nose, curved like a scimitar, and eyes that never seemed to blink. There was an intensity to him that was accentuated by the leanness of his physique and he held himself with the stiffness of a Crown Prince at court. He said, 'I apologise for not greeting you when you arrived. But Elza said you had an excellent ride.'

'Yes, thank you. What wonderful country around here.'

'Yes. The Willems are very kind to let us use it in their absence. But excuse me – I believe I heard a car.'

Nessheim took a bourbon and water from the Chinese man, with lots of ice in a tall glass. He was impressed by the ice – there was no way electricity would have got this far up the mountainside. The lamps in the room held light bulbs, so there had to be a generator somewhere.

He took his drink and turned back to the room; a couple came up and introduced themselves – the man was named Nick and was a writer at MGM, and his wife Jean was an actress under contract to Paramount. They'd been to the ranch once before, they said, and Nick asked what Nessheim did. He hesitated, not sure how to respond. 'I'm working now at AMP,' he said and left it at that.

'Ah, for the legendary Buddy Pearl,' said Nick.

'Legendary?'

Jean swirled her drink. 'Nick really means notorious but is too polite to say so.'

'Honey,' warned Nick.

Nessheim said, 'Don't worry, I don't actually work for him. Feel free to speak your mind.'

'That's big of you,' said Jean sharply.

Her husband rolled his eyes. 'The Mukaseis brought a bottle of vodka along. I fear my wife has mistaken it for water.'

A door opened at the far end of the room, next to a little hall by the front door, and a couple entered, followed by Mikhail again. Suddenly a *frisson* ran through the room like a charge of electricity, intangible but somehow *there*. Jean turned around, as if on command, and Nick tried not to stare but failed, tried not to stare again, and failed again. When Nessheim looked over he saw a dapper middle-aged man, wearing a suit and open-collared shirt, standing next to an absolutely stunning young girl. She wore a tight-fitting silk dress that showed off her precociously good figure. She had deep dark eyes, a cutie-pie dimple in her chin and dyed hair the colour of corn silk. Nessheim would have assumed she was the older man's daughter if they hadn't been holding hands in an interlocking grip that didn't look remotely paternal.

The man let go of the girl's hand to greet Elizaveta and Mikhail, and the girl eyed the room with the innocent confidence of someone very pretty and very young. When her eyes got to Nessheim they lingered for a minute and he smiled at her – she smiled back. It was then he looked at her companion and realised it was Charlie Chaplin. What was he doing here? And where was his wife, Paulette Goddard?

Jean said, 'I didn't know Charlie had *two* nieces.'

Nick spat an ice cube back into his glass and started coughing. Jean turned to Nessheim and said, 'Are you here because of John?' He was about to ask who John was, but then he understood. Waverley had entered the room. He saw Nessheim and nodded. But didn't come over.

Dinner was in a room next door with two silver candelabra hanging over a long table covered with a white linen tablecloth. Here the Old West met new money: the plates were china, the cutlery silver, the wine glasses had been hand-blown, but the food was ranch-style and they helped themselves from an old oak sideboard – steak and fried potatoes, boiled squash still steaming in a large crockery bowl. The Chinese man stood attentively in a corner while they served themselves, then returned to the kitchen through a swing door.

At dinner the conversation down the table was loud and political. A tall bald man in a frock coat and a high-collared European shirt was insisting that the workers of America wanted to join their Russian comrades in the fight against fascism, but were being prevented by Western capitalist bosses sympathetic to Hitler. It sounded like the editorials of the *Daily Worker*, and about as interesting – even Mikhail could only manage a polite nod as the man went on.

Chaplin was in the middle of the table, next to Elizaveta, and now spoke up. 'The free world is with your countrymen, Mikhail. I hope they know that. If you think a broadcast from here would increase morale, you have only to ask.'

Mikhail nodded, but seemed pensive. 'That is very generous of you. Perhaps when the situation is clearer.'

The writer Nick piped up. 'They say Moscow will stand or fall by Christmas. Is that right?'

'I think so,' said Mikhail. 'I am praying the snow continues.'

'It can't help that you have to watch your back in the east as well. Though I see they've pulled General Zhukov back to Moscow. That's a good sign.'

'Why's that?' Chaplin asked mildly.

Nick looked a little abashed, but ploughed on. 'Well, that could mean the Russians have a secret weapon the Germans don't know about.'

'What do you mean?' Mikhail asked sharply.

'More divisions,' said Nick. He explained, 'If the Russians know the Japs—'

A glass suddenly toppled over at the end of the table and broke, the bowl detaching from the stem. A small flood of red wine surged down the tablecloth.

'God, I'm sorry!' Waverley exclaimed, for it was his glass that had been knocked over.

Hearing the noise of the accident, the Chinese man came in with a cloth to clean up. Nessheim felt an elbow dig into his ribs. He turned to find Chaplin's girl looking annoyed. 'It's been getting too serious down there,' she said, rolling her big dark eyes in mock-despair. She smelled of talcum powder and scent. 'Charlie said it would be a fun party,' she complained, brushing her knee against Nessheim's under the table. She smiled flirtatiously. 'So what do you do for fun, mister?'

'Oh this and that,' he said.

She giggled. 'Let's start with this,' she said and her knee brushed his again.

The Chinaman was picking glass from the table, bringing a halt to conversation at the far end of the table. Nessheim gave the girl his full attention.

Her name was Suzette and he rapidly discovered that she would laugh at anything he said, which was slightly disconcerting since he wasn't trying to be funny. Across the table sat Nick's wife Jean, who smoked more than she ate and leaned over, lipstick-stained gasper in hand, to relate deprecating anecdotes of the famous people she had worked with. Awkwardly for Nessheim she spoke only to him, completely ignoring Suzette. He was glad when they finished their dessert of angel food cake and homemade ice cream and were led by Elizaveta back to the living room, where bottles of liqueurs sat on a tray. When some people went outside to smoke Nessheim joined them, grateful for the fresh air.

He walked over to the pond and looked up at a star-infested sky. The cloudless night was nippy and he reckoned the first snowfall would not be far off back in Wisconsin. He was tired and once back inside he didn't stay up very long – before eleven he went out to his cabin. The party was still going strong. Chaplin and Suzette had retired, but the other guests had gathered around the piano in the living room, and while Nick played show tunes and popular songs they all joined in, fuelled by a second bottle of brandy the Chinaman had brought out. Then Jean did a passable imitation of Billie Holiday's 'Strange Fruit', followed by a Russian folk song that Mikhail declaimed in a sombre bass voice. They were hoarsely singing 'Five Foot Two, Eyes of Blue', when Nessheim made his excuses.

In the cabin he turned off the light and put on

pyjama bottoms but no top – it was cool now this high up, but he was still warm from the main house, where the Chinese servant had lit fires after dinner. He got into bed and lay down on his back, able to see a patch of star-studded sky out the window. He thought of his conversation with Chaplin and realised that for the first time since he'd arrived in Hollywood he had felt star-struck – not on his own behalf, but vicariously for his mother, who loved Chaplin and had seen *Modern Times* three times and would start to giggle whenever she described the movie. In his next letter home Nessheim would tell her about meeting her idol, though he would leave out reference to Chaplin's young companion.

Outside crickets chirping filled the air; in the distance an owl gave a long muted hoot. Nessheim felt suddenly drowsy, the effect of his long ride, and was almost asleep when a whisper came from just outside the window.

'*Chim*,' whispered a familiar voice. Was he dreaming? He shook the drowsiness out of his head as the voice spoke again. 'Nessheim, it's me. Elizaveta.'

'Yes?' he said, fully awake now. He sat up and put his legs on the floor. He could see her face, pressed against the screen window.

'Come for a swim? The water's lovely.' She was still whispering.

'Okay. Let me get my trunks on.'

'You don't have to,' she teased, but her face had moved away from the screen.

He got up and put on his trunks nonetheless, then left the little cabin, making sure its swing door didn't bang shut. In the dark he heard a giggle several feet away. He moved towards it and the giggle moved too. Gradually his eyes adjusted to the night and he could make out the reed beds on the edge of the pond, then watched a white figure in a dark bathing suit walk across the sandy edge and disappear into the water.

He edged his way closer to the landing dock, where the land was clear of growth, and walked out into the water. The sandy bottom fell away quickly and the water was surprisingly warm, almost bath-like; he sank into it without flinching. He swam hard in the direction of the float he'd seen in daylight, breaking his crawl only once to readjust direction.

When he reached the float Elizaveta was already there, standing still in the water with one hand keeping a grip on the slats of the float. 'I didn't think I would win two races today,' she said.

'Race you back and you won't win this time.'

'In a minute. But listen.'

He did, but could hear only the soft clink of a glass and the murmur of voices from the main house.

Then the owl hooted again, like the lonely whistle of a night-time train.

He turned, ready to swim back, but Elizaveta put a hand on his shoulder.

'There's something I want to tell you. One day, not so long from now Mikhail will be going home. I would expect it to happen within the next year. Assuming Hitler does not have his way.'

Nessheim sensed their conversation was on the edge of something. He said pointedly, 'I thought his work was too important for him to go back.'

She shrugged her shoulders, pale in the moonless dark. 'You must know what he does.'

'Intelligence, I assume.' She gave a little nod. 'Is he watching other nationalities – Germans?' He thought of Osaka. 'Or the Japanese. Everyone's scared of the Japanese invading.'

'No, no. It's Americans he's focused on. He's supposed

to influence opinion here. Newspapers, and especially the movies.'

Like me, thought Nessheim. He wanted to ask why she was telling him this, though he was starting to sense where she was headed. He asked, 'What about you?'

'Me?' She took her hand off his shoulder, trying to sound surprised, but Nessheim was sure it was an act. 'I am not important – unless I don't go back.'

'Is that what you'd like?'

She didn't speak for a moment, and when he turned to look at her face, little more than a foot away from him, she nodded, her firm jaw dipping down and up like a see-saw.

'It is probably just a dream to think like that.'

'Why?' asked Nessheim, who had seen some of his own dreams dashed without giving up the habit of dreaming.

'Oh, the usual reasons. I am a wife. Wives do as they are told. To stay would be cowardice when my country needs me. Then my government would be very cross.'

'They'll stick the Bruiser onto you?' he asked.

'That's no joke,' she said grimly. 'But anyway, it would be very difficult to persuade your government to let me stay. The Russian quota's full, believe me, and it's not as if I have much to offer.'

She went quiet and Nessheim felt he had been given his cue. 'You know a lot about your government. That's always valuable. Especially if we become allies,' he said disingenuously.

Before she could reply a voice came from the shore. '*Elza!*'

It was Mikhail and he had a flashlight, though its beam was too weak to reach the float.

'I better go now,' she whispered.

'I'll swim with you.'

'No!' She put her hand again on his arm.

'What's the problem? We were only swimming.'

'*Elza!*' came another cry from the shore.

'So far,' she said enigmatically. Then her hand moved under the water and caressed him lightly on his stomach. 'I would like to see you again. I need you to advise me.'

Pushing off from the float she swam towards the shore in a slow, steady crawl, returning dutifully back to her husband. It was only a hundred yards or so and halfway there she was illuminated by the beam from Mikhail's flashlight, which then followed her all the way in.

Nessheim watched as she stood up in the shallows, then walked towards her husband. Enough light came from the house that Nessheim could see the two, and he could hear their voices as each spoke. The Russian words sounded harsh and loud. It was impossible to tell if they were arguing or merely talking volubly. He could have sworn he heard his name pronounced – '*Nessheim*' – by Mikhail as Elizaveta stood beside him on the grass.

Suddenly he saw Elizaveta move towards her husband and he watched as the tall figure fell backwards, landing with a splash in the water. Mikhail stood up, the water knee high, while Elizaveta gave a loud triumphant laugh. She turned and skipped towards the house like a jubilant schoolgirl, her white limbs slipping seal-like through the dark, while her husband emerged, cursing, from the pond. Nessheim waited until Mikhail had gone back into the house before he swam back to shore, hoping this time he could go to sleep.

27

HE HAD BEEN back for an hour on Sunday night when the phone rang. It was Annie Ryerson. Maybe she had changed her mind about Christmas, he thought. He said, 'It's nice to hear your voice.'

'I'm not calling with good news, Jimmy. It's Harry.'

'What's happened?'

'He's been shot.'

It took a second for it to sink in.

'Is he dead?' He didn't trust himself to say anything more.

'Not yet. They say they'll know in twenty-four hours if he's going to pull through. He's at Walter Reed. He was shot twice – once in the back and once in the head. It's the head wound they're worried about, though they say he's lucky – it missed the main part of the brain.'

'When did it happen?'

'Two days ago.'

'But why – ?'

He stopped himself. Now was not the time to complain that he hadn't been told. He thought guiltily of his time with Elizaveta at the ranch, fooling around by the float.

'Marie tried to reach you, but you haven't been at the Bureau. I don't think she had your home number. So I volunteered. I thought it might be easier coming from me. After all, the three of us have history together.'

'Where did it happen?'

'At his house. Isabel had been saying she'd seen a man in the backyard. Harry went out to investigate, and that's when he was shot. Isabel was inside – she'd got worried and somehow managed to get to the back door, just in time to see Harry shot.'

'Did she see the shooter?'

'Not really – it was dark. They say the gunman used a silencer, so no one heard it.'

'Who's looking after Isabel?' He was asking this dutifully, but knew Guttman's first worries would have been for his wife.

'I am. Don't worry – she's okay. Just worried and waiting. Like the rest of us.'

'Do the police have any clue who did it?'

'Not that I know of. There were Bureau people here all day – lots of men with brushes.'

'That's for fingerprints,' he said dully, envisaging the scene. He doubted there would be any evidence left by the shooter. It sounded like a professional job; an amateur wouldn't use a silencer.

As Annie kept talking, Nessheim thought of his last phone conversation with Guttman just a few days before, when Nessheim had called him from home. They'd joked about whether Guttman would authorise the payment for his phone bill. Then Guttman had said, 'Schultz is dead.'

'Max Schultz?' Herr Schultz as he had insisted on being called when Nessheim worked for him at one of the *Bund*'s youth camps in Vermont.

'They found him in his cell in Sing Sing.'

'Tears as big as horse apples are rolling down my cheeks.'

Guttman laughed and Nessheim asked, 'Do you think someone bumped him off?'

'Nope. It was natural causes.'

'Too bad.'

'That's the good news. The bad news is that his car may have been used by whoever killed Thornton Palmer.'

Nessheim said, 'Do you think the *Bund*'s involved?'

'I don't know. But it's making me nervous. I may have some news for you soon. Good news. Just be patient.'

He'd heard that before – he'd stayed in San Francisco for over a year investigating fraud cases while Guttman told him to be patient.

Guttman said, 'And I want you to watch your back, okay?'

'I was watching anyway.'

'Watch it double-time then.'

Now Nessheim contemplated the irony that it was Guttman who had needed to be extra careful. Could the *Bund* have shot him? It seemed improbable – the brotherhood was a spent force now, most of its leaders in jail, most of its followers fallen away. Even the Nazis had disavowed the home-grown American variety, preferring to try and put their own people in place in America and make their own Fifth Column.

Though the Nazis would have wanted Guttman dead. As head of Investigations he had set snares that had caught a lot of Germans trying to operate in America. It didn't help either that he was a Jew.

Now Nessheim said to Annie, 'Would you keep me posted, please?'

'Of course I will. Are you all right, Jimmy?'

'Sure,' he said automatically. He felt awkward and oddly guilty as the image of Elizaveta in her bathing suit during their midnight swim came to mind. *I didn't do anything*, he told himself, then wondered why that mattered. Annie didn't want him.

Then she said, 'I'm sorry about Christmas.'

There was a pause.

'Sure,' he said finally. 'Let me know how Harry gets on.'

* * *

Trauma had never filled Nessheim's dreams, which were usually happy and uncomplicated. But this night he felt haunted as a succession of faces flitted in and out – Ike larger than life behind his eyrie's desk at the casino, followed by the younger Pearl lifting the Hispanic maid, Anita, up in both arms. She was naked. Teitz appeared by the pool house at Pearl's, laughing merrily, only to be replaced by a tall male figure who turned away to hide his face. In the dream Nessheim grew agitated as he decided this must be Osaka, and he raced around the swimming pool, desperate to find out for sure. But as he approached, the figure turned and he found himself staring into the face of Mikhail Mukasei.

He woke up in the early dark hours – his clock said it was only four o'clock. He lay there, trying to sort out this confusion of images, and found to his consternation that he couldn't for the life of him picture Osaka's face. He could see the man walking along the street, flicking his straight black hair out of his eyes with a carefree hand. But the face eluded him. It was as if the mystery of Billy Osaka's whereabouts extended, like the swipe of a chalkboard's eraser, to Nessheim's memories.

Rafu Shimpo occupied a storefront on East 3rd Street in Little Tokyo, a few blocks from the Satake Bank. There was a Japanese girl at the counter and he explained what he had come for. She asked him to wait and went through a pair of swing doors to the rear. As they opened he could see the three editorial desks, covered with papers, and behind them a large printing press that looked like a Victorian piece of ironmongery.

He stood waiting at the counter, which had a stack of the latest issue. He leafed through a copy's English language section, noting that none of its bylines were Osaka's. An editorial caught his eye. It urged readers – in a time of growing tension between America and Japan in the Pacific – to remain loyal to their new country. *Nisei*, in particular, it argued, could have no dual allegiance. Now was the time for all good Americans – of whatever descent – to stand up for their country.

'I'm Togo Tanaka,' said a man as he came through the swing doors. He looked in his mid-twenties and had a floppy fringe of black hair and crew-cut sides.

Nessheim showed his badge. 'I've been looking for Billy Osaka. I wondered if you had a photo of him – he had a press card, didn't he?'

'He did, just in case he had to get through a police cordon or chase a fire engine somewhere. Hang on a minute.' He went back through the swing doors and returned a minute later with a small mugshot in his hand, which he gave to Nessheim.

Nessheim peered at the small picture. Osaka had had a haircut and the shot made him look even younger than he was. He stared at the camera intensely, as if daring it to expose him.

Tanaka said, 'You can have that.'

'Thanks,' said Nessheim, and he put the mugshot carefully into his inner breast pocket.

'You phoned a while ago, didn't you?'

'That's right. Any news of Billy?'

'We haven't heard from him in weeks.'

'Did you know him well?'

Tanaka smiled. 'I got him his job. We were both political science majors at UCLA.'

'Is Billy a good reporter?'

'When he bothers to file.' He spoke with an air of fond chastisement.

'I read the latest editorial,' Nessheim said, pointing

to the paper he'd just skimmed through. 'Was that Billy's view too?'

Tanaka hesitated. 'Pretty much,' he said, then pursed his lips as if to ensure they stayed shut.

'How was it different?' He realised he had spoken in the past tense.

'I'm not saying it was. But he knows a lot of people who are siding with Japan.'

'Do you think he may have gone back to the Islands?'

Tanaka said, 'I doubt it. His folks are dead, and he doesn't have a lot of friends in Hawaii. He never did.'

'Not even from high school?'

'Billy didn't go to high school in Hawaii.' Tanaka looked at him quizzically. 'He's *Kibei*. Someone who goes back to Japan for their schooling.'

'I know that.' Nessheim added with a hint of suspicion, 'Are you *Kibei* too?'

'Jeez no. I can't think of anything worse.'

'Why did Billy go back, though?'

Tanaka thought for a moment. 'I guess his mother wanted him to. Funny, since she wasn't Japanese herself. She probably thought he should know his roots.'

'Would that explain why he knew so many nationalists?'

He was guessing now, but Tanaka nodded slowly. 'Partly, I guess. Though when it came down to it, Billy's always wanted to be a hundred per cent American.' He hesitated, then said reluctantly, 'Look, the thing about Billy is that he's kind of wild.'

'So I've gathered,' Nessheim said. 'Was he in trouble when he disappeared?'

Tanaka gave him a look. 'Tell me when he isn't in trouble.'

'Money?'

'It's always money or women or both.'

'Whatever it is, I need to find him – and before some other people, if you catch my drift.'

Tanaka considered this, then shrugged. 'He came to me early in the summer. He said he was desperate. I'd heard it before, but this time I believed him – he had some gambling debts and he was going to get his legs broken if he didn't pay up. This was a new one for Billy – usually it's nickel-and-dime stuff he owes. If I gave him a sawbuck that would take care of things. But this time he needed a lot of money. I'd have had to mortgage my folks' house to raise it. So I had to say no.'

'What happened?'

'Oh it got paid, just not by me.'

'When was that?'

'The beginning of August – I know for sure because my birthday's August 2nd.' He gestured towards the printing room. 'We had cake in the back and Billy came in – he was filing stories again. He pretended that he'd known it was my birthday. When I asked if he was okay he said the problem had been taken care of.'

'By who?'

'Billy's got this girl. She's head over heels for him.'

'You mean Hanako?'

'The very one.'

'But she doesn't have that kind of dough,' Nessheim protested.

'Maybe she mortgaged *her* parents' house.'

Under Hoover, most of the Special Agents were either CPAs or had passed the Bar, and the qualification often (though not always) steered the kind of work they did – if someone had been passing bum cheques in seven different states it was usually an agent with accountancy credentials who took on the investigation.

In the LA Field Office there was also one accountant

agent, a little dark-eyebrowed man named Gordon, who did the internal bookkeeping – he sat in a windowless room with an assistant who so resembled his boss that Nessheim found it hard to tell them apart. Both were in the office when he knocked on their door, and both ·were happy to answer his questions. He realised that just because they sat day after day, shut in with only numbers for company – everything from payroll to expenses – it didn't mean they didn't yearn for a glimpse of the external world.

He walked back to Little Tokyo feeling better equipped for another visit to the Satake Bank. But at the bank he discovered to his consternation that Hanako had not only resigned from the bank, but had left town altogether.

'She went to Chicago,' announced one of the *Nisei* grocery girls who spoke fluent English.

'Do you have an address?'

The girl shook her head. 'She said she'd write once they were settled.'

In Hanako's absence Mr Satake had not miraculously acquired any English. Nessheim asked the girl to help.

'Tell Mr Satake I'm asking about money coming from New York again.'

She translated and Mr Satake gave his reflexive smile, though Nessheim detected a hint of weariness behind the grin.

'Ask him where the telex machine is, please – you know, the teletype.'

This time Mr Satake looked embarrassed. At last he mumbled something.

'He says we don't have one,' said the girl.

'Ah. Then ask him if he uses the one around the corner.'

Once translated, this had Mr Satake nodding eagerly.

Nessheim laughed, glad at least one of his hunches had paid off. 'Tell him I am most grateful and I won't need to bother him again. Though if anyone hears from Hanako, please inform me at once at the headquarters of the FBI.'

Hearing this, Mr Satake beamed. Nessheim sensed he would have agreed to anything to get this *ganja* out of his private office.

The Yokohama Speccie was unambiguously a bank, uncluttered by its near-neighbour's array of fresh vegetables and bottled soy sauce. It was a squat building, two storeys high but without a second floor – you walked into a large space made larger by a cavernous dome on the ceiling and by ridged pillars that went up to the roof. Nessheim was reminded of the Midwest, where even in the Depression the grandest buildings in small towns were their banks.

A young vice-president named Kinemi, in a banker's black suit, white shirt and sombre tie, saw Nessheim at once. He spoke perfect English. His office had a glass wall that let him watch the customers in line at the tellers. Nessheim explained his mission and the man nodded.

'Fifty thousand – I remember that. We have some well-heeled customers, but that's still a most impressive amount.'

'Is there any chance the fifty would have been split up? I mean in transmission.'

'Not only a chance – it definitely would have been split up. You see, twenty-five is the limit for our bank receiving money, so it would have come in in two lots.'

'Could you tell me how it was split?'

'Give me a minute,' said Kinemi, and went out of the office. When he came back he was holding a paper in his hand. 'Here we go,' he said, handing it to Nessheim.

The mess of codes meant nothing to him. 'I'm sorry but can you help me make sense of this?'

'That's easy enough,' said the young banker, reverting to his professional persona. 'There are two sets of codes, see, for two separate tranches of money. One was going to the account of a Mr Lyakhov at the Satake Bank.'

'I've got that one. It's the other tranche I'm trying to find.'

'It's not that different. Just a cashier's cheque this time.'

'Also for Lyakhov?'

'Of course,' said Kinemi casually. 'It would have to be – the money was wired for Lyakhov.'

'But then why would they treat the two payments differently?'

Kinemi looked bemused. 'Because the Satake Bank – his bank – asked us to.'

'Miss Waganaba?'

'Who?' Kinemi looked puzzled.

'The chief teller of the Satake Bank.'

He was still puzzled. 'It was Miss Yukuri who handled it.'

'Hanako Yukuri?'

'Yeah. But what's the problem?'

'Could she have cashed the cashier's cheque?'

'Sure,' he said. 'Anyone could have. That's how a cashier's cheque works.' He looked questioningly at Nessheim.

'Just one more thing. What was the date of this transaction?'

Kinemi looked flustered for the first time, but it was an innocent reaction, Nessheim realised, as the Japanese banker pointed to the sheet still held in his hand.

'It should tell you right there,' he said.

Nessheim looked down and saw the bank's stamp: **Aug 18 '41.**

Sixteen days after Tanaka's birthday party. So why had Hanako diverted $25,000 when Billy had told Tanaka his problem had been dealt with?

28

HE DROVE BACK to the studio on Wilshire because he liked the boulevard's adolescent palm trees and the sense he got, looking at the new stores, that the city was spreading like spilt milk outside the confines of its dense downtown. When he got to the studio, feeling guilty about his frequent absences, he relaxed when saw that little filming seemed to be going on. As he was waved through by Ernie, the usual traffic of grips, cameramen, extras and make-up artists was nowhere to be seen outside Studio One.

In the Ink Well Teitz was alone at his desk in the office he shared with Stuckey. He had taken off his tie and it sat on his desk like a motionless butterfly, blue spotted with white polka dots. With his shirt open at the neck, Teitz looked older. He was pouring Four Roses bourbon from a pint bottle into a coffee mug when Nessheim knocked on the open door. Teitz's hand jerked and a slurp of whisky hit the desk. 'Shit,' he said without emotion, then added a steadier half-inch into his mug.

'Starting early today?' asked Nessheim mildly. It was only four o'clock.

Teitz stared at him. 'What's it to you?' he asked.

'Not much,' said Nessheim.

Teitz softened. 'Sorry, Jim. Bad day.'

'Something happen?'

'The powers that be don't seem to share my sense of self-worth,' he said grimly. 'My contract's up at Thanksgiving. They've renewed me –' he began, then paused.

'That's good, isn't it?'

'—until Christmas,' said Teitz. He sang, cheerfully, in a decent imitation of Bing Crosby:

'Come the New Year
I'll be out on my ear.'

He stopped and said, 'Pearl's got great ambitions – hell, you must know that, Nessheim. He has this FBI movie in mind that's supposed to carry the place into the big time.'

'Can't you work on this big picture?'

Teitz dropped his chin and looked at Nessheim dolefully over the tops of his glasses. 'I think it's a little late to recast me as a lead writer, Jim.'

'Maybe, but they're bound to need some rewrite men. They always do.'

'The Count has never been a fan of my work.'

'It may not be the Count directing. Let me put my ear to the ground and find out.'

'Would you? That would be swell,' said Teitz, without sounding hopeful at all.

'There's something you can help me with in the meantime. I'm still looking for that kid Osaka.' Teitz looked at him without interest. 'I've been round the houses, but no luck. I remembered you said he had an eye for the girls.'

'Yeah?' Teitz said cautiously.

'Older women. I distinctly remember you saying that.' He ignored Teitz's shrug. 'You made it sound like he'd had a couple of close calls. With husbands, I mean.' He laughed, hoping it didn't sound like a phoney guffaw.

Teitz perked up. 'He never got caught red-handed, if that's what you're asking. If he had he wouldn't be breathing today.'

'I don't know if he is breathing today.'

Teitz looked shocked as this sunk in. After a moment Nessheim said, 'What I was wondering, if you don't mind my asking, is how you knew this. I mean, were you friends with the guy?' Teitz seemed about to protest when Nessheim raised his hand, 'Don't tell me. Everybody knew Billy. I understand that. But I didn't realise you knew him well.'

'I didn't. Not well. But we used . . .' He waved an arm towards the hall. 'You know the Ink Well.'

'What does Billy Osaka have to do with the Ink Well?'

Teitz looked at him. 'But I'm sure I told you. He worked here.'

'*Here?* At AMP?'

'Yeah,' said Teitz, a little flustered. 'It was three or four years back. He was just a runner on the set – he'd fetch water and take messages. Nice guy. Everybody liked him. I'm surprised you didn't know that.'

'Was he active on the older lady front while he was here?'

Teitz shrugged, but it was an evasive movement of his shoulders. 'I'm not going further than that, Jim. Could be more than my job is worth.' He gave a quick, grating laugh. 'Not that my job's worth two bits come Christmas.'

'Your luck will change,' said Nessheim, realising where he had to go next. 'Where's Lolly by the way?'

'Studio Two as of yesterday, my friend.' He looked accusingly at Nessheim. 'I'd have thought you knew that too, pal. She's got a role in the mice movie.'

He didn't want to know. No doubt the Count was directing.

He said, 'I forgot.'

*   *   *

On his way home he stopped at Latham's, a grocery store on Hollywood Boulevard. After his trip to Santa Barbara he was short on supplies. He bought a small porterhouse steak from the meat counter, figuring he might try and barbecue at the weekend. A barbecue for one, he supposed, since he didn't think Lolly was going to want to see his house after all. It didn't bother him now; instead he kept thinking about Elizaveta, wondering if she would be in touch with him soon. She had been friendly but formal when he said goodbye on Sunday, maybe because her husband had been standing next to her, watching them with what seemed to Nessheim a careful eye.

He also picked out some fresh broccoli and leaf lettuce and a bag of mixed fruit (oranges and grapefruits and peaches), amazed as always by the produce you could buy in California year-round. At home there would be apples, more apples, and pears – if they'd kept that year. The only other fruit would be preserved – he thought of his mother's tutti-frutti, summer fruits put in big glass jars with brandy, and pickled peaches in sugared vinegar with cloves and cinnamon sticks. For vegetables, there would be cabbages for sauerkraut, and maybe an acorn squash or too. And that was it. Yet something about this Californian cornucopia seemed awry, like Christmas in the southern hemisphere.

When he got home he put his groceries away and opened a bottle of beer. He was about to go out to the garage to find the barbecue when the phone rang.

'Is that Agent Nessheim?'

'None other,' he said as the line crackled, then he tensed as he understood it must be a long-distance call.

'It's Marie in Assistant Director Guttman's office.'

'We've met, Marie.' As you well know, he thought. 'How is Harry?'

'He's still in a special ward, but they're talking about moving him any day now. They let me see him today for the first time.' She seemed to relax a little over the transcontinental line.

'Is someone looking after Isabel?'

'Oh yes. Miss Ryerson goes over and calls to let me know. His wife's fine. Well not fine, if you know what I mean, but not any worse.'

He was glad someone was looking after Isabel, but discomfited that it was Annie, though he didn't know why.

'There was something else I needed to speak to you about, Mr Nessheim.' She sounded nervous again.

'Call me Jim,' he said.

'Okay, Jim. The thing is, when Mr Guttman had his . . . accident, he'd been typing up some notes. They were for you. He asked me today to make sure you got them.'

'Why don't you mail them to me?'

'That's the thing – he doesn't want them to go by any normal route. He gave me strict instructions about that.'

'Oh,' he said, baffled.

'He wants you to go see Agent Devereux next week.'

'Devereux?' A friend and fellow agent at the San Francisco Field Office. Nessheim hadn't seen him since he'd come to LA. A good guy, straight as a die, but with a sense of adventure – and a love for a party that meant he wasn't going to make SAC while Hoover was in charge. He'd got engaged last time Nessheim had seen him, but Nessheim hadn't heard if he'd got married yet.

'Mr G said, "Tell him to make any excuse he has to, but to make sure he goes and sees Devereux." And Mr G said you were to take your other driver's licence.'

'Other driver's licence?'

'Yes. Those were his exact words. I hope that makes sense.'

'It does, Marie,' he said finally. Not again, he thought, since he knew all too well what this could involve.

In the Ink Well, Lolly's replacement had left three messages on his desk, all scrawled at a left-hander's curious angle, all telling him to call a Mrs Mooksigh. He dialled the number with a mix of apprehension and excitement. Down boy, he told himself.

'Elizaveta, it's Nessheim.'

'You got my messages?'

'Yes.'

He waited awkwardly, not sure what he was supposed to say or do. After the late-night swim in the pond he'd realised she was interested in him, but he couldn't gauge how much was personal and how much he was meant to be her conduit to the US authorities, who might let her stay if her husband went back. Whatever their difficulties it was hard to see how Nessheim could insert himself as a third party to their domestic arrangements and still try to sort out Elizaveta's status as . . . what? Another informant. A defector – that was the term, he thought.

She broke the silence. 'It would be lovely to see you, Nessheim.'

'Likewise.'

'I have a lot to tell you. Have you mentioned our conversation with your superiors?'

'Yes,' said Nessheim. It was only a white lie, he told himself. He would have told Guttman if he'd been able to speak with him.

'And what was their reaction?'

'They want to know a bit more. You can understand

their caution. Your country may soon be an ally in a war, and relations with the US are friendlier than they've ever been before. There's even a rumour Roosevelt is going to extend Lend Lease to your country.'

'So the last thing they want to hear is bad things about a new friend.'

'I wasn't saying that, but they need to know a little more about you.'

'About me or about the information I'd bring?'

'Both,' he acknowledged.

'I see. Is this what you Americans call B.S.?'

She was miffed, but he had nothing more tangible to offer. Not professionally at least. He said, 'You know I'm not like that, Elizaveta.'

He could hear her exhale. 'I know. It's not why I was calling anyway.'

'Oh,' he said, wondering what could be more important to her.

'I was hoping to see you. Privately, I mean. Not about business. The Willems are still away – but they do like those horses to get exercise.'

'When?' he asked, ignoring the mental red flag that was trying to catch his attention. I'm not a fool, he told it.

'I was thinking next week. How would Thursday be? If you took a day or two of your vacation, we could stay through the weekend.'

'Elizaveta, I'm sorry but I'm going to be away then.'

'Anywhere nice?'

'Could be,' he said elliptically, not that he knew himself. Damn, he thought. He could not think of anything much nicer than two nights alone with her at that beautiful ranch. Fleetingly he considered postponing his trip, but then dismissed the idea. He could get up north and back in a couple of days max. He was going to tell her this, but something restrained him. He had better see Guttman's instructions before he promised to be anywhere else. With Guttman you never knew; Nessheim might find himself travelling to Washington or Chicago or even Alaska before he saw LA again.

29

A ROW OF pepper trees lined one side of North Bentley Avenue, with low branches that hung over the sidewalk like a riverbank willow. Nessheim parked further down the hill, then walked and waited under one of them, shaded from the descending sun and from view, resting against a drystone wall that bordered the front of one of the big Bel Air properties. He heard a shout and, turning, saw two kids there, throwing a football on a lawn the size of two gridirons.

He tried to be patient as he waited now, his back turned to the playing kids, telling himself this was unfinished business he needed to wrap up before he went north to San Francisco. But it was another twenty minutes before he saw the small, dark-haired figure moving down the hill. She really was very pretty, he thought, as he watched her again, striding on strong brown legs in the sunshine down the hill from the tree-shaded edge of Pearl's property. He thought of Elizaveta, her sudden touch in the pond.

She was only ten yards away when she saw him. She started at first, then looked straight ahead and kept walking. He pushed off from the drystone wall.

'Anita, I need to talk with you.'

She kept going.

'I don't work for Mr Pearl, Anita. I'm with the FBI.'

This time she stopped. Peering in under the over-hanging branch, she regarded him with distaste.

'Why are you bugging *me* then, G-Man?'

'Just a couple of questions. It won't take two minutes.'

Her sigh was undramatic, but sounded heartfelt. He

sensed he was in a long line of white men who had pushed her around. She ducked under the branch and joined him. 'I don't want to be seen talking to you. I'm on thin ice already.'

'Because of TD? Is he still . . . bothering you?'

She snorted. 'Is that what you call it – bothering?' She laughed again, without inviting him to laugh as well. 'But the answer's no – TD's got himself a girlfriend now. Some actress.'

'Good for TD. But that's not what I wanted to ask you about. His father was looking for a guy – suddenly he's not looking any more. I need to know why.'

She gave him a fierce look. 'How would I know about that? You think Mr Pearl told me his secrets while he was breathing heavy in my ear?'

He took the photo of Billy from his jacket pocket. 'Was this the guy?'

He could see at once that she recognised the picture.

'Does Mr Pearl know?' he asked.

'About what?'

She looked at him with a pretence of innocence, but there was something in his gaze, fixed and not willing to be deterred, that seemed to sink home.

Eventually, she nodded.

'And he went bananas?'

She nodded again, more quickly. 'But Missus denied it and Mr Pearl couldn't prove it.'

He thought about this momentarily. 'Listen, Anita, I think Pearl was after this guy. I know the fella. He's not a bad sort.' Then he added softly, 'All I want to know is whether Pearl found him.'

'I don't know. All I know is that all summer long Pearl and his wife were arguing, but now they're love-birds again. If you ask me I think something's happened to make it okay between them. He keeps talking about a big picture he wants to make.'

I bet he does, thought Nessheim.

'You want a ride home?' he asked, trying not to look at any part of Anita except her eyes.

She looked at him as if he'd said something comical, then shrugged. 'You think there'll be something at the other end?'

'I'm just offering you a ride,' he said and she smiled sceptically.

They stepped out together on to the unshaded pavement and he motioned towards his car down the block.

She nodded knowingly, then suddenly her almond-shaped eyes widened and she jumped back under the overhanging branch. He looked up and saw a blue convertible speeding down the hill. It was flying and at the wheel he glimpsed a handsome woman in sunglasses, a scarf knotted round her throat. Mrs Pearl.

He watched as the car went down the hill.

'You can come out now,' he said cheerfully.

Anita looked shaken as she emerged into the sunlight again.

She said, 'I think I'll take the bus home.'

30

SATURDAY MORNING HE worked in the yard, since he was taking the train north to San Francisco the following day. He raked leaves and lit a bonfire of them – the wind was favourable, blowing the smoke away from Mrs Delaware and down the hill towards Hollywood. He went in and showered but didn't shave, then changed into light khaki trousers and a blue-and-white cotton short-sleeved shirt – it was already in the high seventies according to the radio.

He got the car out and drove to Hollywood Boulevard, where he parked down the block from the barber shop. As he approached it on foot, he saw there were two squad cars outside, and a crowd gathered in front of the rotating candy-cane barber's pole. A tall cop stood in the doorway of the shop, barring the way. Peering past him, Nessheim could just make out a figure in the nearest chair, the one where Nessheim had been planning to get his shave. Whoever sat there had been covered down to the waist by a barber's sheet, which was soaked in big splotches of darkening blood. The floor around the chair was slick with it.

Outside on the sidewalk he saw Albert and the other barbers standing with a policeman, who was taking notes. Seeing another cop, standing by a patrol car, he went up to him.

'What's happened?'

'Read the paper tomorrow and you'll find out.' The cop raised both hands to shoo him away.

'I'm with the FBI.'

'Sure, and so's my sister.'

'I work with your sister. So now will you tell me what happened?'

'You got a badge?'

'No, I'm off duty. I was coming here to get a shave.'

The cop seemed to relent slightly. 'Be glad you weren't here earlier, then. Anyway, Homicide's arrived. He can tell you what happened.'

They were joined by Dickerson, the same detective whom Nessheim had seen at Mrs Oka's apartment.

Dickerson said, 'We meet again. You here for the Bureau this time too?'

'Nope. I was just coming for a shave.'

'So was the stiff. Guy named Lapides – did you know him?'

'We both came here on Saturday mornings. That's about it.'

Dickerson said, 'Kind of strange, don't you think?'

'How's that?'

'Any way you look at it, this spells a mob hit. I mean, a guy comes into the barber shop and sits down, even though there's a chair going. Says he wants to wait for Albert, who's busy with a shave for another customer.

'Then a minute later another guy comes through the door, carrying a .45 the size of your arm. He covers the room, while his friend gets up, takes the razor out of Albert's hand and slices the throat of Mr Lapides like a butter pat. Then they both stroll out of the place, cool as cucumbers.

'This Albert fellow – he's the owner – says the stiff worked in insurance. Lapides lived two blocks away – a couple of kids, nice wife, not much money but they got by. So why does he get his throat slit?'

'Maybe he sold a bad premium.'

'I read that book too. But this Jimmy Lapides

didn't sell insurance; he was a clerk in the payroll department.'

Nessheim glanced over at the barber shop and the sheet-covered corpse. 'Have you talked to Mrs Lapides?'

'Not yet. But if Albert's got it right, she's not exactly femme fatale material.'

The beat cop spoke up, without looking at Nessheim. 'One of the other barbers said the killer asked if the guy was "Jimmy".'

'That was Lapides's first name,' said Nessheim. He didn't like where this was heading.

'The barber said he was called Jimmy One.'

'Yeah,' said Nessheim.

He was about to explain when Dickerson interrupted, 'I'm wondering if the killers screwed up. If Lapides was Jimmy One, then I'd like to find Jimmy Two. I'd put a dollar on a dime it was him they were looking to ice.'

Part Eight

Oahu and Molokai
Late November 1941

31

'I HOPE YOUR trip's been worthwhile,' said Robert
Shivers.

'It has,' said Nessheim. He put down his bag. 'Thanks.
And thanks for showing me the ropes.'

'You better get a move on. You don't want to miss
this flight – the next one's a week from now.'

They shook hands and Nessheim picked up his
pea-green duffel bag. He walked out of the terminal
into the curiously flat sunshine. It seemed to fall from
the Hawaiian sky like a daily coat of paint. There was
a light sea breeze, which exuded a mild perfume of palm
and salt air.

He ambled towards the dock where the Pan Am
Clipper waited. He walked down the steps of the ramp
slowly, towards the open door behind the Boeing 314's
cockpit, where a stewardess was waiting. He didn't
know if Shivers was one of those flying buffs who liked
to watch planes take off, but turning round at the
bottom of the ramp he was relieved to be out of sight
of the terminal.

'Welcome aboard, sir,' said the stewardess. She had
bright white teeth that filled her smile and was wearing
a grey-blue, naval-style jacket and skirt. Nessheim
wouldn't have minded spending eighteen hours travelling
in her company.

He shook his head. 'I'm sorry, miss, but I won't be
flying after all.'

She looked taken aback. 'Is there a problem, sir?'

'Family illness. I've just been paged in the terminal

– it looks like I'd better stick around.' He lifted his duffel bag. 'This is my baggage – nothing to unload.'

'Are you sure?'

'I'm sure. I'd never forgive myself if my mother died before I could get back here. Don't worry – I'll sort out my ticket at the desk inside.'

Concern had replaced her surprise. 'I'm so sorry. I hope your mom gets better soon.'

He stayed on the dock for a good five minutes after the Clipper took off to the west in Pearl Harbor, watching as the great double-decker bird dipped its heavy wings and, slowly turning, lumbered towards California. Then he walked back to the terminal.

There was no sign of Shivers. Nessheim found the men's room and went into one of its stalls. There he stripped down, replacing his suit and tie with cotton trousers and a light coat which had deep side pockets – in one of them he put a taped roll of spare ammunition for his .38. He left his wallet in his suit jacket and swapped his polished Florsheims for a pair of ankle-high canvas shoes. He kept the gun and holster on and exited the stall with his bag, checking for any telltale bulge in the mirrors above the row of basins. Satisfied, he left the men's room and walked over to the lockers in the terminal. Opening one, he crammed in his duffel bag and slotted a dime into its lock, then pocketed the key.

Outside he hailed a cab from the waiting line and told the Hawaiian driver to take him down to the fishing docks. The driver sighed, since the commercial harbour was virtually next door. They passed the edge of the naval base, then moved slowly along the fishing marina, its jetties thrusting out in neat lines from the raised embankment of the shore. At the seventh dock he had the cab pull over, paid the driver, tipping him well, and waited until the taxi had driven off. Then he went back to the first dock off the quay.

Here a fishing boat named *Moana Two* was idling, a solitary rope wrapped around a stanchion on the dock all that kept it tied to the shore. In the boat's open cabin a broad-shouldered Hawaiian with long black hair stood at the wheel. He nodded once, and Nessheim undid the rope and tossed it into the well, pushed the bow away from the dock, then made a quick jump into the boat. Seconds later the pilot throttled down and they surged out towards open water, as Nessheim perched on a flat bench on one side of the hold in the middle of the open deck. There was a faint, slightly sickening smell of dead fish and diesel fumes.

They moved into the water of Mamala Bay, then a few miles out turned south-east and ran parallel to the shoreline of Oahu. To their left Honolulu sat in a cluster of low buildings, mainly houses, that stopped at Diamond Head, the long volcanic ridge that lay like a sleeping lion, its head slightly raised, towards the east end of the island.

As they gradually left Oahu behind them Nessheim lay down with his back against the boat's side. The waves were low and regular, and *Moana Two* cut across them in a lazy chop. Nessheim dozed, using a life preserver as a pillow, trying to make sense of the events of the past week.

He had left LA on a Friday night for San Francisco, taking the Southern Pacific *Lark*. Since the train was all Pullmans, he got a sleeper to himself. He wasn't worried about the expense – that wouldn't get him into trouble; it was the trip itself that would. He'd done his best to cover for himself: at the studio he had left a note for Lolly's dimwit replacement, saying that he had been called to Wisconsin on a family emergency. He figured this would give him seven days' cover when you included the train time to the Midwest and back. As for Hood and the local Bureau, he was crossing his fingers that they wouldn't have any reason to contact him while he was gone.

His roomette was small (the bed folded down from the wall) but comfortable, and on the left side of the train as it moved along the coast. He sat up for a while, not going to the fancy dining and lounge car in case he met someone he knew; instead he tipped the porter fifty cents to bring him a ham sandwich and bottle of beer. West of Santa Barbara, the tracks moved close to the ocean, and as a half-moon moved in and out of cloud he caught glimpses of the Pacific Ocean, rough and unsettled as it moved in on the tide.

He sat gazing towards the shore, wondering where Guttman was sending him this time. He was glad to be out of LA, where puzzle seemed to devolve into puzzle – the more he discovered the more became unclear, a kind of learning process in which he took one step forward and got shoved two steps back. If Ike's debts had been paid off for Billy before the wire transfer of money from the East, then why had half the fifty grand been diverted by Hanako into a cashier's cheque? Who was this Lyakhov and what did he do with the other twenty-five grand?

He thought, too, of the gruesome corpse at Albert's barber shop, wondering if it could really have been a case of mistaken identity. For the first time since Billy Osaka had disappeared, he felt real fear, which was enhanced by guilt over the murder of Jimmy One, who he was certain had not been the intended target.

He had arrived in San Francisco at nine in the morning and gone straight in a taxi to Devereux's house. It sat off Ocean Avenue on a side street that ran sharply up towards Monterey Heights, in an area which even in Nessheim's time there had started to be developed. The lots were filling up quickly with new builds, and Devereux's house had neighbours on either side.

The door was answered by a young woman who introduced herself as Devereux's fiancée, Mona. Explaining that Devereux was busy at the Bureau, she took Nessheim into the living room, which had a bay window with a view of the Pacific down the hill, almost two miles away. On the sofa Devereux had left a large manila envelope. Nessheim sat down to go through it and Mona disappeared into the back of the house. She seemed slightly suspicious of Nessheim and though he hadn't expected a brass band, he could have done with a cup of coffee. At least she was tactful enough to leave him alone with the envelope.

Its instructions were detailed, particularly about the Kalaupapa Peninsula on the island of Molokai, where he was to make contact with agents of the Japanese. He was going to conduct the rendezvous which Popov had failed to make, and his instructions replicated the procedures Stephenson of the BSC had arranged for that missed contact in July. At the Bureau Guttman alone knew of Nessheim's mission. Popov was persona non grata since his disastrous meeting with Hoover, and any operation emanating from the double agent would have never received the Director's approval.

As instructed, Nessheim put the notes back and left the resealed envelope on the sofa, then went and found Mona in the kitchen, where he asked her to phone a cab. While they waited, she warmed up slightly, probably because he would be going soon, and told him about her plans for the wedding that spring. She said that after they were married she and Devereux hoped to move up the hill, where the houses were swankier and the lots larger. The Devereux whom Nessheim used to know would have laughed at this kind of aspiration, but there was a certainty in Mona's voice; it suggested that either his old friend had discovered career ambition, or he was going to soon. It explained, too, why Devereux hadn't been there to greet him: he must be uneasy about his role as Guttman's intermediary – rightly so, since he wouldn't be working for the Bureau much longer if this were discovered.

The terminal on Treasure Island was a vast U-shaped Art Deco building that had been built for the World's Fair two years before. It had a curved concourse that faced west towards San Francisco; next to the main building were the ramps for the flying boats, and behind them the hangars for the aircraft when they were out of the water. Inside, at the wood-panelled Pan Am reservations desk, Nessheim had found a ticket waiting for him. A colourful poster on the wall, 'Fly to the South Seas Isles', showed an enticing picture of palm trees, smiling Polynesian girls greeting passengers, with the *Honolulu Clipper* in the background.

Less than three hours since arriving at Third Street Station, Nessheim took off again, the *Honolulu Clipper* calmly gathering height over the Golden Gate Bridge, flying west towards the sun. Only three of the ten seats were occupied in his compartment, which had thick turquoise carpet and pale-green walls, and was curtained off. A woman in a powder-blue dress and hat to match was playing cards with her companion on the wide table in front of them both; a man in a suit who looked like he'd never voted for a Democrat in his life was reading a copy of the *San Francisco Examiner*. It was luxuriously peaceful. Later on, in the dinner lounge, Nessheim settled down at a table laid with silver cutlery and bone-china plates, and examined the thick card menu, handed to him by the steward in a white uniform.

It was a long flight, slow-paced to conserve fuel, since there was nowhere between California and the Islands to land. When the plane came down at last, almost eighteen hours later, it gently skimmed the surface of the Pearl Harbor loch and idled towards shore, until the pilot turned off the engines as they reached the dock. When Nessheim disembarked, two hula girls stood under one of a dozen palm trees, ready to welcome the new arrivals with fragrant *leis*. He skirted them politely and walked into the terminal, a converted beach house. There was another one next to it for baggage and other cargo. It was midday in Hawaii.

Nessheim had taken a taxi into downtown Honolulu, which seemed as sleepy as Madison, Wisconsin, and not much bigger. He got out at the corner of Hotel and Bishop Streets, half a mile from the beach, and went into the grand-looking Alexander Young Hotel, which had white awnings along its block-long façade. It had over two hundred bedrooms, which would make it easy to come and go unnoticed.

After checking in, he napped for an hour, then changed into a light cotton suit before walking to the Honolulu Field Office. The one request he'd made of Devereux, relayed through Mona, was to send a telex, alerting Shivers that he was coming and citing Guttman's author-isation, although Guttman was still in the hospital.

Shivers turned out to be a soft-spoken Southerner, whose office had Venetian blinds tilted to keep out the high hot sun, a bookcase full of legal texts, a photo of FDR on one wall and a smaller one of Hoover on another.

'I got news you were coming,' he said, sounding cordial. 'What's this all about?'

Nessheim explained what he was doing in Hawaii, and Shivers nodded at first, as if this were reasonable enough. Then he asked, 'Does SAC Hood know you're doing this?'

An early Rubicon. Nessheim couldn't duck the truth, not when ten minutes' teletype would expose him.

'No.'

Shivers weighed this up with a frown.

'The cable said you work for Harry Guttman now.'

'Yes. He would have sent the wire himself, but he's out of commission.'

Word of the shooting must have reached even this remote part of the Bureau; in the LA office there had been talk of little else. Most people there thought the Nazis had plugged Guttman – Cohan, perversely, had opined it was the work of the Brits.

Shivers said, 'It's a damn shame. I've never met the man, but I've always heard he was crackerjack. So I figure he knows what he's doing sending you here.' Again he paused, then said questioningly, 'You wired me before from the LA office, asking about this fellow Osaka.'

Nessheim nodded. 'And a cousin of his, who's called Akiro. He's originally from Hawaii too.'

'It must be something extraordinary these two are up to, if Guttman doesn't want to use the local field office to investigate.'

Shivers sounded slightly peeved, but then nobody liked it when Bureau HQ sent someone in to step on the toes of the local agents. Nessheim said, 'I think it's more a case of their activities occurring in multiple locations. I believe Mr Guttman thought it would be better to have one agent following them to different places, than several agents trying to tie the story together.'

Shivers stared at him and finally shook his head.

'Well, I'll let you get on with it then,' he said in a resigned voice. 'You let me know if there's anything I can do to help.'

Nessheim made very little progress for the first two days. The Osaka home turned out to be a modest bungalow, north of the US naval base at Pearl Harbor, on a street grandly named Maypole Avenue that petered out in a cinder track. The actual house had been sold twice since the death of Billy's mother and the latest owners didn't even recognise the name. The neighbourhood seemed transient, a mix of first- or second-generation Japanese and Filipinos, with a smattering of Chinese and Hawaiian natives. A few people recalled Osaka's mother – she had stood out as a white woman in the district. But no one claimed to have known her well. Billy himself was only dimly remembered; his high-school years as a *Kibei* in Japan meant people in Honolulu wouldn't have seen anything of him for over a decade.

Nessheim also went to the county courthouse in search of Billy Osaka's birth certificate. It was a classical building, covered in white stucco that shone like toothpaste in the bright sun. But inside they were reorganising the archives, and after a fruitless hour combing through a disorganised mountain of files on the floor, Nessheim gave up.

This part of the trip was starting to feel like a big waste of time, but then three days in he found a note from Shivers at his hotel, inviting him to dinner at his house that night. When he showed up at a pleasant brick-and-board ranch house on Black Point Road, close to Diamond Head, he'd been surprised to find that Shivers was a relaxed host, who handed over a lethal glass of Planter's Punch before Nessheim had even got through the front door. Mrs Shivers came out from the kitchen, wiping her hands on her apron. She was trailed by a Japanese girl, who Nessheim figured was the cook.

They all shook hands and Mrs Shivers introduced the girl as Sue Kobatake.

'Sue lives with us. I guess you could say we adopted her.'

The Japanese girl gave a little bow and smile, then retired to the kitchen with Mrs Shivers.

Nessheim sat down with Shivers in the living room, which had family photographs on a pedestal table and watercolours of the Islands on the walls. There was a huge arrangement of brightly coloured Hawaiian flowers, which Shivers proudly named: red-leafed anthurium, white plumeria, yellow ilima, and blue-and-gold bird of paradise.

'That little gal you met just now,' and Shivers gestured towards the kitchen, 'her blood is a hundred per cent Japanese. Yet all she wants is to be an American – she's even changed her name from Shizue to Suzette. And she's taking American citizenship. I'm hoping she'll go to college on the mainland if war doesn't break out.'

'Are the other Japanese here like that?'

'Pretty much. Oh, there's a minority who want the Emperor installed on Waikiki Beach. But we know who they are, and if war breaks out we'll know what to do with them. What I keep telling Washington is that the others are completely loyal. I wouldn't draw up the lists they wanted.'

Nessheim thought about the rosters the LA office had

been compiling. The same lists Osaka was supposed to help create. Things were clearly different here.

Shivers refilled their drinks from a jug on the little bar he kept in a corner of the room. Sitting down he asked, 'So how are you getting on finding this Osaka fellow?'

Nessheim told him the truth, then said, 'I'm going to turn to his cousin next. He may have had more contacts here. There's a chance he had a rap sheet, too. He's a bit of a low life, from what I've managed to find out.'

'Then you'd better take a look down by the harbour.'

The next day Nessheim had walked the waterfront. He dipped into two bars, where he found a tough-looking mix of Oriental fishermen and American sailors drinking hard. Then he saw a place that looked more promising, for its lettering was distinctly Japanese. *Jin Jin* read the big red neon sign, which was blinking from a faulty bulb.

Inside, he peered down a long dark room, which had a heavy teak bar running along one side. The wooden blades of two big ceiling fans circled in a lazy stutter, and some rough-looking natives and a Chinese construction crew sat at tables, drinking from bottles of beer. Most of the bar stools were free.

The bartender ignored him at first, keeping his back turned and polishing a whisky glass as if it were a piece of silver. Through a haze of smoke in the rear of the joint, Nessheim could see a group of Japanese in workmen's clothes gathered around a pool table. He heard a cue chalked, the loud click of balls caroming across the velvet, then a curse from the player of the misplaced shot. As the bartender continued to ignore him, Nessheim got the message: he was the only white man in the bar.

'Help you?' the bartender said, turning round at last. There was a native accent to the voice – American with a funny lilt. But he was Japanese, heavy set, with an upper body shaped like a fireplug. He wore gaudy red suspenders over a white shirt that bulged around women-sized breasts, but no one would joke about his boobs once they'd seen his hands, which were the size of catcher's gloves.

'I'm looking for a guy,' said Nessheim, sliding onto a stool to show he was there for a while.

'What, you in love?'

'It could well be,' said Nessheim cheerfully. 'But we haven't met yet – it's an arranged marriage. Why don't you give me a beer while I try and make up my mind?'

The bartender grunted, then drew draught beer from a tap into an angled glass. He whacked the full glass down in front of Nessheim and the foamy head sloshed over the lip onto the bar's wood top.

'Take it easy,' said Nessheim mildly. 'What do I owe you?'

'We'll call it a dime if it's your last one.'

Nessheim reached into his trouser pockets. He took out a ten-dollar bill and flipped it onto the bar. 'I may want another.'

The bartender looked at him warily. His eyes were disconcertingly far apart. 'If you're looking to mix things up, there's three guys playing pool who will help me out like that.' He snapped his fingers menacingly.

Nessheim leaned forward, letting his lapel fall open enough to show his Smith & Wesson. He smiled. 'You can relax. I'll stick to the one beer and there's a sawbuck sitting there that's yours – if you give me a lead on the guy. His name's Akiro.'

The bartender just stared at the bill on the bar. He must have been used to cops. 'I can't take your money,' he said with a mock show of regret. 'Never heard of the guy.'

Nessheim chucked another ten-dollar bill on the bar. 'Does that help your hearing?'

The bartender gave a phoney laugh and Nessheim suddenly realised two players from the pool table had joined him, one on each side of his stool. The one on his right started to raise an arm and Nessheim slipped off the barstool, which was high-backed with wooden legs. He lifted the stool by its seat and poked it straight into the man's face. One of the barstool legs hit home: the man fell, squealing in pain as he clutched one eye. Behind him, Nessheim sensed the other man move and, dropping the stool, he turned and threw a low hard right hand straight into the man's gut. *Whoof!* the man exhaled, like a blowing whale, and crumpled to his knees.

Nessheim pulled his .38 from its holster, just as the bartender lifted a baseball bat from under the bar. The bartender froze and Nessheim said, 'Put that down or you'll be wearing its splinters. Tell your other friends' – he jerked his head towards the pool table – 'that if I see a fly move down there I'll shoot it out of the air. Got it?'

The bartender nodded slowly and dropped the bat. It bounced noisily on its handle, the only noise in the place now, then rolled on the floor behind the bar. Nessheim took three steps back. The man he'd punched was still on his knees, breathing hard; the other guy had one hand plastered to his eye and was starting to moan.

'Let's start again,' said Nessheim. 'There's twenty bucks there if you give me a lead on Akiro. Simple enough, don't you think?'

'Twenty bucks,' said the bartender with false wonder,

then laughed. 'You'd need a lot more than that to catch a man like Akiro. Starting with a ticket to Japan.' He was suddenly looking cheerful. 'Now get the hell out of my bar.'

32

THE NORTH-WEST TIP of Molokai stuck out like the blunt handle of a .25 calibre handgun. The fishing boat slowed about 500 yards offshore and the Hawaiian idled in the swells. He came out of the cabin with a plate of cold rice and vegetables, which he handed to Nessheim with a friendly nod. He pointed to himself and said, 'Hiapo.'

Nessheim grinned. 'Jim,' he said, keeping it simple.

The light was starting to go and instead of moving on Hiapo cut the engines, then came back and threw the anchor overboard. He chucked an old wool blanket to Nessheim.

'Sleeping time,' he said, with a grin.

Within fifteen minutes, just as it grew resolutely dark, Nessheim could hear the sound of gentle snoring. He could see Hiapo lying on his back, his belly moving like a small bellows, and then he too fell asleep.

There was *poi* for breakfast, a disgusting paste of pounded roots which Hiapo served in wooden bowls, and black coffee in a tin mug, along with fresh pineapple chopped with a hand axe. Hiapo started the engine while Nessheim drew up the anchor. They were less than a mile offshore, and the Hawaiian pointed ahead.

'Kalaupapa,' he said.

Then he steered them further out into the Pacific, until the island of Molokai was little more than a distant southern speck.

After travelling east almost an hour – the rising sun straight in their eyes – they moved south towards

Molokai again. As land neared, Nessheim saw a tree-less shoreline lined with lethal-looking rocks, jagged as sharks' teeth. The point of the Kalaupapa promontory, at the northernmost part of Molokai, seemed unbeachable. But when the boat swung around the tip he saw an inlet sweep of honey-coloured sand and a few straggly palms.

About forty yards out Hiapo slowed the boat, turning it while idling until it didn't rock in the gentle swells. He motioned to Nessheim that he should go ashore. He then came over and pointed to his watch. Hiapo moved the hands around until they said six o'clock and pointed meaningfully at them. He said in halting English, 'I will leave then.' He was smiling, but there was nothing flexible in his voice.

They shook hands, then Nessheim clambered over the side of the boat, jumping down to find himself up to his hips in the crystal clear water. It was bathtub warm, which he hadn't expected. A sudden wave hit him from behind and knocked him over onto his knees. His first reaction was that his gun would get wet, but then his left knee hit a razor-sharp rock on the bottom and the pain was excruciating. He managed to stand and hobble to shore. He turned around and shouted, but already the boat was chugging out further to sea, and Hiapo, standing at the wheel, didn't hear him. The breeze had picked up.

He managed to climb the small incline of the beach, picking his way through a crop of small, black volcanic boulders, then stood on level ground to survey the damage. It still hurt like hell, though he doubted he had broken his kneecap or he wouldn't have been able to walk at all. But it was bleeding profusely, just below it.

He took off his coat and then his shirt and ripped a large patch from one of its sleeves. Doubling it up, he held it against the cut to staunch the flow, which slowed and finally stopped, coagulating into a thick, dark paste. He unfolded the patch of cloth and managed to tie it tightly around his upper calf and shin. It wasn't Red Cross standard, but it would have to do.

He put back on what remained of his shirt, followed by his coat, then tried to check his bearings. Facing him over a mile away was a range of spectacularly high sea cliffs, the *na pali* as the natives called the range. Their tops were heavily wooded in deep furrows of thick emerald growth. The *pali* ran in a forbidding line that blocked off access to the rest of Molokai, to the south; at either side of the peninsula they plunged vertiginously down into the Pacific. He saw now why they'd told Popov to come by boat and why he was duplicating those instructions. It was a natural prison. He felt he had just thrown away the key.

A quarter mile ahead a tall lighthouse loomed like a thin, tapered pencil stuck in the flat landscape. He headed towards it, limping now since each step was painful. It took him ten minutes to go 200 yards, and he was sweating profusely, though it was probably only in the low seventies.

There was no one at the lighthouse. A few hundred yards away there was a turf airstrip, which had been laid down in the early Thirties. But its use was confined to the military and Hawaii authorities in charge of the colony of patients and afflicted residing in Kalaupapa; no other visitors were allowed to arrive by air.

He sat and rested on the inland side of the raised concrete platform that surrounded the lighthouse like a collar. At this rate he would be hours late for his rendezvous; actually, he doubted he could even make it to the village, which was over a mile away according to the map he had seen.

Why he was doing all this? Guttman's instructions – or were they Stephenson's? – had been precise about where he was to go, but there had been nothing about *why* he was there other than the general instruction to receive information from the Japanese. He didn't like the vagueness of it one bit and he was in any case finding it hard to concentrate, given the pain in his leg.

From the lighthouse a dirt path led into the heart of the peninsula. The terrain ahead was flat here, though the path looked rocky and was overgrown in places with low, scrub-like bushes. Then he heard a shuffling noise and, turning his head, saw a small Hawaiian boy standing on another path which led to the lighthouse from the west. He was holding a mule by a sagging length of rope and he was staring straight at Nessheim.

Nessheim beckoned, but the boy stayed where he was, still staring. Standing up, Nessheim took an awkward step and pointed to the bandage below his knee. He didn't have to exaggerate to show he was in pain.

The boy came forward hesitantly and Nessheim smiled, trying to look friendly and unthreatening. He gestured to the south-west, then pointed at his chest. The boy looked at him and his eyes widened.

'Kalaupapa?' he asked timidly.

Nessheim nodded vigorously and said, 'St Francis Church.'

The boy suddenly beamed. 'Mother Julia?' he asked eagerly.

'Yes,' said Nessheim. Whoever she might be.

The boy came closer now, tugging on the rope to make the mule follow him. He motioned for Nessheim to move to the edge of the platform, then drew the reluctant animal alongside. Nessheim crouched down, ignoring the sharp pain from his leg, and swinging his wounded limb to the far side clambered onto the mule's back. The boy laughed at the sight of him there, and then set off along the peninsula's central path, leading the mule and Nessheim.

They travelled at the pace of a slow walk and Nessheim tried to ignore the steady throbbing in his leg. From his position astride the mule he could see for hundreds of yards over the open flat of the peninsula. He spotted a pair of wild spotted deer, which bolted when they heard the mule's lumbering tread, and a bright orange-red bird flitted across the sky, picking minuscule flies out of the air with its attenuated beak. Low stone walks were laid across stretches of grassland, which looked unfarmable, though he saw a small herd of cattle in the distance.

The path turned sharply west and soon Nessheim could see clumps of trees ahead, ironwood and coconut palms, plum and papaya. Then he saw houses and knew he was almost at Kalaupapa, since it was the only village on the peninsula.

As he came to the first street he was surprised to find it paved, and more surprised still to see an old Model T sitting in a concrete driveway of one of the bungalows, since the enclosing cliffs meant you wouldn't be able to drive it very far. The houses were one-storey and well built in the Hawaiian plantation style, with shingle roofs, sweep-around porches and encircling verandas. Their boarded walls were sun-faded, the white or green paint half-stripped by the humid air and high rainfall. One larger house had a wooden portico.

The village was bigger than he had expected, and carefully planned: the streets seemed to form a regular grid and the houses sat in neat rows, divided by picket fences, stone walls or thick hedges of lantana in yellows and pink, and some were obscured by the shady fronds of banana trees. There were huge coconut palms and morning glory, hibiscus, lilies and roses; most of the yards contained tidy vegetable gardens. It all seemed part of a concerted effort to look like a normal Hawaiian village.

They were nearing the ocean. He could smell the salt brought in by a breeze that had suddenly come up. Another street over and he heard the roar of the breakers. They passed a row of shops: the grocery store, which had concrete walls and a corrugated roof, a freshly painted white bakery on Damien Road, squashed between a launderette and a bigger building that had a sign offering the services of a carpenter, plumber and blacksmith. A goat was tethered under a flame-coloured Poinciana tree.

They turned the corner and the boy pointed ahead down the street towards the Catholic church of St Francis, a cream-coloured building built of stone covered in rich layers of plaster.

Approaching it, the boy stopped the mule by the entrance and Nessheim got down very slowly, trying not to put pressure on his hurt leg.

'I'm okay,' he said when the boy tried to help. 'Thank you,' he added, wondering how he would ever get back to the boat. He'd have to find someone to take him there, but Nessheim didn't want to ask the boy to wait when he himself didn't know what he was letting himself in for.

The wood door to the church was slightly ajar. He heard music inside and limped in cautiously. There were half a dozen rows of dark wood pews, divided by a thin centre aisle that led up to the altar. At the foot of the tall white pillars on each side of the nave were wide pedestals which held brightly painted, life-size statues of the Madonna and Child and of St Francis.

The front pews were half-filled with people: men and

women and a few children. The men were dressed neatly in white short-sleeved shirts; the women wore skirts and cotton blouses and hats. It could have been a service held almost anywhere, except that this congregation was barefoot and there was no sign of a priest. Instead a nun stood in front of the altar, in traditional black-and-white habit. She was a tall, imposing woman with weathered skin, probably in her fifties. Giving the faintest of nods as Nessheim came in, she and the parishioners were singing the final verse of a hymn.

The hymn finished, the nun took a step forward and regarded her audience fondly.

'Next week we welcome our new priest, Father Patrick, who will be arriving on the supplies boat from Oahu, and at last we will be able to celebrate Mass again.' She paused to let this sink in, then concluded, 'Please bow your heads. Let us pray.'

There was an unusual cadence to her voice and Nessheim realised she was English. The small sea of heads bowed and the Sister tucked her chin down. As she intoned the words of the final blessing, Nessheim's were the only watchful eyes. The instructions had been vague – no mention of the congregation, only the injunction to sit in the last row and wait for the contact.

'Amen,' the nun declared again, and as the heads lifted she signalled that the service was over. The congregation stood up to leave and Nessheim saw them properly for the first time. He tried not to gawp.

These were the lepers of Kalaupapa, the reason for the community's physical isolation. They all seemed to have something terribly wrong with them – a permanently raised eye, a lip curled in an involuntary grimace, a pus-seeping wound on a nose. And scars – so many terrible facial scars, furrows and cuts and lines etched into their skin. As they came towards him, Nessheim

343

saw that many of them were also crippled – toes missing, fingers gone, an arm amputated at the elbow. They moved down the aisle like the wounded retreating from the front line. There was nothing self-conscious about their procession; they barely gave him a glance.

At last the parishioners had all left and the church sat empty and quiet. The nun had disappeared and when she appeared again she entered by the church's front door – she must have gone through the vestry to greet her congregation as it came out. As she passed Nessheim's pew she said chidingly, 'The lepers are not to be frightened of.'

'I'm not scared of them, Sister,' Nessheim said, and realised he hadn't masked his shock.

'Believe me, they are not the worst cases – those will not even come to church, however much I tell them that the Lord sees people only with eyes of love. Many people do not understand. It is why we do not usually have visitors here. Are you of the faith, my son?' she enquired.

'I'm Lutheran, Sister,' he said, with the deference he had always given nuns – the Lutherans had plenty of them.

She tilted her head questioningly. 'I am Mother Julia. Have you hurt yourself?' she asked, pointing at the makeshift bandage wrapped around his leg.

'It's nothing, Sister. A small accident, nothing serious.'

She took a longer look at his leg. Finally she said, 'Excuse me a moment.'

She walked to the vestry and Nessheim sat and waited tensely. His leg was stiffening badly. After a few minutes the door to the church opened and a balding Japanese man came in, then sidled into his pew.

'What's your name?'

The voice wasn't friendly.

'Rossbach.'

'Noritaka,' the man said.

Nessheim nodded. That was the name he had been given in Guttman's instructions, the same person Popov was supposed to have met five months ago.

'How did you get here?' asked the man.

'I came down the cliffs,' he said, as he had been instructed.

The man said tersely, 'We were expecting you months ago.'

'I don't know anything about that. I was ordered to come here now.'

Noritaka wasn't satisfied. 'No one understands where these orders have come from, including Dr Kuhn.'

According to Guttman's briefing, Kuhn was a Nazi who had been sent to spy for the Japanese in Hawaii, but Guttman's instructions had also said that Kuhn would be arrested on espionage charges well before Nessheim arrived here.

He said firmly, 'Dr Kuhn doesn't have any idea who I am. He was detected by American Naval Intelligence last year. They've read his letters, deciphered his cables and watched every move he's made. The last thing we wanted was for him to know I was here. I'd have been arrested the moment I arrived in Honolulu.'

He could see that Noritaka was taken aback.

Nessheim went on, 'You say I'm too late – why?'

Noritaka was silent. Then he said slowly, 'Because the information has already been supplied.'

'I have come a long way, Mr Noritaka. I can't go back without a message for my superiors.'

'The harbour depths won't change, and we know what the tides will be.' Noritaka added impatiently, 'Though you can't expect us to guarantee clear skies. So –' He stopped suddenly, as if he'd heard something.

'Stay here,' he said abruptly. He got up and went out of the church, pulling the heavy wood door behind him.

A minute later the door opened again. He heard a footstep and Noritaka said, 'There's someone else who wants to speak with you.'

There was another step and a rough voice said, 'Is this him?'

Nessheim turned and saw another Japanese man standing at the end of the pew. He had a rifle cradled in one arm – a 30.06, the kind people used to hunt deer back in Wisconsin. He was wiry, with black hair that was cut in the LA style – a shock in front, short at the sides.

For a split second Nessheim thought it was Billy Osaka. But there was a harshness to the face that he'd never seen in Billy's, an anger that put this man at odds with the world. Nessheim realised he was staring at Akiro.

'You had a long trip down the cliffs,' said Akiro.

'It felt that way.' Nessheim said nonchalantly.

'Schwab guide you down?'

'Was that his name?'

'Did he limp?' asked Akiro, watching him with relentless eyes.

'Couldn't say. I wasn't walking so good myself by the end.' He pointed to his leg and said sheepishly, 'I fell off the mule halfway down.'

Akiro ignored this and barked, 'Where's your identification?'

Nessheim reached slowly in his pocket, then pushed his driver's licence down the bench. He noticed Akiro kept his barrel ready to swing round as he reached for the licence. He looked at it and a thin smile creased his face.

'Nicely done,' he said.

346

'The State of Illinois does its best.'

Akiro flipped the licence back to him; when it fell on the bench Nessheim left it there.

Akiro said, 'Is your real name Rossbach?'

'What else could it be?' He tried to sound indignant.

'Someone who's been looking for me in Honolulu.'

'Maybe you're a popular guy.'

'I think it was you.'

'What makes you say that?'

'The description fits.' Then Akiro said, 'Stand up and take your coat off.'

Nessheim started to stand up. Akiro said tensely, 'Do it slowly.' He had raised the barrel of his rifle.

Nessheim kept his hands out in the open and delicately lifted each lapel of his jacket back, then wriggled out of the coat. Akiro stared at Nessheim's gun and called out for Noritaka. When Noritaka came over, Akiro rattled out something in Japanese and Noritaka moved along the pew in front of Nessheim's, taking care to stay out of the line of fire. He extended his arm and carefully fished out the .38.

Akiro laughed sourly. 'You can keep the holster.'

'You didn't expect me to come here unarmed. I didn't know what I was going to find.'

'G-Men carry the Smith & Wesson, not Germans.'

'Ever try to find a Luger in Honolulu?'

Akiro shook his head impatiently. Noritaka said something to him and Akiro replied sharply. Noritaka answered back more mildly and Akiro said something else. It was clear they were arguing – Nessheim figured it was about what to do with him. From the tone of their voices – one decisive, the other uncertain – Akiro wanted to shoot him and Noritaka wasn't sure.

Nessheim tried to calm himself, but saw that there was a good chance he was about to be executed. It seemed so preposterous – he hadn't learned anything on this foolhardy mission – that it was almost enough to still his mounting fear.

The door to the vestry opened and Mother Julia appeared. She looked surprised to see the three men and came towards them.

'What are you doing here?' she demanded. 'You are not *kama'aina* – I have never seen you before.'

'We are staying at the Japanese clubhouse,' Akiro said.

'On whose authority? You should not be on the island without the superintendent's permission – and mine.' She pointed at Akiro's rifle. 'Take that out of here at once. This is a house of God.'

'All right, Sister,' Akiro said. 'We'll take our friend and be on our way.'

'You're not taking him anywhere.'

'Get up,' Akiro ordered Nessheim.

Two native boys suddenly appeared, coming out of the vestry. They were in their teens, strong-looking, but still just boys. Mother Julia said to them, 'Come along. I want you to help this man to the infirmary.'

Akiro lifted his gun. 'He's staying with us.'

Mother Julia was unfazed. 'Now you listen to me: you can't just barge into my church and tell me what to do. This man can't travel without treatment. The supplies boat isn't due for another week and we don't know when the next airplane will land. If you think you can walk out the way you walked in, you're mistaken. The watchman at the top of the *pali* is armed, so your gun will not impress him, and he won't unlock the gate there for anyone without a pass from the superintendent. The superintendent never gives that out until he has consulted with me.'

Noritaka was looking anxiously at Akiro, and started

whispering. Akiro dismissed him with a wave of his hand, but he too looked uncertain now.

'All right,' he declared at last. 'You may have this man treated. But we will come with you.'

Mother Julia quickly motioned the two boys and they came forward to help Nessheim. It was a good thing too, he thought, for in sitting so long his leg had virtually seized up. He managed to get to the end of the pew, then the boys each took one of his arms around their broad shoulders and led him out of the church.

They moved in a slow and awkward procession down a street and towards the ocean. The nun walked next to Nessheim and the boys, with Akiro and Noritaka right behind them. She turned to one of the boys helping Nessheim and said something. The boy nodded, then spoke to the other boy and they began to sing, loud enough for the nun to speak without being heard from behind.

'Who are you and what are you doing here?'

He whispered, 'I'm with the FBI.'

'But how did you get here? If you'd come down the *pali* I would have been told.'

'I came by boat and put down by the lighthouse. The boat's still there waiting for me.'

Mother Julia said nothing. She was looking thoughtful.

They came to a long one-storey building with a glassed-in sun porch. The wind had picked up and Nessheim could see the spray the big breakers threw up as they hit the rocks by the town's little landing dock. The Pacific here was almost unbelievably blue.

Mother Julia turned back to Akiro. 'This was the old hospital – the new one's next door. Come this way.'

She led the way through an archway into a courtyard that was surrounded by small living quarters for the lepers.

'This is where our patients live,' she said.

A man was sitting at a small table in a corner of the courtyard, reading a newspaper. When he put it down to nod hello to Mother Julia, Noritaka gave a little gasp – the man's face was badly scarred and one of his cheeks flattened, as if it had been crushed in a press.

They moved through another arch at the far end, then climbed some steps into a new building with concrete foundations. At the door Mother Julia turned.

'Wait here,' she told them.

She was back in a minute. 'Now, I am going to take this man through to see the nurse. You can't come any further.'

Akiro shook his head, though Noritaka looked ill at ease. Akiro said, 'We're coming too.'

Mother Julia said, 'If you insist.' Before Akiro could argue, she opened the door and motioned the boys to help Nessheim inside.

They all entered a small atrium. A corridor stretched down either side, with signs for the Dispensary and X-ray room. In front of him, Nessheim could look directly into one of the wards through its swing doors, which had small glass windows. It was a long white room, with two ceiling fans and a dark linoleum floor. On each side of the ward were about ten beds and all were occupied. He saw a nurse sitting at one bedside; another stood in the aisle, holding a tray.

'This way,' said Mother Julia.

She opened another door, next to the entrance to the ward. It gave onto a small office, where a uniformed nurse stood waiting. The room had a desk, a chair and the raised flat bed of a consulting room. There was a wall cabinet, presumably to store medicines, and a trolley that held rolls of gauze, a bottle of rubbing alcohol and half a dozen needles for injections, resting upright in a jar of liquid steriliser. At the back of the room another door led straight into the ward.

She motioned to the boys and they helped Nessheim into the chair, then left the room while Mother Julia stood guard in the doorway. She said fiercely to Akiro and Noritaka, 'The nurse doesn't want you in here. The ward right next door is for severe cases,' she said, pointing towards the swing doors, 'and the risk of contagion is extremely high. One of the patients has just died and they're about to take him to the graveyard. Naturally, all the patients are upset. I won't have you making things worse. Now wait there.'

She closed the door on them. 'We have to be quick,' she said.

The nurse went and opened the rear door of the room into the ward. The two Hawaiian boys were standing by an army stretcher that was lying on the floor. Mother Julia said to them, 'Come help.'

Nessheim struggled to his feet, then with the aid of the two Hawaiians shuffled through the back door and lay on the stretcher. The nurse bent and took off his shoes, while Mother Julia covered him with a large sheet. Then the two boys lifted up the stretcher.

Mother Julia leaned down and put her face close to Nessheim's. He smiled.

'May the Lord forgive me,' she said. 'Now when they take you through the swing doors hold your breath. Dead men don't breathe.'

They waited thirty seconds, then the boys bustled him through the swing doors and didn't stop. They could hear Mother Julia just a few feet away, talking to distract Akiro and Noritaka.

He heard Akiro grunt and Noritaka answering in Japanese. Then Nessheim sensed he was being carried outside. He didn't dare move his head and he was still holding his breath. Suddenly the cot tilted and he flinched, then realised they were taking him down the steps of the building. They moved a few steps on smooth pavement and he felt the front pair of carrying hands let go as the stretcher slid along a floor. A moment later a hand flipped the sheet down from over his head, uncovering his eyes. He took a chance and opened them and realised he was lying in the back of a wooden cart. One of the two Hawaiian boys was looking down at him and nodded, then pulled a canvas tarpaulin over the back of the cart.

The horse and cart made good time. Nessheim reckoned they had at least a few minutes' lead, maybe more if Mother Julia could keep Akiro out of the nurse's room for longer. It was a bumpy ride and Nessheim had nothing to hang on to. He banged his leg twice against the sides of the cart and when he reached down his hand came back sticky and wet.

He sensed the cart turning gradually and imagined their progress: north along the Kalaupapa side of the island, then east and over the aviation field, past the lighthouse and down to the shore. It couldn't be much past noon and he only prayed that Hiapo hadn't decided to go for a spin.

They were riding now on a soft springy surface, which he decided must be the turf runway strip. He figured it was five minutes to go when he heard a low rumble far in the distance. Thunder? No, it was a steady low noise and it was coming closer. A car. The two Japanese must have forced their way into the nurse's room, then gone and taken the nearest vehicle, probably at gunpoint.

The smooth surface ended and the cart jolted and bounced on rough stones, which slowed them down.

He sensed they were very near the water now and a moment later he heard waves breaking. The low throb of an engine was growing louder.

Suddenly the cart slanted and he was pushed against one side as it moved at an angle along the beach and stopped. He heard the cart driver get down and he tried to sit up, but the canvas had been tied firmly. He waited impatiently as the driver worked at the ropes, then threw back the tarp.

The cart driver was an enormous man in a short-sleeved shirt; his forearms looked like hams. As Nessheim struggled to get up, the Hawaiian looked at his bleeding leg with concern, then reached in and hauled Nessheim to the back of the cart, until he was sitting up, his legs dangling. In one quick move the Hawaiian hoisted Nessheim over his shoulder.

The big man carried him down the twenty feet or so and carefully put Nessheim down to stand at the water's edge. He turned to go back to the cart and Nessheim could hear the car coming. It must have reached the airstrip by now.

The *Moana Two* was anchored less than fifty yards from shore and he waded gingerly into the water and swam for it. It was only as he made his last few strokes that Hiapo heard him and then he helped him into the stern with the aid of a grappling hook.

'We have to go right away,' Nessheim said, gasping. He pointed wildly at the shore. When he turned and looked he saw a Model T screech to a halt next to the cart and horse. Hiapo had gone straight to the wheel. There was a low rumble and the diesel engine caught. Hiapo pushed the throttle down hard and they crouched beneath the gunwale level as the boat surged forward. Looking back, Nessheim could see Akiro aiming the rifle in their direction. Then suddenly the big Hawaiian appeared next to him on the beach and Nessheim watched as he launched a punch that connected flush on Akiro's jaw. The Japanese man collapsed onto the sand, and his rifle flew in the air and landed with a splash in the water.

When they were out of range, Nessheim looked at his watch, feeling like he'd aged ten years. Less than three hours had passed since he'd waded ashore.

The cutter in the channel between Molokai and Oahu appeared out of nowhere. The sun had just set when a blinking semaphoric light came out of the dusk and approached at a sharp angle off their bow. The ship was called the *Prairie Schooner* and it was manned at its prow by a sailor tending a thirty-millimetre gun. An American flag was flying from the top of its pilot house. When the vessel was less than twenty yards away a voice rang out, amplified by a megaphone: '*Moana Two*, turn off your engines and keep your hands in the air! I repeat, keep your hands in the air!'

Thank God, Nessheim thought.

He waited to explain until he was brought on board, while a sailor stayed on *Moana Two* with the Hawaiian.

'I'm an FBI agent,' he said.

'Save it for the Marines,' said the skipper, a young lieutenant. He turned to the two sailors who stood, pistols drawn, on either side of Nessheim. 'How about the other one?'

'He's called Hiapo, sir. He's a local fisherman. I think he's okay. We've seen him out here plenty of times before.'

The lieutenant nodded. 'Let him go. If we want to talk to him again we know where to find him.' He pointed at Nessheim. 'This must be Rossbach. Cuff him and take him below.'

'I'm not Rossbach,' Nessheim protested. The skipper shook his head.

Nessheim tried again, but it was no use – when he started to speak for a third time, the young lieutenant threatened to gag him as the sailors led him away. Below deck they attached his handcuffs to a large internal pipe, which didn't budge. Then the cutter started to move again.

They travelled quickly, at probably twice the knots of *Moana Two*. There was nothing to do but wait until they reached Oahu. Nessheim wondered whose attention he would command on a Friday night. His thoughts alternated between anxiety that no one would believe him and fury that he had been betrayed. How else did these Navy men know to look for 'Rossbach'?

It was pitch dark when they came into Pearl Harbor and only a solitary light glowed from the Pan Am terminal on the east loch. They headed towards it in the vast internal waterway, towards the main docks of the naval base. An enormous battleship in war camouflage was berthed there and as they passed it he could just make out the name, painted in bold letters by the bow – USS *Arizona*.

They marched him off the boat, half-lifting, half-dragging him into the command-post headquarters, which were tucked away at one side of the south-east loch of the harbour. He tried to hobble along unassisted, but when he moved too slowly the escorts propelled him by both arms.

He was expecting to be taken to the base commander, and the same two sailors led him along a series of linoleum-floored hallways, through a succession of swinging doors. At last they arrived at one that wasn't swinging. The sailors rapped smartly on the door and an orderly opened it. On the far side Nessheim could see a long corridor, battleship grey, with barred cells on either side.

'Prisoner,' the sailors announced and shoved Nessheim through the door.

33

HE HAD A single cell with a wall of bars facing the corridor, and a small high window on the back wall. If he stood on the little chair in his cell it gave him a view of Ford Island across the east loch. There was no moon, and though his eyes adjusted gradually he could only make out the bulky shapes of the battleships in the harbour and an expanse of even darker grey, which must be the water.

Across the corridor a drunken sailor who'd gone AWOL stood staring through the bars at Nessheim; in the next cell another sailor sat crying on his bunk. When the guards came with dinner trays they must have said something about the new prisoner.

'Nazi bastard,' the AWOL sailor suddenly snarled. 'Wait until we get you in the yard!' an inmate down the corridor shouted. Even the crybaby sailor looked daggers at Nessheim. Soon all the inmates took up the cry of 'Traitor! Traitor! Traitor!' ringing out from the dozen cells.

The stockade CO came down late the following morning. He was a very little man with square shoulders, in a crisp Navy uniform that looked as if it rarely went outdoors. Nessheim stayed seated on his bed in order to look shorter.

'I'm Captain Maston,' the Navy man announced.

'And I'm Special Agent Nessheim of the FBI. I was sent to Molokai to meet with Japanese agents there—'

Maston cut him short. 'Save the horseshit, please. I don't know exactly what you were doing on Molokai, but let's not waste my time, okay Herr Rossbach?'

'My name isn't Rossbach.'

'Why does your driver's licence say it is?'

'My real name is James Nessheim.'

Maston looked amused. 'I saw that movie.'

Nessheim tried to control his rising impatience. 'Please contact the local Special Agent in Charge – he's named Shivers. He can confirm who I am. And while I wait for him, I need a medic.' He pointed to his leg, which had started seeping blood again during the night.

Maston looked around the cell. 'The thing is, Rossbach or Nessheim or whatever your name is, I've already talked with Mr Shivers.'

'Really?'

'I phoned him last night. Shivers said there *was* an agent here last week, named Nessheim.'

'Okay, then.'

'Not so fast.' Maston held up his hand. 'Shivers told me that he personally saw this guy on to the Pan Am Clipper to San Francisco. He said there's no way you can be the same guy unless you parachuted out and swam back.'

Nessheim shook his head furiously. 'He only saw me leave the terminal. I never boarded the plane.'

Maston was unimpressed. 'You can tell that to the Naval Intelligence folks on Monday.'

Nessheim was now fully on edge. 'Listen, please will you call Shivers again? Tell him I can prove I'm Nessheim – all he's got to do is come have a look at me. Tell him I had dinner last Wednesday at his house. We had meat-loaf with pineapple rings. Sue, the Japanese girl, made it. Just tell him that, okay?'

'I'll think about it,' said Maston and went out the door.

*　　*　　*

By the time night fell Shivers had not come to see him and Nessheim was beginning to despair.

A medic did show up, a taciturn man who cleaned his wound in silence, then bandaged it. When Nessheim asked for something to dull the pain, the medic gave him two aspirin in a twist.

'I need something stronger,' Nessheim said.

'You're lucky to get that.' The medic started to leave. 'Heil Hitler to you, pal.'

'*Auf Weidersehen*,' snapped Nessheim.

The calls of 'Traitor! Traitor!' continued sporadically throughout the evening, then at last the cells grew quiet. But sleep was an impossibility: Nessheim lay sweating in his boxer shorts, as his leg continued to throb. He went and stood on the chair, which oddly seemed to ease the pain. He looked over the east loch, towards Ford Island and the large battleship shapes he could just make out in the dark.

What the hell had Guttman been thinking of? He had never understood the man. Guttman would cajole one day and mislead the next; alternately confide secret information, then refuse to say what time it was; dole out effusive praise, before proceeding to chew him out. It was bewildering, exasperating and sometimes point-less. But as infuriating as these vacillations were, Nessheim had always held a sustaining belief that Guttman knew what he was doing.

Not this time. Nessheim looked down at his bandaged leg, totem of his abortive trip to Molokai.

A light went on high in the bridge of one of the ships berthed across the loch at Ford Island. What were the names of the different kinds of battleships out there? Nessheim wondered idly. Cruiser, frigate, destroyer – what else? Aircraft carriers – newfangled and apparently crucial, because they carried planes. He wondered how the planes landed in the fog or when the cloud cover was really low. It must be a lot easier to do in clear skies.

Clear skies – someone else had mentioned them recently. Who was it? He tried to remember, letting the inchoate jumble of recent memories float through his mind. Finally he heard the voice say – *you can't expect us to guarantee clear skies.*

It was Noritaka who had said these words. But why?

Then it came to him, as if he'd crossed a finish line. Depths, tide differentials – these were the facts of a fleet at harbour, and the harbour must be here – why else meet in Hawaii?

Oh, how could he have missed it? The Japanese were going to attack, and the Germans had wanted to know when. It was as clear as day to him now. But he realised that there was no way on earth he could prove it, for he had no evidence any of these Navy people would take seriously. Without Shivers there was absolutely nothing he could do.

He went back to his bed, completely drained. Despite the pain in his leg, or because of it, he finally managed to fall into a deep sleep. As the sun came up, light the colour of plums streamed through his cell, but Nessheim was still only half-awake when he heard the sound of jangling keys. He sat up groggily as an orderly came in. Behind him stood another man, dressed in a green polo shirt and blue checked trousers. It was Shivers.

'Am I glad to see you,' said Nessheim.

'I'm not going to say "likewise".' Shivers looked at his watch. 'My Sunday four-ball tees off in twenty-five minutes.'

'What time is it? My watch got soaked in Molokai.'

'It's just short of seven thirty,' said Shivers. There was

no warmth to his voice. He turned to the orderly. 'You can leave us, sailor. And tell your CO that this man is who he says he is – Special Agent Nessheim.'

Shivers sat down on the chair beneath the grilled window. 'I am assuming you are Nessheim, since I can't for the life of me see why, if you were actually a Nazi named Rossbach, you would have contacted me when you arrived.'

'I'm Nessheim all right. Two years ago, I infiltrated the German-American *Bund* on Harry Guttman's orders; my alias was Rossbach. Guttman resurrected that identity for me to meet with foreign agents in Molokai. At Kalaupapa.'

'The leper colony? Jesus, what were you meeting there for?'

'For the reason you just reacted like you did. Nobody goes there if they can help it.'

'Who were you meeting with?'

Two days before Nessheim wouldn't have told him, but all that had changed. 'I found Billy Osaka's cousin, Akiro. He's a Japanese agent.'

He was disconcerted when Shivers didn't say anything.

'Look,' Nessheim said, 'call Harry Guttman – he'll confirm all of this. I have been acting on his direct orders.'

'Believe me, I've already tried. But Guttman's out of commission again – he's back in the hospital with pneumonia. Without him, there's not much I can do. I can't ask for you to be released, now can I? In fact, when I called D.C. HQ I ended up talking to Clyde Tolson himself. I have to say he's not one of your natural defenders. Or Guttman's for that matter. He said to throw the book at you and sort out the details later.'

'Do whatever you want to me. But please listen first to what I have to say.'

He explained as calmly as he could his sudden revelation in the early hours, and watched as Shivers's face moved back and forth between amazement and disbelief.

Nessheim ended, 'Can't you see? You have to tell them that the Japanese are coming. If I'm wrong, you can throw away the key, but if I'm right there's still time to defend the base.'

Shivers stared at him for a long time. 'All right. I will do that. I give you my word. But don't be surprised if it doesn't make a damned bit of difference. We get a rumour a day here. They may not come from an FBI agent, but then, they don't usually come from a German spy, either.' He shrugged and gave a little smile, then rose to his feet. 'I'll be back tomorrow with the ONI. But I'll see the rear admiral first.' He paused, then held out his hand. Nessheim shook it and the SAC left.

Nessheim sat down again on his bed, suddenly exhausted. He trusted Shivers and that was what mattered. If Guttman didn't make it, Nessheim was looking at a prison sentence, he figured, but right now he didn't care.

It was minutes later that he heard the first dull thud, like a shoe dropped in an upstairs bedroom. Down the hall someone was playing the radio loudly – *Hawaii Calls* with Webley Edwards on CBS – and at first Nessheim though the noise was part of the programme. Then there was a boom, and then a succession of them, each louder than the last.

He grabbed the chair and stood on it by the window. In a cloudless sky the sun spread over Ford Island in a buttery sheen. More booms were coming from Hickam Field, to his left but out of sight, and then there was a cannonade of explosions. Over Ford Island he now saw half a dozen low-flying, unfamiliar planes. There were small red circles on their wings that stood out from the greenish-grey of their fuselages. A plane flew above them like a supervising bird, its entire tail painted red. The planes below were heading straight for the island's airfield, and as they passed over, only a few hundred feet above the ground, they began dropping bombs in clusters. More planes followed them in, dropping their own explosives in the untouched spaces left between the lines of the previous explosions.

He looked to his left and in the south he saw a succession of aircraft, grouped in threes, pass through the entrance to the harbour. From the bellies of the first trio sleek, tube-shaped objects fell like lozenges ejected from a Pez dispenser. Why were they unloading there in the middle of the loch, well short of any obvious target? Then he understood – these were torpedoes, despatched by the airborne equivalent of submarines.

Seconds later one of the ships lying in Battleship Row was hit. A towering geyser of water soared into the air like a theatrical fountain. Another battleship was hit, and then another; the ship closest to him began to list.

Sailors started to appear on the decks, running to man their guns. The hit ships were on fire, one so badly that flames spread along its starboard side like a lit trail of gunpowder. Panicked seamen began leaping into the harbour. Nessheim watched as a watery slick of gasoline caught fire on the harbour surface and engulfed half a dozen of them.

There was a short pause, as the planes regrouped to attack again. Down the stockade corridor the radio was still playing when suddenly the programme was interrupted and the urgent voice of Webley Edwards was shouting, 'Attention! This is no exercise! The Japanese are attacking Pearl Harbor! All Army, Navy and Marine personnel—!' someone switched it off, just as a siren sounded in the distance, howling like a dog caught in a trap. Another siren followed, curiously unmodulated, its high-pitched shriek one long note.

Nessheim could hear orders being shouted over PA systems on the ships in the harbour, and watched as a fighter plane tried to take off on the Ford Island runway. It suddenly shuddered to a halt, just short of an enormous crater that had been created in its runway path. In the corridor orderlies kept running past the cells, while the prisoners were shouting to be let out. Suddenly, just overhead, Nessheim saw a plane appear and as it headed towards Ford Island there was an enormous bang. The walls around him shook as if an earthquake had struck.

Nessheim stood transfixed, finding it almost impossible to take it all in. He looked out again towards Ford Island. The torpedoes had done their job well: already two of the battleships were sinking and a third had lost most of its stern. Smoke swirled like burning tyres from the many small fires, and hundreds of men had jumped overboard.

Then the attack recommenced. He could spy yet more planes circling far up in the sky, at least 10,000 feet up. Bombers. There was an explosion on the USS *Arizona*; he could hear it as if the bomb had gone off in the next cell. Fire broke out on the battleship's deck and quickly spread below, glowing like an elongated hot coal. Suddenly the entire ship seemed to erupt, showering enormous pieces of metal into the air. The fire must have reached the munitions stores.

Then the planes moved on, and within minutes more explosions could be heard from elsewhere on the island. The Japanese seemed to be attacking all the other airfields at once, and from the sound of it Fort DeRussy at Waikiki.

In the stockade the prisoners were shouting, relaying what they'd seen and – in every word they spoke – their fear. From the harbour the noise now was less relentless: a small secondary explosion; a ship blasting its horn as it tried to escape through the small-necked harbour entrance; ambulance sirens; orders shouted from the shore or broadcast on the decks of the crippled ships hit by torpedoes. And a solitary, dreadful scream.

An hour later the Japanese returned.

Part Nine

Los Angeles and San Francisco
Late March 1942

34

THE LETTER ARRIVED on a Tuesday morning. It was marked **Private** in a female hand.

P.O. Box 343
Owens Valley Reception Center
Manzanar, California

Dear Jimmy,
I never thought I'd end up here. Could you come visit me please? I have something to tell you, something I should have told you before. I promise it won't be a waste of time.

Yours faithfully,
Hanako Yukuri

Just what I need, Nessheim thought wearily, for he had his own plans now. He felt in his trouser pocket for the Rossbach driver's licence, which was always with him. It was his ticket out of a life that hadn't given him the answers. And now here was Hanako raising questions.

His return to LA had been a close-run thing. After 7 December, prisoners were not a priority for the authorities at Pearl Harbor. Over 2,000 military personnel had been killed (Nessheim had seen half of them die when he witnessed the bombing of the USS *Arizona*) and the survivors' sense of shock had turned to anger.

There had been no sign of Shivers, and Nessheim was in no position to demand to see the SAC. On the 11th news ran through the stockade cells that Hitler had declared war on America, and an hour later he'd been suddenly yanked out of his cell by two military policemen, taken in an outboard-powered dinghy across the wreck-festooned loch to the back end of Ford Island and put on a requisitioned Pan Am Clipper, which had taken off five minutes later. Blackout blinds had been fitted over the porthole-shaped windows of the airplane; as the sun went down the attendants took them off and Nessheim saw that they were flying without lights. But no one told him where he was going and he was kept handcuffed throughout the long flight; when he needed the bathroom he was taken under guard, even though he could barely hobble there.

It was only when he had seen the Golden Gate Bridge that he knew they'd returned to San Francisco. At Treasure Island he'd been escorted out first by a trio of MPs carrying carbines. He wondered how long he was going to remain a prisoner, and what he would be charged with. He was confident he could establish his true identity, less sure that he could prove he was on a legitimate mission on Kalaupapa. It was critical that Guttman survive his pneumonia, and he tried not think what would happen if the man didn't; he knew traitors were usually shot.

The terminal building was crowded with military personnel, looking dazed that their uniforms were suddenly for real. They stared as his escorts cleared a path for the wobbly Nessheim, then led him down a corridor of Pan Am offices. These rooms had also been requisitioned, and the MPs decided he was dangerous enough to warrant the General Manager's suite. It had a stunning view of the Bay, but the contrast with his cell's view of the watery graveyard in Hawaii was almost too much to bear. He looked away, and it was then that one of the MPs slapped him.

'What's that for?' he asked in surprise.

'Pearl Harbor,' the soldier said without batting an eye.

Nessheim wanted to tell him that it was deserved, but for a different reason. Nessheim wasn't a spy; he was a failure.

He asked mildly, 'So what happens next – you hit me again?' And the soldier was clenching his fist when the door opened.

'That's enough,' said a calm voice.

The soldier said crossly, 'Our orders were to bring the prisoner to an office, and then—'

'Await further orders,' the man said smoothly. 'Your first one is to take those handcuffs off.'

The soldier hesitated, then reluctantly unlocked the cuffs. At last Nessheim turned around.

'Stephenson?' The Canadian stood in front of him, dressed in a brown wool suit and grey fedora.

'You two know each other?' the soldier asked suspiciously. He looked at Stephenson. 'I'd better see those orders.'

'Be my guest.' Stephenson handed over an envelope.

As the soldier read the letter inside, his eyes widened. He looked at Stephenson and saluted smartly. 'Sir!'

'That'll do,' said Stephenson. 'You can leave us now.'

When the sailors had gone Nessheim let out a soft whistle. 'I'm impressed. Who signed the letter – the Pope?'

Stephenson gave a hint of a smile. 'No. Just the President.'

He had come back to LA with Stephenson on a Main train full of soldiers. They eyed the gimpy Nessheim admiringly, as if he must be one of the first casualties of the war. In a way he supposed he was.

He and Stephenson had sat up in the smoker, though neither smoked, drinking rye and ginger while Nessheim related what had happened to him in Kalaupapa and then at Pearl Harbor.

Stephenson shook his head in wonder. 'I knew we were sending you into the frying pan, but I didn't think you'd get burnt.'

At Union Station they walked slowly through a terminal teeming with panicky civilians talking about the prospects of a Jap invasion. Stephenson had put Nessheim in a taxi and paid the fare home after Nessheim had remembered that his wallet was still in a locker on Ford Island.

At first – which meant in the days before Christmas – the entire city had seemed on war alert, recoiling from Roosevelt's 'day of infamy'. Strict blackout regulations were imposed, rationing was introduced, and the Japanese population began to be rounded up. The flame-fanning headlines of the popular press meant that everyone knew what to expect – the worst.

But gradually things calmed down, perhaps because the actions of the war were once again so far away – the Japanese were advancing unimpeded throughout the Far East, while the Germans seem stalled in the Soviet hinterland and had been pushed back from Kursk. There was nothing phoney about this war, but by January there was at least a sense of lull, as America focused on preparing for the part it knew it was going to play. Like an innocent beast wounded for the first time, but now recovering, the United States was gathering strength for worldwide war. Full power had been applied to its internal engine, and the capacities of its existing factories were being maximised, while hundreds of new ones were going up. All to produce enough guns and tanks and ships and planes for a fight which no one thought would be over soon.

At the Bureau office Hood lost interest in Communists in Hollywood, preoccupied instead with rounding up Japanese-Americans, while Cohan was deputed to tour other Western field offices to help them do the same. He left, but not before reminding Nessheim of his promise to show Mrs Cohan around the AMP studio.

There the biopic of Hoover had been deferred indefinitely, while a roster of war movies were rushed into production, boosting the studio's fortunes but leaving Nessheim with virtually nothing to do. He'd had one brief phone conversation with Guttman in February after Guttman had come out of the hospital, but Guttman didn't sound a hundred per cent, and Nessheim had not wanted to keep him long.

Nessheim's social life was negligible, confined to the occasional drink with Teitz. He almost never saw Lolly, for she was no longer working in the Ink Well and had landed a succession of small parts in the studio's flurry of new productions. Recently she had been cast in her first leading role, in one of the new features the Count was directing now that the Hoover film had been put on ice. As a mark of her move up she had been given a new name – Lolly Baker was now Lois Merola.

But it was Elizaveta Mukasei he wondered most about. The Russians were officially allies now, which coincided with her disappearance from his life. His phone calls went unreturned, a note he sent got no reply. Perhaps she now regretted her overtures – if not the flirtatious ones of their midnight swim, then her suggestion of a swap: information about her husband's activities in return for citizenship. It would have been hard to make the deal in any case – the spies the Bureau was preoccupied with were either Japanese or German.

But Elizaveta could relax, he thought. If Mikhail did go back, America was not going to deport his wife when her country was on the same side.

He had returned hoping to find answers to explain his botched mission in Hawaii. If he could not undo the disastrous consequences, he could at least unearth their causes. So many questions remained unanswered. He'd phoned Dickerson, the LAPD detective, enquiring about Mrs Oka's case and the murder of Jimmy Lapides in the barber shop. Dickerson made it clear he had bigger fish to fry, and now claimed Mrs Oka's murder was a botched burglary after all. According to the detective, Lapides's slit throat was a case of 'the wrong guy being in the wrong place at the wrong time'.

The detective went on, 'I heard you were down in San Pedro when they found that fisherman's wife. Check with the cops down there if you want, but they haven't got anywhere either.'

He called the Cleveland Field Office the next day from the studio. He got through to the SAC easily enough by claiming to call on Hood's behalf. He was just double-checking an earlier query, he said, giving Mo Dubin's name and mentioning an associate named Ike.

Sure, said the SAC, and he was happy to explain Ike Winters was a long-time gambling boss with three convictions in Ohio alone. Dubin was even better known to the Cleveland office and was a more sinister character who had started as a small-time Shaker Heights bootlegger, then gradually moved up in life by rubbing out his immediate competitors.

So why had Cohan claimed Ike and Dubin were clean? He couldn't have called the Cleveland office, as he said he had. There was only one explanation (and the only one for his ritzy house in Beverly Hills). He was on the take. Which solved a mini-mystery for Nessheim, not that he had an ounce of proof.

So now as March was ending, Nessheim looked down at Hanako's letter again, strongly tempted to put it in a drawer and forget about it. He'd be in the Forces soon enough, where he could make a new life for himself and forget about the recent past.

But then he thought about Billy Osaka, wondering again what was the real story behind his disappearance. Nobody knew, thought Nessheim. Except maybe Hanako.

35

THE CAMP WAS a vast, stark complex of low-roofed barracks, stretching for almost a mile into the grey salt flats. It was Spartan housing, uninsulated, with tar-papered roofs. The landscape was bleak, though in the distance dramatic, snow-capped mountains lined the horizon on three sides, foreshortened in the clear desert air like tantalising colour postcards held just out of reach.

At the front entrance to the compound a sentry swung the gate back as soon as he saw Nessheim's badge. A twelve-foot fence ringed with triple strands of barbed wire lined the simple vast rectangle, studded at intervals by high watchtowers, which were manned by soldiers carrying vintage Springfield rifles from the Great War. Nessheim parked his car off the main dusty thorough-fare of this newly created 'town', between a general store with shuttered windows and a schoolhouse, which had a pretty little bell tower but no bell. Next to that sat the command post, a larger version of the general store. Two MPs stood guard on either side of its front doors.

Inside, Nessheim showed his credentials and was ushered in to the governor, a New Yorker named Kramer. Nessheim explained why he was there, turned down Kramer's offer of an escort, and drove almost half a mile to Row C, passing monotonously identical tar-papered barracks. It was all a far cry from the Little Tokyo he had known, though since the deportations the LA neighbourhood should have been rechristened Ghost Town.

As he walked towards Hut 11 Hanako appeared in the doorway in a faded calico dress and a scarf to protect her hair from the dust.

'You came!' she exclaimed. He couldn't tell if she was delighted or just surprised.

'Hanako, why are you here? I thought you'd gone to Chicago with your family.'

'I did, but then I came back and then internment started.'

Nessheim looked around at the packed dust, the high, wire-topped fence and the bleak hut.

She shrugged. 'You'll understand in a minute. Come on in.'

He followed her into a small room that had a pine table and a small sink in one corner. She crossed the room and stopped at a doorway that was screened by an old sheet held up by tacks. Lifting a corner, she gestured Nessheim to come through. He followed her cautiously into a darker room, where only a small shaft of daylight came through the solitary window, illuminating a patch of knot-holed plank floor and a few pine slats of the walls. As his eyes adjusted to the gloom he saw that the furniture consisted of a camp bed against the far wall and a stool in one corner, where a man-like figure was sitting. It looked like a tailor's dummy, but dummies didn't wave hello.

'Hey, Jimmy,' said a quiet voice from the stool. Even subdued, the voice had the happy-go-lucky tone that had always made its owner such a breath of fresh air.

Nessheim moved forwards until he could make out the face.

'I thought you were dead,' he said without relief.

'If I don't get out of this place, I will be soon enough.'

'Is the food that bad?'

Billy gave a wan smile. 'I thought I was the guy who made the jokes.'

He didn't look good. Bare-chested and barefoot, he wore only a stained pair of khaki trousers. He hadn't shaved for a couple of days and there were stray black hairs on his cheeks the size of staples. His hair had been cut, but lopsidedly.

Maybe it was because he had been looking fruitlessly for Billy so long, or maybe it was because of all that had happened since Billy had asked to meet (*It's important*), but Nessheim couldn't think of anything to say.

He looked around and found another little stool in a corner. He hooked it with his foot and drew it out, then sat down. When he let his eyes rise they met Billy's, which were animated now, as if Nessheim's arrival had brought him to life.

Nessheim said at last, 'As I remember, you wanted to see me.'

Billy laughed and Nessheim gave a wry smile. He noticed Hanako had left the room.

'Like old times, huh?' said Billy.

No, thought Nessheim. He said, 'I was sorry about your grandmother.'

The smile on Billy's face melted. 'They ever catch who did it?'

'No,' said Nessheim. 'The LAPD's not too good in Little Tokyo. You know that. They say it must have been a burglar.'

Billy shook his head.

'So where did you go anyway?' asked Nessheim casually. 'I've been looking everywhere.'

'I needed a change of scene. I worked with my cousin in Oregon during the salmon run; I picked grapes for a bit in Napa; and I saw the High Sierra at last. Don't tell Hanako,' he added with a wink.

Nessheim nodded slowly. 'That's funny, I've been travelling too.'

'Anywhere nice?' asked Billy. They could have been swapping holiday stories over a beer.

'Hawaii,' said Nessheim, and Billy blinked. 'Unfortunately I was on the job. I saw your cousin Akiro while I was there. He sent his best.'

Billy's eyes didn't waver, but one of his hands was now clenched. If they'd been playing five-card stud, Nessheim would have doubled down.

'How's he been keeping?' Billy managed to say.

'So-so. He lost his wife, you know.'

'I didn't.' The surprise seemed genuine.

'Yeah, someone mistook her for a tuna in the San Pedro cannery. She bled to death.'

Billy paled.

'Still, he's doing okay, I think. They say time heals all wounds, but I reckon money medicine works just as well. And I heard in Hawaii that Akiro's had a big dose of it.'

'Maybe,' said Billy, coolly neutral. 'But Akiro has always been a big spender.'

'Well, he's got something to spend now.' Nessheim waited a moment, then asked as if out of the blue, 'Did you pay him?'

'For what?' Billy looked suddenly alert. 'I might have slipped him the odd couple of bucks now and then. Akiro was always short.'

'Your friend Ike says the same of you.'

Billy whistled air through pursed lips. 'You get around, Jimmy.'

'Akiro was on a different scale altogether. He's come into something like twenty-five grand.'

'How the hell do you know?' Billy was sitting up now.

'I did the groundwork. Ask Hanako. I even met her boss Mr Satake. Did Hanako siphon off the money? You know, twenty-five grand from the Russians?'

'You'd better ask her. I don't know what you're talking about.'

'The Russians must have thought they were smart using a Japanese bank – excuse me, a Japanese-*American* bank.'

'Is there a difference?' asked Billy with a bitterness Nessheim had never heard in him before. Billy gestured to the grim room they sat in and with a wider sweep of his hand to the camp itself. Nessheim could see his point.

'Anyhow,' Nessheim continued, 'it was pretty dumb of them. If the Russians were trying to hide the transfer they couldn't really complain when Hanako lifted half of it.'

'You've learned a lot of things,' said Billy.

'Not that much really. I was hoping to get some more answers from you.'

'Sure,' said Billy, but his eyes were flitting to the door.

Nessheim sat back, making sure his gun hung loose. 'When did Akiro tell you about the plan to attack Pearl Harbor?'

Billy pursed his lips, then rocked his head back and forth. 'Take it easy on me, Jimmy,' he said. He wouldn't look Nessheim in the eye.

'Is that what you were going tell me?'

Billy nodded reluctantly.

'So why the hell didn't you?' Nessheim was almost shouting. He heard Hanako stir in the next room and lowered his voice. 'All those guys who died. I saw it, Billy. It wasn't nice.'

'They were trying to kill me. They still are. They thought I was going to talk.'

'To me?'

A faint hint of a nod.

Billy was trying to pull himself together.

He said, 'Listen, I'll tell you everything you want to know, but first you have to get me out of here.'

Nessheim was still picturing the sunken USS *Arizona*. 'Then play ball, Billy. Who is trying to kill you? I know it's not Ike any more. Is it the nationalists? Or the Tokyo Club? Or are they the same thing? I need to know.'

'If I tell you now there won't be any reason for you to pull strings. Don't bullshit me, Jimmy. I know how it works.'

Billy hadn't lost his cunning. It sat beneath his surface razzmatazz like tracks under a bouncy train.

Nessheim stood up. 'I'll see what I can do. I'll come back in the morning.'

'Hey Jimmy,' Billy said, shivering slightly. 'Any chance you could loan me your gun? Just for the night.'

Nessheim shook his head. 'Sorry.'

Billy hugged himself. 'And I'm sorry, too, that I didn't tell you. But I was scared.'

There was no sign of Hanako when Nessheim left. He drove down the dusty avenue and pulled up at the command post again. Inside, his conversation with Kramer proved unsatisfactorily short; in the base commander Nessheim had run into a classic bureaucrat who was uninterested in individual situations. Kramer wasn't going to be swayed by the fact that people in the camp – nationalists? gangsters? – might want to harm Billy Osaka. Kramer's concern was with authorisation, and he made it clear that here Nessheim fell short.

Lone Pine was an arid, unattractive little town with one hotel on its main street. It was two storeys with a long railed balcony on its upper floor, but had seen better days. He paid for a room, then went and asked for a Western Union office, which turned out to double as the Southern Pacific railway depot, a little north-east of town.

> **OSAKA LOCATED. OWENS VALLEY RECEP-
> TION CENTER INDEPENDENCE CALIFORNIA.
> REQUIRE AUTHORISATION RELEASE IN
> MY CUSTODY ASAP TO BASE GOVERNOR
> KRAMER. URGENT REPEAT URGENT. REPLY
> HOTEL TROUBADOR LONE PINE**
> **JN**

It was only three o'clock, but it would be six out east, too late for Guttman to do anything until morning.

Nessheim read in his room for a couple of hours, then ate an early supper of chicken-fried steak with baked beans in the hotel dining room. After supper, he was half-tempted by the saloon, but went up to his room. It had a radio and he listened to news on KSL, a Salt Lake station, about the Russian push against the Germans, and about the Japanese advance in the Philippines. There was a report, too, of the American soldiers now in Great Britain – a crackly voice said that it was just fine over there and the boys were getting used to fish and chips. Then KSL played religious music until he fell asleep. When he woke halfway through the night it was to a blanket of static.

There were no messages downstairs when he checked out after a breakfast of grits and bacon, and his frustration grew as he sped towards the camp – the MP barely had time to open the gate as he drove in. He parked and jumped out of his car, half-running up the steps into the headquarters, passing a typist who did a double take when he walked straight into the governor's office.

Kramer was at the window, looking out at the dusty parade ground where the internees gathered for announcements and the distribution of parcels.

'Have you had a telegram from D.C.?' Nessheim asked immediately.

Kramer didn't turn around.

'I have,' he said.

'Did it authorise Osaka's release?' he demanded.

'It did.'

'Can I see the internee, please?'

He didn't care if Kramer wanted to sulk. He just wanted to get Osaka out of there. He'd do what he could for Hanako once he got back to LA.

Kramer went and stood behind his desk. He sighed and bowed his head.

'You may not want to.'

Kramer looked at Nessheim for the first time. There was something awful in his eyes, something beseeching. It spooked Nessheim.

'What's happened?'

'Come with me and I'll show you.'

There was no sign of Hanako at Hut 11. The tiny table in the front room still held their dishes from last night's supper. There was an MP in the next room, visible when the sheet hanging in the doorway ruffled in the slight breeze. He looked relieved when they joined him and after entering the room Nessheim saw why.

Billy was lying on his back on the floor, both his arms extended. He wore the same trousers but had put on a shirt; he was still barefoot. He looked smaller and almost frail, stretched out on the plank floor like an overgrown kid. But there was a knife in his chest, which had a long oval handle and was stuck in to a hilt that was covered in phoney little jewels. It looked like a stage prop from a production of *The Arabian Nights*, but it had done its job.

'Who killed him?' Nessheim demanded. He noticed there was very little blood.

Kramer didn't reply. The MP shrugged, then said, 'There're disagreements among the Japs. Sometimes the arguments get out of hand. Somebody gets mad . . .'

'Bullshit. Look at him – he hasn't been in a fight.'

The MP looked uncomfortable.

Kramer said from the window, 'The soldier's right, Agent Nessheim. Osaka wasn't very popular among the *Butoki-Kai*. And they seem to be in charge.'

The reactionary nationalists.

'*Seem* to be? Don't you know?'

Kramer shrugged.

'Where was Hanako Yukuri when this happened?' Nessheim asked angrily.

The MP said, 'The women gather once a week to sort out any problems with the food supply. Last night was meeting night. When Yukuri came back she found him, just like this.'

'I want this looked into right away. Fingerprints and people interviewed. Somebody must have heard something.'

Kramer looked at him glumly. Nessheim could see he was worried about what had happened under his watch, and he wouldn't want another telegram from Washington.

Kramer said, 'There's one other thing you should know.'

'What's that?'

'Somebody cut the fence last night. At the outer perimeter. We've done a roll call and everyone's accounted for. It looks like they were cutting their way in, not out.'

36

NESSHEIM STAYED IN the Owens Valley for two more days, consoling Hanako and starting a process to send her to her family in Chicago. No one in the camp talked, no one claimed to know anything. He returned to LA with a low-grade fever and once home he slept for twelve hours straight. The next day he sat in his AMP office and kept the door closed. Lolly's replacement had the moxie of a timid mole, so he managed to keep to himself while he thought about Billy Osaka.

In a curious way he was mourning him, this extraordinary figure whom he had barely known – until, that is, he had gone missing; then Nessheim had learned more about Billy Osaka than he had ever bargained for. Billy's old teacher Larson had been right; Billy would never have been truly 'one of us' – his deportation to the Owens Valley was proof enough of that. But he'd paid a terrible price for his sheer exuberant Americanness; the nationalists had punished him for that. There seemed little hope of catching the killer, since they must have called in someone from outside to do the job.

Then late that afternoon Teitz poked his head in. He looked like his old self, with a spanking new blue bow tie. 'Coming to the Liberty Bonds party?'

'I hadn't planned to,' Nessheim said without interest.

Teitz pulled a face. 'We've got to do our bit. It's not like we're in uniform – yet. I could use a lift – one of my tyres needs retreading and it'll be a week before they can get it done. I never knew rubber was such a key ingredient for waging war.'

So he drove Teitz to the fundraiser in West Hollywood,

which was being held in a school gym. That meant no booze, so they stopped for martinis at Musso & Frank, where Teitz claimed to recognise half a dozen famous writers as they sat down at the bar.

'So what's new?' asked Nessheim, chewing on his tooth-picked olive. 'Heard from Stuckey?'

'He's still in Basic, apparently.'

Nessheim nodded. 'How goes the great job hunt?'

'Didn't I tell you? They're keeping me on to work on a new comedy. Madame Merola's bid for fame.'

Nessheim smiled. 'She'll always be Lolly to me. I hear she's stepping out with Pearl Junior.'

Teitz laughed. 'I don't reckon it's going to last – apparently Buddy doesn't think Lolly's good enough for his boy. But at least she's got her teeth fixed out of it.'

The benefit turned out to have been hijacked by pink politicos, which meant no band and not much food, just a succession of putatively stirring speeches, lauding the Russian counter-offensive. Waverley was there, and Nessheim thought he saw Nick from the weekend at the ranch near Santa Barbara.

At last even Teitz's enthusiasm for a party flagged. Just as they had decided to go for another martini, Teitz plucked Nessheim by his jacket's sleeve.

'There she is,' he said.

'There's who?' asked Nessheim.

Then he saw Elizaveta Mukasei. She was wearing a knee-length black dress with a twin-strand choker of pearls. Elegant, understated. If she had seen Nessheim she didn't let on.

'You remember the older broad I told you Osaka used to see.'

'Billy?' Nessheim said the name reluctantly.

'Well there she blows.' He pointed straight at Elizaveta. There was no mistaking who he meant.

'Are you sure, Teitz?' Nessheim asked urgently. 'I thought it was Mrs Pearl that Billy was knocking off.'

'I've never laid eyes on Mrs Pearl in my life. So yes, I'm sure.'

He tried to tell himself that Elizaveta could have been just a friend of Billy's. He didn't want to chase answers any more, not unless they could tell the whole story. Maybe there weren't any big answers. Maybe they were like Bishop Berkeley's tree falling in a forest with no one around – it doesn't make a noise if nobody's there. It doesn't even exist.

As the day for his planned departure neared, his sense of detachment grew. When late one day he dropped by the field office in the Federal Building it was after an absence of ten days. He didn't want to see Hood and, thankfully, Cohan was still away on secondment. He'd send them both a copy of his resignation letter to Guttman once he had successfully enlisted.

He went to his desk in the corner, intent on emptying his few belongings into a paper bag. On the desk top he found an envelope addressed to him, postmarked Honolulu.

Inside the envelope there were two folded pieces of paper. One was a copy of a form, the other a handwritten note on official stationery from **The Office of Births and Deaths, Honolulu Hawaii**. He read that one first:

Dear Mr Nessheim,
Sara Kane our high school helper found the birth certificate you were looking for. It was buried with a few others underneath the files in the new record

room. I am so sorry you didn't find it when you were here, but hope the attached Photostat will do in its stead – the Court officials upstairs finally bought a machine!

Yours truly,
Mary Beth Carlyle

Glancing at the certificate with Billy's parents' names, he was glad they weren't alive to learn about their son's wretched end.

Then he looked at the birth certificate again. The name Billy had put down on his FBI form was *Mary Mitchie*. Irish as the Book of Kells. But there could be no mistake: on the birth certificate it said *Maria Lyakhov*.

Suddenly the answers were making lots of noise.

He got through to her at last on the phone. When he proposed a meeting she tried to put him off, but something in his voice must have sounded an alarm bell and eventually she agreed, even offering to come to his house. She seemed to find it odd when he insisted they meet somewhere else.

He parked his car below Griffith Observatory and walked down to the small park at the bottom. It was an open, grassy space of maybe two acres with gravelled paths. There were a few wooden benches, which had their donors' names engraved on little brass plates.

He sat on a bench with his arms spread along its back, trying to look relaxed. He kept his eyes open and after a few minutes he saw Elizaveta begin the trek from the lower parking lot towards the bench. She had come without a coat, which reassured him, and was wearing a smart, cherry-coloured dress and black felt hat. There was no one with her.

He stood up.

'It's been too long,' she said brightly as they both sat down on the bench.

'I wanted to see you before I left town.'

'Really? Have you been transferred?'

'No,' he said, but didn't explain.

'Oh.' She gave a short sigh. 'It is good to see you, but sad to think it may be the last time. At least while this war goes on.'

'Have you changed your mind about staying?'

She looked surprised. 'Didn't I tell you? I will be staying. Mikhail has been told it is crucial that he continues with his vice-consular duties here. He was very disappointed.' She smiled. 'And I pretended to be.'

'Have his duties changed?' he asked shortly.

'No,' she said. 'If you are referring to our conversation at the ranch, I am afraid I was guilty of exaggeration. I was worried about going back to Russia. You see,' and she ducked her head like a schoolgirl, 'I'm afraid I am the most terrible coward.'

He didn't say anything for a moment, but looked across the park. A gardener was planting some roses near a little pavilion. He wore thick canvas gloves to keep his hands from being pricked.

Nessheim turned to Elizaveta. 'I want to tell you a story.'

'Story?' She looked amused.

'That's right.'

Her eyes were scanning the park. 'Why don't you take off your jacket first?'

'My jacket?' It wasn't hot that day. 'Why?'

'Just take it off. Please.'

He stood up reluctantly and took off his jacket, then turned around, thinking of Akiro's similar request. He was wearing his .38. 'You know I carry a gun.'

'Yes, but I didn't know if you were wearing a microphone.'

'It would have to be awfully small. We don't have them like that.'

'We do,' she said flatly.

'I see,' he said. He sat down again and without looking at her, he began to speak:

'Once upon a time there was a boy named Billy. He had a Japanese father and a white mother and in his early years he grew up in Hawaii. His father died when he was young, and after that people were told he went to Japan for the rest of his schooling. His girlfriend here in LA – I bet you never knew about her – thought he was *Kibei*. But he wasn't. He told people he was half-Irish, but in fact his mother was Russian. She didn't send him back to Japan for his education, but to Moscow.'

'Is there something wrong with that?' Elizaveta asked.

'That depends on your point of view. This was the early Thirties and the first Soviet espionage teams were being sent abroad.' Stephenson had told him this on the train. 'A new generation of spies was being trained. Billy was one of them.'

'But he would have been only a schoolboy,' she protested.

Nessheim shook his head. 'It's like the Jesuits. You know, give me your son until he's seven and he's mine for life. I don't think Billy went to a normal high school in the Soviet Union. Or if he did, he had supplementary tutoring in spycraft. He would have kept up his Japanese – he was bilingual after all – but they would have taken particular care to keep his English fluent, because it was America he would be returning to, not Japan.

'When he left Moscow he came to the mainland here, and the first thing he did was re-establish contact with a cousin he'd known as a boy in Hawaii. Akiro wasn't half-Russian – or half-Red for that matter. He was a bit of a crook – most of his friends were Tokyo Club mobsters – and he was a Japanese nationalist. Ideal, if you wanted to connect with the nationalists here and those in Japan.'

'This is a very interesting story,' said Elizaveta. 'Perhaps you have missed your calling.'

'Not if you know what most Hollywood writers get paid,' he said dryly. 'But let me go on. Now, our Billy became more valuable when other agents arrived and started giving him direction. They had specific things they wanted to know. Such as: were the Japanese going to attack America? Or would they move on neigh-bouring territories, like the parts of China they hadn't occupied? Or – and this was the biggest fish of all – attack the Soviet Union?'

'I would call that natural curiosity.'

'Of course, but it wasn't the Vice-Consul who was going to supply the answers. It was Billy, with a large helping of funds. You see, Billy's cousin was very well connected in nationalist circles, but he was also a gambler – he'd bet on anything. I'm sure you've met the type.'

'No doubt. Perhaps Billy did some gambling, too.'

'You bet,' said Nessheim, his lip curling at the pun. 'To cut a not-so-long-story short, Billy told the Russians that if they gave him money to pay Akiro, he could get information out of him about the Japanese plans. They agreed, and he did.'

'So everyone was happy.'

'For a little while, but I'm beginning to see why money doesn't play a part in fairy tales. When this money came in, not all of it went to Billy's cousin.'

'Really?'

'Billy, you see, had started to worry about his own

wellbeing. And there's nothing like twenty-five grand to keep a guy healthy.'

'You think he stole this money?'

'Yes. And I think the Russian running him thought he did.'

'And you believe that was my husband?'

Nessheim shook his head. 'No. It was you.'

She tried to protest, until she saw the expression on his face.

He said, 'Though I don't believe that romancing Billy was part of your assignment. I just think you were sweet on the kid. That's what makes you even more frightening.'

'Frightening?' she asked, as if fear were only something in the movies.

'Yes. You were so in thrall to your ideological masters that you were even willing to kill the man you were sleeping with.'

For a moment he thought she was going to slap his face. When she didn't he said, 'I'll finish my story. I think that after Billy came to live here in America he gradually started to fall for the place – something one of his old teachers at UCLA understood. Ultimately, Billy wasn't interested any longer in being a good Communist. You were starting to see this too, and you saw the potential threat. Billy was right to think his life was in danger. Then Billy went missing and I came along, looking for him. He wanted to see me, said he had something important to tell me. You must have suspected something like that so you had the note put in my house – *Billy Osaka RIP*. It couldn't have been you personally – you were with me at the benefit. I figure your friend Ivan the Bruiser must have slipped out, after bumping into me so I'd think he was there all evening.'

'Maybe you were just being warned off.'

'I like the "maybe", Mrs Mukasei. But when that didn't work, your people did the next best thing – they tried to kill me.'

'We must be very inept then. You seem to be breathing.'

'But others aren't.'

'I never killed anyone.'

'I think you did.'

She started to object, but he cut her off – 'Hitler's never pulled a trigger, but he's killing millions.'

She said disdainfully, 'How can you compare the two? It's ludicrous, just like this story of yours.' Her voice was impatient. 'There is a war out there, you know, which you have only just discovered. My country is fighting for its life, but that's nothing new for us: Mikhail was fighting in Spain while you were chasing petty crooks. So don't lecture me.'

'An old lady's strangled? Akiro's wife gets chopped up like tuna fish? Some poor bastard gets his throat cut in the barber's chair? And you're saying they're all done to protect the Soviet Union?'

'Yes,' she said without hesitation. 'My country was in the utmost danger – it still is. I could not risk news of the Japanese plans reaching your government.' She added, almost as an afterthought, 'There are many inno-cent casualties in war, Agent Nessheim.'

'I have to agree: we both know I was supposed to be the guy in the barber's chair.'

She stiffened and Nessheim gave a caustic laugh. '*Chim*,' he said, mimicking the voice beneath his cabin window in the mountains above Santa Barbara. '*Come for a svim, Chim.*'

The greater his anger, the more futile he felt. He suddenly thumped the bench arm with his fist. 'If it weren't for this goddam war you'd be facing the chair!'

'I don't know about that. There seems very little evidence to your accusations,' she said smoothly. 'And we are allies now, Agent Nessheim.'

She was right. There was little, if anything, he could prove.

Elizaveta took a deep breath. 'I have listened to your story with great interest. Now, is there anything else left to discuss? If not I must be going.'

When he stayed silent, Elizaveta stood up.

'I am sorry this was not a friendlier meeting.' She extended her hand. 'I hope we may meet again.'

'I don't,' he said.

Her face froze when she realised he wouldn't shake her hand.

37

HE DROVE UP the side of Laurel Canyon slowly, still outraged by Elizaveta Mukasei. She hadn't told him anything he hadn't known or guessed already, nor had she seemed surprised by his accusations – it was the matter-of-factness of her acknowledgement of what she'd done that had enraged him in the park, and depressed him now.

He couldn't wait to leave LA. Nessheim wasn't going to miss the house on Mount Olympus Drive, which had only been a transient station for him. Although he liked the space it had provided (and the privacy), he had been too unsettled ever to consider it a home. Not that he'd be settling down anywhere in the near future. Barracks life in boot camp and then – who knew? He hoped it would be combat in a theatre of war, but it was impossible to predict whether he'd be fighting in the Far East or in North Africa. A year before he had only thought of the Nazis as America's enemies, but Los Angeles and then Pearl Harbor had changed that. He wished that the Russians were also on the enemy side.

He parked in the garage, then climbed the stone steps and unlocked the front door. The living room already seemed deserted, even though the furniture wasn't his and would be staying. He had little to pack, really, just clothes and a box he'd gradually been filling with books in the spare room.

He was going to change out of his suit, hang up his holster and .38, but it was a warm day and he was thirsty, so he first went through into the kitchen and filled a glass with water. He stood by the rear window and drank slowly, thinking again of his meeting with Elizaveta Mukasei. He wasn't sure which was worse: knowing she had been responsible for the deaths of so many people or knowing he was powerless to do anything about it. The same feeling he'd had in his cell at Pearl Harbor.

He forgot about changing and opened the back door. He came down the two steps of the porch and crossed onto the lawn. He'd miss the best of the season's flowers, but at least he wouldn't have to cut the grass this year.

'Hello stranger.'

The voice was cheerful. He looked round and saw Mrs Delaware behind him by the back porch. She said, 'I haven't seen you in a coon's age. Been keeping busy?'

'I have.' He wondered if he should tell her he was moving out, but decided against it. He hadn't even told his landlady yet that he'd be breaking the lease.

'Don't tell me you missed your friend again.'

'Which one's that?' he said vaguely, wondering how he could politely get her to go away.

'The man who wasn't from the utility company. He was wearing a suit again. Not as nice as yours.'

He barely heard the compliment. 'When was this?'

'About an hour ago. I asked his name this time, but I didn't really catch it.' Suddenly her face seemed to change, and her eyes widened in surprise as she looked past Nessheim. 'Why there he is—'

He turned around just as he heard a sudden *phit*, like an arrow leaving a bow string. He glimpsed the tall figure emerging from behind the persimmon tree as he threw himself down, already rolling and reaching for his gun. Nessheim let his momentum carry him once, twice on the grass, ending on his belly with his elbows propped, the .38 held in both hands.

Dirt kicked up two inches in front of his nose, spraying

soil all over his face. The tall figure was aiming again when Nessheim fired. His gun roared with a massive *boom* and almost kicked out of his hands. He steadied it and fired again, then again, and finally the man – he could see now it was a man – lurched and fell flat on his back. Then he didn't move. Nessheim scrambled to his feet and approached with his gun extended, ready to fire again.

He looked down and saw an ugly, pockmarked face. Ivan the Bruiser. No wonder Elizaveta had seemed so unruffled. She knew Nessheim would go home, so full of impotent fury that he would be easy to kill. If it hadn't been for Mrs Delaware, she would have been right.

'It's all right, Mrs Delaware!' he called out, still staring down at the Russian assassin. His gun had a silencer attached.

Confident at last that the man was dead, he turned around.

Mrs Delaware was lying on the ground. He walked over to her, suddenly numbed. She wasn't moving. There was a small dark hole perfectly centred in her forehead.

38

HE'D RECEIVED AN invitation to Devereux's wedding the month before, but had written to say he couldn't attend – one encounter with Mona had been enough. So he was surprised to get a phone call one evening at home from his old colleague – other than the invitation, Nessheim hadn't heard from him since he'd collected Guttman's instructions at his house.

'Nessheim, old buddy, you gotta help me out,' Devereux began. 'You remember Tucker?'

'Sure, what about him?' said Nessheim. Tucker had been another agent in the San Francisco Field Office, a CPA who specialised in fraud.

'Tucker was supposed to be my best man. But the son of a bitch went and joined up, and the army won't give him leave to attend the wedding. So I'm in a bind. Please say you'll stand in for him.'

He was too startled to say no right away, and tried to buy time: 'When is it again?' It was Wednesday now.

'Saturday. I know it's short notice, but it's an emergency. Please, Jim.'

And he had agreed, not so much out of any enduring friendship with Devereux, but just to get out of town before he left for good.

This time the *Lark* didn't provide a view of the Pacific, even though Nessheim had a Pullman room on the left side again. The blackout blinds were pulled down and the conductor checked that they stayed that way.

'Can't take any chances,' he said.

He arrived in San Francisco in the morning again and

grabbed a cab. When the front door opened at the house off Ocean Avenue it wasn't Devereux or Mona standing there, but a balding man in a suit that didn't fit.

'Hello Harry,' Nessheim said. 'You've lost weight.'

Guttman looked down at his shirt, which flopped where once it had bulged.

'I'll get it back,' he said defiantly.

Nessheim laughed and Guttman gave a grumpy smile. 'Come on in.'

They went to the living room and sat down. The view through the window was of cotton-wool fog. Nessheim asked, 'Where's Devereux? And what are you doing here anyway?'

'He's at the field office.'

'That's dutiful: he's getting married tomorrow. I'm meant to be his best man.'

Guttman hesitated, then said, 'Mona called it off.'

'Why'd she go and do that? Last-minute nerves?' He wished Devereux had let him know.

'Not quite,' said Guttman, looking sheepish. 'I think it happened a month ago.'

Nessheim stared at him and suddenly he got it.

Guttman said apologetically, 'It seemed the best way to get you up here.' He pretended to look at his watch. 'Say, do you want some cola?'

'Too early for me,' Nessheim said sharply. 'Why couldn't you just come see me in LA?'

'It's kind of complicated.'

'None of this has been simple.'

'The Director doesn't know I'm here. Though, frankly, he's in no position to do anything about it.'

'Why's that?'

'Just before I was shot, the great man decided to transfer me to Mexico. There's no way I could do that, with Isabel not well. I was being pushed out.'

'So what's changed that? Getting shot?'

Guttman laughed. 'No, it was Popov. He gave Hoover some German microfilm that contained questions Popov was supposed to answer when he went to Hawaii – about the harbour layouts, where ships berthed and the location of the airfields. You'd have to be stupid not to see the thrust of it.' He paused. 'Popov's such a libertine that Hoover didn't even look at the questions. But Stephenson did – and he passed the info on to me.'

'Does Hoover know you know this?' When Guttman nodded, Nessheim added, 'He can't like that.'

'He hates it,' Guttman said with relish. 'But I'm not posing any kind of threat. He knows I don't want his job. I just want to keep mine. The first Jewish Director of the FBI awaits a future generation.'

'What is your job now, Harry? San Francisco isn't exactly Latin America.'

Guttman looked at him happily. 'I'm back in charge of domestic counter-espionage.'

Nessheim shook his head with admiration. Guttman was hopeless at politicking in the conventional sense – finding allies, neutralising foes, staying out of hot water. But when he had the goods he could play hardball.

'I'm going to need your help.'

Nessheim yawned ostentatiously. 'I've heard that before.'

'This is different,' Guttman insisted.

'You've said that before, too.' He grew serious. 'Something really went wrong this time.'

'Are you feeling aggrieved, Nessheim?'

He shrugged. 'A little.'

'Who do you blame most – me?'

'Of course,' said Nessheim easily, and he noticed that

Guttman was smiling wryly. 'Though I don't think you were trying to get me killed.'

'That's big of you.'

'But the Russians were. And they kept trying – just like they tried to kill you.' Guttman raised an eyebrow. Nessheim went on, 'I was lucky, Harry.' He found himself feeling emotional, and tried to fight it off. 'I know I'm supposed to be highly resourceful and all that. But it was pure dumb luck I got out alive, and that was thanks to a Mother Superior and a guy with a horse and cart.'

Guttman didn't say anything. He scratched one side of his head, where his hair had been shaved. It must have been where the bullet had hit him, thought Nessheim. It wasn't growing back very well, but then Guttman's hair had never been exactly lush.

Guttman said at last, 'I got your report. I had a question or two.'

'Yeah?' Nessheim said warily.

'Was Osaka a crook?'

Nessheim thought about this for a moment.

'Hard to say. I think he realised that once he told the Russians about the Japanese plans, he was disposable. So he went on the run and took half the money with him – he used the other half to pay his cousin for the information. Once he disappeared the Russians panicked and started killing anybody he might have told.'

'Cheer up,' said Guttman. 'If they try to kill you again, at least the report's on file.'

'That's consolation.' But he said it without anger.

They sat quietly for a minute.

Then Guttman asked, 'When you were banged up at the base in Pearl did you see much of the attack?'

Nessheim hesitated. He had been doing his best lately

not to think about what he'd witnessed, though his dreams wouldn't let him forget. 'Enough,' he said.

Guttman nodded thoughtfully. Then he said, 'So what are you going to do now?'

'I'm going to enlist.' He paused a beat. 'If you let me.'

'What do you mean?'

'I didn't finish college, Harry, but I'm not a dope. The last time I tried to sign up, somebody called the selection board in Wisconsin and told them about my medical history.'

Guttman looked uncomfortable.

Nessheim said, 'I don't want you to do it again.'

'All right already,' Guttman said, then, as usual when he was embarrassed, he got tetchy. 'I know you've still got that driver's licence. But I can't track down every service board from Pasadena to Poughkeepsie, asking if they've got a James Rossbach on their books.' He thought about this. 'Well, I suppose I could. But I'm not going to. If you're that determined, be my guest. Come on, let's go for a ride.'

Outside they got into the big Chevy Guttman had rented and set off. It wasn't clear where they were going and the way Guttman drove it wasn't clear that they would get there, either. At first they didn't talk, then Guttman broke the silence.

'So what are you feeling so bad about?'

Was it that obvious? Nessheim tried to shrug, but when Guttman didn't say anything he felt obliged to speak.

'I feel I failed. If I'd put two and two together on Molokai I could have warned the people at Pearl.'

'You think they would have believed you? What are the odds they would have swallowed some story that the Japs were about to come flying in? The way

I understand it, you're lucky you weren't put in front of a Navy firing squad. You're blaming yourself for something nobody could have prevented.' He snorted. 'Except for Hoover, if he'd bothered to look at Popov's microfilm. He's the one who should be losing sleep.'

He accelerated as the light turned green.

'You've got to let all that stuff go, Nessheim. There's too much else going on you can do something about. The world isn't about you and your guilt, you know.'

The words stung, and Nessheim was about to reply when Guttman gave a sigh and said, 'I've been thinking a lot about Thornton Palmer recently. He's an interesting case. Here's a guy who did a bad thing and then tried to make amends. Yet he only got punished for doing the right thing.'

'I feel the same way about Billy Osaka. Only he didn't manage to make amends – he was too scared.'

'Understandably.'

'They got him in the end anyway – he should have come clean.'

They were driving again, heading towards Golden Gate Park. The fog was lifting.

Nessheim said, 'At least Billy had the excuse that he was recruited as a kid. How did they get to Palmer?'

'I've got a new friend at Yale who did some digging for me into Palmer's past – apparently he had a cousin out in Hollywood. A guy named Waverley.'

'Christ. He's a writer at AMP. And a Communist.'

'Must be – he was a scout for Soviet Intelligence. But I can't prove it. Just like I can't prove the Russians tried to bump me off.' He laughed, almost appreciatively. 'They're crafty bastards, you know. They even used a car they bought from your *Bund* friend Schultz's widow to cover their tracks. Not that I can prove that either.'

'That's the problem,' said Nessheim bitterly. 'If I could prove half the things I know, I'd feel justice was being served. As it is, I can't do a goddamned thing.'

Guttman looked at him, bemused. 'Hey, that's how it is in our country. Would you want it any other way? Stalin's boys don't need proof. Hitler's don't either. Thank the Lord we do.'

'Even if it means the Mukaseis and Waverleys of this world get away with it?'

'Even if they do. Once you let yourself play judge, it's only a matter of time until you become a bad guy too.'

Guttman was in better spirits now, and driving better. He turned right and they moved along Geary. On this side of the peninsula the fog had cleared, replaced by a weak spring sun. They travelled in silence for a while. Then Guttman said, 'So what about it?'

'What about what?'

'This project. I'm not telling you for my health, Nessheim. I've got to find somebody to be in Chicago.'

'There must be plenty of qualified candidates.'

'I don't think so. It's a counter-espionage job.'

'Yeah?' said Nessheim. It was important not to show interest, he told himself.

'I report on it directly to the White House.'

Nessheim looked over at him, but Guttman stared resolutely ahead. He said, 'The President knows we may have a problem.'

'At the Bureau?'

Guttman didn't reply right away, then finally said, 'The reason Kuhn wasn't picked up in Hawaii was because a telex went to Shivers saying that on no account was Kuhn to be detained. It went out under Tolson's name, but it couldn't have come from Tolson – he and the Boss were in New York at the time.'

'Maybe it was a mistake.'

'Maybe.'

Nessheim's thoughts were racing. 'Do you mean the Bureau has been infiltrated?' That would explain how the Navy had been tipped off about 'Rossbach'.

Guttman shrugged. 'We need to tread carefully.'

They stopped at a light, where three soldiers were flirting with a girl in a nurse's uniform. The girl was laughing, enjoying the attention. All four looked as if they hadn't a care in the world. Guttman pointed at the soldiers. 'That'll be you in a little while. Defender of the free world.'

The light turned and halfway along the next block Guttman started to slow down the car. 'I can let you out at the corner. There's a recruiting station just down the block. You might as well get the process started.'

'Where are you going?' asked Nessheim, slightly taken aback.

'Over the bridge to Berkeley to see a physicist – isn't that what they're called?'

'Jesus, Harry, you don't know any science. Physics is hard. I took it in college and it was murder.'

Guttman started to ease the car over. 'You want to hop out here?'

It was Nessheim's turn to sigh. 'No, Harry. Let's keep going for now.'

Acknowledgements

I would like to thank Jocasta Hamilton, Susan Sandon and Emma Mitchell of Random House UK for their encouragement and help as I wrote this book. At The Overlook Press in New York, I thank Peter Mayer, Dan Crissman and Michael Goldsmith for their belief in this series.

At Aitken Alexander my agent Gillon Aitken was supportive as ever, as was Clare Alexander, and I would like to thank Andrew Kidd in particular for his detailed editorial suggestions.

The writer Jacob Epstein corrected errors about Los Angeles (and is not responsible for any that may remain); Christopher Silvester pointed me to many useful sources about the Hollywood movie industry, as did Barry Isaacson; retired Special Agent Larry Wack provided information about the early FBI. Professor Brian Masaru Hayashi of Kyoto University, an authority on the Los Angeles Japanese-American community in the years before the War, patiently answered many questions.

My uncle Willard Keeney shared his remarkable knowledge (and archive) of transport and terrain in pre-War California – and in many other places too; he also made several astute suggestions, and I thank him. Dan and James Rosenheim read chapters with sharp eyes, my daughters Laura and Sabrina both peeked, and their mother helped throughout.